DOWN AMONG THE DEAD

DAMIEN BOYD

THOMAS & MERCER

Text copyright © 2020 by Damien Boyd
All rights reserved.

Published by Thomas & Mercer, Seattle

www.apub.com

Amazon, the Amazon logo, and Thomas & Mercer are trademarks of Amazon.com, Inc., or its affiliates.

ISBN-13: 9781542094276
ISBN-10: 1542094275

Cover design by Dominic Forbes

Printed in the United States of America

For Polly

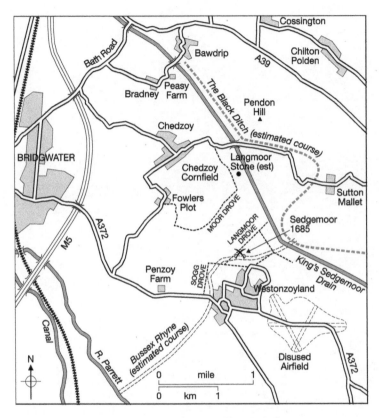

Map of the Sedgemoor Battlefield

When . . . the Duke's army was marching after mid-night into Langmoor with great silence, a pistol was discharged about step stones or Langmoor Stone. Immediately an 'unknown' trooper rides from that place-ward full speed to the camp, calls with all imaginable earnestness, 20 times at least, 'Beat your drums, the enemy is come. For the Lord's sake, beat your drums.' He then rode back with like speed the same way he came. Among some of the King's soldiers, particularly the Scots, there was expectation of the enemy before this, yet all continued quiet. Now the drums beat, the drummers are running to it, even bare-foot for haste. All fly to arms. All are drawn out of their tents and in five battalions stand in the space between the tents and the ditch, fronting the ditch, not having their clothes or arms all on and ready. Thus were they expecting the enemy.

Rev. Andrew Paschall
Rector of Chedzoy
July 1685

Six of our nearest guns were with the greatest diligence imaginable advanced, three upon the right of the Scots and three in the front of the King's first battalion (of Guards), and did very considerable execution upon the enemies. They stood near an hour and a halfe with great shouting and courage, briskly fyring; and then, throwing down their armes, fell into rout and confusion. The number of the slaine with about 300 taken, according to the most modest computation, might make up 1,000. We losing but 27 on the spot and having about 200 wounded. A victory very considerable, where Providence was absolutely a greater friend than our own conduct. The dead in the Moor we buried, and the country people took care for the interment of those slaine in the corn fields.

Extract from the journal of Edward Dummer
Serving in the Train of Artillery emply'd by his Majesty
6th July 1685

Prologue

'The guilt weighs heavy, Master Appleby?'

He paused outside the open window, watching the drunkard slumped in his carved oak chair: head back, mouth open; a flagon on the table in front of him, his tankard upended on the floor beside him.

'And a fine manor house. Tell me, how does a cobbler afford that, I do wonder?'

The fire flickered in the hearth, sparks from the dying embers dancing in the draught as the last of the candles on the table burned out.

'Is that vomit down the front of that fine silk shirt, my treacherous friend?'

He glanced over his shoulder at the sound of hooves behind him, the grey he had turned loose at the crossroads having followed him through the woods, the reins trailing on the ground.

'See what you have done? A horse thief I am now.'

Rebel, slave, horse thief; destined for the gallows as sure as night follows day.

'But not before I have added murder to my litany of trespasses.'

A knife on the table and a sword hanging on the wall above the granite lintel. He glanced down at the rusting hand scythe he had found on the edge of the cornfield at Chedzoy, dropped by one of his band of brothers fleeing the field of battle. Turning the blade in the glow from the fire, he ran his finger along the cutting edge; blunt. A blacksmith, come to this. Still, the point would be sharp enough for the task at hand.

He tried the latch on the door, careful to make no sound.

'You will waken, Master Appleby, when I am good and ready.'

Not bolted either; the door inched open, the hinges well greased. The wet leather soles on his boots made no sound on the stone floor, just as the boots of thousands of good Somerset men marching out on to Langmoor had made no sound that fateful night ten long years ago.

He picked up the flagon and sniffed the dregs. Rum.

Unconscious in drink; a door not bolted.

'A want of care, Master Appleby,' he whispered. 'Did you think I had forgotten you?'

He took off his wide-brimmed floppy hat and placed it silently on the table, watching the last of the raindrops trickle down between the timbers. Two hours in the saddle, lappery all the way; he was soaked through. 'You'll catch your death,' his wife would have said, had she not taken up with another, thinking him dead. Then he sat down opposite the slumbering Appleby, listening to the crackle of the fire, and the snoring.

Fresh bread and cheese on the table were tempting.

'Maybe afterward, when the Somerset men butchered at Westonzoyland have been avenged.'

He picked up the knife from the bread board and dropped it into his coat pocket. A scythe was his weapon of choice this night; a knife would not do at all.

Appleby cut a sad figure: two weeks unshaven, the turncoat had put on weight since last he had seen him that dismal night, galloping away into the fog, his betrayal complete, the battle joined.

2

Ten long years a slave in the Indies, one thing and one thing alone had kept him alive; few survived, fewer still returned home. Perhaps he should be grateful to Appleby for that; for giving him the will to live.

His breathing quickened.

'Vengeance is mine.' He wrapped his fingers around the metal handle of the scythe, the wood long since rotted away. 'The day of your calamity is at hand, my old friend. Or perhaps I should let Judas sleep a little while longer?'

Mixing Old Testament and New; that would be the least of his troubles.

'Yes, there will be a price to be paid. And I will gladly pay it.'

He perched on the edge of the table, his feet resting on the arms of the chair, either side of Appleby. Then he lined up the tip of the scythe with the left side of the drunkard's chest, his left hand taking a firm grip on the handle, his right wrapped in a cloth and holding the curved blade.

He thought about the lines of loyal Somerset men marching out of Bridgwater that night to fight for their proclaimed King Monmouth: blacksmiths, cobblers, graziers, wood-turners; some armed with muskets, some with scythes. All of them betrayed by Appleby for his thirty pieces of silver.

He sent the tip of the blade into Appleby's chest; not far enough to kill – just enough to wake him. The eyes snapped open, recognition turning confusion to fear.

'Cornelius?'

''Tis I,' he said, smiling down at him, listening to the blood gurgling up in his lungs.

He plunged the scythe further into Appleby's chest, inch by inch, his full weight behind it now until the tip of the blade hit backbone deep inside.

He leaned forward and peered into Appleby's eyes, watching the last flicker of terror begin to fade as his gasps shallowed. It was a moment

3

he had contemplated every single day since the militia had found him hiding in the woods behind Moorlinch and he had been shipped to the Indies; a reprieve of sorts. And it was a moment to savour, however fleeting it might be.

He leaned forward and whispered his parting shot in the dying man's ear.

'Beat your drums, Master Appleby. The enemy is come.'

Chapter One

Two weeks *in the field*. It had sounded fun.

'A mass grave on English soil. And it's not often you get to look for one of them,' Colin said, with a broad grin and a clap of his hands.

'Professor Colin bloody Timperley,' Zak muttered under his breath. 'Anyone would think we'd found Tutankhamun's big brother.' The only thing missing was the pith helmet.

'And remember, you're representing Reading University archaeology department.'

Zak Holman could hardly forget it. Everybody on the field trip was wearing the T-shirt, for a start. He let out a long slow sigh. *In the field* had turned out to be a cornfield in the middle of nowhere. The sun was beating down and the surf was up on the north coast – four to five feet and clean. Croyde would have been good; Newquay better still, given that he'd got some study leave due.

Instead, a couple of weeks up to his armpits in mud somewhere on the Somerset Levels was as good as it was going to get. At least there was a pub within walking distance of the campsite.

'We're joined by a couple of members of the local history society,' continued Colin. 'This is Rob Salmon. He'll be going with you year one students and Professor Watkins to look for evidence of the friendly fire incident. I take it you've all read Dr Ashton's notes?'

Zak glanced across at the year ones; keen as mustard, most of them, nodding enthusiastically. He remembered it well.

'You'll be looking for evidence of a short engagement away from where we know the main battle took place, so north of the line of the old Bussex Rhyne; a concentration of musket balls, something like that. Map them if you find any, then we can mark out some trenches and start digging. Right, back on the minibus and Malcolm will drive you round to Bussex Farm.' Colin waited until the year one students had drifted off. 'Year two, you'll be with me; and this is Sandra Smith, local guide extraordinaire.'

Maybe it wasn't all bad, thought Zak, wondering if she went for younger men. Much younger, but what the hell – maybe he'd learn something on this trip after all. No wedding ring either.

'Sandra lives in Westonzoyland and knows the battlefield like the back of her hand. She's also organised the permissions for us. There'll be a couple more joining us later, I'm told, and Graham Ashton arrives tomorrow. I'm sure you've all read his book.'

No, I bloody haven't, thought Zak, nodding all the same.

'Sandra, did you want to say a few words?' asked Colin.

She stepped forward. 'Thank you all for coming,' she said, tying her dark hair back in an elastic band. 'This is the first major dig for years and it's great to have some help. The hardest task you're going to have is trying to imagine what this place looked like in 1685. What we're standing on now is the original Chedzoy cornfield. I've traced the boundary on this map, and beyond that it was open moorland. It hadn't been drained back then.' She handed a bundle of maps that had been tucked in the top of her jeans to the student standing at the front of the group, who took one and passed them on. 'That church you can see over there is Westonzoyland, where the Royal Army was camped for the night. There were no hedgerows then, just the cornfield, the ditch and then it was straight out on to Langmoor. Think thick fog and you'll get an idea of what it was like on the night of the battle.'

Zak was more interested in the old farmer putting up a small marquee behind them on the far side of the field, sheltered behind a red brick barn on the edge of the village.

'Rebels fleeing the battle were caught here in the cornfield by the Royal cavalry and cut to pieces,' continued Sandra. 'Contemporary estimates put the dead at four hundred or so.'

Zak looked down, as they all did, expecting to see the mud at his feet running red with blood.

'Difficult to get your head round, isn't it,' said Colin.

'Is this corn?' asked a student at the front of the group, brushing the shoots with her foot.

'It's maize this year,' replied Sandra.

'And four hundred men died on this spot?'

'They did,' said Colin. 'And we're looking for their bodies. Or what's left of them.'

Sandra waited until most of the group looked up again, their faces a shade paler, even in the sun. 'We know from Edward Dummer's account that the locals were left to bury the dead, and we think it's reasonable to assume they didn't bury them where they grew their corn, so they must have carried the bodies back out on to the moor and buried them there. What we're proposing, therefore, is a series of trenches along the boundary of the old cornfield—'

'You've tried that before,' interrupted Colin, hardly able to contain his excitement. 'Tell them what's different this time.'

'A colleague from the local history society found a diary in the archive at the Somerset Heritage Centre. It dates from 1696 and there's a hand drawn map in it which gives us a much more accurate picture of the original boundary of the cornfield. The locals had started to cultivate the edge of the moor in places, so we'll be digging further south this time, on the edge. Previous digs were too far north, we think.'

'And who knows what we'll find this time?' Colin clapped his hands again, loudly. 'We'll be using metal detectors to begin with, to pinpoint possible dig sites. Buckles, buttons; you know what to look for. Stick a flag in the ground and mark them on the map. We'll be draining the ditches too, so get ready to get down and dirty. Sandbags and a water pump are on the trailer.'

'I wondered what those were for,' whispered Zak, curling his lip. 'Got my name on them, I bet.'

The girl behind him ruffled his hair, playfully. 'Have you ever thought you might not be cut out for archaeology?'

'And to think I'm racking up student debt for this.'

They began to wander towards the van and trailer parked on the track at the edge of the field.

'Before you go,' shouted Colin, 'The ladies from Westonzoyland Women's Institute will be providing refreshments in that marquee you can see over there, so a huge thank you to them. And the TV cameras from *Digging for Britain* will be here in a couple of weeks, so let's make sure we find something!'

'What's with the patch?'

'Laser eye surgery.'

'You look like Captain Pugwash.'

He was a scruffy little herbert. Cheeky too. Ripped jeans, a green hoody; looked about twenty years old, but Detective Inspector Nick Dixon knew the boy was only fifteen. He would have searched his pockets, but the shop assistant had already done it.

They were sitting in the staff room at the back of Hurley's in Burnham-on-Sea, watching through the open door as Detective Sergeant Jane Winter tried to persuade the irate shop owner, Monika, not to press charges.

'You look a bit old for Pokémon,' said Dixon.

The boy folded his arms tightly across his chest. 'I was going to sell it.' He was sitting with his back to the wall, staring at the key in the side door.

'I wouldn't try it, if I were you. There's a dog handler outside.'

Some holiday this was turning out to be. Dixon shook his head. They should have been out on the fells somewhere today. The cottage in Hartsop was standing empty and the weather in the Lake District was perfect, according to the Met Office. Maybe he shouldn't have checked. At least the travel insurance had coughed up for the cancelled booking; diabetic retinopathy is a serious condition and the surgery had been urgent. The surgeon had winked at him when she signed the medical certificate, but it had done the trick.

The certificate had been his second question. His first, 'Am I going blind?', had got a laugh, much to his surprise. 'Of course you're not,' had been the reply, and he still had the bruise where Jane had dug her elbow into his ribs. All that worrying for nothing.

It was just a precaution, the surgeon had said; two small bulges in the blood vessels at the back of the retina. They'd probably be fine, but best to zap them to be on the safe side. Then had come the lecture about watching his sugar levels and checking his blood four times a day instead of once a week. And if that wasn't bad enough, Jane had appointed herself chief of the diabetes police ever since.

They'd been out on the beach after a late breakfast when she got the call from Sandy in the Safeguarding Unit.

'You told her we weren't going away?'

'I had to, in case of emergencies.' Jane had shrugged, as if that made it all right. 'Billy Parker's got himself in trouble again. He's one of my regulars.'

'Do I know him?'

'No.'

'Should you be interfering?'

'Don't start.'

It hadn't taken long to persuade the uniformed officers on scene to look the other way. Monika, on the other hand, seemed to need a little more persuading.

'It's not often you get a pig trying to get you *out* of trouble.' Billy smirked, watching the animated conversation out by the tills at the front of the shop.

Take a deep breath and count to ten; Jane had said he was a good kid. 'She's also my fiancée, so you'll watch your tongue if you know what's good for you.'

'I don't.'

Dixon didn't envy Jane her job in the Safeguarding Unit, even though she was spared hot-desking in an open plan office. She had her own desk, and walls. Looking after those who pose a risk and those at risk. He wondered into which category Billy Parker stumbled and fell.

'I suppose you're a pig too?' asked the boy, his knee bouncing up and down as if operating an imaginary pottery wheel.

Tempting, but Dixon didn't take the bait. 'Tell me about your father.'

'He's innocent.'

'Isn't everyone?'

'Yeah, but he really is. And your lot put him away for life.' Billy sat up. 'It's his appeal next week and he's getting out. Then we'll see.'

Jane appeared in the doorway, her face flushed. 'Monika's not a happy bunny, but she's agreed not to press charges,' she said, looking at Dixon.

'Lucky lad.'

'Now, tuck your shirt in, Billy, get out there and apologise to Mrs Morris.'

The boy looked up at Jane, his look of defiance softening into capitulation.

'I explained about your father and she's prepared to give you the benefit of the doubt.'

Dixon smiled as he watched Billy shuffle out to the tills to eat humble pie. He thought it best to keep quiet about his own close shave in the same shop. The memories came flooding back: of a yo-yo thrust into a pocket in the toy department upstairs; of his friend, Ben, and the hole in his trousers; and a yo-yo rolling off across the floor. They hadn't stopped running until they reached the lighthouse.

'What are you smiling about?' asked Jane.

'Nothing.'

'Right then, I'm off,' said Billy, when they stepped out on to the pavement.

'Oh no, you're not,' snapped Jane. 'You're coming with us.' She was leading him by the elbow towards a raised flowerbed where her half-sister Lucy was sitting on the wall, her arm around a large white Staffordshire terrier that was busy flattening the geraniums with his tail.

'Don't tell me this is the dog handler?' Billy flashed a warm smile at Lucy.

Dixon nodded.

'You said it was a police dog!'

'No, I didn't.'

A couple of matchsticks would have been useful; one under each eyelid.

Detective Chief Inspector Peter Lewis stifled a yawn, glancing around the table to check if anyone had noticed. Assistant Chief Constable Charlesworth, sitting at the far end, certainly hadn't; he was replying to a text message, or playing Candy Crush possibly. Chief Inspector Bateman hadn't noticed either – he looked as if he was about to nod off too.

Budgets. Lewis squeezed his eyes shut, taking the opportunity to undo the top button of his shirt. What the hell does a management accountant know about policing anyway? he thought, as he straightened his tie.

The meeting had started at ten. Much longer and the canteen would have closed.

The pile of reports and spreadsheets on the table in front of him was at least half an inch thick, the oscillating fan on the windowsill periodically flicking the corners and threatening to blow them across the table. Still, it was keeping him awake while the accountant took them through it all page by page. To justify her fee, probably.

If the window had been open any wider, Lewis would have jumped out.

'Look, we can't go on like this all day,' said Charlesworth, placing his smartphone face down on top of his bundle of documents. 'We all know why we're here.'

'Cuts,' muttered Bateman, sitting up. 'How many can we get rid of and when.'

'I wouldn't have put it quite like that,' replied the accountant, the corners of her eyes crinkling with indignation. 'We need to—'

'We?' Lewis couldn't help himself, but immediately wished he had.

12

'Yes, *we*. And let's try to steer clear of the c-word, shall we? It conjures up all sorts of . . .'

Lewis resisted the temptation to finish Charlesworth's sentence for him.

'It's about staying in budget,' said the accountant. 'In a budget that's getting smaller rather than bigger.'

'Well, I'm not sure what savings I can make.' Bateman gave an exaggerated shrug; not a good move, thought Lewis, when you've got your back to the window and sweaty armpits. 'We're already relying on more community support officers than Home Office targets allow, and uniformed cover is pared to the bone. Response times are nowhere near where they should be.'

'What about CID?' asked Charlesworth.

'A couple of major investigations have knocked us for six,' replied Lewis. 'We had to drop everything for the child abductions and then there was the Hinkley thing. The backlog is over six months for serious crime as it is, and we've stopped investigating car crime altogether. It'll be burglary non-residential next.'

'The public won't like that.'

At last, thought Lewis, the press officer had said something useful. He'd wondered why Vicky Thomas was there in the first place, looking down her sharp nose at him, her starched blonde hair rigid even in the breeze from the fan. He had put it down to the fact that Charlesworth didn't break wind without checking with the press office first. That and damage limitation – in case news of further cuts got out.

The c-word again.

'What about reducing the number of officers in each team, rather than the number of teams?' asked the accountant, looking at Lewis.

'Me?' Lewis sat up and took a deep breath. He leaned forward, placing both elbows on the table and interlocking his fingers in front of him. 'We've gone from eight teams,' he began, choosing his words carefully. 'Four at Taunton and four at Bridgwater – each a team of twenty officers led by a detective inspector – to four teams of eighteen. That's less than half. We're covering the same geographical area, with more people living in it and more crime.'

'We know the figures, Peter,' said Charlesworth, trying a disarming smile.

'We've had three major investigations, all of them with national coverage. I've got HQ at Portishead trying to poach my best people, and a backlog that is, quite simply, unsustainable.'

'Well, it won't be your problem for much longer, will it?' Charlesworth's eyes narrowed, his voice loaded with menace. 'When you get your promotion you'll be off to Portishead yourself, as a detective superintendent.'

'You'll have to find the savings somewhere else.' Lewis was trying not to bristle, but had clearly given the game away somehow. Maybe Charlesworth could tell what he was thinking – *we don't need four assistant chief constables for a start*. 'Any more cuts to CID and we'll cease to function at all, let alone effectively.'

'There's only one full-time fingerprint expert covering the whole of Avon, Somerset and Wiltshire as it is,' said Bateman, jumping in.

Lewis had had enough. And, no, he wouldn't regret it later. He knew that. Some things are just too important. 'And if the price of promotion is leaving a bloody shambles behind me, then you can shove it.' He snatched his papers off the table in front of him and stood up, sending his chair slamming into the glass partition behind him.

'Saved by the bell,' said Charlesworth, nodding in the direction of the door behind Lewis, where Detective Constable Dave Harding was hovering behind the small window, more in hope than expectation of catching someone's attention.

'What is it, Dave?' asked Lewis, snatching open the door of the meeting room.

Harding stepped back. It really was remarkable how one suit could have so many crumples in it; someone had even suggested a whip-round to buy him an ironing board. Loyal, reliable, honest as the day is long; just the sort Charlesworth would cheerfully make redundant.

'You know they're digging on the battlefield,' he said.

'I saw it on the local news last night,' replied Lewis.

'They've found a body.' Harding spoke quietly, his eyes downcast – the subject matter of the meeting was no secret and nobody liked sticking their head above the parapet when redundancies were being discussed. 'In a ditch. I thought you'd like to know straight away.'

'They're looking for human remains, aren't they?' Charlesworth was craning his neck to listen.

'Yes, Sir.'

'What's so special about this one then?' Lewis stepped out into the corridor and fixed Harding with a hard stare, his eyes wide. 'Well?' he asked, impatiently.

'Single stab wound to the chest. They found it with a metal detector when they drained a rhyne,' replied Harding. He managed a faint smile before delivering the punchline. 'The pacemaker set it off.'

Chapter Two

'Are you trying to tell me something?' asked Lewis, looking down at the bottle of Avon Skin So Soft in Roger Poland's outstretched hand.

'Mosquitoes; clouds of 'em,' grumbled Poland. 'It's the stagnant water in the rhynes.'

'It's a moisturiser.'

'Best repellent there is. The little buggers can't stand it.'

They had parked at the end of the track at Fowlers Plot Farm, a couple of fields away from a group of people all standing around with their hands on their hips, looking down into a ditch.

'It's as close as we can get,' Poland had said. Further progress along the track was blocked by farm machinery.

Lewis left the bottle on the roof of Poland's Volvo and followed the Home Office pathologist, rubbing the dollop of moisturiser into his arms and the back of his neck. He glanced over his shoulder at two uniformed officers sitting on the bonnet of their patrol car, drinking tea.

'There's somebody watching the body,' said Poland, skirting around a hayturner, his large metal case clattering against the prongs. 'They'll need to get this lot shifted so we can get the mortuary van in.'

They walked in the shallow depression in the ground between two lines of maize, Lewis watching his feet and trying not to tread on the crops. Lumps of mud crumbled beneath the soles of his shoes, the soil cracking in places.

'Could do with a bit of rain,' he muttered.

'Not till we've got her out, for God's sake.'

'Her?'

'Making assumptions from what I've been told,' replied Poland, grimacing as he rebuked himself. 'Sloppy.'

They walked on in silence, through an open gate and then diagonally across a field of deep grass, the only sound the revving of large diesel engines coming from the farm behind them. Lewis watched the swallows flitting in and out of the hedgerows, picking off the mosquitoes with a bit of luck.

Several figures were visible a few fields further over towards Westonzoyland, combing the ground with metal detectors.

'They must be the ones looking for Ashton's friendly fire episode,' said Poland.

Lewis thought it best not to ask.

The crowd parted when they approached, revealing a uniformed officer sitting on a water pump with his back to the ditch. He jumped up on spotting Lewis and Poland.

'Who found the body?'

'Zak did, Sir,' replied the officer, gesturing to a crumpled figure sitting cross-legged in the grass, smoking a hand rolled cigarette. 'This is the group leader, Colin Timperley, and Mrs Smith is from the local historical society.'

'Sandra,' she said, moving her sunglasses to the top of her head.

'What about the rest of them?'

'They were spread out in this field and the next one,' replied Colin. 'They were using metal detect—'

'You've got their names?' Lewis turned to the uniformed officer.

'Yes, Sir,' he replied.

'They can go.'

'Back to the marquee at Chedzoy,' said Colin, raising his voice. 'And get yourselves some tea. I'll ring Malcolm to come and get you in the minibus.'

'Not you.'

Zak sighed at Lewis before slumping back down into the grass.

'And what the bloody hell is that noise?'

'Buckraking, Sir.'

'They're making silage,' said Sandra. 'They use the tractors to roll the grass before they bale it. It squashes the air out of—'

'Do they have to do it now?'

'They can't leave it in case it rains.'

Poland had walked over to the ditch and was standing on the edge. 'It's remarkably well preserved.'

'Are you sure it's modern?' asked Lewis.

'See that square thing on the ribcage, under the skin?' Zak was rolling another cigarette, licking along the edge of the paper. 'It's a pacemaker.' He put the cigarette in his mouth and then pulled his T-shirt down from the neck with both hands, revealing a scar down the middle of his chest.

'Looks like it.' Poland dropped his case in the grass and opened it. 'You shouldn't be smoking that if you've got a pacemaker,' he said, frowning at Zak over the lid.

'Whatever.'

'We stopped as soon as we realised,' offered Colin. 'We thought we'd found the mass grave.'

'Find out where Scientific Services have got to, will you?' asked Lewis, turning to the uniformed officer.

18

The ditch had been drained along a length of five yards or so, the stagnant water held back at either end by plastic sheeting and sandbags. The pump had done the rest, revealing a layer of black sediment in the bottom.

'The sediment's only half an inch deep, then it's clay underneath,' said Colin. 'Zak got in with the metal detector and found her.'

'It's been dredged recently.' Sandra was pointing to the pile of thick grey mud along the far bank. 'I spoke to Chris and he said he did it last autumn. Chris farms Fowlers Plot and it's his field.'

A blue pipe led from the water pump into the ditch; another leading from the pump further out into the field. Lewis followed it, finding an area of sodden grass at the end, freckled with duckweed. 'Scientific will need to search this area,' he said.

'Yes, Sir.'

'Why are you digging here?' asked Lewis, turning to Colin. 'On this particular spot.'

'We think it's just outside the boundary of the old Chedzoy cornfield. They were beginning to cultivate the edge of the moor by 1685, extending the boundary a bit further south, so we're checking along what we think was the boundary at that time.'

'So, this rhyne wasn't here at the time of the battle?'

'No,' replied Colin. 'This was open moorland.'

'Langmoor,' said Sandra.

Poland was wriggling into a white oversuit that looked two sizes too small for him.

'You won't keep them on in that mud,' said Zak, watching Poland unwrapping a pair of latex overshoes. 'Just the wellies, if I were you. It nearly had my trainers off.'

Lewis sat down on the water pump and watched Poland slide down the bank into the rhyne, the overshoes disappearing into the mud at the bottom of the ditch.

'The feet will be about . . . here,' said Poland, sticking a hand trowel into the ground just in front of him. Then he began flicking the wet mud to the side with a brush. 'There we go.' He straightened up and looked up at Lewis, squinting into the sun. 'Painted toenails.' The skull, ribcage and left hand had been partially exposed by Zak, although water was beginning to seep up from the sodden rhyne bed, forming small puddles around the body and submerging all but the ribcage and skull.

'D'you want the pump on again?' asked Colin.

'Thank you.'

'Shouldn't the ribcage be lying flat?' Lewis asked.

'Depends on how long the body's been in the ground,' replied Poland. 'There must still be cartilage holding the ribs in position.'

Lewis stood up as the professor took hold of the starter cord and jerked it back; the water pump started first time, drowning out the noise of the tractors in the distance. Poland placed the end of the pipe lying in the rhyne bed into the shallow grave and waited while the water receded. Then he began flicking at the mud again with his brush.

'Will there be any DNA?' Lewis asked.

'Yes, plenty,' replied Poland. 'There's skin, hair. We might even get a set of fingerprints too. Dental records; pulp in the teeth. How much d'you want?'

'As much as we can get.'

'Well, identifying him or her certainly won't be a problem. There are the hip bones. Now I just need to find the other hand.'

'How old?'

'Teenager probably, judging by the development. That's just a guess at this stage. All right?'

'I won't hold you to it.'

The ditch was wide enough to allow Poland to stand astride the body, so he brushed away the mud to either side of it before stepping forward, placing his feet with precision. 'Let's have the pump on again.' He leaned over, watching the murky water recede from around the skull. 'And if push comes to shove we can check the prescription on these too,' he said, holding up a pair of horn-rimmed glasses. He dropped them in a plastic bag and handed them up to the uniformed officer.

'Let me see them,' said Lewis, his hand outstretched.

Recognition was immediate. He blinked away the film of moisture in his eyes just as quickly, not that anyone would have seen it behind his sunglasses.

'Hands across the stomach,' Poland said. 'Fake fingernails on both hands.' Then he leaned over and examined the ribcage. 'Hand me a torch, will you? My body's casting a shadow.'

Lewis handed him a torch and awaited the verdict.

'There's a large incision between the third and fourth vertebrosternal ribs, left side. It's remarkably well preserved. Goes clean through into the chest cavity.'

Lewis sighed to himself. 'Any idea when?'

'No. Not yet anyway. We'll need to get a forensic anthropologist involved, I think. There's one at Bristol University. I'll give her a call when I get out of this ditch.'

'What about the blade?' Lewis was doing his best to sound calm. 'Can you tell me anything about the blade?'

'Possibly curved,' replied Poland, matter of fact. 'It's difficult to tell without opening the chest up, but I can see a mark on the bone. It would've gone straight into the heart at that angle too, so there's your cause of death, subject to the usual caveats at this stage. A scythe springs to mind. Something like that.'

'Well, that didn't take long.'

'Eh?'

'You'd better have a look.'

Jane leaned over the sea wall and glared down at Lucy and Billy sitting on the steps below, holding hands. 'Right, that's it. I'm not having—'

'She's more than capable of looking after herself. Relax and have your ice cream.'

'You didn't have a Flake in yours?' Jane asked, frowning at him.

'No. And I've only got one scoop. All right?'

'You shouldn't be having it at all.'

'Lunch was four hours ago and my blood sugar was getting a bit low.' Dixon sat down on a bench, deciding that a change of subject might be advisable. 'Tell me about Billy's father.'

'I only know what's on the file, really.' Jane sat down next to Dixon, broke a bit off her ice cream cone and gave it to Monty. 'You ever heard of the Scytheman?'

'The Scythe*men* was the name given to rebels at the Battle of Sedgemoor. All they had were scythes; there weren't enough muskets to go round.'

'That's where it comes from. Only this bloke was a serial killer.'

'Billy's father is a serial killer?' Dixon jumped up and looked over the sea wall. 'They're still there,' he said, puffing out his cheeks as he sat back down.

'His father's got a hearing next week at the Court of Appeal. That's why I didn't want Billy getting in any trouble, really. He's convinced his dad is coming home.'

'And is he?'

'Word is it's unlikely. But I haven't told Billy that.'

'Maybe you should?'

'It's not my place. And besides, it's only gossip.'

'How many?' asked Dixon, giving Monty the last inch or so of his ice cream cone.

'He was convicted of two, with a third not pursued. Plus there are several missing persons believed to be victims. They all came from the area in and around the battlefield and went missing within weeks of each other. No trace of them was ever found. No bodies, nothing.'

'When?'

'Fifteen years ago. Billy was just a baby when his father was sent down. He's in foster care at the moment.'

'Where's his mother?'

'Overdose when he was two.'

'Poor sod hasn't had much of a start in life, has he.'

'That's why I'm determined to see it doesn't get any worse.'

Dixon gestured towards the steps. 'Looks like you might have some help,' he said, watching Billy and Lucy appear at the top, still holding hands.

Lucy was carrying her trainers in her free hand, her feet covered in sand. 'You got any money?' she asked. 'We thought we might get some fish and chips.'

'What time are your foster parents expecting you back?' asked Jane, looking Billy up and down.

'Eight.'

Dixon handed Lucy a ten pound note, then fixed Billy with a cold stare, pointing at Monty at the same time. 'Just remember, he knows where you live.'

'Him?' Billy grinned. 'He's soft as a mop.'

They watched Lucy and Billy wander off along the seafront.

'His father's appeal will be dismissed,' said Jane, shaking her head. 'He'll go off the rails and I really don't want Lucy caught up in it when he does.'

'She'll be back in Manchester by then, if the hearing's next week.' Dixon squeezed Jane's hand. 'Safely out of the way.'

'There's not been a single killing or disappearance linked to the Scytheman since his father was arrested.' She folded her arms. 'What does that tell you?'

'Nothing.'

Jane tipped her head, puzzlement etched on her forehead.

'Think about it,' continued Dixon. 'If you were a serial killer and someone else was sent down for your murders, what would you do? Because I can tell you exactly what I'd do.'

'What?'

'Retire.'

Chapter Three

The helicopter hovering overhead had gone by the time darkness fell, and a uniformed patrol was keeping the traffic moving out on the main road; the crowd that had gathered in lay-bys and field gateways long since moved on by traffic officers. Lewis was still sitting on the water pump when Scientific Services finally lifted the body out of the ditch just before midnight. A large tent had been pitched over the rhyne and the scene lit by bright spot lamps.

'Found one at last, have we?' said Donald Watson, the senior Scientific Services officer, poking his head around the tent flap. 'I saw it on the news when I got home from the pub.'

Lewis was watching a spider in the grass. 'Looks like it,' he said without looking up.

'Found one what?' asked Poland, his frown lost behind his hair net.

'Before your time, Roger,' replied Lewis.

'Male or female?' asked Watson.

'Female, possibly, but I'll need to have a look at the pelvis to confirm,' replied Poland. 'We'll soon get an ID from DNA anyway, so I'm not too concerned at this stage. They're young though. A teenager. See here.' He was pointing at the top of the skull. 'The skin here has decomposed and you can see that the parietal bones haven't fully fused.'

The body had been laid out on a blue tarpaulin adjacent to the ditch, still encased in clay apart from the skull and torso, which Poland had brushed clean.

'There's still a lot of soft tissue, so she can't have been in the ground long, surely?' Watson looked down at two of his colleagues in the bottom of the ditch, carefully digging out the clay around the grave and placing it in trays for forensic examination back at the lab. 'Buried shallow too.'

'Unless she was buried before the ditch was dredged.' Poland stepped back to let the photographer stand over the body. 'The farmer says he dug out about a foot of sludge all the way along, so she'd have been eighteen inches deep if she was buried before that.'

'Very little wax, as well,' muttered Watson.

'Wax?'

Poland turned to a uniformed officer standing behind an arc lamp, who looked on the verge of being sick. 'It's formed by the decomposition of body fat in moist conditions. You'd expect to see a layer of—'

The officer raised his hand, then fled the tent, his other hand over his mouth.

Watson stepped inside, staying by the entrance and ducking under the insects swarming around the spot lamps. 'Any wound marks?'

Poland leaned over and pointed at the ribs on the left side of the chest. 'There's a curved blade mark here. It goes right round—'

'The Scytheman, then.' Watson inhaled sharply. 'Bastard.'

Poland looked at Lewis, puzzled at the revelation and irritated that it had not been mentioned before.

'Long story, Roger,' said Lewis.

'His appeal's up next week, isn't it?' Watson smiled. 'This'll put paid to that.'

'No doubt somebody will tell me sooner or later,' grumbled Poland. 'Right, let's get her in a crate, mud and all. Post mortem in the morning. The forensic anthropologist is coming down for a nine o'clock start. And I'll let you have an ID as soon as we get it.'

'Do we know which one it is?' asked Watson.

Poland straightened up, his hands on his hips. 'Which one what?'

'Misper.'

'Well, there'll be plenty of DNA and I can check the serial number on the pacemaker as soon as I get back to the lab, so it should be easy to ident—'

Lewis raised his hand, silencing Poland mid-sentence. 'There are four missing persons linked to the Scytheman. Only one had a pacemaker.' He hesitated, taking a moment to gather his composure. 'And it's a "he", not a "she".'

Poland picked up a brush and began flicking away the mud from the pelvic bone, careful to ensure that the debris stayed inside the crate into which the body had now been placed, tarpaulin and all. 'Yes, you're right,' he said after a minute or two of brushing, Lewis and Watson watching on in silence. 'It's male.'

Lewis lifted his chin. Time to come clean. 'His name's Rory Estcourt. He's seventeen years old and he loved *Doctor Who*, Eminem and his Xbox 360.' He took a deep breath. 'I always promised his mother I'd find him; never thought for a bloody minute I would.'

'Well, now you have,' mumbled Watson.

'I'm beginning to think that was the easy bit.' Lewis turned away, stepping back into the shadows behind the spot lamps. 'Now I've just got to tell her.'

'Send uniform.' Watson was trying to be helpful.

'Nice idea, but it's got to be me.'

'Tell me about the Scytheman,' said Poland, holding open the tent flap.

Lewis stepped out into the darkness, the flap closing behind them. 'Two hours and twelve minutes the jury took to convict him. And you and I both know they'd have spent most of that time drinking coffee and selecting a foreman.' He was staring up at the night sky, his hands thrust deep into his pockets, talking to himself more than Poland. 'I remember the twelve of them filing into court, looking pleased with themselves. The chief super was sitting behind me, revelling in it.' Lewis sneered. 'If I had a pound for every pat on the back I got I could have retired there and then.'

'Who was he?' asked Poland, trying to join the conversation.

'Daniel Parker. He was convicted of two murders, but there were more; there was blood all over the place at a house on the edge of Sutton Mallet, but we never found the boy's body; and at least three others missing that we know of, including Rory.'

'You were on the original investigation?'

'I was a sergeant back then.' Lewis spun round, looking along the hedgerows – dark shadows in the moonlight. 'I remember the fog; swirling. It seemed to close around me as I ran across the cornfield, just over that way, towards Chedzoy. I found the victim first – Nicola Bond. Then Parker hiding under a hedge, with a hand scythe on the ground next to him.'

'You nicked him?' Poland seemed impressed.

Little does he know, thought Lewis. 'I was in the right place at the right time, I suppose. There was insufficient evidence to proceed with the other victims, so he got the two life sentences: Nicola and her mother.'

'A good result by any standards,' said Poland.

'If he's guilty.'

'And you don't think he is?'

'I couldn't bring myself to stay for the sentencing. There was forensic evidence and, more importantly, the killings stopped. Nobody would've listened to me anyway, so I decided not to rock the boat. Trouble is, I haven't had a decent night's sleep since.'

'Well, this body gives you another chance to have a look at it, doesn't it?' Poland put his hand on Lewis's shoulder. 'Who are you going to give it to?'

'Division are going to want it pinned on Parker with the minimum of fuss,' he replied, talking to himself again as he set off along the track. 'And there's only one person I can rely on not to do that.'

Chapter Four

A little too much Scotch had helped Lewis sleep, but not for long. His wife had seen the television news and had waited up for him, listening to him rambling on and keeping his glass topped up until he fell asleep in the armchair. A body on the battlefield; she knew better than to ask.

Wounds heal and scar tissue may fade, but a mark remains all the same.

A clean shave had woken him up the following morning, although now more than ever he didn't like what he saw when he looked in the mirror. He knew what today would bring: formal identification of Rory Estcourt, and then a trip to see the boy's mother – a trip he never really thought he would have to make – to deliver the death message. It was just one of the many parts of the job he hadn't missed since promotion had turned him from a police officer into an office manager.

He'd kept a bowl of cornflakes down, but it had done nothing for his dry mouth and headache – a real belter. The drive to Burnham had, though; all the car windows wound down in the early morning sun. It was probably a good job he hadn't been breathalysed, mind you.

It had been an easy decision as soon as the press had got hold of the story – a liaison officer with each family until the remains could be identified. Charlesworth would probably grumble about the cost, but that was just tough.

Lewis parked in front of the block of flats opposite the almshouses and checked the time on his phone: two minutes. Then he checked the text message from Roger Poland one more time:

ID confirmed Rory Estcourt. Pacemaker serial number and dental records. DNA to follow. RP

He glanced up at the inshore lighthouse as he crossed the Berrow Road towards the Gothic arch over the front gate, pausing to admire the manicured lawns and flowerbeds in front of Ellen's Cottages: a faded red brick terrace of five single storey almshouses, each with an ornate porch and carved stone windows, all of them sandblasted by the wind over the years.

One minute.

In less than sixty seconds now, three liaison officers would break the news to tearful families that the remains found were not those of their son, prolonging their agony still further.

Who the hell would want to be a family liaison officer?

It was his job to break the news to Rory Estcourt's mother that the remains *were* those of her only son. It was not something he'd had to do for a while, but this was one death message he'd always promised to deliver himself, if and when the time came. She had insisted and he had agreed.

He spotted the movement behind the net curtains, the oak front door opening before he rang the bell.

'I knew you'd come,' she said, leaning on the frame to steady herself. 'I just knew. When I saw the news on the telly, I said to myself, "Peter will be coming."'

Lewis looked down at the wilted figure standing in front of him. Years spent trudging the battlefield in all weathers looking for her boy, coupled with the unrelenting grief, had taken its toll, made worse – far worse – by the uncertainty, the doubt; the not knowing. At least all that was about to end.

Immaculately dressed, as always, her hair had turned a shade whiter, if anything, the fringe stained with nicotine. The glasses were new, but the fire still burned brightly in her eyes, even behind the tears.

'It's Rory, isn't it,' she said.

He nodded. It was all he could muster, his attempt at words sticking in his throat.

'Karen Marsden's here.' She reached out and took his hand, leading him into the hall and closing the door behind him. 'I put the kettle on when I saw you coming.'

'I'm making the tea,' said Karen, emerging from the kitchen.

Lewis followed the old woman's exaggerated limp into the living room. 'Have you still not had your hip done, Doreen?' he asked, with a wince.

'I did, but it's the other one giving me gyp now.' She gestured to the coffee table. 'Cigarette?'

He stared at the open silver box. 'Given up,' he mumbled.

'Good for you,' she said, taking one and closing the lid. 'You don't mind if I do?'

Lewis knew it wasn't really a question.

'I take them out of the packets and put them in this box,' continued Doreen. 'That way I don't have to look at those revolting health warnings they have to put on them these days.'

He watched the reflection of the flame flickering in her eyes as she lit the cigarette. A deep drag, then she blew the smoke out through her nose.

'I have one question,' she said. 'The rest can wait.'

'Go ahead.'

'Did he suffer?'

'No,' replied Lewis, knowing that he couldn't afford even a moment's hesitation. He watched her processing the information, nodding and taking another drag.

'I don't want to see him.' Matter of fact; holding in the smoke.

'There's not a lot—'

'You forget I used to be a nurse, Peter,' she said, with a dismissive wave of her cigarette, the trail of smoke hanging in the air. 'He'll just be a bag of bones now. My beautiful bag of bones, but bones all the same.'

Lewis was struggling to find the right words when Karen walked in carrying a tray of tea. 'I couldn't find any mugs, Doreen, so it's cups and saucers, I'm afraid.'

'There aren't any mugs.' Doreen dropped her cigarette into the ashtray on the coffee table in front of her, leaving it to burn out. 'Here, let me.' She began pouring the tea, giving the pot a swirl before pouring the second cup.

She was deep in thought, that much was obvious. She had said she had one question, but more were coming; Lewis knew that. And he would do his best to answer them. Straight. As much as he dared, anyway; she deserved nothing less. 'Karen, d'you mind if we . . .' He didn't feel the need to spell it out.

'Of course. I'll be in the kitchen,' she replied, taking her tea with her.

Doreen watched the door close. 'Is it . . . *him*?' she asked.

'A single stab wound to the chest from a curved blade, consistent with a hand scythe. So, yes, it's him.'

'Had to be, really. The idea that Rory was still out there somewhere and hadn't got in touch was ridiculous.'

'May I?' asked Lewis, gesturing to the silver box.

Doreen frowned. 'Not if you've given up, no.' She snapped the box shut and put it on the shelf beside her chair, next to a photograph of Rory; the same one Lewis had stared at many times on the police file, of a young bespectacled boy sailing a model yacht on the old paddling pool on Burnham beach, smiling at the camera; his father visible on the far side, ready to catch the boat, turn it round and send it back. Doreen had taken the photograph herself, he remembered that. Rory was an only child born to older-than-average parents, and they had doted on him.

He thought about the last time he had seen Doreen – at her husband's funeral. Her words to him that day still turned his stomach: 'The saddest thing of all is that he died without knowing what happened to our son.'

'This is going to be swept under the carpet, isn't it,' she said, her sudden change of tack jerking Lewis back to the present.

'I promise you, Dor—'

'I had a letter from the victim support people telling me Parker's appeal is up next week. Will he get out?'

'If his conviction is quashed then he'll be arrested for Rory's murder, so he's not getting out, no.'

Lewis waited, watching her mull it over.

'But if his appeal fails then Rory's murder will be dropped, won't it? I mean, what's the point of prosecuting Parker again when he's already got whole life sentences for the other two murders? That's what they'll say, anyway.'

'That would be a decision for the CPS.'

'I know that.' She picked up the photograph of Rory and dusted it with a tissue that had been tucked in her sleeve. 'What I want to know is what *you're* going to do about it?'

'I'm going to see to it that Rory's murder is investigated properly, Doreen. You have my word.'

'Well, I hope he gets out,' she continued. 'I sat through every day of that charade of a trial at Bristol Crown Court, and so did you.'

Lewis shifted uneasily on the edge of the sofa.

'Oh, c'mon, this is me you're talking to.' She leaned back in her armchair. 'You don't think Parker is the Scytheman any more than I do. You didn't even stay to see him sentenced.'

Those eyes burning into his. She was right, of course. And she didn't know the half of it. Not a day had passed since the trial when he hadn't agonised over it. Not only that, but if Parker pleaded guilty to Rory's murder, or worse still, the case was dropped, then Doreen would go to her grave not knowing what really happened to her son, just like her husband.

'The man who killed Rory is still out there, Peter,' she said. 'You know it, and I know it.'

Lewis stood up, buttoning the jacket of his suit. 'This is going to get messy, Doreen. Are you ready for that?'

She moistened her lips with the tip of her tongue. 'I've been grieving for sixteen years, Peter,' she said, screwing the still-burning cigarette butt into the ashtray. 'All that's left is anger. I just want to know what happened to my son. And I don't care how messy it gets.'

Dixon leaned over the sea wall and looked down at Jane, pacing up and down on the sand in front of Lucy and Billy. They were sitting on the bottom step, their backs to him, Lucy's arm around Billy. He could hear voices, but the wind was too strong to make out what was being said.

'It's no good, old son,' he said, when Monty pulled on the end of the lead. 'You're not allowed on this part of the beach and that's all there is to it.'

The previous evening had been an odd one, Lucy giving it the full lovestruck teenager routine. Dixon remembered it well, although his phone had never pinged incessantly throughout *A Night to Remember*. He cringed. Maybe it would have done, if he'd had one back then.

Lucy was a bright kid, despite the 'I thought *Titanic* was just a film?' question. Dixon had paused the DVD, taken a deep breath and counted to ten before embarking on a short history lesson.

The real argument had started when the film finished. Lucy had produced her *Walking Dead* box set with a mischievous grin. 'Not in this house, you'll upset the dog,' Dixon had said.

Then her phone had rung.

He had watched Jane fidgeting throughout Lucy's conversation – scowling, frowning and shaking her head every time Lucy looked in her direction; overprotective, as always. He thought it was guilt, but any attempt to talk about it had always been shut down, so he hadn't pushed it. Guilt that she had been adopted at birth when Lucy hadn't been so lucky; in and out of foster care for much of her childhood, her mother addicted to alcohol and drugs, Lucy hadn't had much of a start in life. It was understandable that Jane would feel guilty, perhaps, having landed on her feet in a loving home with parents who had spoilt her rotten.

Lucy's foster parents, David and Judy, did their best, but she had been a handful, at least until she met Jane at their mother's funeral. Since then Lucy had spent every spare minute down in Somerset, hitch-hiking down from Manchester at one point. She'd even decided she was going to be a police officer; the nose studs and earrings had gone soon after, the black dye in her cropped hair grown out within a few weeks.

Dixon had known what the telephone call was about. He'd seen it on the early evening news but had kept it to himself, hoping Billy wouldn't have spotted it.

The argument had started before Lucy's call had finished, the last straw coming when she agreed to meet Billy on the seafront at eleven.

'And how d'you think you're getting there?' Jane had demanded.

'I'll walk if I have to.'

Then Jane had snatched Lucy's phone. 'Billy, it's Jane. What's going on?' She had turned away, her hand across her forehead. 'Look, nothing's going to happen tonight, is it? I'll find out what I can in the morning and we'll meet you in Burnham, all right? Lucy's not coming out tonight and that's all there is to it.'

'Bitch,' Lucy had muttered. Dixon heard it, but had allowed her that one. It might have been different if he thought she meant it.

The rest of the evening had been a bit frosty, to say the least. Jane had sat up until the early hours, listening for Lucy trying to creep out of the cottage, but all she really achieved was keeping Dixon and Monty awake half the night.

'What can I tell him?' asked Jane, appearing at the top of the steps from the beach. 'It doesn't look good, does it?'

'How's Lucy?'

'She's promised me she won't do anything stupid. And besides, she's back to Manchester on Sunday.' She leaned over the sea wall and looked down, just in time to see Lucy and Billy set off along the beach, hand in hand. 'Poor sod. He'd convinced himself his dad was coming home. Then this.'

'Is there any evidence his father had anything to do with it?'

'Just the scythe mark, I think. I'll have to go in to work and see what more I can find out. Social services are keeping an eye on him and there's not a lot more I can do, really.'

'Who's the senior investigating officer?'

'Lewis hasn't given it to anyone yet, according to Sandy, but she's stuck in the Safeguarding Unit. She was just passing on canteen gossip.'

'Who's handling the appeal?'

'Someone at Portishead. I'm not sure who.'

'Headquarters have got it?' Dixon slid along the bench, uncovering a small area next to him not plastered in seagull shit. 'That explains why we haven't come across it, I suppose.'

'The original trial was in 2005.' Jane sat down, then shuffled along when Monty jumped up and sat in between them. 'I was still at college then.'

'I might google it and see what I can find out.'

'You're supposed to be taking it easy.' Jane frowned. 'Light duties for a couple of months, Charlesworth said. And they don't know about your eye either.'

'They seem to have hit it off,' said Dixon, nodding in the direction of the jetty, where Lucy and Billy were now queuing at the ice cream stand.

Jane sighed. 'It's got disaster written all over it, hasn't it?'

'They understand each other, I suppose. Both in foster care and all that.'

'Fancy growing up and finding out one day your father's a serial killer . . .'

'I don't envy the poor sod who had to break that news to him.' Dixon grimaced. 'And his mother's dead too, don't forget.'

'At least he was too young to remember it.' Jane stood up. 'Can you drop me home so I can get my car? I need to go in to work.'

'What about Lucy?'

'She said she'd ring me.'

Dixon had parked on the seafront, just along from the Pavilion.

'I just can't get over the timing,' Jane said, the bells and whistles of the fruit machines in the background. 'I mean, the week before his appeal and we find another body.' She shook her head, watching Dixon lift Monty into the back of his Land Rover. 'What sort of coincidence is that?'

'Maybe it's not a coincidence at all,' he said, unclipping the dog's lead. 'Have you thought of that?'

Chapter Five

'You haven't changed a bit, Sir.'

You're still an arrogant bloody prick.

Lewis had been warned that Ridley was in the building, but hadn't banked on being cornered in the lift. At least the glass doors had given him advance warning.

Detective Chief Superintendent John Ridley had retired ten years ago, but still managed to swagger along the landing as if he owned the place. The moustache had gone – more grey in it than his vanity could stomach, probably – and the glasses were new. He was even wearing the same old pinstripe suit, although it looked as if it had had a clean.

'And you, a DCI. Wonders will never cease.' Ridley's hand was outstretched as Lewis stepped out of the lift on the first floor at Express Park. 'Up for promotion too, I gather.'

'We'll see.'

'I know what you're thinking.' Ridley winked at him while they shook hands.

I doubt that.

'You're wondering what the hell I'm doing here.'

'The thought had crossed my mind.' Lewis rounded off the barb with a smile.

'David rang me and said I should come in.'

On first name terms with the Assistant Chief Constable now, is it?

'He thought I might have some perspective to add,' continued Ridley. 'I was the senior investigating officer on the Scytheman, in case you'd forgotten.'

'Is the ACC here?' asked Lewis, stepping around Ridley and heading towards the canteen.

'He's got the press officer in with him at the moment.' Ridley pointed to meeting room 2. 'They're in there. He was waiting for you, I think.'

Lewis stopped in his tracks, still out of sight of the occupants of the meeting room. Take the long way around the atrium to the canteen, or double-back to the coffee machine? Decisions, decisions; the smaller they are, the harder they become. Or maybe that was just how it felt today?

'The Chief Crown Prosecutor says Parker's appeal will fail.' Ridley rubbed his hands together. 'Are you going?'

'No,' replied Lewis. Odd, that. He hadn't even thought about it until that point. He hadn't been asked; there'd been no witness summons. So, no, he wasn't going. And what good would it do? Picking at old scars.

'Have you seen the boy's mother?'

'I've just come from there now.' The glare he gave Ridley was enough to wipe the glee from his face.

'How is she?'

'Angry.'

'Daft old bird'll go straight to the papers again.' Ridley shook his head. 'She must think she's helping, keeping it in the public eye.' His voice was loaded with sarcasm. 'Not letting us forget it, more like.'

The sound of a door opening behind Lewis triggered an involuntary sigh, which he allowed to escape silently through his nose.

'Ah, there you are,' said Charlesworth. 'In here, when you're ready.'

Lewis stepped back, allowing Ridley into the meeting room, then closed the door behind them and sat down opposite Charlesworth, the ever-present press officer to his right and Ridley sitting to his left. It felt more like a job interview.

'Have you found out how the press got hold of it so quickly, Peter?' asked Charlesworth.

'Not yet, Sir. It could have been social media. The battlefield was covered in archaeology students, as you know.'

'I got the impression it was one of ours.' Vicky Thomas tucked a strand of hair behind her ear. 'The journalist was being tight-lipped about revealing his sources though.'

'I'll make some enquiries and see what I can find out, but I wouldn't hold your breath.'

'Well, you did the right thing getting family liaison out,' said Charlesworth, folding up his reading glasses and dropping them into his top pocket. 'How was Mrs Estcourt?'

Lewis grimaced. 'Angry.'

'Not with us?'

'With everybody and everything.'

'You'd think she'd be grieving,' said Ridley.

'She's been doing nothing else for the last sixteen years.'

'Quite,' mumbled Charlesworth. 'Will she go to the press again?'

'I expect so, Sir.'

'The timing couldn't be better, could it?' Ridley's obvious delight grated on Lewis. Again. 'I mean, finding another body the week before his appeal.'

'The CPS have asked if there's any evidence relevant to the hearing next week. I'm told it's not likely to succeed anyway, but . . .' Charlesworth's voice tailed off.

'I haven't appointed an SIO yet, Sir,' replied Lewis. 'But he or she will look into that as a priority.'

'Let's cut the crap, shall we?' Ridley rapped the table with his knuckles. 'Whoever is the senior investigating officer needs to be singing from the same hymn sheet as the rest of us. All right?'

Direct as ever, thought Lewis.

'The boy was killed with a curved blade. That makes him a victim of the Scytheman, and Parker *is* the Scytheman. End of discussion. The SIO just needs to make sure he does whatever it takes to—'

'I think what DCS Ridley means, Peter,' interrupted Charlesworth, clearing his throat, 'is that care needs to be taken to see to it that we get the right result. If Parker's appeal fails then the pressure is off; we can take our time to build a case against him and put it to the CPS.'

'Let them take the flak for dropping it.' Ridley folded his arms.

'Is it really in the public interest to prosecute him again now?' asked Vicky Thomas. 'After all these years.'

'Try asking Doreen Estcourt that question,' said Lewis.

'It gets more complicated in the unlikely event his appeal succeeds.' Charlesworth glanced at the press officer, who was still glowering at Lewis. 'Do we have any evidence he was involved in the murder of the boy?'

'None at all.'

'Yet,' Ridley said, testily.

Lewis took a deep breath. 'Various samples have gone off to the lab, so we may find some trace DNA, and I've made it clear we need the results before the appeal hearing. But, as it stands, there is nothing specific to implicate Parker, or anyone else for that matter, in the murder of Rory Estcourt.'

'There's nothing that clears him either.'

'Thank you, John,' replied Charlesworth, massaging the bridge of his nose between his thumb and index finger. 'Look, it's early days and this is a very delicate situation. Parker has to be the prime suspect—'

'He's the *only* suspect,' interrupted Ridley.

'And we need to be in a position to arrest him immediately if the worst happens and he walks out of the Appeal Court next week.'

'What are the chances of that?' asked Vicky Thomas.

'Virtually nil, I'd have thought,' replied Ridley. 'If they quash his conviction, they'll probably order a retrial and he'd be remanded in custody until that took place. So—'

'We can speak frankly within these four walls, can't we?' Charlesworth's eyes darted around the meeting room.

Looking for reassurance, thought Lewis, choosing not to oblige.

'As John says, we all know Parker is the Scytheman and we need to pin this murder on him quickly and quietly, because if it turns out that we put the wrong man away fifteen years ago the press will crucify us.'

'We haven't put the wrong man away.' Ridley spoke through gritted teeth.

'You don't look convinced, Peter,' said Charlesworth, confusion furrowing his brow.

Lewis had never been any good at poker.

'You made the arrest, for fuck's sake,' snarled Ridley. 'And the jury took, what was it, two hours?'

'Two hours and twelve minutes,' offered Lewis.

'That's got to count for something.'

'There can't be any doubt,' said Charlesworth. 'And we can't afford to let any creep in now. We have to avoid a PR disaster at all costs. That's got to be the top priority.'

'Think about it: this body is a bloody godsend for us. If his appeal fails, we're home and hosed.' Ridley leaned back in his chair, his arms above his head. 'All we need is an SIO we can rely on to do the necessary.'

'Who d'you have in mind, Peter?' asked Charlesworth, closing the notebook on the table in front of him.

'I haven't decided yet, Sir.' Lewis put on his best pained expression to cover the lie. 'I'll need to check availability. We're under the cosh at the moment and it's a question of who's got capacity to take it on.'

'Well, let me know.' Charlesworth stood up. 'Just make sure whoever it is knows what's expected of them.'

Chapter Six

'How much longer have you got to wear that thing for?'

'A day or so.'

'You look like Captain Pugwash.'

'What is it with people and Captain bloody Pugwash? He didn't even wear an eye patch.'

'Didn't he?' Lewis sat down on the bench in the porch of Berrow Church and leaned back against the parish noticeboard. 'Who did then?'

'I don't know. What about Long John Silver?' Dixon was standing in the doorway, watching Monty sniffing along the wall on the far side of the churchyard.

'He had a wooden leg,' replied Lewis.

'Maybe one day.' Dixon managed a lopsided grin.

'You're supposed to be on holiday. The Lake District again, wasn't it?'

'Had to cancel it. The eye surgery was urgent, or so they said.'

'Did it hurt?'

'Not really. I'm not sure why I've got to wear this thing either.' He lifted the patch and squinted out into the sunlight. 'The eye's fine.'

'It'll come up at your next medical, you do realise that? They'll get your medical records—'

'If they do, the records will show a successful op and a full recovery.'

'Pleased to hear it.'

'How did you know I was here?'

'I saw Jane at Express Park, and when you weren't at home . . .' Lewis shrugged. 'I did check the pub first, mind you.'

'Is it about the body on the battlefield?' asked Dixon, sitting down on the bench opposite Lewis.

'It was my wedding anniversary. The fifth, so what's that? Wood – or something like that anyway. Not that it matters now.'

Dixon knew when to shut up and listen.

'The twenty-third of October. We were in the Sedgemoor Inn at Westonzoyland, having a meal,' continued Lewis, 'when I got the call. No one else from CID could get there quickly because of the fog, so they rang me. Maybe I shouldn't have told them where I'd be?'

A rhetorical question.

'Late it was; not long before last orders. The clocks were going back that weekend.' Lewis closed his eyes. 'I can see it now. Thick fog. Always bloody is out on the moor.'

Monty trotted into the porch and sat down next to Dixon.

'Obedient, isn't he?' said Lewis, sucking his teeth. 'I left my wife in the pub and drove round to Chedzoy. Took an age – seemed like it, anyway – creeping along watching the grass verge at the side of the car. I tried my lights on full beam but it just reflected off the fog; I couldn't see more than a couple of paces and you know what those bloody rhynes are like at the side of the road. There was already a patrol car on scene when I got there – on the corner by the old red phonebox.' He sighed. 'That's not there any more either. I remember seeing the blue lights in the fog and driving towards them. You drive down through the village and there's a lane off to the right; Frys Lane it's called. I turned in and that's when I heard the screaming.'

Dixon clipped on Monty's lead, all the while watching Lewis fighting to keep his composure.

'There were two farm cottages on the left. They've been knocked down now. The lights were on inside both, the doors open; shafts of lights streaming out into the fog. I remember a uniformed officer vomiting in the yard out the front; the other was sitting in the patrol car, screaming into the radio.' A deep breath through his nose. 'The neighbour was screaming too. I couldn't get a word out of her.'

A spaniel ran into the porch but soon scooted off when it saw Monty. Lewis waited for the owner to walk past and up the track to the golf course before continuing.

'I can't describe . . . you'll have to look at the crime scene photographs for the inside of the cottage. I can't begin to do it justice. That was the mother, Christine. Twenty-seven stab wounds; she'd almost been decapitated.' He leaned forward, his elbows on his knees, staring out at the gravestones. 'I found the daughter in the cornfield. Nicola. She went to school with my daughter, Sam. Peaceful by comparison to her mother, she was; just a single stab wound in the chest. She looked asleep.'

Lewis stood up, thrust his hands in his pockets and turned to face the noticeboard, his back to Dixon. 'Then I heard a noise. It sounded like someone running through the corn, so I went after it, following a trail of flattened stems. I'd had a couple of glasses of wine, so it must have been Dutch courage or something. That's when I found Daniel Parker curled up under the hedge on the far side of the field. I can remember seeing the beam from my torch lighting up the tracks of his tears in the blood spatter on his face. People say it's funny the things you remember, but I remember it all. Every last detail.'

'You made the arrest?' asked Dixon.

'I was the hero of the hour. I got a commendation and was made up to detective inspector within six months of the trial. My wife was delighted.'

'What's the problem then?'

'I don't think Parker did it, that's the problem. Never have.' Lewis spun round. 'C'mon, there's someone I'd like you to meet.'

Ten minutes later Dixon was sitting on the edge of the sofa in Doreen Estcourt's living room, the old lady looking him up and down. 'Is this him?' she screeched, turning to Lewis. 'Doesn't look up to much.' She sat back in her armchair with a dismissive wave of her hand. 'He's only got one eye.'

Dixon took off the patch and stuffed it into his pocket.

'And he's the best you've got?' Doreen shook her head.

'No, he isn't, Doreen,' replied Lewis. 'He's the best there is.'

'Pass me that box, young man,' she said, gesturing to the silver cigarette case on the coffee table.

Dixon did as he was told, watching her eyes fixed on him through the flame of the lighter.

'They've found my son's body on the battlefield,' she said, holding the smoke in her lungs as she spoke. 'Stabbed with a curved blade. Did you know that?'

'I know a body's been found,' replied Dixon. 'That's all it said on the television news.'

'Quite a coincidence, isn't it?' offered Doreen. 'A body being found the week before Parker's appeal comes up. Don't you think?'

'I don't believe in coincidence, Mrs Estcourt,' said Dixon.

'Looks bad for him, though, doesn't it?'

'Only if he's the killer. And he says he isn't.'

'An open mind.' Doreen turned to Lewis. 'I like him.'

'I thought you would,' he mumbled.

'Tea?' asked Doreen, standing up.

'Yes, please,' replied Lewis. He waited until she had left the room, then turned to Dixon. 'I'm appointing you senior investigating officer. All right?'

'It's hardly light duties, is it?'

'Are you turning it down?'

'What d'you think?'

Lewis offered a tired smile. 'You'll need to liaise with DCS Potter at Portishead. She's leading the appeal from our end. Parker is at Long Lartin and you can interview him there. The appeal is Monday and Tuesday next week.'

'What about the original case file? I'll need access to that.'

'I can sort out copies back at Express Park, but I've got the trial transcript in my car. I can take you out to the crime scene too.'

'The sooner, the better.'

'Charlesworth is going to go berserk when he finds out I've given it to you, but you let me worry about that. The original SIO is sniffing about too – DCS John Ridley.'

'I expect he took all the credit.'

'He was welcome to it, the arrogant ponce. He's going to love you.'

'I'm used to it.'

'The expectation is that Parker's appeal will fail. Then they're going to want Rory's murder pinned on him quickly and quietly. There'll be immense pressure from division, and Charlesworth, to see to it that it never sees the light of day, so be ready for that. Pin it on Parker and forget it, that's what they want.'

'That's not the way I—'

'That's why I'm giving it to you,' said Lewis, a scheming glint in his eye. 'Do what I should have done fifteen years ago and blow it wide open. Whatever you have to do, do it, and I'll keep you out of trouble along the way.'

'What about Doreen?'

'They don't give a shit about Doreen.' Lewis lowered his voice to a whisper. 'They'll lean on the CPS to drop it and that will be that.'

'You said you thought Parker is innocent.'

'Read the case file, meet him, and make your own mind up.'

'I sat through the trial too, dear,' said Doreen, bustling in and setting down a tray with three mugs of tea on the table. 'And I don't think he did it either. He's as much a victim of the Scytheman as Rory. You've only got to look at him to see he's not capable of it.'

'I thought you said you didn't have any mugs?' Lewis frowned.

'That was for Karen's benefit,' replied Doreen, a twinkle in her eye. 'Snooty cow.'

'Where did the nickname come from?' asked Dixon.

'One of the tabloids.' Lewis rolled his eyes. 'The scythe was enough, of course, and the fact that Nicola had been "hacked to death" in the Chedzoy cornfield. That was the headline, anyway. It didn't help that all the victims seemed to be connected to the battlefield in some way too.'

'Connected how?'

'They all lived within a mile or two of the area.'

'Seems like I've got a bit of catching up to do,' said Dixon, standing up.

Doreen took his hand. 'Rory's dead and gone. But Parker is still alive.' She gave him as warm a smile as she could muster from behind the tears. 'Let right be done, young man. Let right be done.'

Chapter Seven

'Where've you been?' asked Jane, holding open the door of the cottage.

'The library.'

'And where's your eye patch?'

'In my pocket.' The rear door of the Land Rover was standing open, Dixon following Monty around the yard, inspecting everything the dog sniffed. Even the stinging nettles.

'There's no need to keep checking for poison now, surely?'

'Force of habit.' Dixon slammed the back door of the Land Rover, careful not to drop the two books tucked under his arm. 'What did you find out at Express Park?' he asked, following Monty inside the cottage.

'Lewis saw me, I think,' replied Jane, filling the kettle. 'So he knows we're not away on holiday, I'm afraid. He still hasn't appointed an SIO, apparently.'

'Yes, he has.' Dixon dropped the books on the kitchen worktop.

'*Sedgemoor 1685* by Graham Ashton,' said Jane, reading the title of the first book, her voice sombre. 'Where did he find you?'

'Berrow Church.'

'*Monmouth's Rebels; The Road to Sedgemoor 1685.*' She leaned back against the worktop and folded her arms; a last gesture of defiance before the inevitable surrender. 'What happened to light duties?'

'Lewis was the arresting officer. Did they tell you that?'

'No.'

'You've got two murders – bloody ones – and a suspect covered in the stuff. What d'you do?'

'Arrest him.'

'Of course you do.' Dixon nodded emphatically. 'Two bodies, others missing, and the public living in fear of a serial killer. They were under pressure to make an arrest and Lewis did.'

'I don't understand.' Jane frowned. 'What's the—'

'The problem is he's wracked with doubts about Parker's guilt.'

'And he didn't say anything at the time?'

'That's the one question I haven't asked him yet,' muttered Dixon. 'And I'm not sure I want to know the answer. If he did, he was ignored.'

'What was he, a DS back then?'

'With young kids and a mortgage. He could be forgiven for not rocking the boat . . .' Dixon allowed his voice to tail off, more to hide his uncertainty than anything else. 'Would you?'

'I like to think I'd say something,' replied Jane, rummaging in the cutlery drawer for a teaspoon. 'I know you'd kick up a hell of a stink.'

'Yes, but I've got seniority on my side now. And the fact that I don't give a shit.'

'So, he appoints you SIO to clear up his mess?'

'Something like that.'

She handed Dixon a mug of tea. 'What do we tell Lucy and Billy?'

'Nothing. I'm going to interview Billy's father on Sunday at Long Lartin and Lucy goes back to Manchester on Sunday anyway. The less they know, the better.' Dixon slumped down on to the sofa. 'What else did you find out?'

'Nothing you don't know already, if you've spoken to Lewis,' replied Jane, sitting down on the arm of the sofa next to him. 'The post mortem is likely to take an age, by all accounts. Roger's got some anthropologist down from Bristol.'

'I'll go and see him later.'

'And there's a retired DCS called Ridley sniffing about. He was the SIO on the original investigation.'

'Lewis warned me about him.'

'This is bloody marvellous, this is.' Jane was flicking the edge of the rug with her toes. 'You're the one Charlesworth's going to blame for this. Lewis is basically getting you to do his dirty work for him.'

'I wouldn't put it quite like that,' replied Dixon, not sure how he would put it, though; and Jane was bound to ask.

'How would you put it then?' Right on cue.

'He's appointed an SIO he knows will conduct a thorough investigation into a brutal murd—'

'Yeah, right.'

'He'll watch my back. He always does.' Jane had a point, all the same. 'Nice cup of tea,' mumbled Dixon, trying to avoid her withering look.

'Here he is.' Roger Poland spoke without looking away from the microscope in front of him. 'This is the one I told you about, Helen. I told her it would be you.'

'Thank you,' said Dixon.

'Feeling bold today, are we?'

'Eh?'

'You usually skulk about in the anteroom until I come and get you.'

'It's hardly going to be fresh, is it? And there won't be much of a smell, surely?'

'There isn't,' said Helen, her smile visible even behind her mask. 'You're quite safe.'

'Helen, this is Detective Inspector Nick Dixon.' Poland still hadn't looked away from the microscope. 'Nick, this is Dr Helen Martin, forensic anthropologist.'

'He's told me all about you,' she said, her latex gloved hand outstretched. 'You're getting married, I gather?'

'We haven't set a date yet.'

'Well, congratulations anyway.'

'Thank you.' Dixon had found a mask in the usual drawer outside the pathology lab, and even applied a small blob of Vicks VapoRub under his nose, just in case. He was leaning over the slab, looking down into a large blue crate at the top of the skull, several patches of skin and hair still clinging to the bone.

Poland appeared next to him, holding a clipboard. 'I gave him a rinse before Helen got here, and drained off the water.' He gestured to several large glass jars on the side, the sediment gradually settling in each. 'That lot's going off to the forensic lab for testing.'

Dixon looked back to the crate. 'I've seen lots of dead bodies in my time, but never one that looked like this.'

Grey bones poked through skin that was pale and shiny, some of it split in places where it had been stretched over knees and elbows; it was not the usual shades of brown and yellow Dixon was used to either. The chest cavity and abdomen were all but empty too, revealing the spine and pelvis. He spun round, looking for organs that had been removed from the body. There were usually one or two on a set of scales or in a jar of preservative somewhere.

Nothing. Just a small metal box sitting in a stainless steel bowl. It was about the size of a box of matches, but thinner, with a couple of wires coming out of it.

'That's the pacemaker,' said Poland, picking it up. 'This bit,' pointing into the bottom of the bowl, 'sits outside the ribcage, under the skin. These wires then go into the chest cavity and are fed around to the heart inside the blood vessels. Oddly enough, the student who found him has got one as well.'

Dixon looked away. 'Where is the heart?' he asked.

'I'm rehydrating what's left of it,' replied Poland.

'Rehydrating it?'

'May I?' asked Helen, pulling her face mask down under her chin.

'Be my guest,' replied Poland. He sat down on a lab stool and folded his arms, ready to enjoy what was coming.

'The body's been mummified.'

Dixon was doing his best to take in the information he was being given without appearing flummoxed by it. 'Mummified?' He failed, miserably, the small laugh of disbelief giving him away; either that or the blank expression on his face that followed.

'Not as Hollywood understands it,' said Poland, stifling a chuckle.

'Kept in a warm and dry environment,' continued Helen, frowning at his flippancy. 'It usually happens in deserts, places like that, providing animals don't get to the body, of course. I've seen it a couple of times in this country where someone has died inside a house with the central heating on. The body just dries out instead of decomposing in the conventional sense.'

'When was he buried then?' asked Dixon. 'Do we know?'

'Six to nine months ago at most.'

'Which means it couldn't have been Parker.'

'Parker?' Helen was frowning at Dixon now.

'Daniel Parker. You may know him as the Scytheman. That was the nickname the newspapers gave him.'

'I thought Rory's name was familiar. So, this is Doreen's son.' Helen looked down into the crate. 'I remember seeing her on the telly; she'd be out on the battlefield in all weathers, searching. So sad. She never could let it rest.'

'Would you?'

'If it wasn't Parker who buried him,' said Poland, diving in to change the subject, 'then who did?'

'Perhaps he has an accomplice?' Helen raised her eyebrows at Poland. 'Someone trying to make us think the Scytheman is still out there.'

'Peter Lewis thinks—'

'I know what Lewis thinks, Roger,' interrupted Dixon. 'So, it's mummified, buried, rehydrates and then decomposition starts?' he asked, getting the conversation back to where he wanted it.

'Slow decomposition. Clay is good from that point of view, because it allows comparatively little oxygen to get at the body, slowing the whole thing down,' replied Poland. 'The moisture in the rhyne bed has also allowed the body to rehydrate, as you can see; partially, anyway.'

'Tell me about the mummification,' said Dixon, turning back to Helen. 'How long would it have taken?'

'About a year, probably. There's no evidence of insect activity, so it would have been indoors. Remote too, I imagine. Either that or you'd have your neighbours complaining about the smell.'

'And you're sure?'

'Yes, absolutely. You can see it under the microscope. Do you want to have a look?'

'Not really.'

'It's visible at a molecular level; cells that would usually have ruptured in the first stages of decomposition are still intact, but shrivelled. And there's very little adipocere too. You get that when there's moisture and the body fat is broken down by anaerobic bacteria. It's like a layer of lard, but there's very little here. He didn't have a lot of body fat, which helps, but what little he did have disappeared before he was buried. It would have seeped—'

'I'll take your word for it,' muttered Dixon. 'How long would the rehydration take?'

'About a week,' replied Helen. 'Fully immersed in fluid, that is. There's a doctor in Mexico who does it regularly with bodies found in the desert.'

'But it's not complete here?'

'No.' Poland slid off the stool and walked over to the crate. 'Some of the internal organs haven't fully rehydrated,' he said, pointing into the open chest cavity. 'The heart, for example. Solid muscle, that is.' He clenched his fist. 'Some of the neck muscles, and there are still bits of the diaphragm floating around. The softer tissue has rehydrated and then decomposed.'

'Not enough water seeping through the clay, would be my guess,' said Helen.

'What about the cause of death?' asked Dixon, taking the conversation back to safer ground.

'That was the stab wound.' Poland hesitated. 'But I can't get a proper look at the heart to confirm that until it's rehydrated.'

'There's no evidence of the healing process starting, so we can say that if he was alive he didn't survive the injury,' said Helen.

Poland picked up the stainless steel bowl. 'This is a dual chamber pacemaker; one wire would have gone into the right atrium and the other into the right ventricle. It delivers electrical impulses to the muscle. See this?' Poland was pointing at one of the wires with his little finger. 'That nick was made by a blade. I just need to check for the corresponding mark on the heart, but it looks like a large prune at the moment. If it's there, then death would have been pretty much instant.' His gloves muffled the click of his fingers.

'What about the nails?' Dixon asked.

'The toenails were painted post mortem; two coats. You can tell from the cuticle growth – or lack of it. And there are fake finger-nails too.' Poland lifted the left hand and turned it over, revealing pink nails still glued to the ring and little fingers. 'Forensics have got the rest. They were in the clay recovered at the grave site.'

'No clothes?'

'None,' replied Helen.

'We've got his glasses, though,' said Poland, holding up an evidence bag.

'And it's definitely Rory Estcourt?'

'The DNA's confirmed it.'

Dixon leaned back against the worktop. 'He was kept as a trophy, wasn't he?'

'That's your department,' replied Poland.

'Why else would someone paint his toenails?'

'He has a point,' said Helen.

'And why was he buried nine months ago?'

'Well, now we're back to Parker's accomplice.' Poland peeled back the cuff of his latex glove to look at his watch. 'Either that or the Scytheman is still out there.'

'If he has been kept as a trophy then there's a chance, surely, that we'll find some trace DNA from the killer,' said Dixon, spelling it out.

'Everything's gone or going to the lab,' replied Poland.

Dixon curled his lip. 'We won't find a match.'

'How d'you know?'

'He wouldn't take the risk if he knew he was on the database.'

'True.'

'Parker's house would've been searched from top to bottom . . .' Dixon frowned. 'The timing of the burial must have something to do with the appeal. And the archaeological dig.'

'It could be a coincidence.'

'He was buried there nine months ago in the sure and certain knowledge he would be found by the archaeologists.' Dixon jabbed his index finger in Poland's direction. 'If you think about it, it might explain why Rory was buried rather than one of the other missing victims.'

Poland nodded. 'So his pacemaker would set off a metal detector?'

'I don't buy the "Parker's accomplice" theory either,' continued Dixon. 'He or she would be taking one hell of a risk; offering up another body Parker had killed in the vain hope of making it look like the real killer – the Scytheman – is still out there. An accomplice isn't going to do that, is he?'

'You're right,' said Helen.

'The Scytheman, on the other hand, wants to see to it that Parker's appeal fails, and us finding another victim right before the hearing is hardly going to help his case. And the Scytheman would want to hide the fact the body had been mummified, so where better to bury it than the bottom of a rhyne, where he thinks it will rehydrate?'

'He's not necessarily going to know the clay would slow the decomposition,' offered Poland.

'If it wasn't for the clay we wouldn't be having this conversation at all.' Helen shook her head. 'In a shallow grave in sandy or loamy soil, there'd have been moisture from the rain, insect activity and oxygen getting to the body; decomposition would've been far more advanced by now, if not complete. All we would have found was a skeleton and we'd never have known the body had been mummified, let alone be able to say when the burial took place.'

'Parker was granted leave to appeal this time last year, and anyone following the case would've known that.' Dixon was talking to himself, his voice gathering momentum as he walked towards the door. 'Not everyone would've known about the archaeological dig though.'

'I told you he was a bright lad,' whispered Poland, winking at Helen.

'He's taking a calculated risk, isn't he?' said Dixon, holding the door open with his foot. 'He knows that if Parker's appeal fails, we'll stop looking for anyone else in connection with Rory's murder and he'll be in the clear again.'

'And will you?'

'Over *my* dead body.'

Chapter Eight

It was an ominous sign: the lights still on at gone one in the morning. Not that he would usually complain about Jane waiting up for him. No barking was odd though. Dixon frowned. Perhaps Monty couldn't hear the diesel engine over the shouting?

He switched off the engine, wound down the window and listened. Nothing.

It had been a long day and all he really wanted to do was crawl into bed. Still, it could have been worse. He could have been the one Lewis had got to do all that photocopying. The poor sod. Boxes and boxes of the bloody stuff.

Dixon had spent hours trawling through it all at Express Park, starting with Rory's missing persons file, which was his immediate priority given that he was investigating the boy's murder. It just so happened that it was the thinnest file too. A couple of witness statements from friends on the bus, a few stills from CCTV and a detailed statement from Doreen. It hadn't been much to go on.

What was striking was that there had been no real evidence that the Scytheman had been involved at all, and nothing to connect

Parker to Rory's disappearance either. Just a suspicion, based on the timing – the second in a sequence of four teenage boys all going missing in the three months leading up to the Bond murders.

It was a suspicion that had turned out to be right.

The prosecution files filled two boxes, and the crime scene photographs from inside the Bonds' cottage had been something to behold; the warning from Lewis more than justified. A strong coffee had been needed after flicking through those. Then Dixon had extracted the key witness statements, forensic and post mortem reports, and Parker's interview transcripts.

It made for grim reading and it was easy to see why a jury had convicted him; not so easy to see why Lewis had doubts, although the unidentified fingerprint found at the scene may have had something to do with it.

The bundle of documents for the appeal hearing filled two lever arch files, although it had been obvious from the skeleton argument lodged by Parker's legal team that his appeal turned on the blood spatter analysis. The only slight problem had been that the report ran to ninety pages, with appendices.

It was at that point Dixon had resigned himself to getting home after midnight.

He glanced down at the trial transcript sitting on the passenger seat of his Land Rover. And the two library books. He had been careful to take those with him in case Lucy saw them and put two and two together. She might do that anyway, of course, given that he'd gone back to work, but there was no way round that.

The barking finally started when he slammed the door of the Land Rover. Then the kitchen door opened and a shaft of light lit up the back yard behind the cottage.

'She knows,' said Jane, her hands on her hips.

'How did she take it?'

'Chuffed to bits!' Jane stepped back, allowing Dixon into the cottage. 'She's told Billy you'll get to the bottom of it once and for all.'

'Where is he?'

'At home. She wanted him to stay over on the sofa, but I put my foot down.'

'I'm pleased to hear it.' Dixon opened the fridge and took out a can of beer. 'If it came out that my fiancée's half-sister was in a relationship with the prime suspect's son—'

'They're not in a relationship. She only met him the day before yesterday, and that's being generous seeing as it's gone midnight. They're just a couple of teenagers holding hands.'

'We *are* in a relationship!' The shriek of protest came from the sofa, the top of Lucy's head just visible.

Dixon slammed his beer down on the kitchen worktop. 'That's it then. I'll have to tell Lewis I can't take the case. I've been hauled in front of Professional Standards for not declaring a personal interest once before, and it's not happening again.'

'All right. All right.' Lucy was kneeling on the sofa, leaning over the back. 'We're not in a relationship,' she said, with an exaggerated shrug. 'But we will be when this is over.'

'Just make sure Billy has that clear in his head.'

'I will, I promise.' She gave a sheepish grin. 'What did you find out then?' she asked.

'There's a line, Lucy. And we don't cross it,' Dixon said, taking a swig of beer. 'You know that. We don't discuss the details of any case, let alone this one. Is that clear?'

'What about the appeal?'

'Look, the best thing you can do is go back to Manchester and stay there until this is over.'

'Will it affect the appeal?' Lucy thumped the cushion on the back of the sofa, for emphasis.

'No, it won't; or at least it shouldn't. Billy's father is appealing his convictions for two entirely different murders, and the issues to be decided at the appeal relate solely to those murders. I'm investigating a completely separate case. The publicity won't do him any good, but that's as far as it goes.'

'Yeah, but when you find Rory Estcourt's killer, it'll prove Billy's father was innocent all along, won't it?'

'It might.' Dixon looked at Jane and raised his eyebrows. 'But then again it might not. You have to be prepared for that.'

'It will. I know it will.'

He managed to fit in two chapters of Graham Ashton's book *Sedgemoor 1685* by the light of his phone before finally falling asleep just after two. He skipped the chapters on the background to the rebellion and the pursuit of the rebels around the West Country by the Royal Army, starting to read properly at chapter three, with the arrival of the rebel army in Bridgwater. Some of the detail he knew: the Duke of Monmouth surveying the battlefield from the tower of St Mary's Church; and the fact that the rebels were slaughtered, their night time approach through the fog given away by a lone trooper firing a warning shot.

He had to google the word 'plungeon', which turned out to be a ford across a rhyne. Maybe Lord Grey and his cavalry could be forgiven for not finding it in the dark?

Jane's huffing and puffing had turned to snoring shortly after the battle had started. And the fighting hadn't lasted long; an hour and a half in real time, according to one of the king's artillerymen.

Chapter four – 'Retribution' – was the stuff of nightmares; of rebels tried by the hundred by Judge Jeffreys at the Bloody Assizes and sentenced to death; hanged, drawn and quartered most of them; some shipped to the West Indies as indentured slaves. The Duke of Monmouth himself had been beheaded on Tower Hill on 15th July, nine days after the battle.

Either it was tiredness, or it was the significance of what he was reading, but he read the penultimate paragraph of the chapter three times:

The memories of the Western Rebellion, the battle of Sedgemoor and all the pain and suffering that followed still resonate to this day. Such events leave scars that even the passage of over 300 years cannot fully heal. There are over a million descendants of the rebels of 1685 living in Somerset today, the vast majority of them unaware of the fate suffered by their ancestors.

Maybe one knew, he thought, as he flicked off the light on his phone and rolled over.

◆　◆　◆

Frys Lane at 9 a.m.

Lewis was waiting for him when he arrived; sitting in his car, the windows steamed up, beads of sweat running down his temples.

Dixon parked behind him and tapped on the window.

'What d'you want to see first?' asked Lewis, hiding his bloodshot eyes behind a pair of sunglasses.

'Where they found Rory.'

Lewis slid his key into the ignition and switched on his engine.

'What are you doing?' asked Dixon.

'We can drive round to Fowlers Plot Farm,' replied Lewis, putting on his seatbelt. 'It's quicker.'

'Can we walk?'

'Yes, but—'

'Let's walk.'

Dixon slung his jacket over his shoulder and followed Lewis along the farm track, past a new bungalow on the left and farm buildings on the right.

'We could get a cup of tea on the way back,' said Lewis, gesturing to the marquee against the wall of the barn on the right. Dixon wasn't sure whether it was a serious suggestion or whether he was just making conversation. Not that it mattered.

The track followed the edge of the field, Dixon trying to make sense of where he was. Over breakfast he had read the contemporary account of the battle written by the rector of Chedzoy, Andrew Paschall, in 1685, and wondered where the 'East field Corn' was; where Paschall heard the 'flight and pursuit, 42 killed'. And 'on a corner slaine in the Moor and buried in one pit, 195'.

Which corner?

'Hot, isn't it?' said Lewis, idly. 'I've not seen the post mortem yet.'

'We won't get that until next week.'

They were walking side by side along the farm track, the grass in between them just high enough to flick the underside of a tractor. Swallows were flitting about just above the ground, swifts overhead screeching as they picked off insects on the wind.

'Should've brought some mosquito repellent,' muttered Lewis, swatting the back of his neck with the palm of his hand.

Dixon recognised the Polden Hills away to the north, where Monmouth had fled on the night of the battle. And St Mary's Church was just visible in Bridgwater away to the west, behind an electricity pylon.

'What I don't understand,' said Lewis, 'is why he would bury Rory out in the middle of nowhere like this. He would've had to carry his body in from the nearest road, and if you ignore Fowlers Plot, which is inhabited, then you're looking at half a mile at least. Over rough ground, and it would have to have been at night.'

'What did Roger tell you at the scene?' Dixon opened a five bar gate, then closed it behind Lewis.

'Not a lot.'

'Which way?'

'This way,' replied Lewis, setting off diagonally across the next field. 'Scientific must still be there. You can see the tent over that hedge.'

Dixon followed. 'Rory had been mummified and kept as a trophy.'

Lewis stopped in his tracks.

'And according to the forensic anthropologist,' continued Dixon, 'he was buried six to nine months ago, which is after Parker was granted leave to appeal.'

'Mummified?'

'It took me a while to get my head round that. Dried out indoors, basically. But what it means is that he'd have been as light as a feather. Carrying him out here would've been no problem.'

'Why, though?'

'So he'd be found by the archaeologists. Must be.'

'Parker was in prison then,' said Lewis.

'Of course he was.' Dixon stopped at a rhyne and looked down at the thick layer of duckweed suffocating the water beneath. The steep sides were always off-putting, that and the fact you could never tell how deep these ditches were. Maybe Lord Grey had felt the same when his troopers arrived at the Bussex Rhyne one dark night in July 1685 with orders to attack the Royal Army from the rear, and he was forced to watch his guide fumbling about in the fog trying to find the Upper Plungeon.

'We must've taken a wrong turn,' said Lewis. 'Can you jump it?'

'If I must.'

Dixon landed safely and turned to watch Lewis. 'He buried Rory in the bottom of the rhyne so his body would rehydrate, but he forgot the clay would slow the decomposition down. Either that or he didn't know. If it hadn't been for that, we'd have found a skeleton and never known.'

'He must've known the where and when of the dig though, surely?' Lewis jumped, landing heavily at Dixon's feet.

'He must.'

'His first mistake.'

'He was hoping it'd put paid to the appeal, we'd pin it on Parker, close the file and that would be that.'

'Crafty sod.'

'Do you know where we are?' asked Dixon, frowning at Lewis.

'We cut across one field too early, I think.' Lewis was craning his neck, trying to look over the hedge. 'There's the track from the farm over there.'

'You'll tell Charlesworth, will you?' asked Dixon, dodging the thistles and cowpats as they walked across to the track. 'That was the deal.'

'I was going to have a word with you about that.' Lewis gave an apologetic shrug. 'He's found out and is coming down tomorrow with Deborah Potter. Express Park at midday.'

'Something to look forward to, I suppose.'

Donald Watson was dismantling the tent over the ditch when they finally arrived. 'I was just packing up,' he said. 'I'm going to leave it drained. I've been over it with a metal detector and there's nothing else for them to find. Not here, anyway.'

Two shallow trenches were being dug in the adjacent field, the whole area littered with small red flags.

'Musket balls, probably,' offered Watson. 'There's no shortage of them.'

'He was in the bottom, there,' said Lewis, looking down into the rhyne.

'Get anything useful from the PM?' asked Watson.

'Not really,' replied Dixon, busy surveying the scene; taking it all in. A dark night, nine months or so ago. The Scytheman must have known his way round, but then that was never in doubt. Even Parker had worked the land as a farm labourer. 'When was it dredged?' he asked, pointing at the knee high pile of clay all along the far bank, the tracks of the JCB still visible where it had gone along, digging out the bottom of the ditch.

'Last autumn,' replied Lewis.

'That explains that then.'

'Eh?'

'He wouldn't even have to dig a grave, would he? Just put the body in the bottom of the rhyne and shovel some of that clay in on top. It'd only have taken a couple of minutes.'

Chapter Nine

A single magpie was sitting on the roof of the bungalow when Dixon and Lewis arrived back at Chedzoy.

'Bloody well says it all, doesn't it?' mumbled Lewis, his eyes darting around the farmyard, looking for the other one.

'Since when have you been superstitious?'

'One for sorrow—'

'Bollocks.'

Lewis opened the door of his car and threw his jacket across to the passenger seat. Then he leaned back against the bonnet, looking up at the magpie hopping along the ridge. 'It used to be two cottages, let to farm labourers for a pittance. He knocked them down and built this, after the murders.'

Rendered and painted white, it seemed an odd choice for a bungalow on a farm; even an arable farm.

'Let's hear it then.'

'You've read the statements?' asked Lewis.

'And the trial transcript; the important bits anyway.'

Lewis took a deep breath. 'Christine is lying on the floor in the kitchen of the cottage on the left. Blood everywhere. The neighbour is screaming and I've got uniform throwing up against that barn.' Lewis waved his arm in the direction of the Dutch barn behind their cars. 'The neighbour was Jean Darlison. Her husband worked on the farm, but he was off skittling somewhere. Never got a word out of her, but she did point.'

'Which way?'

'Follow me.'

Lewis walked back along the track towards the cornfields. 'This muck heap wasn't here then,' he said, gesturing to a pile of straw and horse manure on the left. 'They must be doing livery, or something.' Then he stopped on the corner of the maize field on the right. 'Here. There was a trail through the corn going in that direction.'

'Where was the body?'

Lewis walked diagonally across the field of maize, careful not to tread on the fresh green shoots. Dixon followed, listening to the crunching of the dry mud beneath their feet; and the skylarks.

'She kicked off her shoes about here,' said Lewis, stopping after ten yards or so. 'High heels are no good for running at the best of times, let alone across a field at night.' Then he set off again, slowing as he reached the far side of the field, adjacent to the ditch. 'She was here. Lying flat on her back. The corn had been flattened over a big enough area to indicate a struggle.'

Dixon recognised the scene from the photographs – the elderberry in the hedge on the far side of the rhyne was bigger, though, and in the distance, the church tower in Westonzoyland was now almost completely hidden by the conifers. Were it not for that, it could have been any field on the Levels near a ditch.

'It's about three hundred yards back to the cottage,' said Lewis, when he saw Dixon looking back. 'I paced it out at the time. He would've just followed her trail through the corn, so she had no chance of getting away, really.'

'Where was Parker?'

'He'd run along the ditch and was hiding under the hedge in the corner, over there.'

'He said in interview he pulled the scythe out of her chest?'

'That was his explanation for his fingerprints on the handle, and the fact that he'd got it with him.' Lewis blew a sigh out through his nose. 'Despite that, it was the blood spatter that was his real undoing. He just had no answer for that. There was a mist of Nicola's blood on his shirt, face and neck. The expert said it was the residue of impact spatter; only a mist reached him because of the distance between them when he stabbed her. That was down to the handle of the scythe, he said. Stab someone with a knife and you're standing much closer. Right in front of them too.'

'Unless you stab them in the back.'

'Quite.'

'Tell me about the unidentified fingerprint.'

'That's all there is to it, really; it was unidentified,' said Lewis, thrusting his hands deep into his pockets. 'It came from a sequence of three, so you could tell it was the middle finger. The others had insufficient ridge detail for comparison purposes.'

'Smudged, then.'

'The defence said the print came from the real killer, but the jury didn't buy it.'

Dixon looked back along the rhyne, towards Chedzoy. It turned left when it reached the backs of the houses, forming the boundary between the fields and the ends of the gardens. Then it became the roadside ditch beyond the last house. 'Did you pass a car on the road into the village that night?'

'Not that I remember, but it was thick fog and I was concentrating on not ending up in the ditch.'

'You wouldn't have seen a car parked in a field, then?'

'Probably not.'

'Was there a site visit during the trial?'

'No.'

'OK, so you're a juror now.'

Lewis nodded, reluctantly.

'Parker knocks on the door and pushes his way in when Christine opens it,' said Dixon. 'She knows him because he works on the farm and he's got a thing for her daughter.'

'You *have* read the statements, haven't you?'

'It was a late night.' Dixon was pacing up and down between the lines of maize. 'Parker kills Christine in a frenzied attack – revenge because she told his wife he was making a nuisance of himself – and lies in wait for his real target, Nicola. She'd been out on the town with college friends and they dropped her at the top of the lane.'

'You're starting to sound like the prosecution.'

'He's covered in Christine's blood, so Nicola realises what's going on when she arrives home, and makes a run for it. She screams, which alerts the neighbour, Mrs Darlison, who finds Christine. Parker follows Nicola out here, kills her and then hears you coming. He panics and tries to hide under the hedge.'

'I know where you're going with this,' said Lewis. 'He's got Christine's blood on his shirt, impact spatter from Nicola on his face and neck, his fingerprints are on the handle of the scythe; of course I'm going to convict him, even with the mysterious fingerprint.'

'How did he come across in the witness box?'

'Well, I think. He's not the brightest light on the tree, but I believed him.'

'Why?'

'For the same reason as Doreen, I suppose.' Lewis shrugged. 'He's just not capable of it.'

'There's got to be more to it than that.'

'There isn't.'

'Is there anything I need to know?' asked Dixon, watching Lewis closely for a reaction.

'Like what?'

'Interviews not recorded properly, or at all. The odd slap here or there.'

'Certainly not. It was 2005, not the 1970s, for heaven's sake. It was done properly. It's not as if he confessed anyway.'

'So, let's try it the other way round. Parker finds the front door of the cottage open, runs in and cradles Christine in his arms, getting her blood on his shirt from contact transfer.' Dixon was getting into his stride now, his words punctuated by the crunching of the dry earth beneath his feet. 'Then he goes to look for Nicola, follows her trail across the cornfield and finds her with a scythe sticking out of her chest. Dead or dying?'

'There's no way of telling.'

'He leans over her to see if she's breathing,' continued Dixon, his voice gathering pace. 'Then he pulls the scythe out of her chest, hears you coming, and runs and hides. The Scytheman, meanwhile, heard Parker's approach and made his escape along the rhyne—'

'Why the rhyne?' demanded Lewis, the colour returning to his cheeks.

'It explains why there were no other tracks in the corn. His car must have been out on the road, parked in a field, perhaps, so you didn't see it on the way into the village. It must have been close because he would have been planning to carry Nicola's body out.'

'What makes you say that?'

'He kept Rory as a trophy, so it's reasonable to assume he'd have done the same with Nicola.'

Lewis allowed himself a wry smile.

'Ignoring the blood spatter evidence, who d'you believe?' asked Dixon.

'I believe Parker, you know that.'

'His appeal might just succeed.' Dixon squinted into the sun, trying to follow a pair of swifts screeching overhead. 'If the judges believe the new blood spatter evidence, at the very least he might get a retrial.'

'It's a bit thin, isn't it?'

They turned around at the sound of voices behind them to find a car pulled up at the marquee and two elderly ladies unloading plates covered in tin foil.

'Does air escaping from the lungs of a dead body really cause a mist of blood spatter?' continued Lewis.

'The expert says so, although I've only read the skeleton argument so far. It was certainly persuasive enough to get leave to appeal, anyway.' Dixon was checking his pockets for money. 'And if you think about it, we don't know when exactly Nicola stopped breathing, so it might have been her dying breath for all we know. She didn't cough. Parker was asked and would've said so if she had.'

'And that's before you take into account Rory's body and what we know about that.' Lewis took his wallet out of his back pocket. 'Tea's on me,' he said, smiling.

'It'll be down to the forensic evidence. At the original trial it supported the Crown's version of events, so he went down. At the appeal, it'll be consistent with both versions, which means it'll have to go back to a jury to decide. And if that happens, what jury would convict him beyond a reasonable doubt?'

'I suppose it'll come down to which expert they believe,' said Lewis.

'Let's hope it doesn't come to that,' said Dixon. 'If we can find who buried Rory then my guess is we'll find the Scytheman at the same time. And that should see to it that Parker walks free without the need for a retrial.'

'Anything you need?'

'A media blackout on the condition of Rory's body. If that gets out the Scytheman will know we're on to him; there can be no mention of the fact he'd been mummified, or that he was only buried nine months ago.'

'Anything else?'

'A piece of cake would be nice, seeing as Jane's not here.'

Chapter Ten

The drive round to Bussex Farm on the edge of Westonzoyland took ten minutes. Dixon knew he was going in the right direction; left into Kings Drive, then along Monmouth Road. An immortality of sorts, despite being beheaded at the age of thirty-six. He winced. It had been a grisly end for the duke too. Five swings of the axe – some said eight – finally being finished off with a knife. Not the executioner's finest work.

The farmyard was full of minibuses and cars, so Dixon parked in front of the battlefield information board.

'You can't park there!' The shout came from behind him. 'Are you from Reading University?'

'No, Sir.' His police warrant card stopped the approaching busybody in his tracks.

'Ah,' he said. 'Sorry.'

'Not a problem, Sir.'

'I'm guessing you get to park where you like?'

'I do tend to, Sir,' replied Dixon, dropping his warrant card into his pocket. 'It's my only bad habit though.'

Knee-length shorts was a brave move with all the mosquitoes about, thought Dixon, and they looked odd with wellington boots at the best of times. A red T-shirt drenched in sweat and the sunglasses were clip-overs; headphones around his neck and a metal detector in one hand; all of it topped off with a wide-brimmed sun hat. 'My name's Rob Salmon, from the Bridgwater History Society. I'm the treasurer. I see your Scientific lot have finished. Does that mean we can carry on over there?'

'Yes, Sir.'

'Jolly good. I'll let Colin Timperley know. We've got a couple of trenches going in those fields, but the search for the mass grave has stalled rather.'

'D'you have a membership secretary, Sir?' asked Dixon, resisting the sarcastic apology for inconveniencing them.

'She's out on the battlefield. It's Sandra Smith. Have you met her yet?'

'No, Sir.'

'Follow me, then.'

Salmon set off along the farm track lined with trees; all of the puddles bone dry, even in the shade.

'A bit of rain would be useful,' he said, glancing over his shoulder at Dixon walking behind him. 'It'd soften up the ground and make the digging a bit easier.'

'Is it all clay?'

'Around here it is. There are peat beds, but they're east of here. Are you familiar with the battlefield?'

'A little,' replied Dixon.

'This is Sogg Drove we're on now,' said Salmon. 'A drove is basically an old term for a track used to move livestock. It joins Penzoy Drove up there, which leads out to the Westonzoyland Road. That way they could get their animals out to market.' He stopped at a junction. 'That's Langmoor Drove. It goes north-east to meet the Black Ditch. Then you've got Moor Drove, which marked the boundary of the Chedzoy cornfield.'

'It's higher than the surrounding land.'

'It had to be.' Salmon waved his metal detector for emphasis. 'The land between here and Chedzoy was all marshy moorland, remember, and it flooded most winters. Not all of it had been drained and cultivated as you see it today.'

'And the line of the Bussex Rhyne?'

'That connected the Black Ditch to the north with the River Parrett south-west of us. It looped around Westonzoyland. You'll know the Black Ditch as the—'

'King's Sedgemoor Drain.'

'That's right.' Salmon raised his eyebrows. 'The modern drain follows much the same line, although the Black Ditch meandered a bit more. We're standing pretty much where Sogg Drove crossed the Bussex Rhyne now. Previous digs have found sections of the old rhyne and you can still see the ground undulating in the fields opposite the memorial.'

'I'll walk along to the memorial, I think.'

'Fine,' replied Salmon. 'The field behind it is known locally as "the Grave Field". It was always thought that was where the locals buried the dead, but no trace has ever been found there.'

'And the Bussex Rhyne is visible in the field opposite?'

'The remains of it. The Royal Army was camped between the village and the rhyne and lined up along it when the alarm was sounded.'

'Thank you,' said Dixon. 'I'll catch you up.'

'When you've finished, follow Sogg Drove to the end, then into the field on the right. You can't miss us.'

Dixon undid his top button, loosening his tie as he set off along Langmoor Drove, a small copse visible up ahead on the left, framed by two giant oak trees. A nice walk in the countryside;

the only thing missing was his dog. It was far too hot for Monty, though, and the horseflies would have driven him around the bend.

The sun was directly overhead, not a cloud in the sky to offer any respite. Dixon could feel his forearms burning. He listened to the birdsong as he walked; it seemed an ever present feature of battlefields, not that he had visited many. There'd been the school trip to the Somme, skylarks offering the soundtrack that time.

The memorial was small, set back from the drove in a small fenced enclosure. IN MEMORY OF ALL THOSE WHO DOING THE RIGHT AS THEY GAVE IT FELL IN THE BATTLE . . . OR WHO FOR THEIR SHARE IN THE FIGHT SUFFERED DEATH PUNISHMENT OR TRANSPORTATION.

He learned nothing new from the two information boards, took a photo for Jane, then climbed over the gate into the field opposite. He tried to imagine the Royal Army lined up along the far side of a wide rhyne; half-dressed, some of them, squinting into the fog, muskets at the ready. And the rebels approaching across the moor, ready to fight and die for a man who fled the field at the first sign his cause was lost; not even able to rest in peace thanks to archaeologists with metal detectors.

Dixon took out his phone and sent Jane a text message:

When my time comes I want to be cremated Nx

He waited, watching the speech bubble, while Jane tapped out a reply.

Why?

I don't want some twit digging me up in 300 years and trying to work out what I had for breakfast :-(

If you say so Jx

The top of the five bar gate offered Dixon a grandstand view of the battlefield towards Chedzoy. Several students were back in the fields with their metal detectors over towards Fowlers Plot Farm where Rory Estcourt had been found. Others were combing the fields further west.

Dixon stopped at the entrance to the field where the trenches had been dug, watching the students on their hands and knees in the mud. The trenches were shallow, going down in neatly cut steps to a depth of three feet or so, each trench the area of a cricket wicket perhaps, the turf neatly piled up ready to be replaced at the end of the dig.

He saw a metal detector being pointed in his direction. Then a woman came striding across the field towards him.

'Rob said you were looking for me?'

'Sandra Smith?'

'Yes.'

'Detective Inspector Dixon.' He handed her a business card. 'I was interested in the history society. How many members do you have?'

'Just under fifty, but only twenty or so are what I would call *active* members.' Sandra was squinting, holding her hand up to shield her eyes from the sun, her jeans plastered in clay. 'They said the body was a victim of the Scytheman, surely?'

'How many will be joining you on the dig?' asked Dixon, choosing to ignore her curiosity.

'There's me and Rob. He's with the group looking for the mass grave. A couple of others said they might join us on Sunday; that's tomorrow, isn't it? And more will turn up for Dr Ashton's talk. That's on Tuesday night, in the function room at the pub.'

'Is Dr Ashton here?'

'That's him over there,' she said, pointing to a man on his hands and knees in a trench. 'The friendly fire episode is his pet project. And that's Professor Timperley from the university in the other trench.'

'Are you digging any others?' asked Dixon. He was dodging the cowpats as he followed Sandra across the field.

'A couple here, and we've identified what we think may be the grave site over towards the drain, but we'll see. It's best not to get your hopes up.'

'Quite.'

'Graham, this is the police,' she said, when they reached the edge of the trench.

The man stood up. 'I wasn't expecting it to be this hot,' he said, cleaning his sunglasses on his shirt tail; sweat running down his face from under his panama hat. 'How can I help you?'

'How well d'you know the battlefield, Sir?' asked Dixon.

'Not as well as I'd like.' Ashton took his hat off and wiped his forehead with a handkerchief. 'It doesn't help that I live upcountry. Sandra's your best bet. Knows it like the back of her hand, she does.'

'And how did you get involved with this dig?'

'You emailed me, didn't you?' he said, frowning at Sandra. 'When the uni got in touch with you.'

'That's right.' Sandra nodded. 'We got an email via our website, from Colin Timperley I think. Here he comes now. They were interested in digging the battlefield and were asking for our help.'

'When was that?'

'Late summer last year. I've probably got the emails somewhere.'

'It would've been late August,' said Colin, walking up behind them drinking from a bottle of water. 'We'd have been back from last year's field trip to Hadrian's Wall and I was trying to set up this year's. Sending out emails. The hardest part is the permissions – and local history societies, well, they're local, so they know the right people.'

'Have you found anything?' asked Dixon.

Colin held out a plastic tray with several musket balls encased in mud rolling around in it. 'Plenty of these,' he said. 'The main battle was nearer the memorial and we think this is the result of

Lord Grey's troopers being fired on by Wade's Red Regiment as he turned away from the rhyne.'

'He missed the Upper Plungeon in the fog and rode along the Bussex Rhyne until he was fired on by the Royal Army,' said Dr Ashton. 'Probably the Second Guards and the Coldstream Guards. So he turns away, directly towards the advancing rebels, and is fired on here by Wade's Reds; his own men.'

'Turned away?' Dixon tipped his head. 'The Earl of Aylesbury said the horses bolted.'

'That's what I meant, yes. They went right through the advancing Red and Yellow Regiments, some doubling back in front of the entire rebel army.' Ashton raised his eyebrows. 'You are well read, Inspector.'

'I've got your book in my car.'

'Oh, what fun! Would you like me to sign it for you?'

'Best not, Sir. It's the library copy.'

'The irony is,' said Sandra, 'the Bussex Rhyne was only knee deep, so his troopers could easily have ridden across it and attacked the Royal Army from behind, as planned.'

'The rebel foot could have waded across it too.' Ashton shook his head.

'All this history right beneath our feet,' said Colin. 'Musket balls; we've found buckles and buttons at the other dig site.'

'And a set of human remains,' said Dixon, matter of fact.

'Yes, well, that was unfortunate.' Colin grimaced. 'It wasn't exactly the publicity we were looking for, either, and we've had press crawling all over the battlefield ever since.'

'They're only not here now because the pub's open.' Sandra rolled her eyes.

'They'll soon lose interest,' said Dixon.

'Got something!'

The shout came from the bottom of the trench behind them, a student standing up and pointing with his brush.

'What is it?' asked Colin, running over.

'I don't know.' The boy handed the artefact up to Ashton. 'It's metal though.'

'It's difficult,' said Sandra to Dixon, as they walked side by side over to the trench. 'The battle was over three hundred years ago and these fields must have been ploughed countless times. They're grass at the moment, for cattle, but that's not always been—'

'I know what that is.' Ashton dropped down into the trench. 'It's the loop guard from the handle of a sword. Buckled – it may have been trodden on by a horse—'

'Or hit by a plough,' offered Colin.

'Let's see if the blade is still there, lad.' Ashton nudged the student. 'Keep digging.'

'I'll leave you to it,' said Dixon, turning to Sandra. 'I will need to speak to you again about the history society, if that's all right.'

'Of course,' she replied, frowning. 'Whatever you need.'

Chapter Eleven

'Back so soon, dear?'

'Questions, Mrs Estcourt,' replied Dixon. 'There'll be lots of them, I'm afraid.'

'As long as you find the answers.'

'I keep asking them until I do.' He closed the door behind him and watched her hobble towards the kitchen.

'Tea?' she asked, holding on to the doorframe.

'No, thank you.' He pushed open the living room door. 'Are you on your own?'

'I've been on my own every night since my husband died, dear.' She was edging towards her chair, holding on to the back of the sofa. 'Karen Marsden was here, but I sent her home. It's Saturday,' she said, slumping down on to her armchair, 'and she's got a family.'

'May I?' Dixon was standing in front of the mantelpiece, inspecting the photographs lined up along it. He recognised Apex Park and the boy holding a small carp, his grin broader than the fish.

'Alec used to take him fishing when he was younger.'

'What did he get up to that you weren't supposed to know about?' asked Dixon, picking up another photograph, this time of Rory with a pirate. Hell of a way to make a living that, thought Dixon, dressing up as a pirate and having your photograph taken with holidaymakers.

'That was Dawlish Warren, that one. Five pounds they wanted for that one photo.' Doreen frowned. 'And I always knew what he was up to.'

'Really?'

'Yes, really,' she replied, a sudden edge of impatience to her voice.

Dixon watched her defensiveness ebb away as she smiled at a fond memory – all he had to do was wait.

'Even the time he pinched a bottle of sherry from the drinks cabinet and got drunk with his friends.'

'Sherry?'

'It was all we had. He was sick everywhere. So, yes, I always knew what he was up to.' She dabbed a tear from the corner of her eye, then stuffed the tissue back up her sleeve. 'What about you? What did you get up to that your mother wasn't supposed to know about?'

'Lots, but then I was away at boarding school, so it was easier. I did have half a bottle of Scotch once. I woke up the next morning in the squash court. No idea how I got there.'

'Have you seen him?'

'At the post mortem.'

Direct as ever. Dixon had been expecting it, once the small talk was out of the way; Lewis had told him to prepare himself for a cross-examination. Doreen had become adept at extracting information from police officers over the years.

'Karen said you'd got some DNA; from the teeth, I suppose?'

'There's information we can't divulge, Mrs Estcourt,' said Dixon, staring at the rug in front of the electric fire.

'It's Doreen, and don't give me any of that "can't divulge" rubbish. He's my son!'

Lewis trusted her. And so must he, thought Dixon. She deserved nothing less.

'I want to know,' demanded Doreen.

'Have you been to the press?' he asked, suspecting that was the real reason she had sent Karen Marsden home.

Doreen shuffled back into the armchair and began picking at threads where a cat had sharpened its claws.

'It's down to me, isn't it?' she said. 'To keep his memory alive; to find out what happened to him.'

'Not any more, Doreen.'

'Who else is going to do it?'

'I am.'

'I rang a contact at the *Mail on Sunday*.' She reached for her cigarettes on the shelf beside her. 'They sent a photographer over. He was at Westonzoyland anyway so it was no big deal.'

'And what did you tell them?'

'Just that it was Rory's body and there was evidence he'd been stabbed with a curved blade. That was all I knew. They were interested in the human angle, so I laid it on thick. It'll make the front page, they said.'

'You said you sat through Parker's trial at Bristol Crown Court and still don't believe he's guilty?'

'Oh no, you don't get out of it like that.' Doreen wagged her index finger at him, lighting her cigarette with her other hand. 'You were going to tell me about the post mortem.'

Dixon sighed. Token resistance, perhaps, but it had been worth a try. 'Lewis trusts you and so will I, Doreen, but this information cannot go any further if I'm to find Rory's killer. All right?'

'I understand.'

'There's no easy way to—'

'Just spit it out. Whatever it is, it can't be any worse than I've imagined over the years.'

'The body is that of a young adult, between sixteen and twenty years of age, so we believe he was killed the night he disappeared.'

Doreen frowned. 'Why are you telling me that? No one's ever suggested—'

Dixon took a deep breath. 'Because he was buried between six and nine months ago.'

'Nine months?' He was losing her, he could see that. It was too much information, even for Doreen, who had imagined the worst and then some. 'Someone kept my Rory's body for all these years?'

'There's evidence to suggest his body had dried out. He rehydrated when he was buried and then began to decom . . .' His voice tailed off as he watched Doreen struggling to take it all in. Her cheeks flushed, but he couldn't tell whether it was grief or anger. Yet.

She took several slow drags on her cigarette. 'Dried out?'

'Kept somewhere warm and dry—'

'I know the mechanics of it.' She stubbed her cigarette out and reached for the box on the shelf. 'Kept where?'

'That's what I need to find out.'

'Why nine months ago?'

'Parker was granted leave to appeal last summer, which ties in, so I'm thinking it was done to influence that. Rory's pacemaker set off a metal detector and—'

'Whoever buried him must have known about the dig.'

'We're stepping into the realms of highly sensitive information here, Doreen. If this gets out whoever did it will know we know.'

'So, I shouldn't have gone to the press at all?'

'I'm guessing the killer was expecting you to do just that, so it would look a bit odd if you didn't.'

'The Scytheman really is still out there, then.' Her hands trembled as she took another cigarette from the silver box.

'Or someone who wants us to think he is. It was a calculated risk. If Parker's appeal fails then he was banking on us pinning Rory's murder on Parker or just closing the file.'

'Will it influence the appeal?'

'The judges will certainly know about it, if you're on the front page of tomorrow's papers. But it shouldn't, let me put it that way. The evidence to be heard at the appeal is quite specific to his convictions.'

Doreen's face reddened. 'Parker didn't do it.'

'The evidence against him was quite—'

'Have you met him?'

'I'm interviewing him at Long Lartin tomorrow.'

'Not capable of it.' She closed her eyes when the smoke drifted into her face as she lit her cigarette. 'There was that fingerprint, wasn't there? And I wasn't impressed by the witness evidence either. Those women who dropped Nicola off at home – Jennifer Allen and her precious daughter. They said they saw him in Frys Lane with a scythe in his hand, but how could they in the fog?'

'Fog swirls, drifts—'

'That's what the prosecution tried to say. The defence even got a meteorologist to give evidence, but how d'you measure the thickness of fog?' She shook her head. 'It just didn't ring true for me. And we were supposed to accept that Parker killed Rory as well, and "move on". Those were Ridley's words. "Move on". Have you met him?'

'Not yet.'

'The man's a buffoon.'

Not quite the word Lewis had used, but Dixon got the gist.

'Time we had that tea,' said Doreen, getting up from her chair. She reached up on to the shelf by the fireplace and slid out a photograph album from among the books, dropping it into Dixon's lap. 'Have a look through that. I'll be back in a minute.'

Each photograph had been slotted into a sleeve that flipped up to reveal the picture beneath, twenty or so on each side. Dixon flicked through them, as instructed. There were more from Apex Park; the photos of Rory hadn't come out so well, perhaps, but the fish was bigger. Another couple taken at the carnival in Burnham – on the corner by the church, the carts slowing for the turn off the main road. Rory had been a fan of candyfloss too, by the looks of things, his beaming face lit up by the bright lights.

Doreen appeared by the arm of the sofa, looking over his shoulder. 'That one was the day of my mother's funeral, if you're wondering about his black tie.'

'I'm sorry to hear that.'

'She was ninety-six, bless her,' she replied, her expression softening. 'Did you want some cake?'

'Better not. I'm diabetic. And besides, I've already had a piece today.'

'You'll go to hell,' Doreen was shouting from the hallway as she shuffled back to the kitchen.

'I will if my fiancée finds out,' muttered Dixon, turning back to the photograph album.

Rory was younger in the selection on the right hand side of the album; a couple of school uniform shots – poor sod – and some of him astride a racing bicycle, the tips of his toes only just reaching the floor.

Dixon stood up and took the rattling tray from Doreen, setting it down on the coffee table. 'Have you shown this photograph album to anyone else?' he asked, handing it back to her.

'I showed the photos to Ridley back in the day, but he said there was nothing of interest.'

Dixon nodded. 'Tell me about you, Doreen. I want to know what happened the day he disappeared, from your point of view.'

'The day he disappeared?' Doreen was pouring the tea. 'It's in my witness statement.'

'I've read it. I want to know what's not in it.'

'What d'you mean?'

'What were you doing that day?'

'Well, when Rory didn't come—'

'What did you do in the morning?'

'Oh, I went to the supermarket, from memory. We were living over at Moorlinch, so that would've been Asda in Bridgwater. Alec was at work at the ROF. That's the old Royal Ordnance Factory to you. He retired when they closed it in 2008. Rory's bus—'

'What did you do in the afternoon?'

'I was still tidying up over at my mother's place, before we were due to hand it back to the landlord; sorting through her stuff, bagging up clothes for the charity shop, that sort of thing. I got home in time for Rory's bus, but he wasn't on it. I never liked him to come home to an empty house.'

'And when did you know something was wrong?'

'Immediately. He was always on the bus. Always. I reported it, but it was twenty-four hours before anyone did anything. I was told I was overprotective and he'd probably just gone off with some friends. Teenagers do that sort of thing, apparently.'

'Times change,' said Dixon, grimacing.

'They did after that, I can tell you.' She handed Dixon a mug of tea. 'A couple of weeks later they found the scene over at Sutton Mallet.'

Dixon kicked himself, although time had been short, so perhaps he could be forgiven for not getting to that file yet. A murder scene, judging by the amount of blood; no body and no charges brought against Parker; the archive box marked 'Unresolved'.

'Then they found the scythe when Parker was arrested,' continued Doreen. 'The newspapers latched on to that quick enough. "Was Rory Estcourt another victim of the Scytheman?" I remember a journalist firing that question at Ridley in a press conference. That was when he started taking me seriously.'

'What did you do when he wasn't on the bus?'

'I rang Alec and he said to ring the police. He came straight home, but a police officer didn't appear until about eight, took some details and left. We rang everyone we knew – even managed to speak to the bus driver – but no one had seen him. After that it's all a bit of a blur. I had to try to stay strong for Alec; the poor sod went to pieces. A couple more went missing and then, when the Bonds were murdered and Peter made the arrest, we thought that was it; we were praying for Parker to tell us what he did with Rory.' Her eyes glazed over. 'Now you're here,' she said, forcing a smile to hide the tremor in her voice. 'All these years later. And off we go again.'

Dixon took a swig of tea, letting Doreen gather her composure.

'Ridley.' She sneered. 'And his "move on". You lost anyone?'

'Not lately.'

'Were you able to move on?'

'It took me seventeen years and finding her killer.'

'And now you think you're going to do the same for me?'

A sharp edge of scepticism had crept into her voice. Dixon knew where it had come from; he had been tested and Doreen thought he had failed. He watched her out of the corner of his eye, looking him up and down, her look of disappointment thinly veiled. 'Those photos,' he said. 'Have you got the rest?'

'They're in their envelopes in a shoebox at the top of my wardrobe.' She frowned. 'Why?'

'I'd like to see the others taken at the carnival, if I may.'

'Ridley said they weren't of interest.'

It usually took at least one encounter for Dixon to take a dislike to someone; and he hadn't even met Ridley yet. 'Ridley is a buffoon. You said so yourself, Doreen.'

She was sitting up now, perched as near to the edge of her seat as her creaking hip would allow. 'What about the photos?' she asked, her eyes wide.

'The carnival cart in the background, five lorries back and still out on the main road. It's got the Duke of Monmouth up St Mary's Church tower, looking out over the Sedgemoor battlefield.'

'I knew it – it's why I kept looking there all those years. And Ridley laughed at me when I said it might be connected to the battle.' Doreen hauled herself to her feet using the arm of her chair and set off towards the door.

'I'm keeping an open mind and looking at any connection, however tenuous it might be,' said Dixon, draining his tea. 'Have I passed?'

'You have, dear.'

The front door slammed behind him a few minutes later, and he glanced over his shoulder at the old lady smiling at him from behind the net curtains as he walked down the garden path. He wondered what she would have left to hold on to when this was all over, one way or the other.

Or whether just being able to rest in peace with her husband and son would be enough?

Chapter Twelve

The pavement outside the church would have to do; the lane was a tight squeeze and he didn't fancy it in the Land Rover, high brick walls on either side – the churchyard on the left, houses opposite.

A battlefield visitor centre in a church seemed odd, but then perhaps not, given that five hundred rebels had been imprisoned there the night after the battle, several of them dying of wounds on the cold stone floor.

He tried the door – locked – but then that was to be expected on a Saturday night. Sunday morning would be different, no doubt.

Back to Church Lane.

The house was hidden behind a high brick wall; a black gate under an arch had an entryphone and a camera. Shame, that. Dixon preferred to catch people on the hop.

He pressed the buzzer and stood to one side of the lens.

'Hello.' Slightly out of breath, if anything.

It was the right house, but then the sign over the gate had confirmed that: Church Cottage.

'Hello.' Louder and more urgent this time.

'Who is it?' A voice in the background, followed by a loud sigh.

Dixon was definitely interrupting something. Then the front door opened; soft footsteps on the path, barefoot possibly.

'I wasn't expecting you, Inspector,' said Sandra Smith, tightening the belt on her bathrobe. 'Was I?'

'No.'

'What can I do for you?'

'I was after the membership records of the history society. You said you kept them?'

'I do.' She used an elastic band on her wrist to tie her hair back in a ponytail. 'Does it have to be now?'

Dixon stepped forward.

'It's hardly urgent, is it?' protested Sandra, as she closed the gate behind him. 'I mean, Parker's in prison and it's not as if he's going anywhere.'

'His appeal starts on Monday, Mrs Smith,' said Dixon, following her along the garden path towards the open front door. Roses in tubs framed the porch; more in flowerbeds either side climbed up the front of the cottage. It was double fronted with large sash windows, all of them open.

'Come in, Inspector,' said Sandra, when they stepped on to the flagstones in the hall; loud enough to be for someone else's benefit.

Then the living room door slammed shut from the inside.

Dixon looked at Sandra and raised his eyebrows.

'One of the students,' she said, looking in the mirror. She licked the tip of her index finger and smoothed her eyebrows. 'He popped round for a coffee.'

'Don't mind me,' replied Dixon.

'The records are in my office.' She picked up a set of keys off the hall table. 'If you'd like to wait here?'

'I'll come with you, Mrs Smith. It's no trouble.'

He followed her along the passageway, listening to the creak of the living room door behind him as it inched open.

'Zak, isn't it?' asked Dixon, spinning round. Barefoot, a pair of jeans open at the waist, his T-shirt in one hand, shoes in the other. The scar down the middle of his chest was the giveaway.

'Er, yes,' he mumbled.

'There's no need to go on my account. We'll only be a couple of minutes.'

'Oh, for heaven's sake, Zak.' Sandra sighed. 'Just get yourself a beer from the fridge and I'll be back in a minute.'

Dixon watched Zak trudge past them and into the kitchen, much like a schoolboy who'd been caught with his fingers in the biscuit tin.

'It's just a bit of fun, Inspector,' said Sandra, her cheeks reddening.

'And none of my business,' replied Dixon.

'You have to keep it locked, in my position,' she said, opening the door at the end of the passageway.

In my position?

Dixon resisted the temptation, instead working his way along the mantelpiece above the wood burning stove; photographs mainly, with a selection of 'Best in Show' rosettes of various colours pinned to the beam above his head – a fire hazard if and when the stove was lit – the centrepiece a picture of Sandra outside Buckingham Palace holding an Order of the British Empire.

'You've got the OBE?'

'For services to the local judiciary, Inspector.' Sandra took a red ledger out of a filing cabinet and dropped it on to her desk. 'I've been a magistrate for twenty-five years and I'm a Deputy Lieutenant as well.'

'I don't spend much time in the magistrates' court, I'm afraid.'

'So I gather.' She switched on a photocopier on the side. 'I'm assuming you just want the current members?'

Dixon picked up the ledger and began flicking through the pages, all of them handwritten – names and addresses, some crossed through and marked 'lapsed', others marked 'deceased'. It looked more like an old address book than the membership record of a local history society, not that Dixon was entirely sure what one should look like. 'You've never computerised it?' he asked.

'No need. We don't have that many members anyway. And then there's the time involved. I've always got better things to do.'

'Whose is this handwriting?'

Sandra leaned over. 'That'll be Bob Hill. He was my predecessor. In a care home now, poor chap.' She lifted the lid of the photocopier and turned to Dixon. 'Right, which pages would you like?'

He tucked the ledger under his arm. 'You save your ink,' he said. 'I know how expensive it is, these days.'

'Yes, but—'

'You'll get it back.' Dixon glanced through the living room door as he walked out; Zak was stretched out on the sofa, his bare feet on the coffee table, beer can in hand.

'You won't tell anyone about this, will you, Inspector?' whispered Sandra, hesitating as she closed the front door behind him.

'Soul of discretion, me, Mrs Smith,' he replied. 'The soul of discretion.'

Chapter Thirteen

Sutton Mallet was north of the King's Sedgemoor Drain and would have been north of the old Black Ditch on the night of the battle; within earshot of the gunfire all the same.

The Tanner file filled one archive box, the word 'UNRESOLVED' scrawled across the lid in black marker pen.

Dixon flicked on the workstation light at Express Park and started with the crime scene photographs. He hadn't eaten, so there would be nothing to bring up if they were too gruesome. The canteen was closed anyway, and he was relying on fruit pastilles to keep his blood sugar level up. Jane would do her nut.

No body had been found – kept as a trophy, possibly; it was a reasonable assumption given the findings from Rory's post mortem.

Dixon checked the dates. Two weeks after Rory's disappearance and two months before Parker had been arrested at the scene of the Bond murders.

A set of tyre tracks had been found at the scene, but that was the extent of the forensic evidence. Apart from the blood.

It had been identified as belonging to eighteen-year-old Mark Tanner from the DNA, and the pathologist had reported that no human being could survive blood loss of that volume.

The spatter analysis report ran to nearly two hundred pages, with appendices. 'High energy impact spatter' seemed to be the buzz phrase. It started in the hall and continued into the kitchen of the small bungalow. 'Drip trails' from the tip of the blade as the killer followed his or her victim along the hall; low velocity patterns on the ceiling from the swinging blade – the expert had arrived at a comprehensive and convincing sequence of events simply from the blood evidence.

There were even footprints in the blood, but no tread was found.

The substantive problem was that there was no body, not a single eyewitness, nothing found outside the property and no real suspect.

Apart from Parker.

Dixon switched on a computer and read the statements, such as they were, while he waited for it to wake up.

Mark's parents had been away in Venice, leaving their son at home alone. Not that he'd been home alone the whole time: the party had been the night before, on the Saturday, and there were statements from all the attendees.

The neighbours had heard the party all right, even moaning about the noise in their statements, but they heard nothing the night of his murder.

He had last been seen alive on the Sunday afternoon, cycling home from the village shop in Westonzoyland with a bottle of milk in one hand; the 999 call was made by his parents on the Monday lunchtime on their return from Venice.

The satellite view in Google Maps was what Dixon was looking for. He zoomed in, finding the bungalow on a corner plot on the

Chedzoy road. Was that a rhyne at the bottom of the garden? He squinted at it until his phone buzzed on the desk in front of him.

What time you home? Jx

It was gone midnight, so catching last orders at the Red Cow was out.

He tapped out a text message with one hand, switching off the computer with the other.

Now, on way. Nx

Dixon parked in the car park outside Highbridge railway station fifteen minutes before the 0912 train to Bristol Temple Meads the following morning, Lucy fiddling with her phone in the passenger seat next to him.

The bloody thing had pinged incessantly all the way from Brent Knoll.

'I've forgotten my charger,' she said, eyeing up Dixon's hanging in the footwell of his Land Rover.

'That's mine,' he snapped. 'Judy will have one you can borrow, I'm sure.'

'Yeah, but what about on the train?'

'I'm sure you'll survive a few hours.'

'Billy was supposed to be going to see his dad today, but Social Services told his foster parents not to take him.'

'How did he take it?'

'Not great.'

'Just keep him out of trouble, all right.' Dixon switched off the engine. 'That's all you can do for him at the moment. And he'll thank you for it one day.'

'You will get his dad out, won't you?'

'And what happens if I find out his dad really did do it? What then?'

'You won't.'

'Has he ever spoken to his father about it? Asked him about it, in detail?'

'So he says.'

Dixon shifted in his seat to face Lucy. 'And what did he say?'

'That he didn't do it.'

'And he believes him?'

'He's his dad!'

'How often did your mother lie to you?'

Lucy grimaced. 'That's not fair!' She unclipped her seatbelt, pushed open the passenger door of the Land Rover and slid out. 'His dad's not a drug addict, is he.'

'Just keep him out of trouble, Lucy.'

'I know.'

'And yourself as well.'

She slammed the door and stalked off across the car park, putting her earphones in. A few seconds later she appeared on the platform, leaning back against the railings. Dixon waited, watched her get on the train and then sent Jane a text message:

She's on the train Nx

Let's hope she stays on it! Jx

Westonzoyland Church was open, not surprising on a Sunday morning perhaps, so Dixon crept in and spent fifteen minutes or so reading the information boards. Not that he learned anything new about the battle. And he had already seen the videos on the internet.

He tried to imagine the church as it would have been on the night of 6th July 1685, crammed full of prisoners bleeding all over the flagstone floor – five of them dying – the screams of pain and the stench.

He wondered whether the pews were the same ones – probably not.

The replica of the Mary Bridge sword was interesting, the notice on the wall behind it confirming that the original was in the Museum of Somerset. A Royalist officer had been killed with his own sword by a twelve year old girl while he was trying to rape her mother after the battle.

'You're a bit early for Communion.'

'I'm here on business, I'm afraid,' replied Dixon. Black jeans, a black shirt and a dog collar; the vicar was tidying the piles of hymn books on the table by the door – or pretending to, at least. 'Learning about the battle.'

'You'll be a police officer then?'

'That obvious, is it?'

'You haven't seen the Sunday papers yet, I take it?'

'Not yet.'

'The village shop is open till midday and they ordered extra copies, I'm told. It's such a shame, this happening just before Daniel's appeal.'

'Do you know him?'

'I christened his boy, Billy. Or William, I should say. And buried his wife. I visit him in prison from time to time as well. He's one of my flock, whatever he's done.'

'And what has he done?'

'Only God knows that, my son.'

'God and Daniel Parker,' said Dixon.

'Indeed.'

'Did you know the victims?'

'Not the boys, no. Adam Hawley was from Bawdrip and the Tanner boy was Sutton Mallet. Rory was Moorlinch from memory, so that would have been someone else's patch as well. I forget the other's name.'

'James Eastman.'

'I didn't know him either.' The vicar shook his head. 'Perhaps he was a Catholic or something? I knew the Bonds though. It's a team ministry these days, Chedzoy and here, so I knew Christine and Nicola quite well.'

'D'you believe Parker when he says he didn't do it?'

'I do.'

Dixon was about to ask 'Why?' when members of the choir began bustling in, so he made his excuses and a few minutes later parked in the bus stop outside the shop. Several of the headlines caught his eye even before he had wrenched on the handbrake: 'SCYTHEMAN, ANOTHER BODY FOUND' and 'SCYTHEMAN DEATH TOLL RISES'.

He begrudged paying the money, and ignored the shop assistant when she sneered, 'The bastard might get out next week.'

A quick flick through the articles confirmed that Doreen had been true to her word; she hadn't said anything she shouldn't. Then he dropped the newspapers on the passenger seat, took a deep breath and headed for Express Park and the midday meeting with Charlesworth.

Their paths hadn't crossed since the end of the Hinkley investigation. Not many officers recorded their conversations with the Assistant Chief Constable, let alone asked him to confirm his orders in writing, but Dixon had. Jane had said he had made an enemy for life.

No doubt he would soon find out.

Chapter Fourteen

Meeting room 2 was crowded, only one seat vacant. Mine, probably, thought Dixon, watching from the other side of the atrium. Several newspapers were spread out on the table so he could have saved himself a few quid too.

Charlesworth was playing golf later, judging by his clothes. The older man sitting to his left glaring at Dixon through the glass partition must be Ridley. The ever present press officer, Vicky Thomas, was sitting on Charlesworth's right, jeans and a T-shirt making a change from the usual sharp two-piece suit.

Dixon recognised the grey streaks in Deborah Potter's hair, sitting with her back to the glass. That left Lewis sitting next to the empty chair.

'When you're ready, Nick.' The shout came before the kettle had boiled, which was a shame.

Lewis winked at him. 'Ignore Ridley,' he whispered.

Charlesworth didn't wait for him to sit down. 'I must say I'm not entirely convinced by the appointment of you as the SIO in this case, Dixon. I'm not sure you have the sensitivity that's called for.'

'Sensitivity to what, Sir?' asked Dixon, conscious that it was not the answer Charlesworth would be hoping for. He pulled the vacant chair out from under the table.

'The situation in which we find ourselves.'

'We have a murder victim—'

'And we have the killer in prison,' interrupted Ridley.

'You've not met before,' said Lewis. 'Nick, this is DCS Ridley, retired. He was the SIO on the original case.'

Deborah Potter leaned forward. 'We also have the appeal starting tomorrow and while this body is not going to be directly relevant, it does complicate matters somewhat.'

'Does it?'

'Yes, it bloody well does, Dixon, and well you know it.' Charlesworth slammed his fist on the table.

'Rory Estcourt was killed with a scythe, making him a victim of the Scytheman. And Parker is the Scytheman,' snapped Ridley.

'Rory Estcourt was buried six to nine months ago,' said Dixon, spelling it out.

'Bollocks.'

Charlesworth glanced at Ridley. 'It's not an exact science, is it, forensic anthropology?'

'Have you read the post mortem report, Sir?' asked Dixon. 'It came in this morning.'

'Er, not yet, no.'

'Perhaps you should.'

Lewis was fidgeting in his seat next to Dixon.

'It's quite clear,' continued Dixon. 'And I think you would have a very interesting chat with Dr Martin if you tried to tell her she was not a scientist.'

'I didn't say that.'

'If it's right that Rory was buried nine months ago, Nick,' said Potter. 'Why?'

'Why Rory or why nine months ago?'

'Both.'

'Parker was granted leave to appeal a year ago, and the archaeological dig was fixed up just after that. It's hardly rocket—'

'Why Rory and not one of the other missing victims?' asked Charlesworth.

'Two reasons.' Dixon leaned forward and closed the newspapers on the table in front of him, revealing the headlines. 'Whoever did it knew Doreen would go to the press. And there, in big bold print, is exactly the desired result right before Parker's appeal. Then you've got Rory's pacemaker to set off a metal detector.'

'This is all bollocks,' said Ridley. 'Are you saying that we got it wrong fifteen years ago? And that the jury got it wrong?'

'Not necessarily, no,' replied Dixon. 'Just that it needs looking at again.'

'That's the last thing it needs.'

'I think what we were hoping, Nick,' said Charlesworth, his tone conciliatory, 'was that Rory's murder would be investigated with a measure of sensitivity to the fact that we cannot be seen to have *got the wrong man*, for want of a better phrase. If Parker's appeal fails, then unless there is compelling evidence that someone else was involved, the most favourable outcome, from our point of view, would be that it just goes away.'

'I'm sure it would be, Sir.'

'The CPS can be leaned on to take no further action, and Bob's your uncle.'

'All the same, Sir,' said Lewis, 'we do have a body on our hands and a duty to investigate what we now know to have been a murder.'

'Of course we do.'

'More importantly,' said Potter, 'is that we need to be in a position to arrest him for Rory's murder if his conviction for the Bond murders is quashed and he walks out of court on Tuesday.'

'Will you be able to make an arrest in that scenario?' asked Charlesworth. He was looking at Dixon – pleading almost, he thought.

'No, Sir. There's not a shred of—'

'Fucking bollocks,' interrupted Ridley. 'Who does this boy think he is? Fifty officers, eleven months, a three week trial and the jury took two hours.'

'Two hours and twelve minutes.' Dixon glanced at Lewis, who spoke as he was doodling on the corner of the newspaper.

'No connection to the battlefield itself was ever explored,' said Dixon.

'Oh, for fuck's sake.' Ridley sighed. 'We looked at it, but I ruled it out. It was hardly relevant to what we'd got, was it?'

'Assuming what you'd got was right,' said Dixon.

'Here we go again!'

'Perhaps you can fill us in on the appeal, Deborah,' said Charlesworth, turning to her. 'You had a conference with counsel on Friday, I think?'

'He still says it's unlikely he'll succeed. The blood spatter was rehearsed at the original trial and the jury heard evidence from Parker on it. The only difference this time is that the defence now has an expert.'

'There we are then,' said Charlesworth, visibly relaxing. 'I think we can rest easy in our—'

'Not with this idiot raking over it,' muttered Ridley.

'Is there anybody else you can assign to the case, Peter?' asked Charlesworth, turning to Lewis.

'No, Sir.'

'Well, that's it then. Dixon it is. Just be sensitive to the issues at play here, Nick. That's all I ask.'

'Let right be done.' Lewis was still doodling on the corner of the newspaper.

'This isn't *The* fucking *Winslow Boy*,' snarled Ridley.

He knows his films, so maybe he's not all bad? thought Dixon. Bollocks. Even Hitler had a dog.

Within seconds of the meeting breaking up, Dixon heard heavy footsteps behind him on the landing, the reflection in the glass of the lift at the end warning him of Ridley's approach.

'You bloody prick.'

He took a deep breath and counted to ten. Jane, his anger management counsellor, had suggested it in these situations. If he still felt the need to be rude after that, then go for it, she had said.

'Who the hell d'you think you are?'

A count of twenty was called for on this occasion.

'Well?'

'I intend to find Rory Estcourt's killer. And if that turns out to be someone other than Daniel Parker then so be it.'

'And what if that person also killed Christine and Nicola Bond?'

'Then Parker walks free. And rightly so.'

Ridley sneered. 'You're on a hiding to nothing, mate. You wait, not a single officer in this station, or any other for that matter, will lift a finger to help you.' He laughed, brushed past Dixon, and headed for the lift with a dismissive wave of his hand. 'You're pissing in the wind.'

'That went well, I thought.' Lewis had waited until Dixon sat down at a vacant workstation before standing up from behind the computer opposite.

'Well?'

'Compared to how I thought it would, anyway. What did Ridley say? I saw him having a go on the way out.'

'Just that I'm pissing in the wind, which is something I do quite often.'

'Walking on the beach?'

'He also told me that no one would lift a finger to help me,' continued Dixon.

'They probably won't.' Lewis smiled, then disappeared, leaving him staring at his computer screen – open at Google Maps and the satellite view of the bungalow in Sutton Mallet.

He was rummaging in the archive box for the crime scene photographs when he heard footsteps.

'Right then, Sir. What's to do?' Detective Constable Dave Harding was sitting down behind him, turning in his seat to hang his crumpled jacket over the back of his chair.

DC Mark Pearce was sitting at the adjacent workstation, switching on the computer. He grinned. 'Putting the band back together.'

'Shut up, Mark.'

'I've put the kettle on, Sir.' The voice came from behind the partition in front of him, then DC Louise Willmott's head popped up. 'Where do we start?'

The briefing had taken fifteen minutes. They were all familiar with the case and had been waiting for the call as soon as they had got wind of Dixon's appointment as SIO. It had come as no surprise when Lewis had rung them, even on a Sunday morning.

Dixon gave the red ledger to Mark Pearce and asked him to track down each and every member of the local history society, dead or alive.

Doreen's photographs of the carnival he gave to Dave Harding.

'Not cars?' Dave had said, smiling. 'You usually give me cars and cameras.'

'There aren't any yet. But what we do need to know is which carnival club that is, who the members were back then and who is on that cart.'

Louise was busy tracking down the Tanners. A check of HM Land Registry confirmed that they had long since sold the bungalow and moved away. Not that anyone could blame them.

Dixon himself was busy booking a room for the Monday night at a cheap hotel in London – Deborah Potter having suggested that he should attend the appeal hearing.

Chapter Fifteen

There was something oddly chilling about the sound of a steel door slamming shut; more so when it was accompanied by the jangle of keys and the clang of a heavy lock. Dixon glanced at Deborah Potter while he emptied the contents of his pockets into a plastic tray; she was watching a prison officer at HMP Long Lartin rummaging through her handbag.

'What's this?' Another prison officer was gesturing to the slim black plastic sleeve in the tray in front of Dixon.

'My insulin,' he replied, trying not to let his impatience shine through. 'I can't be the first diabetic who's been through here, surely?'

'You'll have to leave it here if there's a needle in it. You can collect it on the way out.'

Dixon's belt buckle set off the alarm when he stepped through the scanner, a cursory wave of a handheld metal detector satisfying the inquisitive prison officer. For Potter it was her wedding ring that did the trick, although she had already explained she couldn't get it off.

'Wait over there. His solicitor's here. Someone will come and get you when they're ready.'

They sat down side by side on the cheap plastic chairs; the collection of torn and out of date magazines on the low table not worth a second glance. Dixon was staring at the blank walls, Potter trying to smooth the creases out of her two-piece grey pinstripe trouser suit with the flat of her hand. They had dispensed with the pleasantries when they had met at the front entrance.

'How's your dog?'

'Fine, thanks.'

'Thought anymore about a move to Portishead?'

'No.'

Now they were waiting to interview Daniel Parker.

'You certainly know how to rub Charlesworth up the wrong way,' Potter said, breaking the silence.

'Thank you.'

'It wasn't a compliment.' She raked her fingers through her hair. 'So, am I to take it you don't think Parker is the Scytheman?'

'Everybody keeps telling me he is.'

'You do realise how we're going to look if it turns out he isn't?'

'What would you have me do?' Dixon wondered where Potter was taking the conversation. Charlesworth would rather it was hushed up – buried – just to avoid a bit of bad publicity. But Potter? He had expected better. Time to find out where she stood, perhaps. 'Sweep it under the carpet?'

'That's not what I'm saying.' She straightened up, shifting in her seat, the legs of her chair screeching on the lino. 'I'm not Charlesworth's hatchet man and I'm disappointed you would think I am.'

'He didn't ask you to lean on me then?'

'Actually, he did. But I'm not going to.' Potter's mouth curved into a half-smile. 'It'd be a waste of time. Just remember, your job is to find who killed Rory Estcourt. And if by doing that Parker is cleared, then so be it. I'd rather that than an innocent man stays in prison.'

'What's the Crown's position on his appeal?'

'Unchanged. The issues arising from the blood spatter evidence were heard by the jury at the original trial, so the CPS takes the view the convictions are safe. I spoke to the barrister this afternoon. The only difference this time is that there's an expert who agrees with him. There's no way the CPS will consent to a retrial on the current evidence. If the Appeal Court orders one, then fine.'

Heavy boots, keys in a lock.

'Remember, it's your interview,' continued Potter, standing up. 'I'm just here to see if anything comes up that might be relevant to the appeal.'

Interview room 1 was behind three steel doors, all of them slammed with gusto by the prison officer. Potter sat down at the table, opposite Parker's solicitor.

'I've told my client only to answer questions relevant to the current enquiry.' Silver hair; corduroys and a polo shirt – but then it was Sunday; a pen behind his ear. He spoke without looking up from his notebook. 'The appeal is off limits. Is that clear?'

'This is Mr Sandbrook, Nick,' said Potter, not bothering to hide her sigh. 'He's instructed by the Innocence Project.'

'They're a charity that funds appeals for those they believe to be innocent. I'm from Sandbrook and Co. We're acting pro bono in this case.'

Formal introductions could wait until the tape was rolling.

'Daniel is expecting to be cautioned?' asked Dixon, dropping his papers on the table.

'He is.'

The door opened and Daniel Parker shuffled into the interview room, his eyes glazed over and fixed on his cheap trainers.

Avoiding eye contact was a discipline he had clearly perfected after fifteen years as a Category A prisoner. All the time protesting his innocence.

His head was shaved, white tape holding his glasses together at one side; a standard issue blue T-shirt and grey jogging bottoms completed the picture of a man broken and staring into the abyss. Dixon waited while the prison officer escorting him took off the handcuffs.

'Daniel, my name is Detective Inspector Dixon of Avon and Somerset Police. This is Detective Chief Superintendent Potter. We'll be interviewing you today in connection with the murder of Rory Estcourt and I am obliged to caution you before doing so. You do not have to say anything but it may harm your defence if you do not mention when questioned something you later rely on in court.'

Dixon had expected defiance, arrogance even, from a man convinced he was going home. Instead, Parker stood motionless, listening as Dixon hammered the last nail in his coffin. At least that's how it felt.

'Anything you do say may be given in evidence.'

Dixon gestured to the vacant chair next to Sandbrook and then sat down opposite Parker. He flicked on the tape machine and watched Parker intently as each of them sitting round the table introduced themselves for the record. Parker was staring at his hands splayed out on the table in front of him, only the tips of his thumbs touching, as if he were attending a seance, perhaps. His breathing was shallow, oddly calm.

He looked as if he had simply given up.

'2005, wasn't it, Daniel,' said Dixon, the question rhetorical. 'I was at university. A good year for Chelsea, if I remember rightly.'

'We won the Premier League,' mumbled Parker, looking up. 'You follow football?'

'The ball's the wrong shape,' replied Dixon, smiling.

Sandbrook had stopped scribbling in his notebook and was watching Dixon intently.

'A rugby man?' Parker was still avoiding eye contact, preferring instead to focus on Dixon's tie.

'Rugby and cricket.'

'You any good?'

'Crap.'

Parker allowed himself a faint smile. 'At least you get to play.'

'Don't get the time,' replied Dixon. 'They give me all the difficult cases.'

'Like mine, I suppose.'

'Like Rory Estcourt's.' Dixon opened the file on the table in front of him and slid a photograph across the table to Parker. 'D'you recognise him?'

Parker leaned forward and looked at the photograph. 'I've seen the photograph before,' he said.

'And the boy?'

'Never.'

'Where were you living at the time?' asked Dixon.

'We had a farm cottage on the edge of Westonzoyland.' Parker looked up. 'I worked on the farm, like, and it came with the job. Only when you lot got me sent down, my wife got kicked out. Then the governor calls me in, says she's dead and hands me a letter telling me that my boy's in care.'

'Does the name Rory Estcourt mean anything to you?'

Parker sighed. 'You mean apart from the fact that most people think I killed him?'

'Before you were arrested, Daniel. What about back then?'

'There was an Alec Estcourt who used to go skittlin'. I'd see him at the Crown at Catcott sometimes. And Moorlinch. I think he played for the Ring O' Bells.'

115

'Did he ever bring his son with him?'

'No.'

'So, why did you kill the boy?'

Parker looked up, slowly, and stared at Dixon. 'I didn't.'

'I'm supposed to believe that you killed him with a scythe, just like you did the Bonds, and buried his body in the bottom of a rhyne out on the battlefield.'

A sharp intake of breath came from Sandbrook, but he clearly thought better of intervening.

'I didn't kill the Bonds, or anyone else for that matter. I've never killed anyone. I hurt some people once, but that was years ago. And it was an accident.'

'Tell me about that,' said Dixon, watching Potter and Sandbrook out of the corner of his eye. Both had sat up and were listening intently.

'6th July 1985, it was. I was seventeen. I was driving the tractor along the main road. Late, nearly midnight. There'd been the three hundred year anniversary of the battle and I hadn't been able to get out to feed the cattle so I had the trailer on the back of the Massey. We had some heifers in a field over Fowlers Plot way.' Parker took a deep breath, focusing his mind. 'The trailer was wider than the tractor and there was no light. I mean there was, but it was broke. It was a farm trailer, these things happen.' Breathing shallow and fast through his nose now. 'There's a long straight past Penzoy Farm and motorbikes use it for a burn. I saw the light, then bang.' Parker wiped away a bubble of snot from his nose with the back of his hand.

Dixon waited, glaring at Sandbrook when he looked about to speak.

'Take your time, Daniel,' he said.

Parker's fists were clenched and he was rubbing his whitening knuckles together. 'They missed the tractor and hit the trailer,' he said. 'They went down the side until they hit the mudguard on the back wheel.' Tears flowing freely now. 'What a bloody mess.'

'What did you do?'

'I stopped, jumped out and ran back, but it was pitch dark. Then a car came along and you could see it in the headlights. She was sitting up in the road – the pillion passenger – and her leg was . . .' His voice tailed off.

'Her leg was what?'

'Off.' Parker buried his face in both hands. 'And his. They both lost their right legs.'

'What happened to you?'

'I was prosecuted for dangerous driving because the trailer wasn't lit, but I pleaded guilty to driving without due care and attention and got five points and a fine. I can't remember how much now. I paid it off at ten pound a week.'

'What about the motorcyclist and pillion passenger. What happened to them?'

'They were local – Bridgwater I think. I heard they got married to each other a few years later. There was a big claim too and the insurance paid out. The premium went right up and Bert was angry. He stopped me driving out on the main road after that.'

'Was Rory Estcourt anything to do with that?'

'No!' Indignant now; arms folded tightly across his chest.

'There were two witnesses who said they saw you in Frys Lane holding a hand scythe.'

Sandbrook puffed out his chest. 'Nothing about the Bonds, I said.'

'It's about the murder weapon, which is common to both. A curved blade and Daniel was seen holding one.'

Sandbrook leaned across and whispered in Parker's ear.

'They must be mistaken. Or lying.'

'Did you know the witnesses?'

'No. I was asked that at the time, but I'd never heard of them. They could never have seen me in the fog anyway. And I never denied I was there.'

'Just that you were holding a hand scythe?'

'Yes. I found it sticking out of Nicola's chest.'

'So, just to recap then,' said Dixon, glancing down at Potter's notebook, the page blank. 'You didn't know Rory Estcourt, didn't kill him and didn't bury his body in the rhyne.'

'That's right.'

'Have you got any evidence that my client did?' asked Sandbrook.

'We have the similarity in the murder weapon,' replied Dixon. He turned back to Parker. 'When you were crouching over Nicola's body—' He raised his hand, silencing Sandbrook. 'Listen to the question first, then object if you must.'

Sandbrook's mouth twitched, but he said nothing.

'Think now, Daniel. When you were running across the field and when you reached Nicola, crouching over her, did you hear anything?'

'I've been asked that countless times before. I walked across the field. I didn't run. It was foggy and I heard no one running or anything like that. Until the police officer came running, that is.'

'What about anything else?' Dixon leaned forwards over the table. 'Think.'

'Eh?' Parker tipped his head, bewilderment etched on his forehead. 'I'm not sure I—'

Sandbrook was busying himself making notes.

'Any sound at all. It doesn't have to be another person moving. What other sounds did you hear? Even some distance away, perhaps.'

'There was no birdsong, or anything like that.' Parker hesitated. 'Maybe, off to the right a bit. It was a still night and the fog was making everything louder; sound travels. There was running water, sloshing, but I just thought it was a drain or a sluice. There's one out on the lane, I think.'

◆　◆　◆

'So, what was the relevance of all that?' asked Potter, leaning on the bonnet of Dixon's Land Rover.

He flicked open the album of crime scene photographs. 'This is the scene of Nicola's murder; the photograph was taken the following morning.'

'I've seen it before,' said Potter.

'This is a picture of the rhyne, adjacent to where she was found,' continued Dixon. 'Look at the duckweed.'

'It doesn't meet in the middle,' said Potter. 'What does that prove?'

'By July most rhynes are covered in a layer an inch thick, and it stays like that until the first frosts kill it off in November. Look in the background, further up – the coverage is solid. And yet here we have a clear line down the middle.'

'You think someone waded along the rhyne?' Potter was trying to slide on her sunglasses and shake her head at the same time. 'It's pure speculation.'

'Any footprints in the mud would be long gone, but Parker said he heard the sound of running water. I didn't make that suggestion to him. He volunteered it.'

'That's true.' Potter hesitated on the way to her car, which was parked behind the Land Rover. She was standing on the edge of the kerb with her back to Dixon, her notebook tucked under her arm. 'You'll need to speak to the CPS in the morning. Before we go in, preferably. But I wouldn't hold your breath on the strength of this.'

Chapter Sixteen

Dixon had managed to get into the cottage without waking Jane up. He had parked out on the main road, so Monty wouldn't hear the diesel engine, but the dog had still started barking, only stopping when Dixon pushed open the letterbox with his fingers and whispered, 'Shut up, it's me, you idiot!'

A turn around the field behind the cottage by the light on his phone, and both were curled up asleep on the sofa when Jane finally surfaced just after six in the morning – just in time to give him a lift to the railway station.

Now he was standing in the queue for the body scanner at the entrance to the Royal Courts of Justice in London, his overnight bag on the conveyor belt. He had taken the precaution of putting his belt in the tray and got clean through, no questions asked about his insulin pen either. Still, they never had before.

It was his first visit to the Royal Courts as a serving police officer, not least because it was the first appeal he had been involved in, but he had been to the High Court many times before as a trainee solicitor for hearings before the registrars up in the Bear

Garden; civil procedural stuff mainly, although the firm had trusted him with more weighty matters in the second year of his training contract.

Dixon remembered the senior partner's words to him the day he qualified and promptly left to join the police: 'What a waste of bloody time that was!' He couldn't have put it better himself, although it had always afforded him a degree of freedom other officers didn't enjoy, perhaps. After all, he could go back to the legal profession in a jiffy, assuming someone would give him a job.

He looked up at the ceiling as he walked across the tiled floor to the daily lists, posted as always on a noticeboard in the middle of the entrance hall, although 'entrance hall' didn't do it justice – it was more like a cathedral without the pews.

Parker, Daniel; 10.30, Court 3.

He dumped his bag in the corner of the empty CPS room and was waiting for the kettle to boil when Deborah Potter walked in, closely followed by a wig and gown. The man wearing them was tall, bespectacled and looked like he had a bad smell under his nose.

'Nick, this is Giles Lambert QC,' said Potter. 'And this is Emma Shah – oh, she was here a minute ago.' Potter was looking behind Lambert. 'She's a Crown prosecutor with the Complex Casework Unit in Bristol.'

'She nipped to the loo, I think,' said Lambert. He had started pacing up and down with his hands in his pockets, his gown billowing out behind him every time he walked in front of the fan on the windowsill. 'DCS Potter tells me you think Parker is an innocent man.'

'My job is to find Rory Estcourt's killer. Everybody tells me it must be Parker because he killed the Bonds, but when I look at it, I'm not convinced.'

'DCS Potter also tells me you believe the real killer made his escape along the rhyne?'

'It's certainly possible,' replied Dixon. 'And there's a rhyne along the back of the Tanner bungalow too.'

'Well, it's a theory, not evidence, and we're under no obligation to disclose it. The Crown's position remains that the blood spatter evidence was assessed by the jury, who found him guilty on both counts. If he's able to persuade their Lordships to grant him a retrial then all power to his elbow, but we will not be agreeing to it. Ah, there you are, Emma,' said Lambert, spinning round. 'I was just explaining the Crown's position to Inspector Dixon here.'

'You're probably wasting your time, Inspector,' said Shah. 'The evidence we're concerned with today is quite specific to the Bond case.'

'Yes.' Lambert smirked. 'You should be down in Somerset. The first seventy-two hours and all that.'

'The first seventy-two hours were fifteen years ago,' replied Dixon, concentrating on stirring his coffee.

'Of course they were.'

'And what about the fact that Rory's body was buried nine months ago, at most? Should we be disclosing that?'

'You've interviewed Parker?'

'A preliminary interview, yes. He denied killing Rory.'

'And you didn't mention the timing of the burial?'

'No.'

Lambert's jaw tightened. 'If it comes up, the Crown's position is that the killer is Parker. And that he had an accomplice who buried the body now to make us think the Scytheman is still out there. It cuts both ways.'

'So does a scythe,' muttered Dixon.

'What did you say?'

'We're supposed to think Parker buried the body fifteen years ago. It's only because of the clay and the anthropologist that we know it was nine months.' Dixon had never had much time for barristers. 'It's an obvious attempt to implicate Parker in another murder just before his appeal.'

'It's not obvious to me.'

'Have you met him?'

'No.'

'Maybe you should.'

'Look, this isn't getting us anywhere,' said Shah, straightening her hair in the mirror. 'We're on in five minutes.'

The corridor was long, with Court 3 at the far end. Dixon couldn't hear much over the sound of leather shoes on the tiled floor and Lambert's Blakey's, but he was sure he heard the words 'bloody troublemaker'.

'Tread carefully, Nick,' whispered Potter, as they waited by the ornate carved oak door of the court, the usher making a note of everyone's name on his clipboard.

'The trouble with our system is that it becomes about winning and losing,' said Dixon, waiting in line. 'What's right gets lost in the games people play.'

Chapter Seventeen

'Be upstanding in court.'

Wood everywhere: the walls, benches, even the ceiling, apart from the ornate skylight window that was open, thankfully. Three judges in black robes filed in and sat down on the bench; in front and below them sat two clerks, each behind a computer screen.

The barrister below and to Dixon's left remained standing when everyone else sat down. 'My Lord, I appear for the appellant in this matter, and my learned friend Mr Lambert for the Crown.'

'Good morning, gentlemen.' The judge sitting in the middle of the three was the Lord Chief Justice, or so the usher had said. 'I think we would all benefit from dispensing with wigs. It is a trifle hot today,' he said, sweating profusely.

Lambert slid off his wig, leaving it upside down on a pile of papers on the desk in front of him. He flattened down his greying hair with the palm of his hand.

'Mr Lambert, what is the Crown's position on the appeal?' asked the Lord Chief Justice, peering down at him from on high as he opened a lever arch file of documents.

Lambert stood up. 'The convictions are safe, My Lord. Taken together with lay witness evidence placing the appellant in Frys Lane with a scythe in his hand, and the statement from the neighbour that she saw him running from the scene out into the cornfield, the blood spatter is merely confirmatory of the Crown's case. It does not turn on the blood spatter evidence alone.'

'My Lord, if I may?'

'Of course, Mr Hughes.'

'The neighbour's statement does not conflict with the appellant's version of events. He too says that he proceeded from the cottage out into the cornfield to look for the second victim, Nicola. That is not in dispute. What is hotly disputed, however, is that he had a scythe in his hand at any time until he pulled it from the victim's chest out in the cornfield. The neighbour says that she saw no scythe, which leaves the testimony of the two witnesses who dropped Nicola off at the end of the lane, a distance of some fifty yards on a dark and foggy night. Taken together with the blood spatter evidence, that was clearly enough for the jury at the original trial, but if the blood spatter evidence is now inconclusive, and we say it is, then can a conviction based solely on that disputed eyewitness testimony be safe? We say not. At the very least we say it should be put to a jury again.'

'So, you're saying it *does* turn on the blood spatter evidence?'

'My Lord will be aware of the effect of forensic evidence on a jury required to deliver a verdict beyond reasonable doubt. The forensic evidence at the original trial supported the Crown's case. Ergo the appellant was convicted. Now it does not.'

The Lord Chief Justice glanced at the judge sitting to his left, then turned back to Hughes. 'But the defence position that the spray came from air escaping Nicola's lungs was put to the jury at the trial, was it not?'

'It was, My Lord, but without expert evidence to back it up.'

'Whose fault was that?'

Hughes rubbed his hands together, nervously. 'My Lord, I am not, with respect, entirely convinced of the relevance of that as an issue here. We are where we are. But if pressed, I would have to point the finger at the original defence team.'

The Lord Chief Justice sighed. 'Well, we've looked at the papers and I have to say we're not entirely convinced by the appellant's case, Mr Hughes. What we have to consider is whether it is such that it renders the convictions unsafe.'

'My Lord, I have the blood spatter expert here, ready and willing to give evidence.'

'Very well.'

Dixon listened to the legal niceties being played out in front of him. The flowery language, the politeness to each other – more often than not forced and loaded with sarcasm. All of it very far removed from a young girl dying in a cornfield, her mother already dead; a police officer running into the fog, scared witless; and a man drenched in blood lying next to the murder weapon. Could he be innocent?

Stranger things have happened.

'Where are you going?' asked Potter, when Dixon stood up and tried to squeeze past her.

'My phone's buzzing,' he said.

Two missed calls, both from Louise. Dixon rang back.

'What is it, Lou?' he asked, pushing open the door of a vacant interview room opposite the court.

'I've got the file on the RTA that Parker was involved in back in 1985. The victims were Robert Perrot and Sally Deale. She comes up on the list of members of the Middlezoy Carnival Club. They're the ones in the background of those photos of Rory. They did the battle scene with Monmouth on the top of the church tower in 2002.'

'Where are—?'

'That's not all,' continued Louise. 'Dave's got the membership lists. She was a member until 2004, then she's listed as deceased. She killed herself, I've since found out, and I'm getting the file from the coroner. Also listed as members at that time are Jennifer Allen and Shelley Allen.' Louise paused, waiting for the reaction.

'Ridley must have known.' Dixon kicked a small metal bin across the room, sending the contents flying across the floor – an empty coffee cup and a Kit Kat wrapper. The question was whether Lewis had known, not that he could bring himself to ask.

'There's nothing on the file, but then the accident was twenty years before. And it's hardly a relevant previous conviction.' Louise was clicking her fingers at someone in the background. 'Dave spoke to the membership secretary; Jennifer and Sally were bezzie mates.'

'Where are they now?'

'I've got addresses for them; Jennifer lives in Bridgwater and Shelley is Taunton way. Shall I bring 'em in?'

'We'll pay them a visit. I'm guessing I'll be back this afternoon. In the meantime, tell no one.'

Dixon tiptoed into the back of the court and along the side of the bench seats until he was adjacent to Lambert, sitting on the front row.

'Can you get a short adjournment, Sir?' asked Dixon.

Lambert frowned at him. 'Why?' he whispered.

'New evidence.'

'What new evidence?' Lambert turned to face Dixon, who was leaning over, his hand on the back of the seat.

Hughes hesitated in the middle of his questioning of the blood spatter expert and looked across.

'Ten minutes, Sir,' said Dixon.

'What is it, Mr Lambert?' asked the Lord Chief Justice.

Lambert stood up. 'My Lord, I wonder whether I might ask the court for a short adjournment.'

'Who is that standing next to you?'

'A police officer, my Lord.' Lambert was speaking while looking at Dixon, his eyes wide. 'I'm told there is a matter of some importance that has just come up.'

Dixon nodded.

'And that it requires my urgent attention,' continued Lambert.

'Is this anything to do with the body that's just been found?'

'I know not, my Lord.'

'Well, you'd better find out. Your junior can keep track of the blood spatter evidence while you're gone.'

'I'm grateful, my Lord.'

Lambert slid out from behind the desk and stalked out of the court, stopping only to turn and bow to the judges at the door. Dixon followed, Emma Shah and Potter close behind, leaving Lambert's assistant at the front taking notes of the blood spatter expert's evidence.

'What is it?' demanded Lambert, when Shah closed the interview room door. He pulled a chair out from behind the table and slumped down, his arms folded.

'On 6th July 1985 Parker was involved in a road traffic accident. A young couple was seriously injured; both of them lost their right legs above the knee. The pillion passenger was Sally Deale.'

'That name means nothing to me,' said Lambert.

'Me neither.' Shah stared blankly at Dixon.

'She killed herself in 2004.'

'I'm sure there's a point to this,' said Lambert.

'She was a member of Middlezoy Carnival Club, with her best friend.' Dixon paused, adding weight to the hammer blow. 'Jennifer Allen.'

Lambert let out a long, slow and menacingly exaggerated sigh. 'Oh fuck,' he mumbled.

'Fuck indeed,' said Shah.

'When did this come to light?'

'I found out about the road traffic accident last night and my team got the file out. We're also looking at some old photographs of Rory taken at the carnival and that led to . . .' Dixon allowed his voice to tail off, watching Lambert take it all in.

'If Jennifer Allen lied about the scythe and got her daughter to do the same, then Parker walks, just like that.' Lambert clicked his fingers. 'And rightly so.'

'And God help any police officer who covered this up,' said Shah.

'Where the hell were you when this case was investigated?' Lambert was looking at Dixon, another sigh – dejected this time – escaping his nostrils.

'Still at university.'

'Who was it who said police officers are looking younger these days?'

'So, what do we do?' asked Potter.

'None of this is confirmed, I suppose?' asked Lambert, still looking Dixon up and down.

'No, Sir,' he replied. 'I need to interview Jennifer Allen and her daughter and they may or may not be charged with perverting the course of justice depending on the outcome of those interviews. I'd also like to take a statement from the membership secretary at the carnival club. And anyone else I can think of.'

'A short adjournment, then.' Lambert stood up. 'Hughes will agree. It looks like his client's case is going down the pan as it is.'

The expert was still in the witness box when they filed back into court.

'Well, Mr Lambert?' said the Lord Chief Justice.

'My Lord, I was right. New evidence has indeed come to light that requires further investigation, and on that basis I am seeking a short adjournment of these proceedings so that those enquiries might be made as a matter of urgency.'

'Can you enlighten the court as to what this evidence might be?'

'I would prefer not to, My Lord. I am conscious that the public gallery is full, and if the matter were placed in the public domain now it might very well prejudice those enquiries.'

The Lord Chief Justice leaned forward over the bench. 'Joseph, what's an adjournment looking like in the daily lists?'

The court clerk pursed his lips. 'Six months, My Lord,' he said, standing up and turning to face the bench.

Lambert coughed, loudly. 'I am conscious of the fact, as I know your Lordships are, that a man's liberty is at stake.' He was choosing his words carefully. 'A man who has quite possibly spent fifteen years in prison for a crime he did not commit.'

Hughes spun round and winked at Sandbrook, sitting behind him.

'You'll have to do better than that, Joseph,' snapped the Lord Chief Justice.

'I've printed off the court list for the next two weeks, My Lord.' The court clerk handed a piece of paper up to the bench.

'How long will you need?' asked the Lord Chief Justice, looking at Lambert while he handed the note to the judge sitting to his right.

'My Lord, half an hour should suffice if the new evidence proves correct. If not then we are back to square one with the appeal as it stands.'

'What d'you say, Mr Hughes?'

'I'm being asked to take something of a gamble, My Lord. If whatever it is the Crown seeks time to explore leads nowhere, then my client faces another six months in prison until this appeal is relisted. On the other hand, he could—'

'We've got a slot on Friday morning at ten,' said the Lord Chief Justice. He was staring down at Hughes, his eyebrows raised as far as humanly possible.

'Very well, My Lord,' said Hughes. He looked over his shoulder at Sandbrook, who nodded emphatically. 'We are content.'

'Good.' The Lord Chief Justice stood up. 'Full reporting restrictions until Friday. This court is adjourned.'

'You've got nerves of steel,' said Potter, sliding her phone back into her jacket pocket.

Dixon was looking up at the departure boards at Paddington station, waiting for something going via Bristol Temple Meads, but praying for a direct train to Taunton to leave first. That way he wouldn't have to make polite conversation with Potter all the way home, and listen to more of her attempts to get him to transfer to Portishead.

'I've spoken to Charlesworth.' She tapped him on the shoulder. 'He said he was delighted that Avon and Somerset Police were focused first and foremost on justice. If a wrong has been done, it must be undone.'

'He's got that line from the press officer.'

'D'you reckon Ridley knew?'

'I don't know him well enough to judge,' Dixon lied. He knew Ridley well enough and his golden rule applied, anyway: assume the worst, then you're never disappointed. Would he assume the worst of Lewis? That was an interesting conversation still to be had.

'It makes a change though, doesn't it?'

'Eh?'

'Proving someone innocent instead of guilty.'

'Ah, there we are,' said Dixon, picking up his overnight bag. 'Platform three: Taunton; Tiverton. Should be home by eight.'

'I'll see you on Friday.' Potter raised her voice as Dixon walked away across the concourse. 'Just stay out of trouble. And don't forget to cancel your hotel room.'

A couple of beers from the buffet car, a takeaway from the Zalshah when he got home and an early night; what could go wrong?

Jane's first text message arrived when he was on the second can and watching Castle Cary station flash by.

Just had a call from social servs Billy's gone missing. His dad's appeal was adjourned. Jx

I got it adjourned. New evidence. It was going to fail anyway. Nx
What time Taunton?

7.24 Thank you :-)

No more text messages arrived, but Dixon wasn't entirely convinced that was a good thing, and his uneasy feeling was confirmed by the look on Jane's face when he walked out of the station at Taunton. She was parked on the double yellow lines outside, her cheeks flushed and her nostrils flaring.

Dixon opened the passenger door and pushed Monty into the back of the Land Rover.

'What's up?' he asked, although he could guess, perhaps.

'Lucy's run away.'

Chapter Eighteen

Fish and chips would have to do.

'You've got to eat,' Dixon had said. 'And so do I.'

Now they were sitting on the sea wall, their backs to Hinkley Point. The memories were still fresh; he'd been able to pick out the crane, and the concrete batching plant was clearly visible. The silo too. The nuclear power station was the backdrop to every walk on the beach, so he'd have to get used to it, but for now he would turn his back on it and enjoy his fish and chips.

'Have you got a trace on her phone?'

'Her foster parents have got the Manchester lot doing it.'

'Let's take Monty for a walk and you can find her in the morning.'

'A walk?'

Dixon smiled. 'She's a smart kid. I reckon she'll be in touch to let you know what's going on. Billy's done a runner and she'll be trying to keep him out of trouble.'

'I've left umpteen messages.'

'Who's she going to turn to if she gets in trouble?'

'You, probably.'

'There you are then.' Dixon closed the polystyrene box and dropped it in the bin, wiping his fingers on his trousers. 'Try to relax tonight. She'll be travelling anyway.'

'Hitch-hiking.'

'She's got money, so let's hope not.'

Jane frowned at Monty. 'Have you given him a chip?'

'Yes,' replied Dixon.

'You've had some, you cheeky sod.' She handed the remains of her fish and chips to Dixon, who dropped them in the bin. 'I don't know what to do for the best,' she said. 'We've got a trace on her phone. Dave and Judy are going mad with worry; not that she hasn't done it before, of course, so they're struggling to get the local lot to take it seriously.'

'Think about it,' said Dixon. 'She's in Manchester and Billy's here. What's midway between the two?'

Jane shook her head. 'What?'

'Get up early.' Dixon stood up, unclipped Monty's lead and watched him tear off down the steps to the beach. 'And go and wait for them outside Long Lartin prison. They'll be along at some point during the day.'

'Oh, for fuck's sake.'

'Quite.'

A long walk on the beach, followed by *The Winslow Boy* – it had been at least six months since Dixon had watched the film, and Jane never had. Her phone pinged just as the trial was starting.

We're fine. Don't panick.

Jane tapped out a reply with Dixon looking over her shoulder. *Where r u?*

'You're wasting your time,' he said. 'She's not going to tell you that. Not yet anyway.' He waited five minutes for the speech bubble to appear telling them that Lucy was typing a message, but it never did, so he restarted the film. 'What time did she go missing?'

'She never got home from college. Her tutor said she left at four.'

'Worcester it is then.'

'You're right,' replied Jane, setting her alarm for six in the morning. 'Idiot.'

◆ ◆ ◆

Too hot for Monty in the car, so Dixon left him at home with the TV on, and was halfway through the file on the 1985 crash when Louise walked along the landing at Express Park just before eight in the morning.

'You found it then,' she said, flicking on the kettle. 'The bit I found odd was that the motorcyclist said he was drawn to the lights. Surely you'd make a conscious effort to steer away from them?'

'Depends how fast you're going, I suppose. The collision investigator never arrived at a figure for the motorcycle's speed. At or near the speed limit was the best he could say.'

'On a Kawasaki Z1000? Hardly. That road's notorious for it. There have been several fatalities in the past few years, all of them on the bend at Penzoy Farm.'

'Did you get a statement from the membership secretary at the carnival club?'

'Dave did. It's on the system.'

'What about an address for Jennifer Allen?'

'She'll be at work by now,' replied Louise. 'She works in the village shop in Westonzoyland.'

'Does she indeed?' Dixon had met her on Sunday morning, the encounter making its mark. 'Dave and Mark can interview her daughter at ten and we'll do Jennifer at the same time so they can't warn each other. If she admits lying about the scythe, tell them to let us know and bring her in. We'll do the same with the mother.' Dixon was looking across the atrium at Lewis walking along the landing on the far side. 'There's someone I need to speak to.'

◆ ◆ ◆

'I heard,' said Lewis, stopping in front of Dixon, who was blocking the door to his office.

'Heard what?'

'About the adjournment.' Lewis brushed past him and opened the door. 'You'd better come in.'

'Did you know?'

'Straight to the point as ever.' Lewis sat down behind his desk, took out his phone and placed it face down in front of him. 'What d'you think?' he asked, looking up at Dixon, a hint of disappointment in his eyes.

'I don't think you can have known, but I need to hear it from you.'

'I didn't know.' Lewis rubbed the back of his neck. 'Whether I would have had the courage to do what you did if I had known is another matter.'

'You would,' said Dixon.

'I hope so. It's the first time I've ever heard of a police officer bringing an appeal hearing to a standstill; deliberately anyway.'

'Ridley interviewed Jennifer Allen, according to her witness statement, but I don't know the officer who took the statement from her daughter, Shelley.'

'Ridley certainly never mentioned anything if he knew, but there's no real reason to believe he did. If Jennifer decided to lie to frame Parker and avenge her friend Sally, there's no reason why she should or would have told Ridley.'

Dixon had to agree, albeit reluctantly, wondering why Ridley had ignored the photographs of the carnival, all the same. 'Why wasn't Ridley interested in the battle? He seems to have shut down any suggestion of a connection.'

'Far be it from me to defend Ridley, but it was over three hundred years ago, for God's sake, Nick.' Lewis threw his hands in the air. 'And when we'd got Parker there was no need to worry about it anyway.'

'Somebody called Lorraine Hardy interviewed the daughter,' offered Dixon.

'She was a DS; died a couple of years back.'

'Who else would I know who was on the original investigation?'

'No one here. They've all retired, died or been made redundant.'

'What about Potter?'

'She was in Manchester back then.'

'Charlesworth?'

'He was always uniform. Never CID.'

Always assume the worst and you are never disappointed. And, yes, sometimes you are pleasantly surprised. Dixon looked down at Lewis. Tortured by years of guilt and regret, by his own failure to speak up when an innocent man had been sent down for two life sentences, Lewis had stayed silent, despite his own doubts. Dixon could see it now, the weight on his shoulders, the sadness. There had always been something about him; something dark – hidden perhaps.

He had trusted Dixon with it, and he would not let him down.

'So, what happens now?' asked Lewis.

'We tip Jennifer Allen upside down and see if anything falls out of her pockets.'

'Don't forget the Scytheman is still out there.'

'I haven't forgotten.'

Chapter Nineteen

Dixon slowed on the kink in the road at Penzoy Farm, pulling over to the nearside to allow a motorcycle to sweep past.

'He wouldn't be doing that if I had the blue light on top.'

'Yeah, he would.' Louise was staring out across the battlefield from the passenger window, glancing down every so often, presumably at the rhyne perilously close below her. 'You'd never catch him in this.'

'Did you get his number?'

'No.'

'Me neither.'

He parked in the bus stop again outside the village shop in the middle of Westonzoyland and checked his watch: five to ten. That was near enough.

'Jennifer Allen?'

'Yes.' Blue jeans and a grey sweatshirt, several rubber bands around her wrist, mousey brown hair swept back in a band.

'Remember me?'

The blank expression told him she didn't. Either that or she played poker.

'I bought some newspapers on Sunday morning and you gave me the benefit of your wisdom about Daniel Parker. Something about the "bastard" getting out soon, if I remember rightly.'

'What about it?'

Time for the warrant cards; Dixon dropped his on the pile of papers on the counter and Louise followed suit.

'You're here about the body they found?'

'No.'

'What's this about then?'

'Is there anywhere more private we can have a chat, perhaps?' asked Dixon, looking over his shoulder when the bell on the front door rang, an elderly lady shuffling in.

'I'm on my own.'

'Is there anyone you can ring, perhaps?'

'Mike's upstairs, but he was up at five to do the papers. He's probably asleep.'

Dixon waited until Jennifer picked up the telephone, watching the number she dialled. It took three sighs, but she got there in the end.

'Mike, can you come down? The police are here and they want to talk to me . . . I don't know what about.' She held the phone to her chest. 'He says can you come back later?'

'No.'

She winced, then replaced the handset. 'He heard that. He's on his way.'

The storeroom was small and piled high with boxes, most of them chocolate or sweets; it was no place for a diabetic to linger. Louise was standing with her back to the door, her notebook resting on a box of Quavers.

'You gave a witness statement in 2005. Do you recall what that statement said?' asked Dixon.

Jennifer avoided eye contact, beads of sweat forming on her temples. 'It was late; I'd picked the girls up in Bridgwater and was dropping Nic home.'

'The girls?'

'My daughter Shelley, and Nicola. It was foggy; everybody knows that.'

'And what did you see?'

'Daniel Parker standing outside the cottage in Frys Lane with a scythe in his hand. One of the small ones, you know.' She was watching Louise making notes and listening for anything that might tell her what was coming.

Time to put her out of her misery, thought Dixon. 'And was this before or after Nicola went into the cottage?'

'After. She went in and he followed her.'

'Does the name Sally Deale mean anything to you?'

The hesitation was longer than comfortable, even Jennifer knew that, trying to cover it with ers and ums; juggling the implications of what her answer might be. Dixon knew the signs.

'It's either yes or no,' he said, trying to appear helpful. Actually, he was just turning the screw.

'Yes.' She busied herself closing boxes, folding the flaps over and smoothing them flat.

'How well did you know her?'

'Not that well. We'd been at school together years before. And Bridgwater College.'

'What happened to her?'

'I don't know. We lost touch.'

'Really?'

'Yes.' The feigned indignation was painful to watch. No BAFTAs here.

Dixon slid a photo out of his pocket and unfolded it. 'This is a photo of the Middlezoy carnival cart from 2002. See if you can see yourself on it,' he said, leaving it on the box in front of Jennifer.

'I wasn't on that one,' she said, without looking at it.

'Was Sally?'

Silence.

'Because you were both members of the Middlezoy Carnival Club, weren't you?'

'I can't remember. We may have been, I suppose.'

'According to the membership secretary you were best friends.'

'He's got that wrong.'

'What happened to Sally?'

'She killed herself in 2004. She couldn't take the . . .' Jennifer's voice tailed off, the realisation she was saying too much arriving a whisker too late.

'Constant pain,' said Dixon. 'Was it the phantom limb pain or her shattered elbow? Her suicide note didn't say.'

'Both,' mumbled Jennifer.

'Very sad,' said Dixon.

'It was. And it was all that bastard's fault.'

'He was a seventeen year old boy and it was a road traffic *accident*, Jennifer.' Dixon stepped forward. 'It was your chance for revenge and you took it, didn't you? Said you saw Parker with a scythe in his hand.'

Jennifer's face flushed. She was picking at the corner of a box, tearing off strips of cardboard and dropping them on the floor. 'No, I—'

She stopped when Dixon's phone pinged in his pocket, the volume turned up for maximum effect.

'A man has spent fifteen years in prison for a crime he did not commit, Jennifer. Thanks to you.'

'No, he did it. I know he did.'

'And what's more, the real killer is still out there.' Dixon slid his phone out of his pocket and read the text from Dave Harding:

Shelley has admitted it. They lied. Arrested and on way to Express Pk. Dave

'Jennifer Allen, I am arresting you on suspicion of perverting the course of justice. You do not have to say anything—'

She pushed the box on to the floor, several bars of chocolate spilling out at Dixon's feet. 'I haven't done anything wrong!' she screamed.

'But it may harm your defence if you do not mention when questioned something that you later rely on in court.'

'Fuck you.'

'Anything you do say may be given in evidence.'

Jennifer slumped back on to a box of crisps, crushing them beneath her as she fell.

'Your daughter has admitted lying, Jennifer,' said Dixon, hauling her up by the arm.

'Has she been arrested as well?'

'Yes.'

'It was my idea. I made her do it.' Sobbing uncontrollably now. 'She was just a kid.'

'The same age as Daniel when he was driving the tractor.'

Chapter Twenty

'Do you want to wait? Either that or we can ring you.'

'I'll wait.'

'This way then.'

Jane followed the prison officer along the corridor to a meeting room at the far end. 'There are no magazines down here, I'm afraid, but I can get you a coffee from the machine, if you like?'

'Thank you.'

Blank walls, a table, four chairs and a bin, all of them screwed to the floor. Probably a good thing, thought Jane, doubting that she would really have wrapped one around Lucy's head, but it would have been nice to have had the option. At least she hadn't had to take the day off; Billy was on the safeguarding list so it counted as work, not that she had a supervisor watching her every move anyway.

A paper cup, one sachet of sugar, but nothing to stir it with even if she wanted to. It didn't smell much like coffee either.

It seemed like a lifetime before the prison officer opened the door again. 'They're here,' she said. 'Shall I just show them in?'

Jane's expression softened. 'Do they know I'm here?'

'We haven't told them anything yet.'

'Good.'

Jane leaned back against the wall behind the door and sipped her coffee, listening to the footsteps coming along the corridor. Then the door opened, Billy shuffling in behind Lucy.

'I'll leave you to it then.'

'Thank you,' said Jane, loud and clear.

Lucy spun round. 'Oh, for God's sake.'

Billy sat down, letting his forehead rest on his arms folded on the table in front of him. 'How did you know?'

'Nick,' said Lucy.

'I just want to see my father.'

Jane sat down opposite Billy. 'They're not going to let you see him. You know that,' she said. 'So what's the point of running away?'

'His appeal hearing was adjourned,' sobbed Billy, without looking up.

Lucy stood over him, rubbing his back.

'Nick got it adjourned.'

'Nick?' demanded Lucy, glaring at Jane. 'Why?'

'You have to trust him, Billy. He thinks your father is innocent and he'll prove it too. You just have to be patient.'

Billy looked up, his eyes bloodshot. 'He was coming home.'

'He wasn't. His appeal was failing until Nick intervened. It would've been thrown out.'

'He told me he was going to get out.'

'He was telling you what you wanted to hear,' said Jane. 'Look, I probably shouldn't show you this.' She took her phone out of her handbag, opened a text message and slid it across the table.

Both witnesses arrested perverting course of justice. They lied. Nx

'That's it then,' said Lucy, leaning over Billy's shoulder to see the screen.

Jane smiled. 'It looks like it.'

'See, I told you.' Lucy threw her arms round Billy.

'You can't tell anyone yet. You must be patient, keep your nose clean and stay out of trouble.'

'Can I see him then?'

'Not yet.' Jane sighed. 'There are procedures, and you're still a ward of court.'

'How long will it take?'

'Days, that's all. Now, Social Services are on the way to take you back. You've run away before so you know what's got to happen.'

'What about me?' asked Lucy, frowning at Jane.

'You're coming home with me.'

You were right. They're here. Security have got them. Social servs on way to pick him up. Bringing Lucy home. Jx

Jane's text had arrived in the middle of the interviews. Both Jennifer and Shelley admitted lying about the scythe, Jennifer doing her best to take the blame. They had seen Parker in the lane after they dropped Nicola off, despite the fog, but saw nothing to implicate him in the murders.

'Did they lie about everything or just the scythe?' Lewis had crept up behind Dixon while he was scrolling through his emails at a workstation in the CID Area. 'Just the scythe, which means their statements now corroborate Parker's own statement. He never denied being in the lane, did he?'

'So, he's innocent then.'

Dixon knew that wasn't a question.

'Are you charging them?' continued Lewis.

'Just waiting for the CPS to make their minds up.'

'About what?'

'Shelley was a minor at the time, so it'll be whether we charge them both or just Jennifer.'

Lewis perched on the desk behind Dixon. 'Just so you know, I've spoken to Charlesworth about a referral to Police Complaints. Parker's solicitors are bound to do it anyway, and the original investigation needs to be looked at again to see whether we could or should have known.'

'Or *did* know.'

'I told you—'

'I was thinking of Ridley.'

'Charlesworth also suggested a major investigation team taking over under Deborah Potter,' said Lewis, picking at his teeth with a paper clip.

'What did you say?'

'I told him you could handle it.'

'I bet that went down like a lead balloon.'

'Actually, he's a big supporter of yours, when you don't rub him up the wrong way.'

'You do surprise me.'

'Just keep your Policy Log up to date,' said Lewis, dropping the paper clip in the bin. 'So, what's next?'

'It's Dr Ashton's talk on the battle in the function room at the Sedgemoor Inn tonight.' Dixon looked at his watch. 'I wouldn't miss it for the world.'

Standing room only at the back, but then that was more to do with the size of the room than the audience.

Two lecturers and twenty or so Reading University students, there under orders no doubt, and a handful of local history society members, Louise busy copying their names out of the visitors' book on the table.

Dixon spotted the furtive glances passing between Zak and Sandra Smith, but said nothing.

Ashton had dressed for the occasion, rolling down his sleeves and putting a tie on. His trousers were still covered in clay though, all of it lit up in glorious technicolour when he stood in front of the slide projector.

'Right, let's make a start,' said Sandra, standing up and turning around to face the audience. 'Dr Ashton needs no introduction, I think, the world's leading authority etcetera, etcetera, so without further ado, Dr Graham Ashton.'

She was sitting down again by the time the ripple of applause subsided.

'Tonight, I'm going to focus on the dig, what we've found so far and what it tells us. Then, if you're lucky, I'll tell you about two of the most enduring mysteries of the battle. You're all familiar with how the battle unfolded, who won and all of that, so I don't need to go over that, do I?'

'I'm not,' whispered Louise, over the murmur of agreement from the rest of the audience.

'The rebels lost,' said Dixon.

'Who were they rebelling against?'

'The king.' Dixon sighed. 'I've got a book you can borrow in the car.'

The next hour consisted of a rather dry run-through of the various finds made over the previous week or so: musket balls, a few buckles, the sword handle; and that, sadly – thought Dixon – was about it. Apart from *that which may not be mentioned*, as Ashton had described Rory Estcourt.

Either way, Ashton was convinced the evidence proved his theory about the friendly fire incident, when Lord Grey wheeled away from the Bussex Rhyne and was fired on by the rebel infantry moving forward. Then he moved on to questions.

'You were going to tell us about the enduring mysteries.' Dixon didn't see who asked the question, but they had only just beaten him to it.

'I was,' replied Ashton with a flourish. 'Of all the mysteries, legend and myth swirling like the fog around that night, two have always fascinated me. I've solved one and am close to solving the other; and, yes, before you ask, there's another book in the pipe-line.' Ashton paused while the audience erupted in more polite applause, led by Professor Timperley.

'Let me tell you about the one I've solved – that's the identity of the Royal officer who was killed by Mary Bridge with his own sword. Is everyone familiar with the story? Twelve-year-old Mary got hold of his sword and killed him while he was trying to rape her mother?'

'Got what he deserved,' muttered Louise.

'The big reveal will come in my book,' said Ashton, 'so I'd be grateful if you didn't put it on social media or publish it anywhere.' He wagged his finger at the audience. 'You're all sworn to secrecy. Agreed?'

'Yes.' That was Timperley again, thought Dixon, the students maintaining a polite silence.

'We know that after the battle, Lord Churchill occupied Bridgwater with his cavalry and Feversham marched to Wells on his way back to London. He was at the head of the Guards and the Wiltshire Militia; they stopped at Glastonbury on the way and hanged six rebels from the sign on the White Hart. Is the pub still there?'

'It is.' Sandra that time.

'I've been back through the records of every parish they stopped at along the way and found nothing – we're back in the days well before there was a register of births, deaths and marriages. But at Compton Dundon there's an entry dated 7th July 1685, the day after the battle: *An unidentified officer of the Second Guards; died of wounds received at Sedgemoor; buried in an unmarked grave; Rector Wm. Marters.* A gravestone was later erected by his family, which gives us his name, but it's long since been lost to the ravages of time.'

'The Second Guards were on the extreme left of the Royal line,' interrupted Timperley. 'They never came into contact with the rebels, except for firing on Lord Grey as he rode along the rhyne. And we know Grey never returned fire. He turned away into the path of his own infantry.'

'Exactly. Hucker is his name and where did he get his wound, if not from young Mary?' Ashton picked up a piece of paper. 'William Hucker, fourth son of William and Elizabeth Hucker, of Farringdon House, Surrey. We know that Mary Bridge was pardoned by Colonel Kirke, so it's reasonable to assume Hucker was under arrest and may well just have been left for burial by the locals when he died en route to London.'

'Wouldn't they have returned the body to the family?' One of the students. All Dixon could say for sure was that it wasn't Zak.

'Possibly, but that would've meant carrying it all the way – in high summer and without means of preserving it.'

'Pure speculation,' whispered Dixon.

'It's pure speculation,' said one of the local history society members sitting at the front. Dixon could just see the back of a bald head. 'He might have been helping Bishop Mews move the Royal guns into position. Or he could have gone to reinforce the right wing when Lord Churchill—'

'Yes, well,' Ashton cleared his throat. 'The second mystery is more compelling. Picture the scene.' He was waving his arms around. 'The dead of night, thick fog; the rebel army is marching

149

out of Bridgwater as silently as they can manage. Six thousand men; the horses' hooves are wrapped in cloth; silence is golden. They skirt round Chedzoy and follow the line of the Black Ditch out on to Langmoor. Lord Grey is ahead of the main column with his five hundred horse, stumbling about in the dark looking for the Upper Plungeon so he can cross the rhyne and attack the Royal Army in the rear. Then bang!' he shouted. 'A shot is fired and we know from Andrew Paschall that a lone trooper rides up to the Bussex Rhyne shouting, "Beat your drums, the enemy is come." And the rest, as they say, is history. The element of surprise was lost and the battle soon followed. So . . .' Ashton paused, teasing his audience. 'Who was that lone trooper?'

'You'll never find that out now.' A male voice from the front of the room; it could have been Timperley, or the bald chap again.

'You're all familiar with Andrew Paschall, the rector of Chedzoy between 1662 and 1696. He was a prolific letter writer and diarist, as we know. Indeed, much of what we do know about the battle comes from his letters and his 1685 diary entries. Then there's Edward Dummer's account, of course. And the king's, but that was written later.' Ashton took a sip from a pint on the corner of the table at the front of the room. 'I found a letter in the archive at Cambridge University. Misfiled. I'm not sure anyone there really understood its significance, but it was from Paschall to his friend, Durling, in London. It's dated September 1696 and tells the story of a rebel, shipped to the West Indies as an indentured slave, as we know some were, who made his way back to England and was hanged for murder.'

'Who did he kill?' That voice at the front again.

'I don't know. Yet.' Ashton was hanging his head in mock contrition. 'But I have reason to believe it was the trooper who gave the game away on that fateful night in 1685; the turncoat, or traitor, if you will.'

'Does the letter give a name?'

'It names the rebel hanged for murder, not his victim.' Ashton bowed. 'You'll forgive me if I don't reveal more at this stage. There's a lot of work to do on it before I can go public, and, as you might imagine, I would hope to do so first in my new book, which should be out next year. Exciting though, isn't it?'

'What other evidence could there be still to find after all this time?'

'Andrew Paschall's 1696 diary is still missing,' said Ashton, tipping his head. 'But you'll forgive me if I say no more about that now.'

'Well,' said Sandra, standing up. 'How exciting!' She clapped her hands. 'Does anyone have any more questions?'

No hands went up – mercifully, thought Dixon, looking at his watch; Jane and Lucy should be home by now.

Chapter Twenty-One

'What number was it?'

'Fourteen,' replied Louise.

Dixon looked at his watch. They were ten minutes early. 'Better wait,' he said. 'They might not be out of bed yet.'

Louise walked over to the railings adjacent to the flats and looked out over Torbay. It was a grandstand view.

'Nice place to retire to, I suppose,' she said.

Dixon still hadn't forgiven her for her joke the previous night as they had walked across the car park outside the Sedgemoor Inn. 'You should have been a historian. You're good at speculation.'

Bloody cheek.

'Remind me that I need to go and see Doreen before Friday. If the court lifts the reporting restrictions I don't want her seeing it on the news first.'

'Can I come? I'd like to meet her.'

'Are these retirement flats?' he asked, leaning against the railings. The block sat on the hill overlooking the bay, but he had his back to the sea.

'There's a warden on duty,' replied Louise. 'If that's what you mean. She did say her husband had had a stroke.'

'What's the time?'

'Five to.'

Dixon pressed the buzzer.

'Is that the police?'

'Yes, Mrs Tanner.'

'Come on up. Third floor.'

He snatched the door open when the lock clicked and held it for Louise. Mrs Tanner was standing outside the open front door of her flat when they reached the landing.

She waved at them. 'Cooee!'

Dixon had his warrant card at the ready as he walked along the landing.

'There's no need for that. Come in.' The door slammed shut behind them. 'You'll need to watch out for Florence.'

'Florence?' Louise hesitated.

'She's out on the balcony at the moment I think, but she'll be in to give you the once-over.'

'Mine's about ten times the size,' Dixon said, at the sight of a black and tan chihuahua jumping on the sofa.

'What've you got?'

'A Staffie.'

'Is he all right? They can be a bit . . .'

'That's the owners, Mrs Tanner. The dogs are fine.'

'So they say.' She smiled. 'And is yours?'

'Soft as a mop, I'm told.'

'You'll have to forgive my appearance,' she said. 'I have better things to be worrying about these days.'

Dixon hadn't noticed much beyond the bags under her eyes. 'Your husband had a stroke?'

She nodded. 'A nasty one, I'm afraid. He understands me, I think, but he can't speak. And his left side's gone. He's having physio, not that it's doing any good.'

'I'm very sorry to hear that,' said Dixon.

'He's still in bed. It takes me a couple of hours to get him up. The carer usually comes in at nine, but I put her off until ten today, when you said you were coming.'

'Have you told him what's going on?'

'I told him you'd found Rory Estcourt, but apart from that I don't really know what's going on.' She sat down on a reclining chair, pressing a button on the side until her legs were raised. 'It's my back,' she said, with a roll of her eyes. 'It's all the lifting and turning. It's making me old before my time, Inspector.' The words caught in her throat. 'Although I wish Mark had had the chance to get old.'

'We intend to find him this time, Mrs Tanner,' said Dixon, perching on the edge of the sofa next to Florence. Louise sat down at a table in the window.

Her eyes welled up. 'You intended to find him last time.'

She had a point. And the answer was far too complicated. Best to duck the issue. 'You need to prepare yourself and your husband for Parker's appeal succeeding. The likelihood is that he'll be released on Friday. There are reporting restrictions in place at the moment, but those may be lifted. If they are, you'll see it on the TV news.'

Mrs Tanner clicked her fingers and Florence darted across Dixon's legs, jumping on to the arm of her chair. Then she curled up on Mrs Tanner's lap. 'She keeps me sane.'

Dixon knew what she meant. 'Dogs can do that.'

'So, Parker didn't kill the Bond girls?'

'No.'

'I can't tell Bob. It'll kill him. I'm sure the stress of it all caused his stroke.' She sighed. 'All he really wants is to bury his son before it's too late.'

For once, Dixon was not sure what to say. It was a cold case, stone cold, but suddenly time was of the essence, for the Tanners anyway.

'Are you any further forward in finding who did it?' Mrs Tanner's voice was loaded with sorrow, but she was holding back the tears. Years of practice, no doubt.

'We have several lines of enquiry.'

'Do you?'

'No.' Dixon immediately kicked himself; that answer hadn't meant to come out loud.

'An honest policeman,' said Mrs Tanner. 'You're wasted; you should've been a politician.'

'We've got a large team on it, Mrs Tanner,' said Dixon, back-tracking. 'The whole case is to be re-examined from scratch—'

'Please don't give me the "no stone left unturned" line. You weren't going to say that, were you?'

'No.'

'Thank God!'

Dixon could forgive her scepticism. Her God willing, Mark's mummified body was out there somewhere for him to find and bring home, but that would be too much information for now, far too much information. 'Can you tell me about the day you got home from Venice?'

'Must I?' Mrs Tanner shook her head. 'We got home about midday. The front door had the chain on it, so Bob walked round the back and found the patio door was open. I was by the front door with the suitcases and I could hear him calling out Mark's name. Then he screamed. I remember banging on the front door, and then it opened.' She took a deep breath, exhaling slowly. 'I'll never forget the look on his face as long as I live.'

She paused – not for Dixon to ask another question, that much was obvious.

Her eyes glazed over. 'There was blood on the sofa, the coffee table and the rug. Bob was running from room to room, screaming his name.' Then she was gone, reliving the moment again. 'A neighbour came round and called the police.'

'Take your time, Mrs Tanner,' said Dixon.

'I'm all right, Inspector,' she said, with a lopsided smile. 'I don't cry any more. There are no tears left in me.'

'Did you find anything outside?'

'No. I don't think your lot did either.'

'And the trip to Venice, was it just a holiday?'

'I'd always wanted to go and Bob booked it as a surprise. He thought it might cheer me up after my father died.' She leaned over and began fumbling in the bottom of a bookcase next to her chair. 'I've got some photos somewhere.'

'I've never been,' said Dixon.

'It's overrated.' She sat up. 'No, can't find them. They might be in the wardrobe, I suppose. It was the first time we'd left Mark. He was eighteen and we thought it'd be all right.'

'It should've been, Mrs Tanner,' said Louise, looking up from her notebook.

She bit her lip. 'We had no idea that two other boys had gone missing from the local area. They kept that quiet. There was the Eastman boy over at Middlezoy and then poor Rory. We'd never have gone and left Mark on his own if we'd known.'

'Did you see anyone before you went to Venice, anyone hanging around you'd not seen before?'

'The same old questions.' Mrs Tanner was rubbing Florence behind the ear. 'No. We saw nothing out of the ordinary. At all.'

'How deep was the rhyne at the back of your garden?'

Mrs Tanner looked up, fixing Dixon with her tired eyes, her attention caught by a question she'd not been asked before, no doubt.

'Only about a foot. We had it fenced off when Mark was a toddler. He was fascinated with the frogs and tadpoles in the summer.'

'Did the farmer dredge it?'

'Once in a blue moon.'

'On Google Earth you can see a patio.'

'We put that down. Then there was Bob's vegetable patch. Is that still there?'

'Looks like it.' Dixon slid his phone out of his pocket. 'Would you like to see?'

'No, thank you.'

A few minutes later Mrs Tanner opened the front door of the flat, allowing Florence out into the corridor. 'She won't go anywhere,' she said, stepping back and taking hold of Louise by the elbow. 'You will find Mark this time, won't you?'

'If anyone can, Mrs Tanner,' whispered Louise, nodding in Dixon's direction. 'It's him.'

'What are you doing?' asked Louise, stifling a chuckle.

'Testing out a theory.'

'Shouldn't you have taken your shoes and socks off first?'

'God knows what's in the bottom of these things.' The water was over his knees, leaving a layer of duckweed stuck to his trousers as he waded along the rhyne. 'And there's a tap on the back of the barn over there.'

Three ladies from the Westonzoyland WI were watching him from the marquee on the edge of the Chedzoy cornfield, shaking their heads and laughing.

'How deep's the mud?' asked Louise.

'It's over my shoes, but once you're through the sediment, the ditch has got a firm bottom.'

'Could you carry a dead body?'

'Not easily, but it could be done. Either that or you could drag it behind you, letting the water take the weight.'

Dixon scrambled out of the rhyne and began flicking the duckweed off his trousers.

'You are not going to be popular back at the station.' Louise was holding her nose as she followed Dixon along the rhyne towards the back of the houses.

He stopped on the corner. 'See, it goes all the way to the road. And you can even duck down below the high sides.'

'On a foggy night, no one would see you anyway.'

'Exactly.'

'They're scary places, these rhynes.'

'That's the steep sides and because we usually see cars upside down in them, but it's just a square cut ditch.' Dixon turned on the tap on the back of the barn and began rinsing off his legs. 'There we are, I'll have dried off in the sun by the time we get back to the car.'

'Ridley's on the prowl,' said Harding, when Dixon and Louise walked along the landing at Express Park. He frowned. 'What's with the tide mark?'

'Don't ask.' Louise rolled her eyes.

'I do wonder how that bloke gets in here sometimes,' Dixon said, checking his trousers for duckweed before he sat down. 'He's supposed to have retired.'

'He's advising Charlesworth on the Scytheman investigation,' replied Lewis, who had arrived from the direction of the canteen, a sandwich in one hand and coffee in the other. 'Or at least he was. Charlesworth was going to tell him to stay well clear now Police Complaints are involved, I think.'

'Well, he hasn't yet,' said Harding. 'I saw him half an hour ago talking to DCS Potter.'

'What's she doing here?' Dixon sighed. 'Is the old incident room still set up on the second floor?'

'They dismantled it last week,' replied Harding. 'When you were on holiday.'

'What about the whiteboards?'

'They're still up.'

'I'll be upstairs then, but if anyone wants me I've gone home.'

A blank whiteboard, a box of papers and a roll of Sellotape. It all helped the visualisation, not that it wasn't clear in his head. After all, there wasn't a lot; exclude Daniel Parker and the original investigation had found precisely nothing of use, all other lines of enquiry dropped after Parker's arrest.

Dixon pinned a picture of Rory Estcourt on the left, and stared at it for several minutes before concluding that he had nothing to add underneath it. Likewise a picture of Mark Tanner and pictures of the Bonds. Then there were the pictures of the two missing persons of whom no trace had ever been found: James Eastman and Adam Hawley, both smiling at the camera, one playing football, the other on a skateboard.

'Not a lot to go on, is it, Sir?' Mark Pearce was standing behind Dixon, although quite how he had got there was a mystery. 'As cold cases go, it's frozen bloody solid.'

'Let's warm it up a bit then. We need to start from scratch and go over everything again. I'll focus on the burial of Rory's body.'

'Yes, Sir.'

'The rest of you can go back over the original investigation. Speak to everyone at Mark Tanner's party the night before he disappeared – the neighbours, college tutors, everyone. The same for the Bonds and Rory.'

'Just as if it were happening now and the killer was still out there somewhere,' said Pearce.

'He's out there, and he thinks he's got away with it.'

'He's in for a bit of a shock then, isn't he?'

'I'll have a look at the missing persons too; see if there's anything—'

'Congratufuckinglations.' Accompanied by a slow hand clap.

Dixon glanced at Pearce. 'That's Ridley. Stay and witness this, will you, Mark.'

'My pleasure.'

'Parker walks and my investigation is going to be pulled to pieces by you and the fucking IOPC.'

Dixon turned to face the fast-approaching Ridley. Any angrier and he'd be foaming at the mouth.

'You got the wrong man. That's all there is to it.' Dixon stood his ground. 'The evidence was there and you chose to ignore it.'

'And you're sure of that, are you?' snarled Ridley, his forehead inches from Dixon's face.

'His convictions are unsafe; I'm sure of that. Another thing I'm sure of is that we shouldn't be having this conversation. There's a clear conflict of—'

'I was warned you were one of those *by the book* arseholes.'

'By the book?' laughed Pearce. 'Hardly.'

'Answer me one question,' said Dixon. 'Just for my own peace of mind. Did you know Jennifer Allen lied?'

'Fuck you.'

'I've had better offers.' Dixon turned his back on Ridley. 'Show him out, will you, Mark. Before he says something he might regret.'

Chapter Twenty-Two

'Not now, Inspector.' Colin Timperley jabbed his finger in the direction of the small radio on the earth step cut into the side of the trench. 'It's an LBW review.'

Three feet deep and covering an area the size of two snooker tables, the trench contained the professor and two students, all of them on their knees and craning their necks to hear the commentary.

'*There's no bat involved,*' said the voice on the radio. '*Front on spin vision, when you're ready, please.*'

'*Test Match Special?*' asked Dixon, pacing up and down too near the edge.

Colin glared at him when the side wall started to crumble beneath his feet. 'I can't bear that limited over nonsense,' he said. 'They're not even properly dressed. Cricket should not be played in pyjamas.' Hands on his hips now. 'Even the ball's the wrong colour.'

'W. G. Grace would turn in his grave.'

'Do I detect a note of sarcasm?'

'Not at all, Sir,' replied Dixon.

'*Impact in line; wickets – umpire's call. Kumar, you can stay with your original decision. You're back on camera . . . now.*'

'Thank God for that.'

'One of ours?'

'I take it you don't follow cricket?'

'I'd love to have the time, Sir.' Dixon squinted, even behind his sunglasses. The sun was directly overhead, heat haze shimmering in every direction; it was too hot even for the mosquitoes.

'Which are you, Inspector?' asked Colin, climbing out of the trench. 'A mad dog or an Englishman?'

'Both, Sir.'

'Me too. I take it you wanted a chat.' Colin slid off his panama hat and dabbed his forehead with a handkerchief. 'Let's sit under the gazebo. There might even be some Pimm's left.' He moved two rickety deckchairs into the shade, sat down gingerly on the one with a small rucksack hanging over the back, and then dragged the cool box towards him. 'Yes, Pimm's. Or there's a bottle of water, if you'd rather?'

'I'm fine, Sir, thank you.'

Colin was cleaning his clip-over sunglasses with his handkerchief. 'What was it you wanted to ask me?'

'I'm interested in the arrangements for this dig, Sir,' replied Dixon. He was moving the deckchair from side to side, trying to stop it wobbling. 'I'd like to know who knew about it and when.'

'It was Malcolm's idea, from memory.' Colin was emptying a can of Pimm's into a glass. 'That's Prof Watkins. He's over at the other dig site looking for the mass grave. We were driving back from Hadrian's Wall and he suggested a battlefield dig for this year's field trip. It makes a change from the Roman stuff. And we've introduced a new battlefield archaeology module to the course too, so it was a good fit actually.'

'Opportunities are fairly limited, I should imagine.'

'You'd be surprised.' Colin took a sip from his glass. 'We've got a student doing a thesis on Battle of Britain crash sites on the South Downs; desperately hush-hush that is, mind you. If the metal detecting lot got hold of it, it'd be a free-for-all. But you're right, most of the major battlefields are protected heritage sites.'

'When was this?'

'We finished at Hadrian's Wall last July. After that I had a couple of weeks off and must've sent out some exploratory emails maybe early August. Hang on,' he said, trying to sit up. 'Hold this.' He passed his glass to Dixon, then reached round for the rucksack hanging on the back of his chair. 'I can check my emails on my phone, can't I? I never delete sent items.'

'And when would you have informed the students?'

'That wouldn't have been until after Christmas. Staff knew early on, but not the students.'

'When did the staff find out?'

'At a meeting before the autumn term started, so that would've been late September possibly. They need to know for lecture planning and such like.'

'How many are there?'

'Four, but only three of us are full-time,' replied Colin. He was scrolling through his emails. 'There's me and Malcolm, then there's Trudy Philips, and Dale Mulling is the part-timer. He's the battlefield specialist, really. He would've been here, but he's gone to Crete for the summer. Local lad too, I think.' He passed his phone to Dixon. 'Here it is. I sent an email to info at zoylandheritage and Sandra replied.'

'What happened then?'

'She got the permissions – that's Bussex Farm and Fowlers Plot – then it was just a matter of finding a campsite.'

'And who involved Graham Ashton?'

'Sandra did. She knew him and thought he might like to be involved, which is fine as far as we're concerned. The more, the merrier. He's also given us something specific to look for in his friendly fire incident, as well as the mass grave, of course.'

'Have you found the grave site?' asked Dixon.

'We've got an area the size of a double bed, maybe, that's throwing up a lot of buckles and buttons. It's very close to the King's Sedgemoor Drain, but would've been in a bend in the Black Ditch at the time of the battle. It makes me wonder whether they found the mass grave when they were excavating the drain and just dumped what was left in a pit.' Colin shrugged. 'They weren't quite so sentimental about things back then.'

'Can I see it?'

'Yes, of course. You'll need to drive round, but you'll be fine in your Land Rover. It's a couple of hundred yards from the eastern corner of the cornfield. You can see their gazebo. Can't guarantee any Pimm's though.' Colin raised his glass. 'You're more than welcome to join us tonight too.'

'The anniversary of the battle?'

'We're doing a night time dig under floodlights, then gathering at the memorial at one in the morning, when the battle started. The vicar's coming out to say a few prayers and I'm going to read the roll.'

Malcolm Watkins was young for a professor, thought Dixon, although he'd lost count of the times he'd been told he was young for a detective inspector. Watkins was clearly an old hand at digging all the same, even equipped with a well worn pair of knee pads; the gazebo pitched over the small trench enabling him to work in the shade. No deckchairs and cocktails here.

The size of a double bed was optimistic too; more like a pool table. And deep.

Several students were sitting cross-legged, cleaning items in large plastic trays with toothbrushes, cans of lager propped up in the long grass. Dixon recognised a belt buckle, buttons and what looked like the sole of a shoe, the leather ridged and cracked.

The King's Sedgemoor Drain was twenty yards away at most, the steep bank shelving down to the water's edge that was lined with lily pads. The last time Dixon had seen it up close had been on a cold dark night in the depths of winter. And he had run down the bank and jumped in. The cold shiver running down his spine was almost a relief in the baking sun.

'Inspector Dixon?' Watkins had stood up, his head just popping up above the parapet, despite him being well over six feet tall. He squinted into the sunlight, plucking his sunglasses off the top of his head and putting them on. 'Colin rang me and said you were on your way over.'

'Must've taken some digging,' said Dixon, looking down at Watkins.

'It's a bit of a shame, really. It's not the mass grave we were hoping for, that's for sure.' Watkins climbed up a small aluminium ladder and slumped down into the long grass. 'Chuck me a can of Coke will you, Layla?'

A girl opened a cool box, took out a can, shook it and then threw it to him, grinning at the students sitting opposite her.

'That's a D you'll be getting for your dissertation.' Watkins sighed as he opened the can, losing half the contents in the grass in front of him. 'They're a good bunch, really,' he said.

'What have you found?' asked Dixon. It was the old ploy: get the witness talking and keep them talking.

'What's left of the mass grave, I think. There's no fabric, or human remains; just buckles, lots of buttons and a few bits of leather.' Watkins took a swig of Coke. 'We think they found the mass grave when they were excavating the KSD and dumped what was left in this pit. It was piled up – we've found stuff all the way down, so there may have been a bit more in the way of remains at the time. Not now though, sadly.'

'Professor Timperley said there was a loop in the Black Ditch just here?'

'As far as we know, yes. There's a rhyne on the other side that seems to follow the line of it, but they straightened it when they dug the drain.'

'Is there anything on the other side?'

'We can't get permission from the landowner over there, which is a crying shame. I can't believe there'd just be the one grave for that many dead, so it'd be worth a look. This loop in the old ditch wasn't cultivated so it's a reasonable burial site, if you think about it.'

'Did he or she give a reason?'

'Not that I know of. Sandra was going to have another word with them.' Watkins scrunched up the can and dropped it into a bin liner. 'That's Sutton Hams you're looking at, and that hedge follows the rhyne that I think is what's left of the old Black Ditch. I may sneak over there with my metal detector when it gets dark. No one's ever looked over here before and certainly not over there.'

'Whose idea was the battlefield dig?' asked Dixon. He was standing under the gazebo, looking down into the pit.

'Mine,' replied Watkins. 'My family are from Taunton and this place has always fascinated me, so when Colin said he wanted to do a battlefield dig, it seemed the ideal place. We were in the car on the way back from Northumberland.'

'And when did you tell your students?'

'I told mine at the start of that term, so that would've been the October. I'm afraid my excitement got the better of me.'

'May I?' asked Dixon, gesturing to the ladder.

'Be my guest.'

He climbed down the ladder and stood in the bottom of the pit, staring at the side walls.

'We go down layer by layer,' said Watkins, appearing on the edge. 'I'm not sure we can go much deeper, though, without shoring up the side walls. Health and safety and all that.'

'Quite.' Dixon brushed the wall with his hand, watching the mud crumble into the bottom.

'We'll expand it that way,' said Watkins with a wave of his hand towards the drain. 'That seems to be where most of the stuff is.'

'Any weapons?'

'No. Just that sword handle they found the other day. All of the weapons would've been recovered after the battle, don't forget.'

'You said this place fascinated you?' asked Dixon, as he climbed back up the ladder. 'Did you come here often?'

'All the time when I was a kid. My father was a detectorist and used to bring me with him. It's what got me into archaeology, really.'

'And where were you in 2005?'

'Reading University. I never left.'

'Did you know about the Scytheman?'

'I followed the story in the newspapers like everyone else, I expect. It seemed surreal at the time. Still does, to be honest.'

'Did you know any of the victims?'

'No, mercifully not.'

'Were you a member of the local history society?'

'My dad was and he used to take me to some of the talks. I must sound like a real anorak?'

'He is an anorak!'

'Thank you, Layla. It's an E now.'

'Not at all, Sir,' replied Dixon. 'Thank you. I'll leave you to it.'

Dixon was aware of footsteps in the grass behind him as he walked back to the drove, where his Land Rover was parked behind the minibus.

'I'll tell you what really bugs me about the whole thing. The bloody media.' Watkins opened the back of the minibus and threw in the bag of rubbish. 'They blew it up into something it wasn't, all for the sake of selling a few newspapers. The haunted battlefield.'

'Haunted?'

'It's supposed to be. You know what people are like. It's just because so many people died here, but they had to turn it into some sort of circus. Are you coming tonight?'

'Yes, Sir.' Dixon was standing by the open door of his Land Rover.

'You may see the lady in white then,' said Watkins, with a bitter laugh. 'Her fiancé was captured by the Royal Army and told he'd be freed if he could outrun a horse. When he did, they hanged him anyway, so she drowned herself in the Bussex Rhyne over by the memorial. She can still be seen wandering the battlefield to this day, blah, blah, blah. The tabloids loved that one.'

'You don't think the murders had anything to do with the battle, then?'

'Of course not. And that was proven when Parker was convicted, surely?'

Chapter Twenty-Three

The text from Louise arrived just as Dixon was walking across the top floor of the car park at Express Park.

Beware welcoming committee mtg rm 2 ;-)

He had watched her drop the box she was carrying and snatch her phone off the workstation when she saw him waiting for the steel gates to open at the bottom of the access ramp. The huge floor to ceiling windows on the first floor had their uses, although they usually worked against him.

He didn't have to wait long for someone to open the door from the inside, allowing him to slip in without swiping his card. Sometimes it worked, and it was worth a try.

Not today though; Lewis had been keeping an eye out for him, and short of crawling along the landing, there really was no escape.

'Just don't blame me,' whispered Lewis, holding the door of the meeting room open.

Charlesworth, Potter and Lewis. At least there was no Ridley this time.

'Things are moving fast, Nick,' said Charlesworth, watching him sit down.

Nick? Since when have we been on first name terms?

'Deborah's had a telephone conference with Lambert and the CPS,' continued Charlesworth. 'Fill him in, will you, Deborah?'

'The Crown will not now be opposing Parker's appeal,' said Potter, snapping the case of her reading glasses shut. 'Both of his convictions will be quashed and a retrial ordered, which means Friday morning's hearing essentially becomes a bail application.'

'Our main eyewitnesses being charged with perverting the course of justice may have something to do with it,' mumbled Charlesworth, holding one arm of his spectacles between his teeth while he rubbed his eyes.

'The Crown will oppose bail, but if he gets it, then he's out,' continued Potter. 'If the court is minded to let him out, then Lambert will be asking for bail conditions; to a hostel out of the area, that sort of thing. Otherwise, he'll be straight on the train home to Westonzoyland.'

'And who can blame him,' said Dixon.

'Lambert will also be asking the court to continue the reporting restrictions.' Potter leaned back in her chair and folded her arms. 'But if they don't, he'll walk out of Long Lartin into the arms of the press and it'll be plastered all over the front pages. And, more importantly, the Scytheman will know you're after him.'

'Which brings me on to what happens now, Nick.' Charlesworth smiled at him – unsettling to say the least, thought Dixon. 'I've spoken to the Chief Constable and the Police Commissioner, and both are convinced that we need to be seen to be taking this seriously.'

Dixon shifted in his seat. Charlesworth was building up to something and he felt sure he wasn't going to like it.

'The Incident Room is going back in upstairs as we speak and we're allocating resources for a major investigation team. This is not something you will hear me say often' – Charlesworth forced another lopsided smile – 'but no expense is to be spared.'

'Are you leading it?' asked Dixon, turning to Potter.

'No.'

'It does need to be a senior officer,' said Charlesworth. 'And I've convinced the chief con that you're the right man for the job. So, with immediate effect, you are now acting detective chief inspector. All right?'

'Yes, but—'

'No buts.' Charlesworth raised his hand. 'We simply can't have people of your quality languishing in the junior ranks. And you're on the fast track programme anyway. What the hell are you doing on that if you don't want promotion?'

Dixon's sharp intake of breath was cut short by Potter. 'We need this sorted out quickly, Nick,' she said. 'And you're the man for the job. You'll report to me, and Peter will help you with staffing.'

Dixon turned to Lewis. 'I'll need Louise, Dave and Mark.'

'They're already upstairs.'

'I'm sending two teams of eight down from Portishead in the morning,' said Potter. 'Let me know if that's going to be enough. And you'll need to liaise with Professional Standards and Police Complaints as and when the need arises. They'll no doubt have questions about the original investigation; cooperate with them at all times, but your priority is finding the Scytheman.'

'Yes, Ma'am.'

'There'll be a press conference on Friday morning when we know whether or not Parker's been released,' said Charlesworth. 'Seniority brings with it additional responsibilities and you'll need to be there for that, I'm afraid.' He raised his eyebrows. 'Is that clear?'

'Yes, Sir.'

'Have you made any progress, dare I ask?'

'Not yet, Sir,' replied Dixon. 'I'm convinced it has something to do with the battle, but I'm not sure yet how or why.'

'One of your hunches, I suppose?'

'Yes, Sir.'

'Well, you haven't let us down yet.' Charlesworth stood up. 'Right then, keep your paperwork up to date and go and do whatever it is you do.'

Chapter Twenty-Four

Do I have to call you chief now? Jx

News travels fast.

Dixon poked his head around Jane's office door to find her shutting down her computer.

'I was just off,' she said, smiling at him. 'Congratulations. We should open a bottle of something fizzy.'

'Maybe when this is over,' he mumbled, hoping his reluctance was obvious to no one but Jane. 'Where's Lucy?'

'She's at home with Billy.'

'On their own?'

Jane shrugged. 'They're watching one of your old films. What else could I do?'

'Nothing, I suppose.'

'She's got an exam on Friday so she's going back to Manchester tomorrow.'

'And back again on Saturday, no doubt.'

'Friday night actually.'

'Tell Billy to ring his father.' Dixon winked at Jane. 'Don't ask me why. And I'll be home late. There's a candlelight service on the battlefield at one in the morning.'

'Can I come?'

'I'll pick you up then. Monty can come too – the walk will do him good. The poor sod's been stuck indoors all day.'

'What about food?' Jane stood up and pushed her chair under her workstation. 'Have you eaten anything?'

'Yes, Mother,' he replied, heading for the stairs with a wave.

'We've only just taken this bloody lot down.' The workman was lying on his back under a desk, a screwdriver in his hand, talking to himself as Dixon arrived in the Incident Room.

Five blocks of four workstations on the top floor, only three of them occupied – Dave, Mark and Louise.

'May I be the first to—?'

'No you may not, Mark,' interrupted Dixon, smiling. 'I'm only "acting", which means it's temporary.'

'Lewis said you asked for us?' Louise grinned.

'I don't know anybody else.'

'Ah, that's it,' said Dave, keeping his head down behind his computer screen. 'I said it would be something like that.'

'How have you got on with the Tanner case?'

'Not very well,' replied Dave. 'I've spoken to a couple of those at the party the night before he disappeared, but they can't really add to what they said at the time. It'll take me a few days to work my way around the rest of them.'

'Well, the cavalry will be here tomorrow morning.' Dixon sat down on a swivel chair. 'What about the other missing persons?'

'Not a lot to add, really,' replied Louise. 'I've only spoken to the families though.'

'And the local history society?'

'The lapsed members are all either dead or in a care home, as far as I can see,' replied Mark. 'It's taken ages to track them down and I haven't spoken to any of them yet.'

'Did you get anywhere with the dig?' asked Louise.

'It's a waste of time.' Dixon's expression hardened. 'It was organised in the August and just about everybody knew about it by early October. All the staff at the uni knew and Watkins told all his students at the start of that term. Sandra was getting the permissions too, so just about everybody and their bloody dog would've known about it.'

'Where do we start then?' asked Dave.

Dixon glanced up at the whiteboard, still blank except for the photos of the dead and missing pinned along the top. 'We need to tread carefully until we know what's happening with Parker on Friday. If he gets bail with conditions that keep him out of the area, and the reporting restrictions are still in place, then the Scytheman may not find out we're looking for him and, if we can, we don't want to do anything that might alert him.'

'How the hell do we avoid that?' Dave's head popped up from behind his computer.

'It means we can't go wading in with search dogs,' said Mark. 'And he may already know anyway.'

'He may, but then again he may not.' Dixon sighed. 'It's more about what we can't do at the moment, which is go in with all guns blazing. As far as the general public is concerned, Rory's just another victim of Parker, and it needs to stay that way for the time being.'

◆ ◆ ◆

Dixon arrived back in Brent Knoll just after 10 p.m. He had called in to see Doreen on the way, breaking the news to her that Parker's convictions would be quashed on Friday, and as expected, she had been delighted. It had been a struggle, but he had managed to get out without telling her why, which was a bonus.

The barking had started right on cue when his diesel engine rattled to a standstill, and he walked in the back door of the cottage to find Jane sitting in between Lucy and Billy on the sofa, all of them with their arms folded tightly across their chests.

'You've spoken to your father?' asked Dixon, standing in front of the television and looking down at Billy.

The grunt sounded positive.

'What did he tell you?'

'There's going to be a retrial and he may get bail on Friday, he may not.'

'That is what we call in the real world, *good news*,' said Dixon.

'I tried explaining it to him.' Jane nudged the boy and smiled at him.

'I'm going to microwave a curry, then we'll drop you home, Billy,' said Dixon, walking into the kitchen.

'It's all right, I'll stay,' said Billy.

'It wasn't an offer.' Dixon was stabbing the film lid of a frozen curry. 'It was a statement of what is going to happen. Tell me you understand the difference.'

'He does,' said Lucy. She appeared in the doorway of the kitchen, leaning on the frame.

'What's his problem?' asked Dixon.

'His social worker says he's still a ward of court and can't see his father unsupervised even if he gets out.'

'That'll only be temporary.'

'He knows that.'

'As soon as his father is acquitted he can apply for residency and the wardship will come to an end. He just needs to stay patient.'

'I'll tell him.'

'Make sure you do, Lucy. His father's been through enough without him mucking it up now.'

◆ ◆ ◆

They had dropped Billy back to his foster parents' house in Bridgwater on the way back out to Westonzoyland, Dixon spending most of the journey wondering whether he had been quite so monosyllabic as a teenager.

The only word he had got out of the boy that had more than one syllable in it was 'whatever'.

Still, patience was not a virtue that teenagers had in abundance and the lad had been through a lot. Jane was prepared to give him the benefit of the doubt, and so would Dixon. Although that benefit did not extend to allowing him to sit next to her sister on the sofa, Jane having caught them kissing when she got home after work.

'How old were you when you had your first kiss?'

'That's not the point,' Jane had huffed at him.

Dixon always knew just what to say.

He parked in front of the information board at Bussex Farm and let Monty out of the back of the Land Rover. Then they set off along Sogg Drove towards the memorial, lights visible in the distance across the fields.

Bats were flitting in and out of the farm buildings, silhouetted against the moonlight, the full moon reflecting off Monty's coat as he sniffed along the track in front of them. Voices and laughter carried on the breeze from the direction of the memorial, more from the field at the end of the drove where the trenches had been dug in the search for the friendly fire incident.

Dixon recognised the smell of a barbecue too.

'You can understand his disappointment,' he said, breaking the silence. 'He'd pinned his hopes on his dad walking out of court on Friday and then he finds out that even if he does, he can't see him.'

'I know.'

'He's not a bad kid.'

'Are you going to catch the Scytheman?' asked Jane, taking his hand as they walked side by side along the track.

'Charlesworth will have my guts for garters if I don't.'

Dixon clipped on Monty's lead when they arrived at the field gate. It was either that or risk him eating the food straight off the barbecue.

'I've only got sausages left, I'm afraid, Inspector,' said Timperley, gently swaying from side to side, a glass in one hand and a hotdog in the other.

Dixon squinted into the beam from the head torch on Timperley's panama hat. 'I've eaten, thank you, Sir,' he said.

'How about you?'

'This is Detective Sergeant Winter,' said Dixon.

'No, thank you,' she said.

The barbecue was sizzling in the bottom of one of the trenches, a group of students in T-shirts gathered around it for warmth.

'It gets pretty cold out here at night, Inspector,' said Watkins. 'It explains the fog.' He gestured to the hedgerow on the far side of the field, where the first wisp was forming along the rhyne.

'Is it fog or mist?' asked Dixon.

'Is there a difference?'

'Not when you're in it.' Ashton chuckled at his own joke from the comfort of his deckchair.

'When you're ready, everybody?' The shout came from behind them, where Sandra Smith was standing with the local vicar, his robes lit up by the moon and the beams from several torches. 'Shall we make our way along to the memorial? It's twenty to one.'

'Somebody put that barbecue out,' said Timperley.

'I'll do it,' replied Zak. Dixon recognised the voice in the darkness. 'I'll catch you up.'

Dixon and Jane hung back, watching the group shuffle along the drove towards the memorial, the giant oak trees visible even in the darkness. Lanterns had been placed on the fence posts; some hanging in the trees.

'Spooky, isn't it?' said Jane.

'Only because you know what happened here.'

'And the ghost stories. I know someone who swore blind they saw—'

'Not you as well?'

'I was kidding.'

The vicar, professors and members of the local history society filed through the gate into the memorial enclosure, while the students lined up along the fence. Dixon, Jane and Monty were watching from the drove, and were soon joined by several members of the public and a photographer from the local newspaper.

They waited in silence, the vicar periodically checking his watch.

Then, in the distance, a loud bang.

'Beat your drums, the enemy is come,' said the vicar, loud and slow. 'Beat your drums, the enemy is come. And so started the last battle fought on English soil. Tonight we gather to remember all those who fell, whether fighting for their king or rebelling against their king. We remember all those who fell during the battle on this very place, or after the battle, of wounds suffered here. We remember those who were executed or transported to the West Indies as indentured slaves. We remember the dead; however, wherever and whenever they met their death.'

Dixon looked out into Grave Field, behind the memorial, where the fog rising from the rhynes seemed to glow in the moonlight as it reached out to envelope the few cattle grazing in the middle, oblivious to the ceremony going on behind them.

Battlefields have an aura about them, reserved for those who take the time and trouble to understand what happened there. To everyone else it's just a field, or a wood. Dixon had felt it on the Somme. And now he felt it again.

He joined in the Lord's Prayer, saying 'trespass' when everyone else said 'sin'.

'I thought you weren't religious,' whispered Jane.

'We have an understanding, me and God.'

Then it was back to watching the murk rising in Grave Field, and the field behind them where the Royal Army had lined up on the far side of the Bussex Rhyne, the smoke from their muskets hanging in the fog, thickening it and leaving them firing blind into the darkness.

'Abide With Me' was a bit of a struggle without an organ to keep the congregation going, but the vicar did his best.

'And now Dr Ashton will read the roll.'

Ashton stepped forward. 'Taken from the *London Gazette*, 1st April 1686, a list of those executed at Lyme, Bridport, Weymouth, Melcombe Regis, Sherbourn, Pool, Wareham, Exeter, Taunton, and several other places.' A lantern would have been more fitting, but not as bright as the torch on his phone, perhaps. 'Executed at Lyme: Abraham Holms, Josia Askew, William Hewling . . .'

Dixon listened intently as Ashton read the names slowly and loudly – a pause between each for the man to answer; men who had stood on this very spot probably, fighting for the Duke of Monmouth; men who had been lucky enough to escape the carnage of the Chedzoy cornfield, only to be arrested later, tried by Judge Jeffreys at the Bloody Assizes and hanged on gibbets constructed by the local people at their own expense.

It was a long list.

The names echoed across the battlefield, much as their own shouts had done all those years ago.

'It really is spooky, isn't it,' Jane said.

'Don't be ridiculous.' The cold sweat in the small of Dixon's back told him otherwise, although he would keep that to himself.

'And lastly,' said Ashton, his solemnity forced. 'Executed at Bridgwater on 22nd October 1696, Thomas Cornelius.'

Then it was back to watching the fog while the vicar said prayers, before a chorus of 'The Lord's My Shepherd', punctuated by the flash of a camera, the photographer from the local paper clearly unable to contain himself any longer.

'Did you hear that?' Dixon spun round. Some of the students did too, so he couldn't have been imagining it.

'It came from over there, I think,' said Jane, pointing back towards the friendly fire trenches in the field at the top of Sogg Drove, a lantern still lighting up the gazebo. 'It sounds like there's someone in a rhyne.'

Too much splashing about for running water, and it was impossible to tell where it was coming from in the darkness. Then it stopped.

'Sound carries miles on a night like this,' said Dixon, tipping his head.

'There it is again,' said Jane.

'Call it in.' Dixon handed Monty's lead to Jane. 'I want backup out here now. And keep everyone here. No one leaves. It's for their own safety.' Then he turned and sprinted back along the drove towards the junction, keeping track of the sound off to his right now.

Distinct splashes. He grimaced. Someone wading along a rhyne. It had to be.

Sirens screaming out of Bridgwater echoed all around. He stopped at the junction where Langmoor Drove joined Sogg Drove and craned his neck, listening for the splashes over the noise of the sirens.

The smell of the barbecue again.

More splashing. Dixon ran on towards the gazebo, the fog swirling all around him as he sprinted through the gate into the field. Blue lights out on the main road flashed by towards Westonzoyland, one turning along Sogg Drove, the diesel engine of a four wheel drive instantly recognisable.

Dixon ran along the edge of the rhyne on the far side of the field, the splashes directly ahead of him now. Placing his feet carefully, trying not to trip over the piles of mud left behind when the ditch had been dredged, he ran as silently as he could, the fog getting thicker the further out on to the moor he went.

He stopped and listened.

Ten yards at most; he could just about hear the splashing over the sound of his heart pumping in his ears.

Ready, alert, he crept forward. Close enough for the torch now, surely. He held up his phone and flicked on the light.

Oh, fuck it.

Chapter Twenty-Five

The police Land Rover had turned into the field, its blue light flickering through the fog. Then he heard footsteps lumbering up behind him in the darkness.

'One for the fire brigade, I think, Sir?' said PC Cole, grinning from ear to ear.

Dixon looked down at the cow in the rhyne. 'Stand everyone down,' he said, with a heavy sigh.

Number 271, according to the tag in her ear; the old girl was plastered from head to toe in clay and duckweed, the water in the rhyne churned to a thick, smelly soup. She looked up at him, blinking furiously in the light from his phone.

'I'll get the farmer out too,' said Cole, stifling a chuckle.

'It's either Fowlers Plot or Bussex,' replied Dixon, glaring at him.

'Control, this is QPR three-twelve; stand down. It's a cow in a rhyne. Over.'

'Please tell us it's not Ermintrude, QPR three-twelve. Over.'

'She's not wearing a hat, Control, so it can't be Ermintrude. Over.'

'Daisy, then. Over.'

'Just get the bloody farmer out here,' snapped Dixon, brushing past Cole and stalking off in the direction of the gazebo. He leaned back on the bonnet of the Land Rover and tapped out a text message to Jane: *It's a cow! Everyone can go.*

He watched the lights drifting back along Langmoor Drove as the congregation walked back from the memorial, the fog clearing now, if anything.

'You're never going to hear the last of this,' said Jane, her hand on his shoulder. 'You do know that, don't you?'

'Thank you for reminding me.'

A group of students were crowding around the cool box, one rummaging in the bottom for the last of the beers.

'I've got a hip flask, Reverend,' said Timperley to the vicar, now standing alongside the trench. 'If you'd care to join me for a nip?'

'I'd be glad to, thank you. I'll never sleep after all this excitement.'

'At least they finished the memorial service,' whispered Jane in Dixon's ear.

'That's something, I suppose.'

Sandra Smith walked back from the direction of the cow, still splashing about in the rhyne. 'It's a Bussex cow. I'll give Bert a ring.'

'Thank you,' said Cole.

She was standing on the edge of the trench, looking down at the barbecue still glowing in the bottom. Then she started checking the students one by one. She spun round, still holding her phone to her ear, and stared at Dixon, the moisture in her eyes glistening in the torchlight.

'What is it?' he asked.

'Where's Zak?'

Chapter Twenty-Six

The dive team turned into Bussex Farm at dawn, just as the helicopter was leaving. It was one advantage of Dixon's new rank and he had ordered a sweep of the area with their thermal imaging camera as soon as it had been confirmed that Zak was not where he should or could have been.

The pub was shut and he was not back at the campsite. Sandra Smith discreetly confirmed that he was not at her house either.

'Sorting out the barbecue then going off to smoke a joint,' was the best anyone could get out of the students. Zak hadn't said where, apparently.

Uniformed police officers were combing the fields in the immediate vicinity of the memorial and the dig; sniffer dogs too. Not that they could smell anything over the stench coming from the cow that had been unceremoniously dragged from the rhyne with a tractor.

Dixon's suggestion that she be taken back to the farm and hosed off had been met with laughter from the farmer. 'It's her own bloody silly fault. The old bugger can damn well wait till it rains.'

Jane had gone, taking Monty with her, leaving Dixon on the battlefield, directing the search. A fingertip search of the rhynes was next on the list.

'I'm going to have to ring his parents,' said Timperley. He had sent the students back to the campsite with Malcolm Watkins in the early hours and then stayed behind to help, although he had spent most of the night asleep in a deckchair having polished off the last of his hip flask. 'I've never lost a student before,' he muttered, his head in his hands. 'I'll have to ring the vice-chancellor's office.'

'His mobile phone's dead, Sir,' said Cole. 'It's not hitting any masts anywhere.'

'And we've got *Digging for Britain* filming next week.'

Dixon glanced down at Colin Timperley, still slumped in his deckchair. 'Why don't you go back to the campsite, Sir,' he said. 'I'll let you know if there's any news.'

'I'd rather stay.'

'Maybe the cow was a diversion, Sir,' said Cole, his back to Timperley. 'Pushed in to cover the noise of—'

'The thought had crossed my mind, thank you.'

'Who's in charge?' A farmhand, probably, sitting astride a quad bike. Filthy jeans, steel toecap boots and a sleeveless T-shirt.

'I am,' replied Dixon, hoping it was mud caked in the man's stubble.

'The gate to the slurry pit's open,' he said.

'Is it usually locked?'

'Aye, the chain's been cut off, like.'

'Have you touched it?'

'Nope, left it where 'twas.'

The Scientific Services team arrived, bagged up the chain and began dusting the gate for fingerprints, just as the divers were getting ready to search the slurry pit. It had taken some persuading

186

to get them to do it, Dixon ignoring their protestations that the fire brigade usually searched slurry with their breathing apparatus.

The farmhand was watching on from a safe distance, still sitting astride his quad bike.

'How deep is it?' asked the dive team sergeant.

'Five feet or so. It was a mild winter and the cattle weren't in for long.'

'And the muck comes straight out from the cowshed and into here?'

'You can see the pipe over yonder.'

'When did you put the cows out?'

'Just afore Easter. I would've spread it by now,' he said, gesturing to a muck spreader lying idle on the far side of the yard, 'but we decided to leave it until after this lot had done their digging. Wouldn't have been very nice for 'em otherwise, would it?'

It looked like a huge above-ground concrete swimming pool, circular and surrounded by a steel fence, the gate standing open. Just inside, a set of steel steps led up to a walkway that ran around the lip of the pit. Five feet deep, maybe, but still not full to the brim; the muck was perhaps a couple of feet below the lip.

'Breathing apparatus on before you go up,' said the dive team sergeant, looking across as the first diver began climbing the steps.

'It's not too bad until you mix it with water, ready for spreading,' said the farmhand. 'Then the gas'll kill you just like that.'

Full face masks, mercifully, thought Dixon, but even so . . . the dive team would earn their money today. He watched them from a safe distance, the smell unmistakable. It had taken some getting used to when he moved down from the city – muck spreading in the fields behind his rented cottage.

Two divers went in, walking in opposite directions around the slurry pit, prodding the muck in front of them with a stick. Both were on safety ropes held by a colleague on the walkway above them. It reminded Dixon of the Alps in winter, wading through deep snow.

'If he's in here, he'll be near the edge,' said the dive team sergeant. 'He'll have to have been thrown in from the walkway.'

Then the diver on the far side of the pit stopped wading and reached down, feeling with his hand, craning his neck to keep his face mask clear of the muck.

His sigh was visible even from fifty yards away; the exaggerated heave of the shoulders and the sudden misting up of the inside of his mask. The signal Dixon had dreaded soon followed, cow muck dripping off the end of the diver's upturned thumb.

The body had been recovered on to the walkway above the slurry pit by the time Roger Poland arrived at Bussex Farm, short blonde hair and a green T-shirt visible from Dixon's vantage point fifty or so yards away, despite the muck.

'I heard about your promotion,' said Poland, smiling. 'And Ermintrude.'

'She was led into the rhyne as a diversion,' growled Dixon.

'You're probably right.' Poland dropped his case on the concrete plinth behind the cowshed. 'What've we got then?'

'It's the boy who found Rory Estcourt.'

'With the pacemaker; we've met.' He stepped forward when the mortuary van pulled into the yard. 'Looks like I'm about to meet him again.'

Dixon watched as Zak's body was lowered off the walkway into a large plastic crate. Then Poland leaned over with a bottle of water and washed away the muck on his breastbone.

'There's the top of the scar from his heart op, whatever it was. No doubt I'll find out,' he said. 'It's the same lad I met the other day.'

'Wallet?'

'Give me a second.' Poland pulled on a set of latex gloves and reached into the back pocket of Zak's jeans. 'There's a photo ID on his student union card.' He held the card up adjacent to Zak's head. 'Yes, it's definitely him.'

'What about a cause of death?'

'Give me a chance. I'll need to clean him up.'

'Just the chest. Left side, lower down. Have a look, will you?'

Poland emptied the bottle of water across the left side of Zak's T-shirt, revealing the Reading University logo. 'No cut marks,' he said. Then he gently lifted the T-shirt. 'There's his pacemaker. No incision.'

'Anything else?'

'Petechial haemorrhaging and some bruising on the neck.'

'Strangulation?'

'Possibly.'

'Quick as you can and text me as soon as you know, will you?' asked Dixon, his voice increasing in volume as he walked off across the yard.

It was just before eight when Dixon rang the entryphone at Sandra Smith's cottage in Westonzoyland, this time standing directly in front of the camera. He pushed open the door when the lock buzzed, to find Sandra waiting for him on the front step.

'Have you found him?'

'I'm sorry,' he said, nodding slowly.

'You'd better come in.'

He followed her into the kitchen, noticing an open bottle of wine and a glass half full on the side.

'That was last night, in case you were wondering,' she said. 'Coffee?'

'No, thank you.'

'Where was he?'

'In the slurry pit.'

'Don't tell me he drowned in it?' Sandra was filling the kettle, talking with her back to Dixon. 'He had an exotic taste in tobacco, as you know, but falling into a slurry pit—'

'He didn't fall.'

'Oh.' She turned around and leaned back against the sink. 'What happened to him then?'

'I'm not at liberty to say, I'm afraid.'

'He was murdered?'

'Yes.'

'But we've got *Digging for Britain* coming next week.' Sandra's brow furrowed, her face flushed. 'What will happen about that?'

'Well, it's entirely a matter for you whether you think it appropriate to continue with the dig. Certain parts of the site will be sealed off for several days—'

'I know what you're thinking,' she said, turning her face away from Dixon.

'I'm sure you do.'

'Look, it was just sex, if you must know.' Two pieces of toast popped up from the toaster on the side, Sandra using her hand to waft away a small plume of smoke rising from crumbs in the bottom. 'Only a couple of times at that, and he wasn't even very good at it.'

'Did he say anything unusual to you, anything odd?'

'No. Nothing. He was just a lad trying his luck and it suited me. I'm old enough – *was old enough* – to be his grandmother, for heaven's sake.'

'Was your relationship a secret?'

'It was hardly a relationship, but I had asked him not to tell anyone, yes.'

'And did he?'

Sandra scowled. 'Am I a suspect?' She laughed. 'He wasn't blackmailing me, if that's what you're thinking. And you're my alibi, aren't you? We were at the memorial together.'

'I'm not suggesting for a moment that you killed him—'

'I'm pleased to hear it.' Sandra waved a butter knife in his direction for emphasis. 'It sounds harsh, but I'm more concerned at the moment with where this leaves the dig.'

Dixon arrived at Express Park just after nine to find the workstations in the Incident Room on the second floor all now occupied. Sixteen new faces – some he recognised from the hunt for the missing children, most he did not.

'Dave and Mark have gone out to the battlefield, Sir,' said Louise. 'Here you've got two teams of eight, each led by a DS.' She snatched a piece of paper off the desk in front of her. 'Linda Classon and Paul Reardon.'

'Linda,' said Dixon, turning around to face the newcomers. 'You've heard what happened overnight?'

'Yes, Sir.'

'We need statements from everyone at the memorial service. Start at the campsite with the students and university staff. If they call off the dig, they'll all head home, so it's best we get it done now. Leave Dr Ashton; I'll speak to him.'

'Yes, Sir.'

'Paul, where are you?' Dixon turned to look at the tall young sergeant who jumped to his feet. 'We need to re-interview everyone at the party the night before Mark Tanner's disappearance. All right?'

'Yes, Sir.'

It took a moment, but Dixon got there in the end: Rodney from *Only Fools and Horses*.

'What about Zak's parents?'

'I got the duty inspector in Bristol to pay them a visit. Then Professor Timperley rang them. They're on their way down now to make a formal identification. They're pretty cut up about it, he said.'

'Their son is dead, Lou.'

'Yeah.'

'I'll be in the Safeguarding Unit if anyone wants me.'

Dixon took the back stairs to avoid Lewis, who he had seen striding along the landing with purpose, and sat down at the workstation opposite Jane. He put his phone face down on the desk, leaned back in the chair and closed his eyes.

'Have you had any sleep?' asked Jane.

'Nope.'

'And he was in the slurry pit?'

'I thought I'd find you here,' said Lewis, leaning around the door. 'Deborah Potter wants a chat. She wants to know where this new murder leaves us with Parker's bail application tomorrow morning.'

'I'll speak to her,' replied Dixon, snatching his phone off the desk and reading the text from Roger. It must have arrived when his phone was in his pocket. Either that or he had nodded off for a few minutes.

Zak was strangled. Dead before he went into the slurry. Report to follow. RP

Chapter Twenty-Seven

Dixon turned into the car park at the Walnut Tree in North Petherton just before lunch. A shower at Express Park had woken him up a bit, but he'd had to put the same clothes back on again, the stench of fetid rhyne water and slurry still following him everywhere. Louise was sitting in the passenger seat of his Land Rover, under strict orders to give him a nudge if he fell asleep.

The conference call with Potter and Lambert had gone as well as could be expected. There was no evidence to suggest that Zak's murder was connected to the Scytheman investigation, meaning it did not offer grounds to oppose Parker's bail application, according to Lambert. The best they could hope for was conditions. Lambert was equally pessimistic when it came to reporting restrictions. 'The bar is high,' he had said. 'Justice must be seen to be done.' Was it in the public interest to restrict reporting? That was the test and Lambert thought not, but he'd ask the court anyway.

Dixon pulled on the handbrake and checked the time. Sandra Smith would be at Express Park at three o'clock, with her solicitor. Initial enquiries into Zak's murder had failed to turn up a motive;

either there wasn't one and he had just been in the wrong place at the wrong time, or his relationship – and it was one, whether she liked it or not – with Sandra Smith had a part to play. She had protested – Dixon would have been surprised if she hadn't – but he had insisted.

After that it would be five o'clock at Musgrove Park to meet Zak's parents, then home to bed.

'What about the other missing persons?' asked Dixon as they walked across the car park.

'I thought we could see James Eastman's mother in the morning, seeing as you're not up to London for the appeal hearing,' replied Louise. 'And that just leaves Adam Hawley. His parents have moved away, but I've left a couple of messages asking them to ring me.'

Dixon stopped. 'That name sounds familiar,' he said, frowning.

'You've read the file, surely?'

'That's not it.'

Dr Ashton was waiting for them in the lounge, hiding behind a broadsheet newspaper. 'There's nothing in here about it,' he said, folding up the paper and dropping it on to the coffee table.

'Is there somewhere more private we could talk?' asked Dixon. 'Your room, perhaps?'

'I've ordered coffee,' Ashton protested. 'I slept through breakfast. It was a bit of a late night, you know.'

'I'm sure they'll bring it—'

'Here it is now,' said Louise, the sound of a rattling tray behind her.

They squeezed past the room service trolley in the corridor and followed Ashton, stopping at a door with a 'Do Not Disturb' sign hanging on the handle.

'Did you know Zak, Sir?' asked Dixon, sitting down on the sofa.

Ashton leaned back in the armchair and stirred his coffee, one eye on Louise who was sitting at the table in the window, opening her notebook. 'I'm afraid not. He was just one of the students, really. I think he was part of the group looking for the mass grave anyway, and I was leading the friendly fire dig. I've got to know some of the year one students, but not the year twos.'

'When was the last time you saw him?'

'At the barbecue. He was the one who volunteered to stay behind and put it out when we all walked over to the memorial. You were there. You saw the same as I did.'

'And you've never met him before?'

'No.' Ashton scowled. 'What are you suggesting?'

'Nothing, Sir.' Time for a disarming smile, thought Dixon. 'We have questions we have to ask, boxes we have to tick.'

'Of course you do. Sorry.'

'How well d'you know Sandra Smith?'

'I don't know her at all, really. She came to a lecture I gave once; that was a few years ago now when my first book came out, and we've kept in touch via email since then; purely about the battle, you understand.'

'What were those emails about, specifically?'

Ashton took off his glasses and rubbed his eyes. 'The diary,' he said.

Dixon waited.

'One of the local history society members unearthed it in the Somerset archive. She was particularly interested in hand drawn maps of the Chedzoy cornfield from 1696, which appeared to show the cultivated area extending beyond Moor Drove. It showed new rhynes not seen on previous maps, which would have drained the land and enabled them to cultivate it. Her point was that the mass grave must have been further south, out on the moor proper.'

'Did you agree?'

'Oh, yes.' Ashton sat up. 'Assuming the maps were genuine, of course; and there was no reason to believe they weren't.'

'Who was the author of the diary?'

'Andrew Paschall.' Ashton was watching Dixon for a flicker of recognition. 'She was trying to organise a dig, but it came to nothing. It was 2005 and the Scytheman was on the loose.'

'Have you seen the diary?'

'Not personally, and it's been lost, sadly.'

'And who found it in the first place?'

'She never said.'

'Presumably the original is still in the Somerset archive, though?' asked Dixon.

'They've got no record of it. I checked. I saw facsimiles of the maps and they looked plausible enough, but I've not seen the originals.'

Dixon stood up and walked over to the window, disappointed at the grandstand view of the car park. There weren't even any photographs to stare at. 'This dig, when did you get involved in it?'

'Last year. Sandra emailed me out of the blue and asked if I'd like to tag along. That would've been late September, I suppose. I posted on my blog about it, so you could get the date from that.'

'That was my next question, Sir,' said Dixon, grimacing. 'Whether you told anyone about it, but it seems you told everyone.'

'I did, sorry. Why, shouldn't I have done?'

Dixon waved away the question with the room service menu. 'Does the name Adam Hawley mean anything to you?'

Ashton slammed down his coffee cup, the disappointment at finding it empty proving too much for him. 'Yes, and it should to you. You heard me read the roll at the memorial service. Executed at Wareham,' continued Ashton. 'He was named in the *London Gazette*.'

'Do you have a copy of the list?'

'It's available online.'

'It was dated 1686 and yet included Thomas Cornelius, who was executed in 1696.'

'Ah, you *were* listening.' Ashton smiled. 'That was my private tribute to the man named in Paschall's letter to Durling, the one I found in the Cambridge archive.'

'Cornelius was the slave?'

'He was; tried at Taunton, he was reprieved and shipped to the West Indies in 1685. Then he makes his way back to England and is hanged for murder in 1696.'

'You said in your talk at the pub the other night that you hadn't identified his victim.'

'Ah, that was a little white lie, I'm afraid. I was saving it for my book. His name was William Appleby and he was a cobbler from Taunton. He was known to be loyal to the king, and by 1696 was living at Rumwell Manor. How did he afford that? I ask myself; hence my belief he was the trooper who sounded the alarm in return for a handsome reward. Apart from that, the details I've found thus far are fairly sketchy, sadly, and I was hoping Paschall's diary might shed more light on it. That's if it still exists.' Ashton licked his lips. 'It would be worth a bob or two as well.'

'Do other Paschall diaries exist?'

'He died in 1696 so that would've been his last, but they exist from 1647 onwards. Some of the early ones are missing, but it would be reasonable to assume—'

'Do you know when in 1696 he died?'

'No, sadly not. We know that he wrote to Durling in the September. There's a lot of speculation in historical research, Inspector, I know that.'

'Much like police work, Sir.'

Chapter Twenty-Eight

'They've got his diaries from 1662 when he became the vicar of Chedzoy, right through to 1695, but as far as they're aware, there isn't a 1696 diary,' said Louise, plugging her phone into the charging cable hanging in the passenger footwell of Dixon's Land Rover.

'Do they keep records of people rummaging about in the archive?'

'D'you want me to ring them back now?'

'Don't bother,' replied Dixon. 'We'll see what Sandra Smith has got to say about it first.'

He thought he hadn't kept them waiting long, not that you'd know it from their reaction when he walked into interview room 1, Sandra Smith and her solicitor sighing in unison.

'You are not under arrest, Mrs Smith, and are free to leave at any time,' said Dixon.

'I've advised my client of that, thank you.' Her solicitor's collar was far too tight; he had clearly put on weight since he had bought the shirt. It explained the red face; either that or it was the slight whiff of alcohol and cigars.

'And you are?'

'Pollard from Whittears in Yeovil.' Another new one on Dixon. Still, he'd remember the smell.

Louise took over for the questions concerning Sandra's relationship with Zak – Dixon only intervening once, when tempers flared.

'We are not here to judge, Mrs Smith. All we are interested in is whether there might be someone with a motive to kill Zak.'

Zak had made it clear he was 'up for it', and it suited her. It was just a bit of fun and, no, there was no one in her life and hadn't been since her divorce five years ago; no jealous boyfriends or stalkers. No ex-husbands now either, her first husband having left her a widow and her second having died during the divorce. She had been divorcing him, and it had been perfectly amicable.

He had changed his will leaving everything to his children, which was fine by her, and she hadn't seen them since the funeral anyway. As for her own son, he didn't know about the 'relationship' – she used the word with exaggerated reluctance – and she thought it highly unlikely he would have travelled all the way from Adelaide.

As far as she was aware, nobody knew about her and Zak.

Her hesitation when Dixon took over the questioning and asked about the diary took him by surprise. As did her blunt response.

'I lied.'

'Lied about what?'

'There is no diary.'

'And the maps?'

'I drew them.'

Dixon waited for the explanation. Sandra was working up to it, her eyes fixed on the table in front of her where she was picking at a mark with her thumbnail.

'It's a field of battle. Men died fighting for what they believed in.' She paused for a sharp intake of breath, blown out through her nose as she continued. 'We'd spent sixty thousand pounds on a battlefield visitor centre no one was visiting. And all because of the bloody Scytheman. The last battle fought on English soil, and all the area was known for was his bloody murders. I thought it might generate a bit of interest in the battle again. And it has. Don't forget, we've got *Digging for Britain* coming next week.'

'You forged the maps to get people interested in the battlefield?'

'Yes.' Sandra folded her arms. 'And it worked. Look, I was the local councillor at the time and I organised the funding for the visitor centre. I told everyone it would bring tourism to the area, but it never did. People came, but for all the wrong reasons.'

Dixon shuffled his papers, playing for time.

'I know what you're thinking, Inspector,' said Pollard, smiling. 'I can't think of a criminal offence my client has committed either.'

'Fracture of the hyoid bone,' said Poland, his right hand clamped around his throat tight up under his chin. 'Takes some force and it's a sure sign of strangulation. Plus there's petechial haemorrhaging on the face, and the bruising, of course.'

Dixon looked down at Zak lying on the slab in the mortuary at Musgrove Park, all cleaned up and ready to meet his parents for the final time. A green sheet had been draped over his body and pulled up under his chin to hide the bruising.

'Can I see his neck?' Dixon asked, turning to Poland just as the intercom crackled into life.

'Mr and Mrs Holman are in reception.'

'I've photographed the bruises, don't worry,' said Poland. 'It'll all be in my report.'

Dixon ripped off his latex gloves and dropped them in the bin on the way out to reception, spotting two figures hunched over in the corner, holding hands. The man was wearing a suit and tie; maybe he had come straight from work, thought Dixon, or was unsure of the dress code – not that there was one. He stood up when he saw Dixon approaching.

'Are you the policeman?' he asked, still holding his wife's hand.

'Inspector Dixon,' he replied.

Mrs Holman looked up, her eyes bloodshot and glazed over. 'He was dead before he went into the slurry pit, wasn't he?' she asked. 'I can't bear the idea of him drowning in that.'

'He was,' Dixon answered solemnly, careful to look her straight in the eye when he told her what she wanted to hear. It was not a question to dodge.

'Thank you,' she said, appearing to accept he had told the truth.

'The pathologist, Dr Poland, is here to answer any other questions you have. Please just ask.'

'What are you doing about it?' asked Mr Holman, helping his wife to her feet.

'It's a murder investigation, Mr Holman. We have a major investigation team working on it and Scientific Services are still at the scene looking for anything that might—'

'Is it connected to the Scytheman?'

'It's early days.'

'Zak was the one who found that other body, wasn't he? Rory somebody.'

'We've got no evidence of a connection. Yet.' Dixon was leading them to the double doors, beyond which a long corridor led to the mortuary. 'But if you're asking me whether I believe it's connected, then yes I do.'

'Who is in charge?'

'I am.'

'You're very young,' said Mrs Holman, giving him a haunted look as she shuffled through the door Dixon was holding open.

The youngest DCI in Avon and Somerset Police history, or so Jane had said, but Dixon thought that was probably too much information.

'Mr and Mrs Holman?' Poland was striding along the corridor to Dixon's rescue. 'I'm Roger Poland,' he said, gesturing to an open door. 'Let's take a moment in here.'

Comfortable chairs, a coffee machine; magazines, not that many people would be in the mood for reading them.

'Mrs Holman was anxious to know that Zak died before he went into the slurry,' said Dixon.

'He was, Mrs Holman,' said Poland, taking her hand. 'I found nothing in his lungs or windpipe. I can assure you—'

'What was the cause of death?' asked Mr Holman.

'Asphyxiation, caused by strangulation,' replied Poland. 'There are no other injuries on his body at all.'

Mr Holman glanced up at the ceiling, fighting back the tears.

'We've undertaken a full post mortem and there are certain matters that have come to light that you need to be prepared for.'

'Like what?'

'Toxicology tests found—'

Holman dismissed Poland with a wave of his handkerchief. 'We know,' he said, smiling. 'I even caught him growing his own in my shed, would you believe it? He'd got the lights and everything set up in there.'

'In John's shed.' Mrs Holman managed a faint chuckle through the tears.

'Purely for his own use,' said Mr Holman, with a concerned look at Dixon. 'He'd say it was medicinal, and it never seemed to do him any harm, so we turned a blind eye.'

'When did you last hear from him?'

'I got a text message a week or so ago, I think. He was grumbling about missing the surfing. He liked to cultivate this image of a rebel, but actually he was a straight A student and would probably have come away with first class honours in Archaeology.'

'He rang the night he found Rory Estcourt,' said Mrs Holman. 'He wanted us to record the news.'

'And did you?' asked Poland.

'Yes, but he wasn't on it.'

'Can we see him now?' asked Mr Holman.

The formal identification took seconds. 'That's my son,' was all it needed. Then they stood in silence for several minutes, staring down at him.

'Have you put his pacemaker back in?' asked Mrs Holman as they trudged towards the door. 'We'd like him to go off in one piece.'

'I have,' replied Poland.

A slightly out of breath Karen Marsden was waiting for them in the corridor. 'Mr and Mrs Holman, this is Sergeant Marsden, our family liaison officer,' said Dixon. 'I'll leave you with her for now, if that's all right.'

'Fine, thank you.'

'Find whoever did it.' Mrs Holman was staring at Dixon, tears streaming down her cheeks.

'He will, Mrs Holman,' said Poland. 'He will.'

Dixon called in at Express Park on his way home, leaving his Land Rover in the visitors' car park to save time. And to avoid swiping his access card. Hopefully, he could get in and out without being spotted. The Incident Room was all but deserted; Louise was still there, and a couple of workstations were occupied by faces he didn't recognise.

'Where's everyone else?'

'Still out taking statements,' replied Louise. 'Scientific have finished at the slurry pit. They've got some boot and tyre prints, but that's about it.'

'Any news about the dig?'

'They've suspended it for the weekend. The students are all going home tomorrow and *Digging for Britain* have pulled out anyway.'

'Get on to Ashton and ask him to email us a copy of that Paschall letter, will you?'

'How is that relevant?'

'I don't know; I haven't read it yet.'

'Really?'

'What time are we seeing James Eastman's mother?' asked Dixon, choosing to ignore Louise's quizzical look.

'I haven't fixed anything up yet. Are you sure you want to go? I can go with Dave or Mark.'

'Yes, I'll come. Make it the morning. I'd be climbing the walls if I was her.'

'I'll ring her now.'

'Full team briefing at eight, so anytime from nine onwards. Where is she?'

'Yeovil.'

'Ten then.'

Lewis intercepted Dixon in the car park. 'And so this whole bloody mess claims another victim,' he said, holding open the door of the Land Rover.

'It's not your fault.'

'We spend our lives making bad decisions and living with the consequences. Only, this time, other people are living with the consequences of mine.'

'What decision?' Dixon slid out of his car. 'You weren't the SIO.'

'I made the arrest.'

'And so would anyone in the same situation. He was covered in blood and the murder weapon was—' Time to give voice to his nagging doubt. 'Unless there's something you're not telling me.'

A flicker of hesitation. 'There isn't.'

'If you say so.'

'I do.' Indignant. 'So, how's it going?'

'The key to it is in the past,' replied Dixon, allowing Lewis to change the subject. 'It's just a question of how far we have to go back: 2005 or 1685.'

'The battle?'

'Possibly.'

'There's Charlesworth,' said Lewis, turning his head to follow a car that had turned into Express Park. 'You go and I'll deal with him.'

◆ ◆ ◆

Jane had left a note on the kitchen worktop: *Taking Lucy to station. Wait for me at Berrow Church! Jx*

'I must be getting predictable, old son,' he muttered, lifting Monty into the back of the Land Rover.

Twenty minutes later he was asleep in the porch, leaning back against the noticeboard, when Jane tapped him on the knee, waking him with a start.

'Where's Monty?'

'I let him off the lead,' replied Jane. 'He's just out there. Standing guard, he was, while you were snoring your head off.'

The dog was already halfway along the path at the back of the graveyard, so they followed him, Dixon putting him on the lead before they crossed the thirteenth fairway, although he let him off again when he saw the golf course was deserted.

'How's Lucy getting on with Billy?' asked Dixon, as they weaved through the bullrushes behind the dunes.

'He's on the edge of his chair about the bail application tomorrow, I think. He's at home, and she got on the train.'

Dixon watched Jane sit down on *their* tree stump and smiled to himself, thinking about their last visit when he'd asked her to marry him. 'We haven't talked about a date yet,' he said, kicking Monty's tennis ball along the sand.

'I rather thought you'd got other things on your mind at the moment.'

'Good point.'

'How's it going?'

'It isn't really. I've got a mummified body buried nine months ago; Parker's convictions will be quashed and he's likely to get bail in the morning. And now a student's been strangled.'

'At least you haven't upset Charlesworth as much as I thought.'

'Not yet.' Dixon's phone pinged in his pocket. 'It's an email from Lou,' he said, opening the attachment to find an image of a handwritten letter dated 28th September 1696, the address at the top given simply as The Rectory, Chedzoy. '*My dear Durling*,' said Dixon, reading aloud.

'What is it?' asked Jane.

'A letter written by Andrew Paschall that Ashton believes names the trooper who alerted the Royal camp on the night of the battle. It's more out of interest, really, I think.' Dixon was scrolling down through the letter, glossing over the pleasantries. 'Here we go. Do you want me to read it?'

'Go on then.' Jane stood up and looked down at the screen in Dixon's hand. 'It's that flowery olde worlde handwriting.'

'*About sunset on the twentieth I was called upon to visit Thomas Cornelius a rebel from my parish who I had known before he did march with the Duke of Monmouth. Taken prisoner after the battel he had been tried by My Lord Jeffreys and sentenced to be executed, later fortunate though to be reprieved and transported to the Indies.*'

'I'm sure this is all very interesting . . .' Jane's voice tailed off.

'It is,' said Dixon. '*Having worked his passage by way of the Kingdom of Spain, Cornelius, with consent, returned to Chedzoy as I do recall seeing him. Then he visited upon William Appleby of Rumwell and did bloody murder upon him by a sickle.*'

Dixon froze.

'What's the difference between a sickle and a scythe?' asked Jane, frowning.

'God knows. *Due to be hanged the following morn,*' he continued, reading aloud, '*I did worship with him and he took Holy Communions. He did not repent for the murder of Appleby, a man whose conduct deserved no less of him. He did repent though for not allowing the rightful burial of Appleby's body as he might and ought to have done. In its stead keeping him in his house until he had all but dried out.*'

Chapter Twenty-Nine

Jane had put her foot down when they got back to the cottage. 'You haven't slept for thirty-six hours and I bet you haven't eaten properly either.'

Dixon's mumbled response about a sandwich at lunchtime hadn't placated her.

'You need some food and some sleep or you'll be no use to anyone.'

And that was that. Twenty minutes later he was fast asleep with his dog curled up on the end of the bed.

His alarm went off at six, although he was already awake, reading Paschall's letter again on his phone. By eight he had been at Express Park for over an hour and half and was up to date with all the statements the team had taken the day before.

'Have you read that letter yet?' he asked, when Louise appeared at the top of the stairs.

'Not yet.'

'Where's Dave?'

'In the canteen.'

Dixon intercepted him and took him to one side. 'Have you finished the statements at Bussex Farm?'

'Yes.'

'I want to know if there are any living descendants of William Appleby of Rumwell.'

'When did he die?'

'1696, or possibly 1695, I suppose.'

'You're kidding?'

'Use a genealogist if you have to; Charlesworth said no expense was to be spared. And focus on Dr Ashton. I want to know everything about him, all right? Bank records, phone records, social media, family, everything.'

'Haven't you spoken to him?'

'I have.'

'What are you looking for?'

'I don't know.'

'How far d'you want me to go back?'

'2005.'

'I meant how many weeks? We'll never get—'

Bail granted on condition that he resides at the Vicarage, Church Lane, Westonzoyland. You can thank the vicar for that!

Deborah Potter's text had arrived just as Louise rang the doorbell at the small terraced house in Yeovil.

'That's bloody marvellous, that is,' growled Dixon. 'Right in the eye of the storm.' Her follow-up text did nothing to improve his mood.

Reporting restrictions lifted. Not in the public interest. Good luck!

The word 'decluttering' had passed Diane Eastman by. It was a small hall, made smaller by the hoarding, although Dixon had seen worse on the TV. He followed Louise past the piles of magazines at the bottom of the stairs and into the front room, which seemed oddly clear by comparison. Beatrix Potter figurines and soft toys appeared to be her preferred living room clutter, but then she had lost her husband and her son, so who was Dixon to judge?

He looked along the mantelpiece and in the glass display cabinet next to the television while Louise took out her notepad, Mrs Eastman busying herself stubbing out the cigarette that was alight in the ashtray.

The photographs on display were mind-boggling: a large montage above the fireplace taking pride of place.

'They're all photos of my Jamie,' said Mrs Eastman, smiling. 'I had them in a box but couldn't bear to keep them hidden away any longer.'

'How old was he when he went missing?' asked Dixon.

'Eighteen.'

'Tell me what happened.'

Her eyes glistened at the memory. 'It was just an ordinary day, really. He went off on the bus in the morning and then never came home in the evening. It was February, so it was dark by five or so. I can't remember what time I rang the police, but it wasn't late.'

'Five-thirty,' said Louise.

'That sounds about right. I know I didn't wait long.'

Birthday cards were lined up along the mantelpiece, propped up in between more photographs. 'They're his,' said Mrs Eastman. 'I send him one every year.'

'Where were you living at the time?' asked Dixon.

'It's all in my statement.'

'I've read it, Mrs Eastman,' he replied. 'We're just going back over everything, as you might imagine.'

'We had a bungalow in Nethermoor Road, Middlezoy. He was at Bridgwater College and it was on the number sixteen bus route. It dropped him out by the pub, so it was ideal.'

'Did he know any of the other missing boys?'

'Not that I know of.'

'May I?' asked Dixon, his hand on the latch of the display cabinet.

'Of course.'

The line of books on the top shelf had caught his eye, and in particular the copy of *Sedgemoor 1685* by Graham Ashton.

'My husband bought that,' said Mrs Eastman. 'There was all that talk about the Scytheman and the battle and he wanted to know what it was all about. That was after Parker was arrested.'

'Have you seen the news yet today, Mrs Eastman?' asked Louise.

'No, why?'

'Daniel Parker's convictions have been quashed and he's been released on bail pending a retrial.'

Dixon wasn't sure what he had expected when Louise broke the news, but laughter wouldn't have been top of his list.

'Clive always said he didn't have anything to do with it.'

'What made him think that?' asked Dixon, spinning round, Ashton's book still in his hand.

'I don't know, really. It was just a feeling he had.'

Louise took over the questioning while Dixon put Ashton's book back on the shelf. Several orders of service toppled over and it took him a moment to stand them back up, the photos on the cover of each facing forward, as before. One for Jamie, a memorial service rather than a funeral given that his body had never been found; Clive Eastman, beloved husband of Diane; and Mrs Winifred Eastman – must have been his mother, thought Dixon.

'How did your husband die?' he asked, when Louise was wrapping up the interview.

'Heart attack. It was only six months ago. He was at work; dead before he hit the ground. He wasn't far off retirement, not that he was looking forward to it. More time to stew, he used to say. At least he was spared that. Would you like a cup of tea?'

'I'm afraid we don't have time, Mrs Eastman. Will you be all right?'

'Oh, don't worry about me,' she said. 'I'll be off to work this afternoon. I do three afternoons a week at the library. I'll be fine.'

The door closed behind them and Dixon stood on the pavement, watching Louise walk off in the direction of his Land Rover.

It was the display cabinet. There was something about the display cabinet; a bewildering array of knick-knacks, figurines and clutter – all of it valueless, except perhaps to Mrs Eastman – its only purpose to give her comfort. And collect dust.

He spun round and knocked on the door, listening to Louise's footsteps running back along the pavement.

'What is it?' she asked, her eyes wide.

'May I have another look at your display cabinet, please, Mrs Eastman?' asked Dixon, when the door opened.

'Yes, of course.'

He opened the door and reached in for the orders of service, picking up Winifred Eastman's.

'That'll be your mother-in-law, I'm guessing, Mrs Eastman,' said Louise.

'That's right, Clive's mum. She was eighty-one when she died.'

Dixon passed the booklet to Louise. 'May I keep it, Mrs Eastman?' he asked.

'Provided I get it back. It's my only copy.' She frowned. 'Is it important?'

Louise frowned too, asking the same question, albeit unspoken.

'Look at the date, Lou,' he said.

Chapter Thirty

'Where's Dave?'

'Busy, Mark,' replied Dixon, watching Louise through the open door of meeting room 2. He could see the top of her head behind a computer screen across the atrium; checking dates.

'Everything all right?' asked Lewis, poking his head around the door; curiosity had clearly got the better of him.

'Sit down,' said Dixon, gesturing to a vacant chair. 'It saves me going through it all again.' He glanced around the table, watching the puzzled glances between Mark Pearce and Lewis. Linda Classon's eyes were closed; Paul Reardon frowning at his phone – checking the weather forecast, judging by the reflection in the window.

'There's a press conference at two,' said Lewis, his voice almost apologetic.

Footsteps running along the landing, then the door of the meeting room slammed shut. Louise sat down next to Dixon and slid a piece of paper along the table.

We spend our lives making bad decisions and living with the consequences, Lewis had said. Ridley had made one, focusing the original investigation on Parker. That he had made that decision wasn't the problem, just that it was wrong. And now Dixon faced a decision; soon to be recorded in his Policy Log for all to see.

Fuck it.

'The Scytheman was selecting his victims at funerals.' He paused, letting the statement hang in the air, watching the lines on Lewis's forehead deepening by the second.

'He's a funeral director?' asked Pearce.

'Possibly. There are a lot of people involved in a funeral.'

'The Tanners were in Venice,' said Lewis. 'The boy's grandfather had died and the father had taken the mother to help her get over it.'

Dixon nodded. 'Rory Estcourt had been to the funeral of his grandmother, as had James Eastman. Both of them within four weeks of their disappearance.'

'What about the Bonds?' asked Lewis.

'Christine's brother died young,' replied Louise. 'Taunton Crematorium, that one.'

'And Christine and Nicola both went to the funeral?'

'According to their old neighbour.'

'What about the other missing person, Adam Hawley?'

'His parents have moved away,' replied Louise, 'but I finally got hold of them on the phone.' She shrugged. 'It was an aunt. I didn't ask the cause of death. The funeral was at Weston Crem.'

'All of them.' Lewis was staring out of the window, shaking his head. 'We never found a connection between them. We looked, but never found it.'

'Going to a funeral is hardly a connection,' said Pearce. 'They didn't even go to the same funeral.'

'What happens now?' asked Lewis, turning to Dixon.

'Where have you got to with the witness statements, Linda?' asked Dixon.

'All done. The students have gone home for the weekend and I think they're planning to call off the dig now anyway. *Digging for Britain* are going to some Viking burial on Salisbury Plain instead.'

'Did anyone see—?'

'Nobody saw or heard anything, no,' she interrupted.

'Paul, your team was going back over the attendees at Mark Tanner's party.'

'All done, Sir. Nothing to report, I'm afraid.'

Dixon sighed. 'Things are going to be complicated by Parker popping up in Westonzoyland this afternoon, closely followed by any photographer and journalist who hasn't got anything better to do. We'll need a visible presence out there day and night.'

'Leave it with me,' said Lewis.

'Linda, your team can take the mourners. We need to speak to anyone and everyone who went to these funerals. Some we've spoken to already, but we'll need to speak to them again. Get a list off each family and I'll double-check against the list of donations when I speak to the funeral directors. All right?'

'Yes, Sir.'

'Leave the immediate family, Louise'll do them. You wanted to meet Doreen. Find out who officiated while you're about it.'

Louise had her head down, making notes.

'Paul,' continued Dixon, pausing to allow him to put his phone down. 'The wake, funeral tea, lunch, whatever you call it, speak to all the staff at these places; anyone on duty on the day – I want to know who they are and what they've got to say for themselves.'

'Yes, Sir.'

'Mark, crematorium staff. It'll be Weston-super-Mare and Taunton, remember. The new one at Pawlett didn't open until 2013.'

'What's happening about Zak?' asked Lewis.

'We're waiting for forensics,' replied Pearce. 'We've got prints and DNA from the herdsmen at the farm for exclusion purposes.' He curled his lip. 'We checked them against the database – nothing. So, we're waiting for Scientific, really. House to house along Monmouth Road and Liney Road turned up nothing and there's no CCTV anywhere to check.'

'What d'you think?' Lewis looked at Dixon.

'Are you asking me what I think, or what I know?'

'What you think?'

'Zak was killed by the Scytheman. He didn't use a scythe because that would've blown any pretence about Parker. Remember, it was still under wraps then that his appeal was likely to succeed.'

'Motive?'

'No idea. You asked me what I think.'

Lewis smiled. 'I did.'

'Right, let's get on with it.' Dixon stood up. 'It'll be all over the news by now that Parker's been released, but justice must be seen to be done, according to the Lord Chief Justice. And who are we to argue?'

'Big decision,' said Lewis, when the room cleared, leaving him alone with Dixon.

'Goes with the territory.'

'It does.' Lewis shook his head. 'It's just that you seem to make it look easy.'

'It's just a line of enquiry.'

'Who's William Appleby?'

Dixon frowned.

'I had to approve a genealogist for Dave,' said Lewis.

'If you believe Dr Ashton, Appleby was the trooper who raised the alarm on the night of the battle. He was murdered by Thomas Cornelius.' Dixon hesitated. 'Stabbed with a sickle and found mummified in Cornelius's house.'

'A sickle?'

'It was the weapon of choice back then for those who couldn't afford a musket.'

'A sickle is a hand scythe, isn't it?'

'Sort of. Just keep it under your hat, will you?' Dixon closed the meeting room door behind them and set off in the direction of the canteen.

Dixon hated press conferences. He'd become quite skilled at avoiding them in recent months, but his new rank had put a stop to that.

'Look at it as a way of communicating with the general public,' Charlesworth had said. 'Use the media as a tool.' Another phrase he'd picked up from the press officer, no doubt.

Charlesworth opened with a prepared statement, written by Vicky Thomas, agreed by the force's solicitors, and read out with exaggerated solemnity. 'The Court of Appeal has expressed concern at some aspects of the evidence upon which Daniel Parker's convictions were based, and Avon and Somerset Police are more than happy to look at it again in conjunction with the Crown Prosecution Service.'

Then came the reminder that it would be wrong to examine the evidence in public when the matter remained subject to a retrial on a date to be fixed.

'Is it true that two of the witnesses have been charged with perverting the course of justice for lying at the original trial?'

Charlesworth ignored the question shouted by a journalist at the front and carried on reading his prepared statement.

'A major investigation team, led by Detective Chief Inspector Dixon, sitting to my right, will be looking again at all the evidence, old and new, in the so-called Scytheman investigation.'

'What about the murder of Zak Holman?'

Charlesworth stifled a sigh. 'Ladies and gentlemen, I would be grateful if you could let me finish my statement. Then we will take questions.' He made them wait while he took a swig of water before continuing. 'All the evidence, including the forensic evidence, will be looked at again and the file submitted to the CPS in advance of the retrial. Now, questions.'

'Chief Inspector Dixon, what can you tell us about the murder of Zak Holman?'

'Mr Holman was found dead in the slurry pit at Bussex Farm and we're asking local residents to think about anything unusual that they may have seen on the afternoon or evening of the fifth of July. Anything at all, however insignificant – please call us on 101 or ring Crimestoppers.'

'Is he another victim of the Scytheman?'

'All I can say is that we have various lines of enquiry and our investigations are ongoing.'

'Is there a connection to the Battle of Sedgemoor?'

'I'm not ruling anything out at this stage.' It was the dodging of questions he hated; journalists asked them and his only task was to answer them without giving anything away. *You have very little to gain from these things and a lot to lose*, Charlesworth had said. *Your only job is to get in and out without making yourself look an idiot.* That gem had come from Lewis.

Dixon frowned. He felt sure that training for DCIs included a module on handling the media, but that didn't extend to acting DCIs, obviously.

'Do you believe that Daniel Parker is the Scytheman?'

Dixon hesitated. The stock response would be that *it's not for me to judge, I just gather the evidence*, blah, blah. He could feel Charlesworth's eyes burning into the side of his head as he leaned forward to the microphone slowly.

'No,' he said. 'I do not.'

'Does that mean the Scytheman is still out there?'

'It means that the killer of Christine and Nicola Bond and also Rory Estcourt may, and I emphasise *may*, not have been apprehended. I would urge all members of the public to remain vigilant at all times and to report anything unusual, however insignificant it may appear.'

'Is it right that Rory Estcourt had been stabbed with a scythe?'

'He was stabbed with a curved blade and a hand scythe has a curved blade. His body was found buried in the bottom of a rhyne on the battlefield and I am asking members of the public to cast their minds back to last September or October and to come forward if they saw anything out of the ordinary on the battlefield at that time; most likely at night.'

'What is the significance of last September or October?'

'That is when Rory's body was buried.'

The calm before the storm; it lasted a split second before the camera flashes exploded as one. Dixon was watching Charlesworth to his left, shifting furiously in his seat, no doubt blurring all the photographs; his assurances of a high profile police presence on the Levels almost drowned out by the camera shutters.

Chapter Thirty-One

'Communicating with the general public, I said.' Charlesworth slammed his papers down on the table in the small anteroom behind the media suite at Express Park. 'Not scaring them bloody witless.'

'They needed to know,' replied Dixon. 'There's already been Zak's murder – that happened while there were reporting restrictions in place – but now it's public knowledge Parker is out, what would happen if the Scytheman started killing again and we hadn't told anyone?'

'He's right,' said Vicky Thomas, clearly terrified at the prospect of disagreeing with the Assistant Chief Constable.

'At least you didn't mention the mummification.' Charlesworth leaned back on the windowsill, his hand across his forehead. 'And thankfully I had the chance to calm things down a bit after you dropped your bombshell.'

'But did the public really need to know Rory's body was buried nine months ago?' Vicky Thomas was staring at her phone, scrolling with her thumb.

'That was for the Scytheman's benefit,' said Dixon. 'He needs to know we know. And it means we can start a proper search too.'

He watched reporters filming pieces to camera outside Express Park as he rode up to the second floor in the lift, their vans parked on the access road opposite the station. Some were recording segments for the local evening news; the BBC and Sky broadcasting live for their rolling national news channels.

A phrase involving a cat and a bag sprang to mind, although he preferred the one about a cat and some pigeons.

'There's someone to see you,' said Louise, when he stepped out of the lift.

'Who?' he asked, flicking on the kettle. He glanced around the Incident Room, all the desks occupied, the phones buzzing.

'Xander somebody. Bit of a hippy, if you ask me.'

'He's here?'

'Sitting down in reception.'

'What have you lined up for this afternoon?'

'Lockwood Funeral Services. We're at their Burnham office first, then Latham's in Bridgwater after that. Mark's lining up interviews with the priests. The Bridgwater vicar who did Mrs Eastman's mother-in-law is still there. And the Estcourt funeral was in Moorlinch but done by the Westonzoyland vicar for some reason.'

'Him?'

'He did Nicola Bond's uncle too.' Pearce's head popped up from behind his computer. 'Mrs Tanner's father had a Humanist, whatever that is.'

'Non religious,' offered Dixon, his finger on the lift button.

The glass lift gave him advanced warning; it must have been over two months, but Xander Dolphin was still wearing the same shirt and leather waistcoat. There may even have been a new tattoo, or perhaps it was just the angle?

A clairvoyant. Dixon shook his head, hoping the journalists and photographers outside hadn't spotted him. Them and the drug squad.

He opened the security door at the side of the reception desk. 'Xander,' he barked. 'This way.'

'Nice to see you too.'

'You stink like a cannabis factory,' said Dixon. 'So, we'll talk out the back if you don't mind.'

'What's wrong with the front?' Xander hesitated by the security door.

'It's crawling with journalists.'

'Will I get out?' he asked, staring at the lock.

'Yes.' Dixon let the door slam behind him. 'The sniffer dogs are out today.'

Xander smirked as he loped along the corridor, looking into the open plan offices on either side, both of them full of uniformed police officers. 'I don't recognise any of this lot. I've got to know the Glastonbury lot pretty well.'

'I bet you have.'

Through two sets of double doors, then a locked security door using Dixon's swipe card, and out into the sunshine at the back of the station. Xander stared at the large caged enclosure adjacent to the custody suite, a prison van parked inside with its rear doors standing open.

'Maybe one day, eh, Xander?'

'You're my "get out of jail" card,' he replied.

'Am I bollocks.'

'Oh, c'mon, I helped you find those kids, didn't I?'

Best to be polite. Whatever it was, Xander had thought it worth a bus ride over from Glastonbury to tell him. 'You were brought in by the family, if you remember.'

Dixon remembered all right; Roger's ex-wife, to be precise. 'All tie-dye and joss sticks' had been his warning.

'What I said was right,' protested Xander.

'Half right,' replied Dixon, forcing a smile to soften the blow. 'And we only found out after the event.'

'What d'you mean "after the event"?'

'After we'd found them anyway. Look, what was it you wanted to tell me?' asked Dixon.

'Oh, yeah, well Parker's out; I saw it on the news this morning. Is he the Scytheman?'

'I don't think so.'

Xander's breathing quickened. Either it was the sight of a dog van parked in the shade on the far side of the car park, or it was the memory of what he'd seen.

'The dogs are in the kennels, Xander. Now what was it you saw?'

'A dead body,' he mumbled, leaning back against the wall, his eyes closed. 'Sitting at a kitchen table. It's like a skeleton, but covered in brown shrivelled skin; like paper. His mouth is open and the eyes are all sunken. There's a fireplace behind him, flickering. And a candle on the table, the wax running down the side, like, y'know.'

Dixon waited.

'His hand's on the table, like a claw,' continued Xander, his hand out in front of him, the fingers curled over.

'When did you see this?'

'A week or so ago. I didn't know what to make of it to be honest.'

'And why are you telling me?' asked Dixon, trying not to appear interested.

'There's a scythe sticking out of his chest.'

Chapter Thirty-Two

Half an hour later Dixon parked outside Lockwood Funeral Services in Burnham-on-Sea. It was an odd shopfront, sideways on to the road with parking bays in front; but then an attractive shop window was hardly essential for an undertaker, perhaps; most seemed to stick to a promotional poster or two, some flowers, and a couple of urns. Lockwood's was no different.

They had spent the drive from Bridgwater in silence. Twice Louise tried to ask what the hippy had wanted, and both times Dixon had been deep in thought. Then she had given up, much to his relief.

He switched off the engine and waited until the rattle had stopped.

'He's not a hippy, he's a clairvoyant.'

'You've used him before?'

'I wouldn't say "used", no. He gave me some information once that turned out to be half right-ish, after the event.'

'And what's he said this time?'

Dixon undid his seatbelt and turned to Louise. 'Breathe a word of this to anyone, and I'll have your guts for—'

'I know.'

'He's seen a mummified body sitting at a kitchen table with a scythe sticking out of his chest. Some trip that must have been.' Dixon raised his eyebrows as far as he could. 'And we've kept the mummification under wraps, haven't we?'

'William Appleby or Rory Estcourt?' she asked.

'God knows.'

'What does it mean?'

'I've no idea, but I expect we'll find out.'

The undertakers seemed deserted. There was no bell on the door, but there was a camera on the wall, behind the reception desk.

White shirt, black tie, and the thick grey and black herringbone suit trousers; it was as much a uniform as khaki. 'Can I help?' he asked. Grey hair, dark horn-rimmed spectacles; the well-practised look of sympathy soon evaporated at the sight of a police warrant card. 'Ah, come through, won't you?'

'Mr Baker?' asked Dixon, following the man into a small room; artificial flowers and a box of tissues on the leather topped desk.

'Yes. I've already spoken to one of your lot and given them the details of the celebrant.' He opened the drawer and took out a thin file. 'The Tanner family went for a Humanist because the deceased wasn't particularly religious, although they did say the Lord's Prayer at the end. Just in case, I suppose. These are my notes from when I first met them,' he said, dropping the file on the desk. 'The bill and a copy of the order of service. The funeral tea was at the daughter's house in Sutton Mallet. That's all we keep these days. It's the storage space.'

'Did you know the family?' asked Dixon, sitting down.

'Not before they came in, no.'

'So, why you?'

'Personal recommendation, I expect. That's the way we get most of our business.'

'Do you remember anything unusual about the funeral?'

'Nothing, I'm afraid. I was there, according to my notes, but I've done so many over the years, only a couple stand out, and those more often than not for the wrong reasons.'

'Like what?'

'We had an old gentleman die and it was a long standing joke that any car he got in broke down. Needless to say, the hearse broke down. Mercifully, the family saw the funny side. Then there was the beekeeper; halfway through the service a swarm of bees invaded the church, flew once round the vestry and then out again. There have been a couple of fights too, usually outside the crematorium; although I did have one at the graveside a long time ago. But there was nothing remarkable about Mr Tanner's funeral, at least not from our point of view.'

'Who was working here at the time?'

'I can give you a list of names. There would've been me; a part time receptionist probably, and Brian used to drive the hearse. We might have had an apprentice doing his City & Guilds back then too. I'll need to look up his details. And old Mr Lockwood, of course.'

'Old Mr Lockwood?'

'He's retired now. This was his business for years, then he bought Latham's in Bridgwater and when he retired I took them both on. We still trade as Latham's in Bridgwater, but it's the same business.'

'Where would I find Mr Lockwood?'

'He lives in Chedzoy these days.'

It was oddly satisfying, watching the pained expression on her face melt away; first the eyes, then the phoney smile. Even his warrant card seemed to come as a relief.

'Sorry,' she said. 'I hate covering reception and I thought you were here to—'

'We're the other end of death today,' Dixon said, determined not to put her at ease, although he found himself wondering what 'the other end of death' was.

'I'm just the secretary. Mr Skinner's had to go out on an urgent.'

'We did have an appointment,' said Louise.

'It was a care home, and if you don't go they get someone else.' She was biting her lip, looking from Dixon to Louise and back again. 'He shouldn't be long. The doctor's given the certificate so it's just a collection.'

Latham's in Bridgwater was sandwiched between a newsagent and a chemist in a small parade of shops on the outskirts of town; on the Westonzoyland road, as it happened.

'What's your name?'

'Tracey Vincent.'

'How long have you worked here, Tracey?' Dixon was admiring the bewildering array of urns on display, his own mortality suddenly in sharp focus. He'd never really thought about it before; not in the sense of what would happen afterwards. 'Excuse me,' he said, sliding his phone out of his pocket and tapping out a text message to Jane.

Scatter my ashes on the beach with my dog's. Nx

He watched the speech bubble, waiting for Jane's reply, at the same time ignoring the puzzled looks passing between Tracey and Louise.

Will tomorrow do? :-) Jx

He turned back to Tracey. 'You were going to tell me how long you've been here.'

'Only six months. My kids have gone to school so I'm doing a bit of part time work. They said I'd get used to it, but it's not really happening to be honest.'

'Get used to what?' asked Louise.

'Death.' Tracey sat down behind the reception desk. 'Being around it all the time gets you down.'

Dixon glanced at Louise, watching her nodding in agreement.

'Can I ring you when he gets back?'

'We'll wait,' he said, picking up the coffins brochure. He began flicking through it, trying not to wince visibly at the prices. 'Who else works here?' he asked, filling the time.

'They're a funny lot, but don't tell them I said so. Mr Skinner's all right, but the rest are a bit weird, if you ask me. Goes with the territory, I suppose.'

'Weird how?' asked Louise.

'I don't know; they just seem to wallow in it. They're miserable all the time. I'm dreading the staff Christmas party, although I'll probably be gone by then anyway.' She stood up. 'There goes the van. They go into the yard round the back.'

'We'll walk round,' said Dixon.

The large gates were still open; a black van with tinted windows reversed up to the back door of the funeral parlour. Two men, both in black jackets and herringbone trousers, slid a trolley out of the back of the van and dropped the wheels down, ready to slide the body out on to it.

'Mr Skinner?'

'Can we just get her inside?'

'Of course.'

Dixon and Louise squeezed past the open rear doors of the van and followed the two men as they wheeled the trolley – now with body bag on top – into the back of the funeral parlour.

Dixon had seen a few pathology labs in his time, but never the business end of a funeral parlour: a white tiled floor criss-crossed by drains; one wall covered with what looked like large stainless steel fridge doors, the others white tiled to match the floor. The ceiling was painted white too.

And a strong smell of disinfectant.

'Right then, you wanted a chat.'

Skinner's outstretched hand took Dixon by surprise. He glanced at the stainless steel sink against the far wall, a bottle of antibacterial gel in a dispenser mounted above it. 'Yes, Sir,' he replied, shaking Skinner's hand. How bad could it be? 'How long have you worked here?'

'Ten years or so. I used to be over at Honiton, but we moved over here to be nearer my wife's mother. Then the old bird went and died anyway.'

'Always in the funeral business?'

'Yes.'

'What about your colleague?'

'Vic's been here for donkey's years. Worked for Mr Latham before he retired.' He looked across at the older man, who was about to unzip the body bag. 'Leave that,' continued Skinner. 'I'm sure they don't want to watch you tidying up Mrs Burridge.'

'Tidying up?' Dixon frowned.

'There's a daughter,' replied Skinner. 'She's coming over from Canada and wants to view the body.'

'A colleague rang earlier and asked about two funerals that you conducted—'

'Not me personally; I wasn't here,' interrupted Skinner, a little too quick for comfort, thought Dixon, but then getting defensive when questioned by the police wasn't entirely unheard of. 'I've got the files out, such as they are,' continued Skinner. 'Mr Latham's notes and the bill. That's about it, I'm afraid. They're in the office, if you'd like to follow me.'

Leather topped desks and boxes of tissues. Standard stuff.

'Mrs Eastman was a cremation at Taunton, ashes scattered in the garden of remembrance, and Mr Walton was cremated and his ashes interred. There's a monumental mason's bill with that one too. I've done copies of everything.' Skinner passed the few sheets of paper to Louise, who had sat down at the desk.

'DC Willmott will take a statement from you, Mr Skinner,' said Dixon, edging towards the door. 'I'd like to have a word with Vic, if I may.'

The body bag was open now, revealing an elderly lady lying on her back; eyes closed, mouth open.

'Went in her sleep,' said Vic, looking down at her. 'They're the lucky ones. If I could pre-book that . . .' His voice tailed off.

'How many is "donkey's years"?' asked Dixon.

'Forty-two. I started straight from school.'

'And always here?'

Vic nodded. 'With Dennis Latham to begin with, then when he retired, Mr Lockwood took over. Now it's Mr Baker.'

'Seen some changes, I imagine?'

'Not that many, to be honest. Health and safety is the biggest thing. A right pain in the arse it is. Substances hazardous to health, manual handling.' He rolled his eyes. 'Sometimes, it'd be nice just to be left to get on with the job.'

'You remember the Scytheman murders?'

'You always remember the murders, and the young ones. We don't get many of either, mercifully.' He sighed heavily. 'Nicola stayed with me for weeks afterwards; sort of peaceful she was, and tragic at the same time. Her mother was a different matter, although she'd been tidied up by the pathologist before she came to us.'

'Have you always done the embalming?'

'I'd worked here a couple of years before I was trained up by Mr Latham. He needed to know I had the stomach for it, he said.'

'Were there any other employees?'

'We use part-timers just for the funerals; drivers and stuff. There have been a couple of full time staff over the years, but they never lasted. Tracey won't either. You can tell those that can and those that can't.'

'What happened to Dennis Latham?'

'He's in a care home over at High Ham. I go and see him from time to time; the poor old sod's got no one else.'

'May I?' asked Dixon, gesturing to the antibacterial gel.

'Be my guest.'

'One last question.' Dixon was watching Vic wriggle into a pair of overalls. 'Have you ever dealt with a mummified body?'

Chapter Thirty-Three

'I'll be down in Safeguarding,' Dixon said as he slammed the door of his Land Rover on the top floor of the car park, thankful that he had managed to get there without being intercepted by Charlesworth, who was on the prowl, according to Mark Pearce.

The Safeguarding Unit consisted of four workstations in their own office; for confidentiality reasons, or so Jane said. Dixon closed the door behind him, craning his neck to check the other desks as he did so.

'There's no one here,' said Jane, smiling.

'I need your help,' he said, sitting down on the vacant swivel chair next to her. 'I need a Social Services file sharpish and if I go through the usual channels it'll take days. You know what they're like.'

'Have you got a name?'

'No.'

Jane reached for a pen and paper. 'How are we supposed to find it then?'

'I've got a date. Well, a year: 1995, but it could be a couple of years either side,' said Dixon, trying a smile to soften the blow. 'Someone may remember the case though, if there's anyone still there from back then. It'll be a thick file too, I expect.'

'What's it about?'

'Social Services intervened at a house in Bradney, where a fifteen year old boy was looking after his bedridden mother. He was taken into care and she was sectioned.'

'And? There has to be more to it than that.'

'The mother was lying in bed next to the mummified body of her dead husband; two years, apparently.'

'God, can you imagine it?' Jane winced. 'The smell and the bodily fluid—'

'I'm going to try coming at it from the other end and see what the coroner's got. There must have been an inquest into the husband's death. But what I really want to do is find the son.'

'I bet you do.'

'Louise has gone over to the coroner's office in Taunton, but even if we get a name, he may have changed it.'

'Well, I'll do what I can for you, but it's Friday afternoon, don't forget.' Jane looked at her watch. 'Five-thirty on Friday afternoon. And I'm picking Lucy up from the station at eight-thirty.'

'What is it, Lou?' asked Dixon, holding his phone to his ear.

'They say there's nothing they can do without a name. That far back it's just a card index.'

'They'll have to go through them one by one then. There can't be that many, surely?'

'What do they look for?'

'Anyone with an unspecified date of death. There's no way a pathologist could say with any degree of accuracy, and I doubt the wife or son gave statements at the time.'

'Leave it with me.'

233

'The coroner's officer is going in tomorrow to go through the records,' Louise had said, dropping her handbag on a vacant work-station in the Incident Room.

Dixon had spent the last hour catching up with the witness statements being uploaded to the system. He'd also updated the Policy Log, the text arriving from Deborah Potter within ten minutes:

Seems logical. Good work.

'One last call to make,' Dixon said before they drove out towards Westonzoyland, Louise following in her own car so she could go straight home afterwards.

Close to the church, but modern; Dixon guessed the old rectory had been sold off some years ago, and the 'Vicarage' sign looked oddly out of place on the new red brick porch. At least there were roses in a pot growing up the front.

'Reverend Philpott?'

'Good evening, Inspector.' The vicar's voice was loud enough to startle Dixon, as well as alert whoever was skulking in the kitchen. Dixon could guess.

'Round the back, Lou.'

He arrived in the kitchen just as Louise was leading Billy in through the back door. Daniel Parker was leaning against the sink, holding a mug of tea.

'Seems I've missed the tearful reunion,' Dixon said, smiling.

Parker stepped forward, his hand outstretched. 'I know I wouldn't be here without you, Inspector,' he said. 'Thank you.'

'Don't thank me,' replied Dixon. 'I'm just doing my job. And what did I tell *you*?' His voice grew louder as he turned to Billy.

'Can we say I'm supervising the contact, if anyone asks?' The vicar spoke quietly, unsure whether he should intervene.

'I'm afraid that wouldn't work without a court order to that effect, Reverend.'

'Jonathan, please.'

'Social Services may allow supervised access at a contact centre, but the best thing you can do, Daniel, is get a solicitor who deals with family matters lined up to apply to the court when you're exonerated. All right?'

'When?' asked Parker, his eyes welling up. 'You said "when".'

'I did.' Dixon turned to the vicar. 'Is there somewhere we can have a chat?'

'The sitting room?'

'You two have got until I've finished with Reverend Jonathan, then I'm giving you a lift home, Billy.'

'You're a good man, Inspector,' said Jonathan, closing the door behind Louise.

'I'm not even a good police officer,' replied Dixon. 'I don't tick the right boxes.'

'I'm sure that's not true.'

'It's not,' mumbled Louise.

'How long have you been the vicar here?' asked Dixon.

'Since 2001.'

'So, you were here right through the Scytheman killings?'

'I was.'

'You conducted the funeral of Simon Walton in 2004. Do you—?'

'I conduct lots of funerals,' he said, shaking his head.

'Simon Walton was Christine Bond's brother; Nicola's uncle. He was cremated and his ashes interred in the churchyard.'

'I do remember it, but only because it was the last time I saw Christine and Nicola. Not for any other reason, sadly. There was a service at St Mary's, then we went to the crematorium, I think.'

'What about the funeral of Doreen Estcourt's mother? The service was at Moorlinch.'

'I remember that one too, but only because I've got to know Doreen so well. I'd have been standing in for the funeral. The pall-bearers had a bit of trouble on the steps down to the hearse, from memory.' Jonathan leaned back in his chair. 'Maybe Rod was away or ill or something.'

'Rod?'

'Rodney Marks. He was the vicar over there. I'm not sure who it is now.'

'Do you keep any records of eulogies you've given, in note-books or diaries, anything like that?'

'I sit down with the family and make notes about the deceased and their life, of course I do, but I always destroy them after the service. A lot of it is highly personal, family stuff, so I got into the habit of shredding it.'

'And there's nothing you can remember about either funeral service?'

'Not really, I'm afraid. I'm sure I'd remember if anything unusual happened, so it probably means nothing did.'

'Keep him out of trouble and out of the way of journalists,' had been Dixon's parting shot when he left the vicarage.

'I may struggle with that,' Reverend Jonathan had replied, his eyes fixed on the doormat as he showed Dixon and Louise out. 'Doreen has invited him to Rory's funeral on Monday, then after-wards at the Sedgemoor Inn. I did say it might not be such a good idea, but you know what she's like, I imagine?'

'We do,' Louise said, filling the uncomfortable silence that followed.

Dixon had still been counting to ten when he had dropped Billy at his foster parents' house on the way home.

He flicked on *The Winslow Boy* again while he fed Monty and waited for Jane and Lucy to arrive home from the station, hopefully bringing with them fish and chips for three. Jane had said they would.

He wondered, as he listened to Monty pushing his stainless steel bowl around the tiled floor in the kitchen, what effect watching his father's body decompose next to his bedridden mother would have had on a thirteen year old boy, keeping them hidden for two years until Social Services finally intervened when he was fifteen. Some formative years those must have been.

It was a powerful reminder of how reassuringly normal Dixon's own home life was and had been, excluding Fran, of course. He thought about her less and less these days, her ghost laid to rest. Keeping busy helped too. And catching her killer.

Random thoughts, popping into his head as he followed his dog around the field behind the cottage. It was still far too hot for a walk on the beach. Much hotter and he'd have to buy a paddling pool for Monty to lie down in.

Maybe a fascination with mummified bodies was not surprising; a collection of them, even? Perhaps it gave him enough for a profiler? Charlesworth would certainly sanction the cost.

Psychological profiling – it had always sent shivers down his spine. It was an option, and might buy him some time perhaps. And, come to think of it, a profiler had never been asked to look at the Scytheman before; Ridley had always resisted it, although it may have been forced on him had Lewis not made the arrest.

Yes, a profiler; first thing in the morning.

The smell of fish and chips wafted around the corner of the cottage. Then Jane and Lucy appeared.

'I know,' said Lucy, holding up her hand as Dixon drew breath. 'Billy sent me a text message. I'll sort it out this weekend. Jane's given me the name of a solicitor.'

'How did your exam go?' he asked.

'Well, I think.' Lucy dropped her bag inside the back door. 'Did you speak to his father?'

Dixon nodded.

'How was he?' she asked.

'Innocent.'

'I don't know how they do it,' said Dixon, with a heavy sigh, his head back on the pillow. The end of *The Winslow Boy* had been followed by a walk on the beach in the half light of a midsummer dusk, the sun below the horizon. They'd left Lucy fast asleep on the sofa.

'Don't know how who do it?' asked Jane.

'Funeral directors. Their whole lives revolve around death.'

'So does yours.'

'Not really; not all the time anyway.'

'Go to sleep.'

'Can you chase someone up about arranging contact for Danny and Billy? It'll have to be supervised at this stage, I imagine, but they really need to get on with it, if only so Billy knows it's in hand.'

'Leave it with me.'

'And I need that file.'

'I've got someone looking for it, don't worry.'

Chapter Thirty-Four

The bungalow was large and pink, the glass of a conservatory at the back visible over the flat roof of the single garage. It backed on to the cornfield, the view south across the battlefield to Westonzoyland almost certainly uninterrupted.

The smell from the farm opposite was pretty ripe, which explained why all the windows at the front of the bungalow were closed. Mixing the slurry ready for the muck spreading. Dixon winced. Country smells – some you get used to, some you don't.

'Mr Lockwood?' he said, when the front door opened.

The old man had been careful to close the inner door of the porch before opening the outer.

'Come in,' he said, not bothering to inspect their warrant cards. He waited until Dixon and Louise had both squeezed into the small porch, then he closed the outer door and opened the inner. 'He always bloody well does it when the wind is blowing in this direction. I swear it's deliberate.' He slammed the inner door behind Louise and reached for a can of room spray on the side.

'And he always spreads it when the weather's fine too. Never when it's going to rain.'

Dixon closed his eyes; pine forest was marginally better than slurry. And less likely to be fatal.

'It's part of the reason I smoke a pipe,' continued Lockwood. 'Still, it's only once a year and it's a lovely place to live, so I mustn't grumble.'

'Don't you find the battlefield spooky?' asked Louise, following him through to the conservatory.

'I've been around death all my life,' replied Lockwood. 'It holds no fears for me.' He sat down on a wicker chair and picked up his pipe from the ashtray next to him. 'You don't mind if I—?'

'Not at all,' said Dixon. He was standing in the window at the back of the conservatory, looking out across the battlefield. Fowlers Plot Farm was visible off to his right, the stack of silage bales bigger.

'Use them,' said Lockwood, gesturing to the windowsill, where a pair of binoculars was lying on a pile of magazines; *Funeral Director Monthly*. 'I did a loft conversion a while back and I've got a telescope in the window upstairs. That's a much better view.'

'It's supposed to be the most haunted place in England,' said Louise.

'I've never seen anything.' Lockwood was holding his lighter over his pipe, sucking hard and blowing the smoke out of the corner of his mouth. 'But then you've got to be looking for it. And you have to *believe*.'

The dig site adjacent to the drain was out of view, hidden behind high hedges.

'How long have you lived here?' asked Dixon, still looking through the binoculars, this time at the gazebo, the top of it just visible over the hedgerows.

'I bought it in 2006,' replied Lockwood. 'I dealt with the old lady's funeral and bought it off her executors. Got it for a song, to be honest.' He waved his pipe in the direction of the garden. 'Nobody wants a murder scene at the bottom of their garden, do they?'

Dixon replaced the binoculars on the pile of magazines. 'And it doesn't bother you?'

'When you've seen what I've seen, what's one more body?' Lockwood was pointing his pipe at Louise now. 'And I'm sure you could say the same.'

Not quite, but some points aren't worth taking. 'How long were you in the funeral business?' Dixon asked.

'Straight from national service; 1963, that was. I was one of the last. I started out as an apprentice with K. J. Flack in Torquay, then moved to Burnham in '76. I took over Horlake's when he retired, renamed it Lockwood's eventually and then bought out Dennis Latham when he'd had enough.' The old man was holding his pipe between his teeth. 'Car accidents were the worst. And the children. But it wasn't a bad way to make a living. Someone's got to do it.'

'Talk me through a funeral,' said Dixon, sitting down on the windowsill.

'We collect the body, usually from the hospital mortuary, or their home perhaps. I'd always try to go for that. Then we have to get them ready; d'you want to know what that involves?'

'That would be too much information.'

'Sometimes relatives want to view the body. Then there's the funeral itself. Book the crematorium and the vicar. It's all about what the family wants though; horse drawn hearse, you name it and we can pretty much do it. Regulations have changed over the years, which complicated things; manual handling regulations made life difficult for us, but it's all trolleys these days to avoid the lifting.'

'When did you take over Latham's?'

'2002.'

'Was there anything unusual about it?'

'Not really.' Lockwood frowned. 'Not that I can remember.' He was sucking on his pipe, the last of the tobacco long gone. 'We took on all the staff, as you do, not that there were many. Vic was off sick and it was a couple of months before he came back to work.' He hesitated. 'There was a case going through the employment tribunal at the time as well. It held things up for a while, but Dennis paid the lad off. It was an unfair dismissal case, from memory.'

'Can you remember what it was about?'

'Never knew. Dennis sorted it all out before I took over so it was no concern of mine.'

Dixon glanced around the conservatory; no television. 'D'you sit in here at night?' he asked.

'Sometimes,' replied Lockwood. 'Depends what's on the telly; it's in the living room.'

'Can you recall seeing anything unusual out on the battlefield last September or October time? It would've been at night.'

'Someone burying Rory Estcourt, you mean?' Lockwood was watching Dixon staring out of the window. 'I saw your press conference.' He paused, waiting for a reaction, but got none. 'If I'm in here at night then I've got the lights on and you can't see anything outside,' he continued. 'There's the odd light out there, from a dog walker, probably. And Fowlers Plot allows lamping on his land sometimes.'

'What's lamping?' asked Louise.

'Shooting rabbits, Lou,' replied Dixon.

Lockwood flicked open a tin of pipe tobacco. 'So, it's not Parker then?'

No reply.

'I never thought it was, to be honest,' he continued. 'You met him?'

'I have.'

'I buried his wife. He was there in handcuffs for that.'

242

'May I?' asked Dixon, opening the door to the garden.

'Close it behind you,' replied Lockwood, stuffing tobacco into his pipe.

Large enough for a tennis court; the grass had been freshly mown. Dixon stopped at the rhyne at the bottom of the garden, fifty yards at least from the bungalow. And if she had heard anything on that night in 2005, the old lady who had lived here at the time was dead, according to Lockwood.

Dixon looked along the back of the houses towards the marquee behind the barn. The tables had been taken down and were leaning against the wall, the side walls of the tent flapping in the breeze.

'Would you like to have a look through the telescope?' asked Lockwood, as he showed them to the front door. 'You'll have to crawl under my train set, I'm afraid. Bit of a Hornby nut,' he added, apologetically.

'No, thank you, Sir.'

'D'you want me to contact the employment tribunal?' asked Louise, after they had squeezed out of Lockwood's porch.

'We'll see what Dennis Latham's got to say about it first,' replied Dixon.

Ham Lodge looked more like a posh hotel than a care home, set down a long, tree lined drive off the main road. Under a grand colonnaded entrance porch, the steps up to the large oak front door were hidden beneath a wheelchair ramp, testament to the building's new purpose perhaps. Its four floors and original sash windows made the single storey new-build red brick annexe on the left look a bit out of place. The car park was full too, although most of the cars were small and parked in spaces marked 'Residents Only'.

Dixon would be ready for it if and when his time came – two years at boarding school had seen to that; one residential institution was much the same as any other.

'My granny's in one of these places,' offered Louise. 'Not like this though.'

'Mr Latham's in suite nineteen,' said the receptionist, pointing along the corridor and into the new annexe. 'It's on the ground floor along there on the left.'

'I'm in the wrong business,' said Dixon, glancing into the rooms to either side as they walked along the long corridor.

'It'll be a rabbit hutch for the likes of us,' said Louise. 'If we're lucky.'

Dixon stopped opposite an open door. 'Suite nineteen, she said.' He knocked and called out, 'Hello?'

'In here,' came the reply. 'Don't stand on ceremony.'

The en suite was bigger than Dixon's kitchen, and marble tiled with a granite sink and huge mirror. The hospital bed was new too – as was the flat screen TV. The old man was sitting in a reclining chair by patio doors opening out on to a private terrace.

'Five grand a month,' whispered Louise.

And the rest.

'Would you like tea or coffee?' asked Latham, pressing a red button on the arm of his chair. 'I like to keep them on their toes.'

'Thank you,' said Dixon.

'It's a nice place,' Louise said, sitting on the edge of the bed.

'When my money runs out I'll be in a cardboard box at the bus station, if I live that long.' Latham grinned the grin of a man accustomed to death. And resigned to his own. 'You're here about Parker?'

'Yes, Sir.'

'You don't mince your words, do you?' said Latham, smiling. 'You really let them have it at that press conference. Did you get in trouble for it?'

'Not really.'

'I thought the bloke sitting next to you was going to lay an egg!' Latham's laugh morphed into a coughing fit, although he regained his composure in time to shout, 'Tea for three!' to the carer who appeared at the door, stopping her in her tracks.

'Tell me about Vic,' Dixon said.

'Victor Hardy. He's a good friend. Worked for me for years.'

'He told me about a mummified body at Bradney. Do you remember that one?'

'There are some you don't forget.' Latham sighed. 'We did the funeral, although there was no bugger there – apart from the social worker.'

'Can you remember the social worker's name?'

'No chance, sorry. It was a man, that's all I can remember now. The widow had been sectioned and the son was in care. It was a cremation with no fuss; ashes interred at Chedzoy. I was a pall-bearer on the day.' He sniffed, then wiped his nose on the back of his hand. 'It was a light coffin.'

'What state was the body in when it came to you?'

'We got him after the pathologist had finished, but he was dried out. All the body fat had liquefied and seeped away, so he was basically just a skeleton covered in dried out skin. It goes brown, you know.'

Dixon opted for his best non-committal smile.

'We didn't bother embalming him, so it was straight in a coffin and off to meet his maker.'

'Was there any press coverage of the case?'

'Social Services managed to keep it out of the papers. We weren't even allowed to place the usual bereavement notice.'

'Who was he?' Dixon was standing in the doorway with his back to the window, glancing at the television; shame, he'd have left the tennis on for Monty if he'd remembered.

245

'A farm worker; post mortem never arrived at a cause of death. The mother couldn't bear to be without him. She was a bit eccentric, by all accounts, and the whole thing tipped her over the edge. We did her funeral too, a couple of years later. She went into Tone Vale psychiatric hospital and never came out.'

'Can you remember a name?'

'As I said, there are some you never forget.' Latham took a deep breath. 'Bagwell; Frederick and Doris Bagwell.'

'What happened to the son?'

'I always felt sorry for him. I first met him at his mother's funeral, then he popped up again a few years later looking for work. Vic was on long term sick leave at the time; I needed someone, so I gave him a job.'

'A job?'

'Yes. I had to let him go in the end, though, and d'you know the little shit even took me to the industrial tribunal.'

Dixon closed the patio doors while he waited for the carer to unload the tea from the trolley. Then he closed the door to Latham's room behind her.

Latham watched him, the wrinkles of his frown growing deeper by the second.

'This is 2002,' said Dixon. 'Just as you were selling to Lockwood?'

'That's right. I paid him off in the end, just to settle it so the sale of the business could go through.'

Dixon glanced across at Louise, busily making notes, her pad resting on her knee. 'Why did you sack him?' he asked.

Latham hesitated, taking a deep breath through his nose, his nostrils flaring as he did so. 'None of this was ever proved,' he said, wiping his nose with his index finger. 'We had complaints; well, a complaint. Tea?'

'In a minute,' said Dixon, trying to hide his impatience.

'I was away and a family wanted to view a body on the morning of the funeral. He refused and the cremation went ahead. Later, they tried to say the coffin was empty and he'd stolen the body, which was ludicrous when you think about it. Grief does strange things to people.'

'It does,' muttered Dixon.

'We had a letter from solicitors and settled with a confidentiality agreement in the end. Anyway, I had to let him go, to keep the family happy more than anything.'

'What can you remember about the deceased?'

'Oh, that was sad. The family name was Picton. The boy had a congenital heart defect no one knew about and he dropped dead on the football pitch.' Latham was sucking his teeth. 'He was only seventeen years old. Just about to take his A levels too.'

'And the Bagwells' son, was he living at Bradney?'

'No, the family home had been sold – I think they even knocked it down in the end. He had a flat on the Sydenham estate, I think.'

'What happened to him?'

'No idea, I'm afraid. I never saw him again after that.'

Dixon had one last question to ask; he waited while Latham dropped a sugar cube in his tea and stirred it.

'What was his name?'

'He'd changed it. The lad I met at the mother's funeral was called Simon, then he popped up again fifteen years later called James Scott. I pretended I didn't recognise him – who could blame him for wanting to leave all that behind? I never let on I knew who he was.'

'We drop everything and find him, Lou,' said Dixon. He was sitting in his Land Rover in the car park at Ham Lodge, looking out over the Somerset Levels, at the same time tapping out a text message to Jane:

The file should be in the name of Bagwell. Mother Doris, son Simon. Nx

'He's probably changed his name again,' replied Louise.

'Almost certainly, but it's a start.'

'And you think he's the Scytheman?'

'Let's assume he did steal the Picton boy's body; maybe he was starting his collection?' Dixon switched on the engine, turning in his seat to reach for his seatbelt. 'Then he loses his job at the funeral director's; how does he get his hands on the next one?'

'He kills.' Louise clicked her seatbelt into the buckle.

'Exactly.'

'What's the significance of James Scott, I wonder?'

'That's easy.' Dixon was allowing the Land Rover to freewheel down the hill towards Middlezoy. 'He was James Scott to his friends, but you and I know him as the Duke of Monmouth.'

Chapter Thirty-Five

'It's all getting a bit . . .' Charlesworth's voice tailed off.

'Ignore the battle, for a minute,' said Dixon, glowering around the table in meeting room 2, still bristling at the ambush. 'We've got a man called Simon Bagwell with a history of issues – arising *probably* from the mummified body of his father – who is alleged to have stolen a dead body from an undertaker's. The last name we have for him is James Scott. All right?'

'And the connection to the murder of William Appleby?' asked Potter.

'We're waiting for the genealogist,' replied Dixon, 'but the reality is it's probably all in his mind. The chances of him being a direct descendant of Thomas Cornelius are miniscule.'

'What are you doing about it?' asked Charlesworth.

'Latham gave us a description of what he looked like in 2002 and we've got a sketch artist going to see the old boy this afternoon, so we'll see what that looks like. Detective Sergeant Winter is helping us track down the old Social Services file, and everything else that can be done on a Saturday is being done.'

'What can't be?' Potter frowned.

'The employment tribunal file. The courts are closed.'

'What about the Pictons?' asked Charlesworth.

'Louise Willmott has tracked them down to an address in Minehead and we're going over there this afternoon.'

'And you've got a profiler coming in tomorrow, I gather.'

'Yes, Sir.' Dixon glanced down at his notebook. 'A Dr Spurway.' He caught a glimpse of Lewis watching from the other side of the atrium, walking slowly along the landing towards the canteen.

'DCI Lewis is to be kept out of this, Dixon. Is that clear?' Charlesworth was watching him watching Lewis. 'He's subject to an IOPC investigation as part of their enquiry into the conduct of the original case.'

'Yes, Sir.'

'We all know how he feels about it and I'm sure he'll be exonerated.'

'He was a junior officer at the time,' offered Potter.

'But for now he's out of the loop,' continued Charlesworth. 'Right, is there anything else we should know about?'

Dixon thought it best not to mention Xander Dolphin and his drug-induced visions. 'No, Sir,' he replied, sliding his chair back and standing up.

'There's a campsite up here?' asked Dixon, the diesel engine of his Land Rover making short work of the gradient as they climbed out of Minehead.

'North Hill,' shouted Louise. 'Mr and Mrs Picton manage it and live on site in their van.'

Dixon changed down to first gear and floored the accelerator. 'I'm surprised they could get up here in a motorhome.'

'It's a nice site. Camping and Caravanning Club; we brought Katie a few weeks ago for a weekend away.'

He pulled up at the entrance and leaned over the steering wheel; motorhomes hooked up to electricity, giant awnings, tents bigger than his cottage.

'The loo block is over there,' said Louise, pointing.

Dixon preferred not to look. 'It's camping but not as we know it,' he said, under his breath. A field of knee deep grass near the pub in Bosherston was the last campsite he'd stayed at, on his final climbing trip to the Pembrokeshire sea cliffs. Then there'd been the night out on the Aiguille du Midi in the French Alps, the ledge no bigger than a bath – *now that's proper camping*.

'They'll be in the office,' said Louise, dragging him back to the present.

'What did you tell them on the phone?'

'Nothing.'

'Have you booked?' asked the man standing behind the counter.

Dixon glanced around the office: a fridge in the corner offering milk, eggs and bacon; the shelves to the side covered in maps and gas canisters, matches, tin openers and corkscrews; all essential camping supplies.

'Mr Picton?' he asked. 'My colleague Detective Constable Willmott spoke to you earlier on the phone.'

'Yes, of course. Faith's in the van, if you want to talk to us both.'

'We do.'

'We'll go next door,' he said, lifting the counter.

There was a sadness to the man, although maybe Dixon only saw it because he knew. He appeared relaxed enough: knee length shorts with bulging side pockets; sandals and a red polo shirt. On the face of it, living the dream. No doubt he would say it was more of a nightmare. And Dixon was about to bring it all back.

Picton flipped round the sign in the window – 'In Van, Please Knock' – then locked the office door behind them. 'D'you want to sit out?' he asked, gesturing to the chairs set up under the awning.

'Best not, Sir.'

Picton was staring at Dixon over his shoulder as he climbed the steps up into his motorhome. 'Faith, the police are here.'

The driver's and passenger seats had been turned around to face a small television mounted on the wall; someone else watching the tennis, although Faith was jabbing the gizmo to turn the sound down.

'You'd best sit there,' she said, gesturing to the seats. 'We can sit on the bed.'

'What's this about?' asked Picton.

Dixon took a deep breath. 'There's no easy way to broach the subject, I'm afraid, but we need to talk to you about your son.'

'Our son?' Picton put his arm around his wife. 'We thought it'd be about someone who'd stayed on the campsite.'

'I'm afraid not.'

'What about our son?' asked Faith, already struggling to keep her composure.

'It's about his funeral.' Dixon spoke quietly, as if that would soften the blow.

'Can we talk about that?' asked Picton. 'We signed a confidentiality agreement when we settled the complaint against Latham.'

'You can, Sir.'

'It was that James Scott,' Picton sneered. 'Creepy, he was. He seemed to relish death; enjoyed it far too much for someone with that job. It was unhealthy.'

'What happened?'

'It was the morning of the funeral and Faith wanted to see Matthew one last time before he was cremated. Not an unreasonable request, I thought, but Scott refused.'

'What reason did he give?'

'He said he'd not been embalmed, so he couldn't open the coffin. He said it would be far too upsetting for us. Then he quoted something to do with substances hazardous to health at us; said the regulations wouldn't allow it.'

'And what happened?'

'The cremation went ahead.' Picton shook his head. 'We didn't have a lot of choice, really.'

Faith's chest was heaving, her head bowed. 'I'm sorry,' she mumbled. 'It's bringing it all back.'

'I knew it would,' replied Dixon. 'And I can assure you I wouldn't be asking if it wasn't important.'

'What's it all about?' asked Picton.

'I really can't say at this stage.'

'We bought the van after the funeral and haven't stopped running ever since,' Faith said, oddly calm now.

'We're here April to October,' said Picton, 'and in the winter, when the site closes, we drive down to Spain. We have a home; we just can't bear to spend any time there.'

'It's still full of Matty's stuff.' Faith was sobbing now.

'You said in your complaint against Latham's that you thought the coffin was empty.'

'We had no evidence for that,' replied Picton. 'Our real complaint was that Scott refused to allow us to see Matty one last time. We said for all we knew the coffin was empty – it was his attitude, really. We threatened to go to the press and police.'

'Did you?'

'No. We tried the press, but they wouldn't print it without evidence; and what could the police have done?'

'So you settled?'

'Latham sacked Scott, which was what we really wanted. And he offered us two thousand pounds to sign a confidentiality agreement. What else could we do?'

'It was a way out,' mumbled Faith.

'Did you see Matty's coffin before the cremation?'

'Not on the day, no. Scott wouldn't let us anywhere near it. It was in the hearse when the cars picked us up, then the next time we saw it was inside the crematorium.'

'Then the curtain goes across and . . .' Faith's voice tailed off.

'One last question,' said Dixon. 'Then I'll leave you in peace.' He looked at Picton, still with his arm clamped around his wife's shoulders. 'What happened to Matthew's ashes?'

Chapter Thirty-Six

'Under the bed?'

'How would you feel if it was Katie?' asked Dixon, crawling down North Hill in first gear.

'I'd never let her out of my sight.'

'There you are then.'

The urn had been hand painted enamel with a screw top. 'We can't risk it tipping over if we have a crash,' Picton had said, with a shrug of his shoulders.

Dixon sighed. He had briefly considered the idea of getting the ashes tested for human bone fragments, but had ruled it out if only because trying to explain it to the Pictons would have been difficult, to say the least.

If he was right, they would find out soon enough. And have another funeral to prepare for.

'Do you think Matthew's body is still out there?' asked Louise.

'Yes.'

Louise got the message from Dixon's monosyllabic reply, and the rest of the drive back to Express Park was spent in silence.

'Go home, Lou,' he said, when he dropped her back to her car. 'Spend some time with your family and I'll see you in the morning.'

'Are you going in?' she asked.

'I'm going home.'

'What time tomorrow?'

'The profiler's due at ten, so any time before that's fine.'

Half an hour later he was standing on top of the sand dunes watching a walker down by the wreck of the SS *Nornen* throwing a tennis ball for a large white dog, the sun setting behind them. The tide was lapping at the spars of the old ship, the yellow marker buoy beyond it afloat, the one at the front still resting on the smooth sand.

The first few notes of the theme from *The Vikings* did the trick as he strolled across the beach; Monty's head shot up at the familiar whistle and he came running, his tennis ball still in his mouth.

Then Dixon wrapped his arms around Jane and held her tight.

'What's up?' she asked.

'Too much death,' he said, throwing Monty's ball towards the water.

'You're a murder detective. And a bloody good one at that.'

'Usually I'm after the killer among the living, but this time even the bloody witnesses are funeral directors.'

'I heard.'

'And now I've got a couple who think they've cremated their son, but if I'm right they probably haven't. They even think they've got his ashes under their bed. How am I going to break the news to them when I find his—'

'None of this is your fault, you do know that?'

256

'Where's Lucy?' he asked, his arms still wrapped around Jane's waist.

'She's gone out with Billy. I gave her the money for a taxi home and told her eleven at the latest.'

'Any luck with that file on the Bagwells?'

'Not yet. I think it may have been destroyed, but I won't know until Monday now, I'm afraid.'

'Have you eaten?'

'Not yet. I was waiting for you.'

'C'mon then,' said Dixon. 'The pub stops serving food in twenty minutes.'

Early morning or late evening; for the rest of the time Monty was confined to barracks. Dogs die in hot cars, and all that.

They were home by eight, and it was only Monty's barking at his empty food bowl that woke Jane the next morning. She'd had a late night, waiting up for Lucy.

'What time did she come in?' asked Dixon, dropping two pieces of bread in the toaster.

Jane was yawning and scowling at the same time; no small feat. 'Two.'

Dixon winced. At least the shouting hadn't woken him up.

'She's grounded,' continued Jane. 'Until tomorrow anyway.'

'What's tomorrow?'

'Rory Estcourt's funeral.' Jane was tying her hair back in a ponytail. 'Billy's going with his father and Lucy's going with Billy. What could I say?'

'No.'

'I tried that.'

'Are you going in to work today?' asked Dixon.

'I'm staying to keep an eye on this idiot,' said Jane, watching Lucy when she appeared at the bottom of the stairs. 'And where d'you think you're going?'

'Out.'

Dixon's toast popped up just as the argument got going; butter, marmalade – seeing as Jane wasn't looking – and then he crept out of the back door with a piece in each hand. 'Sorry, old son,' he whispered when Monty stared at him. 'You'll have to stay and umpire.'

Sunday morning was always quiet at Express Park, not least because of the overtime cost, although the Incident Room on the second floor was busy. Most of the workstations were occupied, the sound of tapping on computer keyboards filling the air.

'I don't suppose we've found him yet?'

'Not yet, Sir,' replied Pearce, the only one who looked up. 'And Dr Spurway's here.'

'Already?'

'He's down in meeting room one with DCS Potter. She knows him, I think.'

'What the bloody hell's she doing here?'

'Came down specially to see him.'

Dixon didn't knock, but then both Potter and Spurway had seen him through the glass partitioning anyway.

'Here he is,' said Potter, standing up. 'Maurice and I go way back, so I just popped in for a chat. I'll leave you to it.'

Dixon sat down and watched Potter close the door behind her.

Spurway was looking him up and down as he closed the lid of his laptop. 'She said I wasn't to let your obvious youth put me off.'

'And does it?'

'She says you have a gift.'

Dixon was listening for the sarcasm in Spurway's voice, but couldn't hear it. Not yet, anyway. Long white hair, swept back behind sunglasses clamped on the top of his head; collarless shirt, linen jacket; Dixon couldn't see his shoes under the table and looking would be too obvious. Boat shoes, probably. Or espadrilles.

'You've made some progress since we spoke on the phone, I gather,' said Spurway.

'Simon Bagwell was the fifteen year old son of a farmhand. The family lived over at Bradney. His father died and his mother took to her bed, next to the dead body of her husband. They were found two years later. The boy had been her carer throughout.'

'And you think he's the Scytheman?'

'The father's body had become mummified over time, and you've seen Rory Estcourt's post mortem?'

Spurway nodded.

'He popped up years later calling himself James Scott,' continued Dixon, 'and got a job at a funeral director's in Bridgwater. Then he got sacked, the suspicion being that he stole a body.'

'Not proven?'

'No.'

'Have you got the Social Services file?'

'Not yet, and there's a chance it may have been destroyed anyway. We won't know until tomorrow.'

'How does the battle fit in?'

Dixon took a deep breath. 'All of the victims lived close to or on the battlefield, and Rory's body was found there, as you know. Then we've got Paschall's letter about Cornelius murdering Appleby with a scythe and keeping his mummified body.'

'I've seen it.'

'We're waiting for the genealogist's report but it looks like neither Cornelius nor Appleby have any living descendants.'

'So, it's all in his mind.' Spurway grinned. 'He must know about Cornelius and feel some sort of affinity with him.'

Dixon hated psychologists. Charlesworth had forced him to see one after the factory fire and it had made for a very uncomfortable afternoon, dodging questions and lying through his teeth.

'It's my belief that Simon Bagwell is keeping the mummified bodies as trophies,' Dixon said. 'He was able to steal one, possibly more, when he was working at the undertaker's, then when he lost his job, killing became his only option. By my reckoning he had at least five when Rory's body was buried, leaving him with four.'

Spurway's eyes widened. 'They're his family,' he said, leaning back in his chair. 'There is no way on God's earth he would willingly have parted with Rory's body. He'd rather die, or risk capture even.'

'So, someone else buried Rory?'

'Must have done. Think about it.' Spurway's obvious glee took some getting used to. 'He looks after them, loves them, talks to them, paints their toenails . . .' His voice tailed off, his point left hanging.

'We know his age and we've got a description that's years out of date.' Dixon stood up and walked over to the window. 'I need you to fill in the gaps.'

'It's a shame about the Social Services file,' Spurway said. 'There'd almost certainly have been a psychological evaluation done when he was taken into care. He lives on or near the Levels, that's immediately obvious. And he's obsessed with the battle.'

Dixon smiled, trying to disguise a look of irritation.

'He's highly intelligent, but hides it from people, just like he does every aspect of his life.'

'And the mummified bodies.'

Spurway ignored him. 'He's never come to the attention of police before—'

'He's not on the fingerprint or DNA database,' said Dixon.

'But he will have committed previous offences. Arson would be my best guess, starting when he was in his early teens; remote barns, outbuildings, things like that.'

'I'm hoping you'll tell me he's single.'

'That side of his life is lived through a computer screen, if at all.' Spurway sat forward and opened his laptop. 'I'm working on my report now and will let you have it by the end of the day.'

'Why the obsession with the battle?' asked Dixon, opening the meeting room door.

'I'm not entirely sure. The family home at Bradney was close to the route of Monmouth's march out of Bridgwater, but that's the best I can come up with at the moment.'

Chapter Thirty-Seven

Dixon left Louise looking for reports of unexplained fires on the Levels in the early to mid-1990s and drove out to Bussex Farm. Sunday afternoon would usually be busy on the battlefield, with dog walkers and sightseers. Today there were the ghouls to contend with too.

Colin Timperley and Dr Ashton were on their hands and knees in a different trench this time; same field, not too far from the gazebo and the cool box.

'We've sent the students home, Inspector,' said Colin, standing up. 'And we've told them not to come back. The dig's off. We thought it only right and proper, really.'

'Quite so, Sir.'

'We're going to stay though. All the stuff's here and we've got the permissions until the end of next week so we might as well.'

'Are you staying, Sir?' asked Dixon, turning to Ashton, who was squinting up at him.

'I thought I would.' He shrugged. 'It's the chance of a lifetime for me. And I wanted to stay for the re-enactment next Saturday anyway.'

'At the village fete?' Dixon had seen the signs on the grass verges.

'That's right.'

'What about Professor Watkins?'

'He's still over at the mass grave site,' replied Colin. 'He said he'd got permission to have a go with his metal detector on the other side of the drain, in the loop of the old Black Ditch.'

'Is he staying all week?'

'I think so. Sandra's over there helping, and Rob Salmon from the history society.'

'It's not usually a spectator sport,' said Ashton, pointing with his trowel at a line of people leaning over the field gate.

'Have you found anything?' asked Dixon.

'A good concentration of musket balls,' replied Colin. 'I think we've proved his theory.'

'The Red Regiment under Wade never engaged the Royal Army, Inspector,' said Ashton, beaming. 'So, who were they firing at, if not a retreating Lord Grey and his troopers?'

'While I think about it, Sir,' said Dixon, 'have you shown that letter to anyone else – the one from Paschall to Durling?'

'Colin and Malcolm. You've seen it, haven't you, Colin?'

'Most interesting.'

'And a couple of the locals. Sandra and Rob. And there was an older couple at the Sedgemoor Inn last week who seemed very interested in it. I swore them to secrecy, of course. Got to protect the new book.'

'Have you told them we've seen it?'

'I did mention it, I think.' Ashton scrambled to his feet in the bottom of the trench. 'Why, shouldn't I have done?'

'They haven't got permission,' said Sandra, her shovel covered in a layer of mud an inch or so thick. She slid the earth into a large sieve and began shaking it; panning for gold – Dixon couldn't remember the film.

It was a new trench, only two feet at the deep end.

'Found anything?' he asked.

'Not in this trench. Not yet anyway.' Sandra wiped her brow with the back of her muddy hand, leaving a smear across her fore-head. 'We'll go as deep as that one, just in case,' she said, gesturing to the other hole, which was more of a pit than a trench. 'But I'm not holding my breath.'

Dixon walked over to the top of the bank and looked across the King's Sedgemoor Drain, two figures visible in the fields opposite, on either side of a hedge; headphones on, metal detectors sweeping the ground in front of them.

'You're not going to arrest them, are you?' asked Sandra.

'Trespassing isn't a criminal offence,' replied Dixon.

'They said they were just going to have a look, and if they got any hits then they'd pester the landowner again.'

'How did they get over there?'

'They drove round to Parchey and followed the anglers' path along the bank. It's not far,' replied Sandra, climbing out of the trench.

'This letter from Paschall to Durling that Ashton is basing his next book on: is it genuine, d'you think?'

'I'd love it to be, but even if it is, I'm not sure it tells us who fired the shot and alerted the Royal Army. Thomas Cornelius could've got back from the Indies and found Appleby in bed with his wife.' Sandra laughed. 'My money's still on Bramston.'

'Even though he was executed anyway?'

'*Because* he was executed anyway. It saved them paying his reward.'

Dixon glanced over at the fields on the far side of the drain, where Rob Salmon had disappeared behind the hedge. 'If he's digging, then he is committing a criminal offence.'

'Are you going to arrest him?'

'If the landowner complains, I'll have to.'

'I'll ring them,' said Sandra, pulling her phone out of the back pocket of her jeans. 'Rob, are you digging?' she said when he answered her call, his head popping up from behind the hedge. 'Well, there's a policeman here watching you.'

'Tell him trespass is a civil matter, but if he causes any damage it becomes a criminal offence.'

'Did you hear that, Rob?' Sandra rang off. 'They're coming back, he said. They haven't found anything anyway.'

'Who is the landowner?' asked Dixon.

'It's Sutton Hams Farm,' replied Sandra. 'Steve Humberstone.' She rolled her eyes. 'A difficult bugger at the best of times.'

Over a five bar gate, then down the bank and along the rough path at the water's edge – Dixon watched Salmon and Malcolm Watkins trudge back towards the bridge, their metal detectors over their shoulders like marching troops. Or retreating ones, perhaps.

'I'll hang on for them,' he said, watching Sandra kneel back down in the trench. 'I never said – I was sorry for your loss.'

'What loss?'

'Zak.'

'Look, it was desperately sad, Inspector. It always is when someone of that age . . .' Her voice tailed off, a measure of premeditation to it. She was trying hard to hide her impatience. Too hard. 'But let's not make out my relationship with him was something it wasn't.'

Dixon turned at the sound of a car sliding to a halt on the track behind his Land Rover.

'Parker's not the Scytheman, then?' asked Watkins, striding towards the dig site. He dropped down into the new trench next to Sandra and sat down on the edge, snapping open the ring pull on a can of Diet Coke. 'Which means he's been out there all this time.'

'That's not for me to say in advance of the retrial,' replied Dixon. The usual drill was that the detective asked the questions and the witness answered them, but Dixon knew he could often learn as much from the questions the witness asked. Or didn't ask. 'We're re-examining all the evidence.'

'We all saw your press conference, Inspector,' said Salmon. 'So, poor Rory Estcourt was only buried nine months ago?'

'Yes, Sir,' replied Dixon. 'Right around the time this dig was organised.'

Watkins laughed, almost drowning out Salmon's sigh of indignation.

'You can't be serious?' demanded Salmon, giving Watkins a frosty stare from behind his dark sunglasses. 'It's hardly a laughing matter.'

'The idea that one of us is involved is.' Watkins took a swig of Coke. 'We're not even local.'

'I thought you said your family came from Taunton, Sir,' said Dixon, matter of fact.

'Yes, but I live in Reading now.'

'So, you're saying it's one of us?' asked Salmon, puffing out his chest.

A retired bookkeeper and treasurer of the local history society; Dixon had read Salmon's witness statements. He'd given two – one at the start of the investigation and then another dealing specifically with the night of Zak's murder. Neither had been particularly enlightening.

Salmon took off his panama hat, revealing a thick head of white hair. The collar of his polo shirt was turned up to shield his neck from the sun. White shorts and black ankle socks were an odd choice too.

'I should bloody well hope not,' continued Salmon. 'It's Parker, everyone knows it's Parker. He's always been trouble, ever since that crash out on the main road.'

'You remember the accident, Sir?' asked Dixon, watching Salmon pour a cup of tea from his flask.

'I was travelling back from a meeting in Bridgwater. It's one of the trials of being a bookkeeper – you end up treasurer of whatever organisation you join.' He sat down on a folding chair under the gazebo. 'That night it was the hospital friends, I think. Anyway, the crash had only just happened. It was back in the days before we all had mobile phones, so I got the car behind me to go back to the pub at Dunwear and ring 999, then I tried to help. Parker was no bloody use. He was just sitting in the cab of his tractor with his head in his hands.'

'Did you know him?'

'I'd seen him around. Westonzoyland is a small place.'

'What did you do?'

'I used my belt as a tourniquet for the girl; God, the blood was pumping all over the road.' He waved away the memory; either that or it was a wasp. 'Then I took the boy's belt off him and used that on his leg. He was screaming about his arm – his elbow was smashed; I don't think he could feel his leg, which was probably a blessing. Your lot told me later I'd saved their lives.'

'Did you know the motorcyclist and pillion passenger?'

'No.'

'What about Christine and Nicola Bond?'

'No.'

'And what do you think of Dr Ashton's letter from Paschall to Durling?'

'You asked me that,' said Sandra, emptying her sieve on to the pile of mud next to the trench. 'Is it relevant somehow?'

'Only to the extent that Cornelius killed Appleby with a scythe.'

'You surely don't think there's some connection?' asked Salmon, trying not to scoff.

'And kept his mummified body.'

The questions they asked, or didn't ask, and their reactions to new information, always spoke volumes. The assessment of a witness was an art, rather than a science, which perhaps explained why there were twelve people on a jury, thought Dixon, as he drove back to Express Park.

The profiler hadn't exactly helped either – the psychological profile of the perpetrator made without the benefit of having met him or her. Again an art, surely, but no doubt Spurway would claim it was a science.

And the hunt for the Scytheman had suddenly turned into the hunt for the Scytheman and someone else as well.

Nice.

'Have you thought about geographic profiling?' asked Spurway, when Dixon poked his head around the door of meeting room 1.

'He lives in the rectangle.' Dixon smiled over his grimace. 'Even I can work that out.'

'What rectangle?'

'It's created by the main roads, with the battlefield slap in the middle; the motorway to the west, A39 to the north, A361 to the east and A372 to the south.'

'Have you searched it?'

'We've done house to house and are using dogs in the remoter areas.'

'I tell you what's really interesting,' said Spurway, dropping his pen on the keyboard of his laptop, 'and that's the fact he hasn't killed since Parker was convicted.'

'What about Zak?'

'If it was him who killed Zak then the motive must have been different; that would explain the change of method and disposal.' He picked up his notepad. 'What else can I tell you?'

Dixon waited.

'He was an only child, with a close – controlling – relationship with his mother, distant with his father.'

'Who controlled who?'

'His mother dominated him. I think that must be self-evident from his continuing to care for her when his father died. There's almost certainly an element of obsessive compulsive disorder and paranoid schizophrenia too. I mentioned arson, but there'll be cruelty to animals and he might have been the school bully as well, although that's less likely given his intelligence. He'd have known he'd get in trouble for it and he prefers to keep things hidden from other people. He's secretive. And arrogant.'

'Arrogant?'

Spurway rubbed his chin. 'You'll never catch him – at least, that's what he thinks. You're not smart enough.'

'You're sure he didn't bury Rory Estcourt's body?'

'More than ever. He'd never have parted with it.'

'Which means there's someone else out there who knows exactly who he is and what he's done.'

'They won't be an accomplice in the true sense. The Scytheman works alone and wouldn't share his newfound family with anyone.'

'Share?' Dixon frowned.

'That's the way he would see it.'

'His victims have always been male, until the Bonds,' said Dixon, pulling out a chair from under the meeting room table. 'Why the change?'

Spurway sniffed, rummaging in his pocket for his handkerchief. 'The male victims were him replacing his father—'

'If that was right, surely he'd have picked older victims?'

'Not necessarily.' Spurway turned away, blowing his nose. 'We can draw two conclusions from it, I think. Firstly, he's slightly built. That's why he's picking on immature victims he knows he can overpower. And your theory about him dragging his victims along rhynes also fits for that reason. Secondly, and I've checked this with the forensic anthropologist, Dr Martin, once a body reaches a certain point in the mummification process it becomes almost impossible for the layperson to tell the age anyway.'

'And the switch to female victims?'

'He needed a maternal figure to complete his new family. Or, to put it another way, he missed his mother.'

Chapter Thirty-Eight

A walk on the beach before breakfast; yet another sunny morning, the tide in but turning. Dixon usually left Monty to decide which way they went, but this morning he turned his back on Hinkley Point and walked towards Brean Down, jutting out into the Bristol Channel with its limestone cliffs towering over the beach. Monty soon caught up.

Dixon pulled his tie – black – out of his pocket and tied it as he walked along. He hated funerals. Maybe he'd send a text message to Jane, telling her he didn't want one when his time came? Then again, perhaps not. He wasn't in the mood for flippant replies today.

Rory Estcourt's funeral would draw a huge crowd: friends, well-wishers, ghouls, and journalists, lots of journalists; TV crews too, probably. Traffic police would be on hand to close the roads if needs be.

Dixon had tried to persuade Daniel Parker not to go, but he had been adamant, and so would Dixon have been in his position. Parker had been right, of course: 'How would it look if I didn't go?'

Billy was going to keep an eye on his father; Lucy to keep an eye on Billy; and Jane to keep an eye on both of them.

It was when the credits were rolling at the end of *Brighton Rock* the previous evening that Dixon had worried Jane even more.

'Just be careful,' he'd said. 'We have reason to believe that the Scytheman was identifying his victims at funerals.'

'He'll be there?' she had said.

'I doubt it, but he might be, yes.'

'Now you tell me.'

Parking outside St Mary's Church had been the problem, the main road through Westonzoyland lined by TV vans and police patrol vehicles moving everyone on. A wave of his warrant card had done the trick and he'd parked on the double yellow lines opposite the pub.

Dave Harding and Mark Pearce were mingling with the photographers, taking pictures of the mourners and the spectators lined up along the pavement opposite the church. It was a large crowd.

Some had jeered when Parker arrived, but soon shut up when Doreen stepped out of the car and glared at them. Then she had taken his arm, Lewis on her other arm, and led them both into the church.

Lewis had seemed broken, thought Dixon, as he watched from behind a TV van. Pale, gaunt, he had the look of a man whose past had caught up with him. *We spend our lives making bad decisions and living with the consequences*, Lewis had said. And he was certainly living with them now.

Poor sod.

Doreen was already sitting at the front of the church, flanked by Lewis and Daniel Parker, when Dixon walked in. Jane, Billy and Lucy were sitting a few rows back, Jane in the aisle seat.

The ornate oak ceiling was providing a distraction for several of the mourners, craning their necks to look at the carvings, some even taking photographs. Dixon preferred to look at the stone floor, running with the blood and tears of five hundred men on that night in 1685. One had made his escape through a side door when the guards were dozing. Tempting, but he thought better of it.

He walked to the front of the church and squatted down in front of Doreen.

'You came,' she said, smiling at him. 'I don't know who most of these people are.' She winked at him, releasing more tears to cascade down her cheek. 'These two are keeping me sane,' squeezing Lewis and Parker's hands in her own.

'It won't be long now, Doreen,' said Dixon, grateful that she didn't want to know what wouldn't be long.

Then the organ music started.

'I'll see you later,' he said, straightening up and going in search of an empty seat. He walked down the outside of the pews, watching the pallbearers carrying Rory down the centre aisle, three on either side; he recognised Vic and Skinner from Latham's at the front of the coffin. They were hardly straining under the weight of it.

The men placed it carefully in front of the altar on a table draped in a purple cloth, and then walked slowly back down the aisle, their eyes downcast, hands crossed in front of them. A well rehearsed routine.

'Dearly beloved,' said Reverend Jonathan, standing on the steps behind the coffin. 'We are gathered here today to give thanks for the life of Rory Christopher Estcourt, beloved son of Doreen and her late husband Alec, with whom he is together in everlasting life.'

The vicar paused, just long enough for the sound of Doreen sobbing to carry to the back of the church. 'And we begin with hymn number six-four-eight, "The Day Thou Gavest, Lord, Is Ended".'

Dixon spent the hymn discreetly glancing around the church; some faces he recognised, some he didn't.

Timperley and Watkins were there – representing Reading University, they had told Dave Harding outside. 'After all, we found his body so it seems only right.' Salmon was there too, as a friend of Doreen's apparently; they had met when he helped with her search for Rory's body over the years.

No sign of Dr Ashton, or Sandra Smith, not that Dixon could read anything into that. Neither had any real reason to be there.

A couple of other members of the local history society whom Dixon recognised from Ashton's talk at the Sedgemoor Inn were there too. He could find out why later. And lots of mourners of the age Rory would be now; old classmates, probably.

The eulogy was given by Rory's former teacher at Bridgwater College. Rory had been a bright student, destined for medical school and intent on a career as a heart surgeon. A great loss to all, let alone all who knew him.

Prayers; then the organ stuttered into life once more for hymn number thirty, 'All Things Bright and Beautiful'. A popular choice, which the congregation really put their backs into.

Dixon crept out ahead of Doreen and was grateful to find that uniformed officers were keeping the media out of the churchyard, the funeral car pulled up across the lychgate ready to take her the short distance to the Sedgemoor Inn. He waited in the graveyard, standing behind a headstone, and watched two women giving an interview to camera on the far side of the road. A quick call to Dave Harding and he was despatched to find out who they were and what they were talking about.

Then he felt a hand on his shoulder. 'Are you going to the pub?' asked Jane.

'No.'

'Billy and Lucy are, so I'd better go. I'll let you know if anything interesting happens.'

Shouts of 'Murderer!' and 'Scum!' from the small crowd on the other side of the road greeted Doreen when she finally emerged from the church – aimed at Parker, who was holding her arm, no doubt.

Dixon was about to bark orders at the uniformed officers in attendance, but they had reacted quickly and were moving the crowd down a side road. The shouts continued, this time accompanied by a selection of hand signals – only the number of fingers varied – and the occasional obscenity.

Relatives or friends of other victims, perhaps, they were certainly convinced of Parker's guilt; unlike Doreen, who smiled throughout, resolutely clinging to his arm as she hobbled down the path to the funeral car.

'When's the cremation?' asked Jane.

'He's being buried. Just in case we need to—'

'I get it.'

'It's a private ceremony at Bridgwater Cemetery tomorrow morning.'

'Where are you off to?' asked Jane, setting off down the path after Billy and Lucy.

'Zak's inquest.'

'D'you need to go to that?'

Jane was out of range for a reply and Dixon wasn't shouting across the gaggle of mourners shuffling down the path. She was right, of course; the inquest was a formality and he didn't really need to go. The coroner would open it, then immediately adjourn it pending the police investigation into his murder.

The truth was that Dixon didn't know where he was going. He was drifting; they were gathering evidence, lots of it, but none of it was leading anywhere. Or if it was, he couldn't see it for looking.

If the Scytheman really did live in the 'rectangle' then he was right under his nose. And if he didn't bury Rory in the bottom of the rhyne, who did?

His phone buzzed in his pocket and he slid it out to find a text from Jane:

Take Monty for a walk :-) Jx

◆　◆　◆

An acting detective chief inspector bunking off in the middle of a high profile multiple murder investigation to take his dog for a walk; the press would love that, he thought, as he lifted Monty into the back of his Land Rover.

And where to take him? A crystal clear blue sky with the midday sun beating down; only one thing for it.

Half an hour later he parked in the quarry at Cleeve and opened the back door of the Land Rover. It was a new one on Monty and he looked lost for a split second before setting off along the path into the trees.

It had been a while since Dixon had been here too; his last time rock climbing with Jake on the cliffs at Goblin Combe. Thinking about it, it had been one of his last climbing trips with Jake, before he went to London and before Jake was killed.

He wondered what Doreen would think as he followed the path up through the woods, the canopy sheltering Monty from the sun as he sniffed about in the undergrowth.

Then he followed the steep and narrow path up to the foot of the limestone cliffs. Yet another trip down memory lane; of a rock dislodged from the top of the cliff – Jake shouting and him ducking – and the rock hitting him on the back of the neck, a fraction of an inch from his spine.

Narrow margins. There'd been a few more lately.

Random thoughts, jumbled, popping into and out of his head. It only seemed to happen when he was out with Monty. The rest of the time everything followed a strict order; logical. Maybe it was his legal training?

He thought about Thomas Cornelius, hatred a powerful motivator; if the story was true, his hatred for William Appleby had driven him to survive ten years as a slave in the West Indies and then work his passage home with only one intent: to kill. Of the hundreds transported as slaves, only a handful made it back, and Cornelius was one of them. No doubt he had Appleby to thank for that.

And the hatred on the faces of those outside the church, all of them convinced that Parker must be guilty.

The funeral; he'd seen something at the funeral. He knew that. *What, though?*

Dixon frowned at his phone buzzing in his hand. An 01278 number.

'Nick Dixon.'

'Nick, it's Peter. Where are you?'

Dixon's uncertainty was noticed at the other end.

'Peter Lewis. Now we're the same rank you call me Peter.'

It would take some getting used to. 'Yes, Sir.'

'Where are you?'

'Thinking,' he replied, buying a little time. Lewis still had questions to answer and maybe now was as good a time as any.

'Out with your dog then. Where?'

'In the woods up behind Cleeve,' replied Dixon. 'Should we be talking?'

'Since when have you worried about that sort of thing?'

'You're at home?' he asked, his mind racing.

'Yes.'

Now it is then. 'I'll meet you at Berrow Church in half an hour. Leave your mobile phone at home.' Dixon hesitated. 'Peter.'

277

Chapter Thirty-Nine

Monty was on his lead, lying on the cool flagstone floor in the porch at Berrow Church, growling softly at the approaching footsteps.

'Did you see those bloody people at the funeral?' asked Lewis, sitting down on the bench opposite Dixon. 'I don't know how Doreen kept her cool.'

'She's a remarkable woman,' replied Dixon.

'Social media is covered in all sorts too. I can't bring myself to look at it.'

'You've made your peace with Parker?'

'I went to see him at the vicarage over the weekend. The vicar said it would be all right.' Lewis shrugged. 'He doesn't blame me. In fact, oddly enough, he doesn't blame anyone.'

'Did you tell him the truth?'

'What d'you mean, the truth?' Lewis arched his back, trying indignation; soon deflated by the coldness of Dixon's stare.

'You knew—'

'I've already told you I didn't know about Jennifer Allen and her daughter lying. Neither did Ridley.'

'Why the guilt, then?' Dixon folded his arms. 'None of this is your fault. There's not a police officer living or dead who wouldn't have arrested Parker that night. And it's not your fault the jury didn't believe him either. So, tell me, why the hair shirt?'

'It's complicated.'

'No, it isn't.' Dixon waited, watching Lewis wringing his hands; much more of that and he'd snap his own fingers. Time to put him out of his misery. 'You remembered every last detail, you said, so when did you tell Ridley you heard movement in the rhyne?'

'What?'

'Parker heard it and so did you,' said Dixon, coldly. 'The sound of water sloshing about.'

Lewis took a deep breath, nodding to himself. 'The phrase I used was "consistent with someone wading along the rhyne". It was in the first draft of my witness statement,' he said, his eyes fixed on the ceiling above him. 'Ridley told me to take it out; convinced me I couldn't be sure and said it would "muddy the waters". I thought he was taking the piss at first, but he said I'd done a good job and it'd be a shame to ruin my career over it.'

'You were a junior officer at the time of the original investigation. If anyone's going to take the fall it'll be Ridley.'

'Somehow that doesn't make it all right. And whichever way you look at it, it's still gross misconduct.' Lewis looked at Dixon, his eyes welling up. 'It's almost a relief to say it out loud. There was someone else there that night, I know there was. The duckweed was still moving on the surface of the rhyne – closing over, y'know. Trying to meet in the middle . . .' His voice tailed off.

'Did you go to the Sedgemoor Inn after the funeral?' asked Dixon, changing the subject; Lewis had suffered enough and he'd got the answer he was looking for.

Lewis nodded. 'Nothing to report, really. Doreen was holding court, telling anyone and everyone that Parker didn't kill her son.'

'Journalists?'

'Several.' Lewis jumped up and started pacing up and down, stepping over Monty each time. 'Then there was the obligatory photo call outside the pub.'

Dixon waited, watching Lewis working up to asking what he really wanted to know.

'Tell me about the letter.'

Lewis listened intently, his frown furrowing into his forehead. 'A scythe, and he kept the mummified body,' he mumbled.

'Then he was hanged for his trouble,' said Dixon.

'It's either one hell of a coincidence or the Scytheman knew the story all along; fifteen years ago he must have known about it.'

'Longer.' Dixon folded his arms. 'That's if he's Simon Bagwell and got sacked from Latham's for stealing a body. That was 2002.'

'People collect the weirdest things,' said Lewis, sucking in his cheeks. 'Where was the letter?'

'In the archive at Cambridge University. Dave's checked with them and they don't keep records of who's looked at what. There's a visitors' book, but they don't verify ID either, so the names are meaningless. We checked and none match anyone of interest.'

'What else?'

'Someone else buried Rory's body, according to the psych profiler. There's no way the Scytheman would've parted with it, apparently. And that's about it, really.'

'You've got to find him, Nick, for my sake as much as Parker's.'

'When's your interview with Police Complaints?'

'Friday morning. And I couldn't care less about Police Complaints!' Lewis lashed out with his foot, kicking the stone wall. 'It's all about Parker now and putting his life back together.'

◆　◆　◆

'Ridley's in for interview. He's got his solicitor with him,' said Louise, when Dixon appeared at the top of the stairs. She was gesturing along the landing to the Professional Standards department at the far end of the second floor.

'Where's everyone else?'

'Dave and Mark are still over at Westonzoyland.' Louise glanced over her shoulder at the vacant workstations behind her. 'I'm not sure where everyone else is.' She ducked down behind her computer. 'There he is,' she said.

Dixon looked across the atrium at Ridley, waiting for the lift at the far end with someone in a suit. The doors opened and they both stepped in, turning around to face Dixon, Ridley's solicitor pressing the button to close the lift doors.

Ridley's hand gesture was unmistakable.

'He's giving you the bird,' said Louise.

Dixon watched Ridley raise his hand as the lift descended. It was the second time that day he'd seen a raised middle finger.

Or was it the third?

Chapter Forty

Dixon parked across the gates at the back of Latham's, the hearse and the funeral limousine glinting in the sunlight as water dripped off them. He flung open the back door of the funeral parlour. The preparation room was empty, but voices were drifting along the corridor from the front office, where he found Skinner comforting an elderly lady in tears, a box of tissues in one hand and a coffin brochure in the other.

Nice work if you can get it.

Dixon's self-appointed anger management counsellor would be proud of him. He counted to ten three times before he started pacing up and down, and another three times before he finally knocked on the glass.

'I'm with someone at the moment,' said Skinner, poking his head around the door.

'Would you prefer to be arrested for obstruction?' Dixon folded his arms, if only to stop himself grabbing Skinner by the scruff of his neck.

'If you'll forgive me, Mrs Ballard,' said Skinner, at his simpering best. 'I won't be a moment.' He closed the door behind him and turned to face Dixon, his eyes wide. 'What is it?' he asked, a slight tremble creeping in.

'When I asked you for a list of those who worked for you, you gave me a list of four people: yourself, Vic, Tracey on reception, and your driver.'

'That's right. We've only got four on the payroll.'

'What about the pallbearers today?'

'There was me, Vic, Jim our driver, and we got three more in for it.'

'In from where?'

'I've got a list of phone numbers.'

'And you didn't think to tell me about them?'

'They're not employees. And we use them so rarely these days.'

'Cash in hand, I suppose?' demanded Dixon, a heavy sigh escaping through his nose.

'Look, it's once in a blue moon. A client has to request it, otherwise we use the trolleys for health and safety reasons.'

'And Doreen Estcourt requested them?'

'She did.'

'Do you keep a record of the funerals where they've been used in the past?'

'Not specifically.' Skinner was leaning back against the door; cowering, actually. 'I could tell by looking at our fee because it'd be a bit higher than usual to cover the cost, but it'd mean going back through them all one by one. The tax man will crucify us!'

'The tax man will be the least of your worries,' muttered Dixon. 'I want you to check the Walton and Eastman funerals.'

'When?'

'Now.'

Dixon listened to the filing cabinets opening and closing in the back office, punctuated by the sound of crying from the front office, the door ajar. 'For God's sake, offer her a cup of tea or something,' said Dixon, glowering at Skinner.

'It won't take a sec,' he replied, flipping over the pages of a lever arch file. 'Here's one. Yes, to Mrs Eastman.' More flipping. 'And yes to Mr Walton.' He looked up at Dixon. 'Does this mean—?'

'Names,' he said. 'Now.'

A page torn from a little black book in the top drawer of the desk. Names and mobile phone numbers only; some crossed through, others current.

'Addresses?'

'Haven't got them,' replied Skinner.

'Mark the ones who were at Rory's funeral today.'

Skinner did as he was told.

Dixon watched him highlighting each one with a fluorescent pen, his breathing quickening at the vision of a hand steadying the back of Rory's dark oak coffin, the fingers splayed out in front of him.

'Now mark the one who's missing the tip of his middle finger.'

Chapter Forty-One

Dixon was sitting in his Land Rover, still parked across the gates at the back of Latham's; not that the funeral cars were going anywhere at this time of day, unless they got another 'urgent', of course.

He had ended the call and hit the redial button three times already when the voicemail cut in. Leaving a message was no damn good at a time like this.

'What is it?' asked Poland, in a gruff voice and at the fifth time of asking.

'Where have you been?'

'Doing a post mortem. Couldn't you have left a message?'

Dixon recognised the twang of elastic as Poland ripped off his face mask. 'The bruises on Zak's neck—'

Poland sighed. 'What about them?'

'Could they be consistent with the killer missing the tip of his middle finger?'

'I'll check and call you back.'

'I'll wait, don't worry,' snapped Dixon, anxious to catch Poland before he rang off.

'It'll take me a minute.' Then the clunk of Poland's phone being dropped on his desk followed by the familiar sound of a filing cabinet drawer opening. Paper rustling; photographs being flipped over in an album. 'Yes, they are,' shouted Poland, without bothering to pick his phone up. 'It's quite obvious when you know what you're looking for. What put you—?'

But the rest of Poland's question was lost in the rumble of Dixon's diesel engine.

◆　◆　◆

'Are you on your own?' asked Jane.

'It's an unregistered pay-as-you-go mobile,' said Dixon, with a dismissive wave at his computer.

'What is?'

'The pallbearer's mobile.'

She sat down at the vacant workstation opposite him, the only light on the second floor coming from the windows, where the sun was setting outside, and Dixon's screen. 'I know that look,' she said, smiling.

'A pallbearer at the funeral today was missing the tip of his middle finger, and the bruising on Zak's neck is consistent with the killer also missing the tip of his middle finger, according to Roger.'

'Haven't you got a name?'

'Tom somebody. That's all they had. And it may not even be his real name.'

'Well, it's more than you had before.'

'The only forensic evidence at the Chedzoy murder scene, apart from the blood, was a sequence of fingerprints. All of them were smudged with insufficient ridge detail for comparison purposes, except for an identifiable right middle finger. But there was no match, not even with Parker. So, what does he do? Bearing in mind he's intelligent enough to stop killing when Parker is arrested. What's the one thing he can do that will guarantee he won't get linked to the scene if he's ever arrested for anything else and fingerprinted?'

Jane frowned. 'You're not suggesting he cut his own finger off?'

'Just the tip; the distal phalanx. And that's exactly what I'm suggesting,' he said, nodding for emphasis. 'Wouldn't you?'

'No, I—' Jane hesitated. 'Possibly. But he certainly would.' She frowned. 'So, all you've got to do is find someone, possibly called Tom, with a missing fingertip.'

'We've fingerprinted hundreds of people in the last week or so and I'm going to go through them all, one by one, until I find what I'm looking for.'

'What about Monty?'

'He's at home. I left him watching the tennis; fed and walked.'

'Right then,' said Jane, switching on the computer in front of her. 'I'll search by date entered on the system and scroll through looking for an empty box at right middle. It should be simple enough.'

'I'll start with anyone called Thomas.'

Twenty minutes later and Jane could stifle her yawn no longer. 'Coffee?' she asked. 'The machine's still on, I think.'

'Ta.'

When she arrived at the top of the stairs five minutes later, Dixon was leaning back in his chair, staring at the computer screen.

'What is it?' she asked, still standing on the top step.

'Thomas Quintin, he's the bloody herdsman at Bussex Farm. I remember him, bold as brass, sitting there on his quad bike, watching us while we fished Zak's body out of the slurry pit.' Dixon sneered. 'He's even taken the name of a rebel executed at Ottery St Mary. I thought it sounded familiar, so I checked the *London Gazette*. Timperley read his name out when he called the roll, would you believe it.'

'What about his right middle finger?'

'Absent.'

Chapter Forty-Two

Dave Harding was arriving at Express Park just as Dixon and Jane were leaving.

'A trace on that number, Dave,' said Dixon, pressing a piece of paper into his hand. 'It's unregistered, but I need to know where it is. Ring me when you get anything.'

'Yes, Sir.'

'And eat some mints before someone breathalyses you.'

'Do we need those?' asked Jane, glancing over her shoulder into the back of the Land Rover. Two stab vests slid across the floor as Dixon took the corner at the bottom of the car park ramp too fast, his tyres squealing on the tarmac.

'Let's hope not,' he said, his fingers drumming on the steering wheel while he waited for the ponderous electric gates to creep open.

'What about some backup then?'

'We'll start at Bussex Farm and see what they say there. At the moment, we're just interviewing witnesses, aren't we?'

'What is it, beef or dairy?' asked Jane.

'Both, I think. Why?'

'If it's dairy, they'll all be in bed by now.' Jane looked at her watch. 'They've got to be up at dawn for the milking.'

'Tough.'

Twenty minutes later Dixon parked by the battlefield information board at Bussex Farm and looked across the yard in his rear view mirror. The dull glow from an outside light on the corner of the cowshed reflected off some liquid or other running in the drains. It hadn't rained, so Dixon thought it best avoided, whatever it was.

Lights were on in the farmhouse, shafts coming from a gap in the curtains; flickering.

'They're watching telly,' said Dixon.

'Old episodes of *Countryfile* probably.' Jane flashed him a mischievous grin.

He switched off the engine and slid out of the driver's seat, leaning against the door until it clicked shut.

'What do we do if he's in there?' asked Jane, wriggling into her stab vest.

'Arrest him.'

'What for?'

'Watching *Countryfile* will do for starters.'

The house was sideways on to the lane, the faded red brick garden wall keeping the farmyard at bay, an old Land Rover Discovery and a quad bike parked along it, the offside wheels of both on the grass verge.

They walked along the front of the cowshed, on a raised concrete plinth to keep their shoes clear of whatever it was running in the gutters in the yard. The smell was familiar; fresh too.

Then past an open barn that was knee deep in clean straw, old steel five bar gates lashed together with orange baler twine keeping the cattle in, both of them new mothers by the looks of things, their calves lying in the straw just visible in the light from the corner of the cowshed.

The picket gate to the front garden was hanging off its hinges, the white paint flaking off the splintered wood. Dixon pushed it open with his foot and then turned to Jane. 'Wait behind the Discovery. You can see the back door from there.'

He was halfway along the garden path when the dog started barking; the unmistakable yap of a Jack Russell.

Dixon stepped forward and banged on the front door, at the same time watching for movement through the frosted glass.

A face appeared at the sitting room window, the frayed curtains sagging in the middle. 'Who is it?'

'Police,' replied Dixon, listening for the sound of running.

'All right, all right.'

'We're looking for your herdsman, Thomas Quintin,' said Dixon when the front door opened, his warrant card at the ready.

'He's not here.' Well over six feet tall, even with a slight stoop; the cloth cap didn't quite match the pyjamas, a tartan dressing gown hanging open, the cord belt trailing on the floor.

'What's his address?' asked Dixon, following the man into the living room. He noticed several cats lying along the back of the sofa and the remains of a dead mouse on the hearth.

'He lives over Sutton Hams in an old static caravan.'

'That's on the other side of the drain?'

'Aye. This time of year he swims it.' The old farmer yawned, revealing several missing teeth. ''Tis the only bath the bugger gets.'

'Do you have an address?'

'Not sure there is one. It's just a caravan in a field; the farm's been derelict for years.'

Jane appeared in the doorway. 'No one came out the back,' she said.

'I told you he's not 'ere.'

'What farm is derelict?'

'Hams. Forty year since. The land was sold off. I rent some of it from a bloke in Stawell.' The farmer leaned back in his fraying armchair and poured the last of a can of stout into a glass. 'Thomas has his post sent here.'

'How long has he worked for you?'

'A while. He just turned up one day. A good worker, he is.' The old farmer gestured to the sofa. 'Sit down,' he said.

'How did he lose his middle finger?' asked Dixon, glancing down at the torn cushions, an inch deep in cat hair. Then he walked over to the window.

'Dehorning cattle. I do mine young when they're just buds, like – you can burn 'em off then, but I bought some at market and they came with 'orns. Small ones.'

'Shouldn't it be done by a vet?' asked Dixon.

The old man's dismissive wave knocked his glass of stout off the arm of his chair. 'Betsy'll clean it up,' he said, picking up the glass while the black and white Jack Russell terrier licked up the beer.

'Did he go to hospital?'

'I took him to Musgrove.' He held up his left hand, the tip of the thumb missing. 'Goes with the territory,' he said, smiling. 'Farm machinery can be a bugger.'

'Did they try to sew his finger back on?'

'We never found it, so he had a skin graft and that was that. He soon got over it.'

'Did anyone see the accident?'

'Nope.'

'And when was this, exactly?'

'God, I don't know.' The old farmer curled his lip. '2005, maybe? Edna said he may have done it on a scythe; joking, like.'

'Who's Edna?' asked Dixon.

'My late wife,' the old man replied, gesturing to a photograph on the mantelpiece.

An old woman was just visible through the dust and cat hair.

'Who else works here?'

'Just me and Thomas. I uses contractors for the hay baling and silaging.' He leaned forward, pointing the gizmo at the television and jabbing at the button with the stump of his thumb.

'Where do we find his caravan then?' asked Dixon.

'Hold on,' he said. 'Just let me pause this. It's the long range weather forecast. I always records *Countryfile* for the weather forecast.'

Chapter Forty-Three

Dixon flicked on his torch and looked at the map unfolded across the steering wheel of his Land Rover.

'It's just beyond the loop in the Black Ditch, over a small hill, looking at the contours. The track stops and then further on there's a building standing on its own.'

'That'll be the remains of the farm?' said Jane, unzipping her stab vest.

'Best leave that on.'

'You are going to call this in?' she asked, turning in the passenger seat to face him. 'Please tell me you're going to call this in.'

'I'm not,' he replied, switching on the engine. 'You are.'

'Thank God for that,' sighed Jane.

'I'm not inclined to go in without Armed Response if I can help it, so see where they are and how quickly they can get here. No sirens either.'

Mist was creeping along the rhynes as Dixon drove past Fowlers Plot Farm and into Chedzoy. Lights on the battlefield twinkled through the haze; dog walkers possibly, or perhaps Timperley and his cronies were still digging.

'The nearest Armed Response car is answering a shout in Yeovil,' said Jane, ringing off as Dixon drove over the King's Sedgemoor Drain at Parchey.

'Tasers it is, then.'

'We've got backup though. I've told them to meet us at the church in Sutton Mallet.'

Dixon slowed outside what had been the Tanners' bungalow on the edge of the village, Quintin's caravan less than two miles away across country. Surely it would have been searched at the time of the boy's disappearance? He shook his head. Maybe not, given that Ridley had called off the search when Lewis arrested Parker.

It was just after ten and pitch dark when Dixon drove around the village green and parked outside the church in Sutton Mallet, behind a patrol car that had beaten them to it. He was relieved to see PC Cole sitting behind the steering wheel, drinking from a thermos.

Cole was a reliable soul; unflappable. Taser trained too. Dixon couldn't think of anyone he'd rather have at his shoulder when he went into the Scytheman's caravan. After all, Cole had already saved his life once, jumping into the King's Sedgemoor Drain on an icy winter's night to pull him to safety.

'Is it him, Sir?' asked Cole, his finger on the button that wound down the window of the patrol car.

'Looks like it,' said Dixon.

'There's another car on the way. They're five minutes away, but no Armed Response.'

'We'll go in without,' said Dixon. He didn't recognise the uniformed officer sitting in the passenger seat, but she looked as if she was about to puke up. 'Are you all right?' he asked.

'She's fine, Sir,' replied Cole. 'Just a bit nervous. It's her first week on the job.'

Blue lights and a siren out on the A39 on the hill above them; Dixon spun round. 'If that's them, tell them to switch that bloody siren off.' He walked back to his Land Rover, leaving Cole shouting into his radio, the siren falling silent as the car dropped down into Stawell, still two minutes away.

'You could wait for Armed Response,' said Jane, sliding out of the passenger seat of the Land Rover.

'No need. We've got no evidence he's got a gun, and if he comes at us with a scythe, Cole can hit him with his taser.'

'If you say so.'

The second patrol car stopped behind the Land Rover, its engine still running. 'Taser trained?' asked Dixon, leaning in to the passenger window.

'I am, Sir,' replied the driver.

'You're with me and Cole.'

'Fork left on the way out of Sutton Mallet,' the old farmer had said. 'Then follow the lane to the end, through the gate and keep going straight across the fields.' Dixon was creeping along the lane using sidelights only, the two patrol cars behind him, when his phone started buzzing on the dashboard. He snatched it from Jane's hand when she picked it up, and held it to his ear. 'What is it, Dave?'

'His phone's hitting the Vodafone mast on the Walrow Industrial Estate.'

'Highbridge?'

'That general area,' replied Dave. 'I can't be any more specific at the moment.'

'Let me know if you get anything else.' Dixon rang off.

'I heard,' Jane said.

He accelerated along the lane, flicking his headlights to full beam, the patrol cars behind following suit.

The five bar gate was open, so Dixon raced through it and followed the track across the middle of the field, the tyre ruts close together. 'Quad bike tracks, must be.'

Through another open five bar gate on the far side of the field, a derelict farmhouse loomed out of the darkness up ahead; the windows were boarded up but the roof was intact, patched with new slate tiles by the looks of things.

The cars screeched to a halt adjacent to a rusting static caravan shrouded in darkness behind the hedge on the left, the patrol cars stopping either side of Dixon's Land Rover.

'He's not there,' he said, thumping the steering wheel with the palm of his hand.

'Police, open up!' Cole was banging on the door of the caravan. Then he stepped back to allow the officer behind him to swing a battering ram at the lock.

The door flew open.

Cole drew his taser and stepped inside, immediately enveloped by the darkness. Seconds later he appeared in the doorway, holding up a hand scythe in an evidence bag.

'Right place, wrong time,' muttered Dixon. 'Fuck it.'

'What about the house?' asked Jane, lighting it up with the beam of her torch.

Grey stone with carved lintels, chipboard and planks across the windows, two either side of the front door and three upstairs. The door itself had been replaced with a steel shutter, bolted on either side.

The garden had long gone too, the property sitting on the edge of the field; not even any outbuildings had survived.

'Doesn't look as though anyone's been in for ages,' said Cole, following Dixon and Jane around the back, his taser at the ready.

He stopped by another steel shutter that had been bolted in place across the back door.

'How the bloody hell do we get in?' whispered Jane.

'This window hasn't got any planks across it,' said Dixon, stepping up on to a small pile of breeze blocks. 'And steps up.'

'D'you want me to go first, Sir?' asked Cole.

'He's not here,' replied Dixon. He was standing on the windowsill feeling along the edge of the piece of chipboard with his fingers. Then he pulled and the board swung open, revealing a perfectly intact sash window behind.

'It's not locked,' he said, sliding the bottom sash up.

Cole was right behind him – torch in one hand, taser in the other – as Dixon shone his torch around what had once been the kitchen; anything metal long since salvaged. The cupboards were still there, gaps left where the cooker and fridge would once have stood. And the sink had gone, replaced by two buckets.

Two Campingaz stoves were sitting on the worktop. Dixon picked one up and shook it; half empty.

He squatted down and looked at the date on the newspapers covering the floor.

'They're recent,' whispered Cole. 'You can tell that by the headlines.' He shone his torch at the sports pages under the kitchen table. 'That's the last Rugby World Cup.'

Absolute darkness in the corridor – almost; it reminded Dixon of a cave, without the sound of running water. It was warmer too, an orange glow flickering under a door at the far end.

'Oddly clean for a derelict farmhouse, wouldn't you say?' muttered Dixon, shining his torch along the skirting board.

The stairs had gone – burnt for firewood, probably, but Scientific Services could check the first floor with a ladder easily enough.

Cole stepped past the closed door and stood with his back to the wall. Then he thumped it with his fist. 'Police, open up!'

'They can't hear you,' said Dixon. 'They're all dead.'

Cole opened the door, still with his back to the wall, the only sound the crackle of the open fire in the hearth. 'Someone's added wood to that in the last hour or so,' he said. 'And there's someone sitting in an armchair.'

'I can count three sitting around a table,' said Dixon, looking through the gap by the hinges.

'Are they moving?'

'No.' Dixon stepped forward and shone his torch into the room. It was exactly what he had expected to find, only worse. Far worse.

The body in the armchair was sitting with his or her legs crossed, carefully posed next to a small table, a decanter of red liquid and a glass reflecting the glow of the fire.

Three chairs were occupied at the dining table, two one side and one the other; the seat at the head of the table was vacant, a full ashtray and several beer cans on the place mat in front of it. The remains of candles were sitting in saucers, cascading drips of wax testament to them having been lit at some point, although when was another matter.

The curtains were drawn, presumably to hide the wooden boards from his house guests. Nice touch, that.

'Call it in,' said Dixon to Cole, who turned away, talking into his radio. 'Knives and forks,' Dixon sneered. 'He's even got them holding knives and bloody forks.'

He shone his torch at the empty chair to the side of the dining table, the seat heavily stained; Rory's resting place for the last fifteen years until he was buried in the bottom of the rhyne. No wonder Doreen had never found him.

Odd that there was no smell. He pulled on a pair of latex gloves, picked up one of the candles and sniffed it: scented.

Brown skin, shrivelled and pulled tight over the bones; it was impossible to tell the age of the victims, or male from female even.

DNA testing would sort who was who: the Tanner boy, Jamie Eastman; four funerals and four families who could bury their dead. Dixon wondered whether Latham's would charge the Picton family for cremating their boy a second time.

'Everybody's on the way, Sir,' said Cole, clipping his radio back on his stab vest. 'Scientific Services are sending all available vans, Dr Poland's bringing his assistant and we've got five cars en route to seal off the area. Even ACC Charlesworth is on his way apparently.'

'What about the helicopter? We could do with its thermal imaging camera.'

'Coming over from Yeovil.'

'Have you checked the other rooms?'

'They're all empty, Sir.'

'Any sign of Quintin?'

'Not yet. The shout's gone out so he won't get far.'

'Well?' asked Jane, when Dixon returned to the open sash window in the kitchen.

'Three bodies sitting round a dining table like mannequins.' He sighed. 'And one sitting by the fire with a glass of port.'

'You're kidding? The sick . . .' Jane's voice tailed off. 'Lucy rang. She was after a lift, but I told her she'd have to call a cab.'

'Where was she?'

'She's with Billy at Highbridge railway station. They're putting his father on the train to Bridgwater.'

Dixon climbed out of the window and rang Dave Harding, pacing up and down in the light of Jane's torch. 'Where is he now, Dave?' he asked, when Harding answered.

'I've still got him on the Vodafone mast at Walrow, but he's showing up on the O2 one now as well – that's junction 22 on the motorway – and the Three mast at West Huntspill. My guess is he's slap in the middle; which puts him somewhere in Highbridge.'

Chapter Forty-Four

Through Stawell with his foot flat on the floor; then he was accelerating up Puriton Hill, listening to Jane frantically dialling Lucy's number.

'She's not answering!' Jane screamed, trying the number again.

There were sirens in the distance as they raced down the hill towards junction 23, blue lights screaming out of Bridgwater and behind them on the A39 too.

Dixon turned at the motorway roundabout and headed north, the click of the pedal slamming into the floor of the Land Rover as he raced down the slip road.

'Shouldn't you have gone along the old road?' asked Jane, glancing over her shoulder.

'Find out where the nearest car is.'

Lights flashed by on the other carriageway, heading south, as Dixon listened to Jane on the phone.

'We're nearest,' she said, ringing off. 'There are others behind us and cars coming over from Cheddar and Weston.'

'Try Lucy again.'

'She's not answering,' said Jane.

'What time's the train?'

'Ten-forty.'

He looked at his watch: five minutes. Then he screeched to a halt on the hard shoulder. 'Drive round,' he said, jumping out of the driver's seat. 'I'll meet you there.'

'Where are you going?' asked a bewildered Jane, sliding across from the passenger seat.

'Along the River Brue. It's only a couple of hundred yards on foot.'

◆ ◆ ◆

'Control, this is QPR three-ten. Over.'

'Go ahead QPR three-ten. Over.'

'We've got him. There are fucking bodies everywhere – I've seen it all now – mummified bodies sitting around a dining table for fuck's sake.'

Lewis sat bolt upright in the driver's seat of his car and looked down at the police radio in his hand.

'Location, QPR three-ten. Take a deep breath and calm down. Over.'

'Ham Farm. It's derelict, in the middle of bloody nowhere, down a lane out of Sutton Mallet. Suspect is Thomas Quintin, otherwise known as Simon Bagwell or James Scott. Inspector Dixon says there's an old photograph on the system. Over.'

'All units, this is Control, respond grid reference . . .'

Lewis smiled. It was sort of inevitable, really, as soon as Dixon had been given the case; he was more sniffer dog than detective – running around in circles sniffing everything until he found what he was looking for. Shame he hadn't been around in 2005, but then he was probably still at school.

Lewis had known something was up when he left Express Park, so he had stolen the radio to keep track. Not stolen; borrowed. He'd never stolen anything in his life. Now he was sitting outside a bungalow in Edithmead waiting for Denise to finish her book club meeting. Ten-thirty or so, she had said. He looked at his watch and grimaced. It must be a long book.

Eavesdropping. He'd never felt comfortable doing it, and unauthorised monitoring of police radio traffic was a disciplinary offence.

'QPR three-ten, backup en route. Scientific Services have been notified. Stand by. Over.'

Thomas Quintin. Who was he? And where the bloody hell had he been in 2005?

Lewis wound down the window of his car and listened to the sirens in the distance, all converging on Sutton Mallet. The worst part was that he wouldn't be in at the finish. He had always promised himself he would be. And Doreen. He had promised her too. Still, maybe now he'd be able to sleep at night.

'Control, this is QPR three-ten, respond Highbridge railway station, suspect believed to be in vicinity. Daniel Parker present. Possible threat to life. Over.'

He turned the key and floored the accelerator, spinning his wheels on the gravel drive just as the front door of the bungalow opened behind him, a shaft of light catching his eye in his rear view mirror.

Denise would understand. And he wouldn't be long.

A scythe in one hand and a shotgun in the other.

The rest of the scene took a moment to come into focus in the harsh lighting when Lewis sprinted on to the platform at Highbridge railway station.

302

Daniel Parker was sitting in the open shelter on the opposite platform next to a girl of fifteen or so; she looked remarkably like Jane Winter – they could be sisters even, thought Lewis. Three phones lay on the ground in front of them, smashed to pieces under a boot, judging by the splinters of glass twinkling in the platform lights.

A boy of fifteen – Billy; they'd been introduced at Rory's funeral – was climbing down on to the tracks, the barrels of the shotgun digging into his ribs to overcome his hesitation.

Parker stood up and edged forward along the platform. 'It'll be all right, Billy,' he said.

'Stay back!' The shotgun pointed at Parker now. 'Or I'll blow his brains out here and now!'

'Thomas Quintin,' shouted Lewis, walking along the opposite platform, keeping pace with Billy as he backed away along the tracks.

'Who the fuck are you?'

'Police.'

Quintin jumped down on to the tracks behind Billy, his steel toecap boots clattering against the rails, and grabbed him around the neck, the scythe across Billy's chest, the shotgun now pointed at Lewis.

'It's over, Quintin,' he said, dropping down from the opposite platform. 'Or whatever the hell your name is. We've found Ham Farm. We've found them all.'

Quintin was backing away towards the bridge over the River Brue at the far end of the station, dragging Billy with him, the sound of sirens in the distance growing louder by the second.

'That'll be Armed Response,' said Lewis, taking another step forward, this time over the rail and into the gap in between the northbound and southbound lines, the brown stained gravel crunching beneath his feet.

Lights were approaching fast from the south, the telltale sound of a horn confirming it was a train; seconds later an InterCity 125 roared past. Lewis glanced up at the faces in the window, some turning in their seats to get a better look, most staring into space. Then the blast of air hit him and he was struggling to keep his balance.

Slowly, the clatter of the train receded and the sirens took over again. Louder this time.

'They're getting closer, Quintin,' said Lewis, taking another step forward.

Quintin raised the shotgun and fired into the air.

'Take another step and I'll kill you!' he screamed, his face contorted with rage, nostrils flaring. 'Just one more step.'

Dixon ran down the bank, wading through waist deep stinging nettles, and climbed over the post and rail fence. Then he jumped down on to the bridge embankment above the River Brue.

More stinging nettles, and thistles this time, then he was on the fisherman's path along the river: narrow, overgrown and weaving in and out of the trees. It would still be quicker than driving round.

He flicked on the light on his phone and began running along the track as fast as he dared, the smell of the burnt out factory on his right catching in his nostrils, the brambles tearing at his trousers as he ran. Then he was at the gap in the fence; he knew the way from there.

A shotgun blast drowned out the sirens fleetingly as he cleared the end of the trees and began following the tarmac path behind the houses. Breathing hard now, he arrived at the back entrance of the railway station to find Lucy and Daniel Parker sitting with their backs to him in the shelter, their heads turned, watching something further along the platform.

Dixon stepped out into the lights.

'They're down on the tracks!' screamed Lucy, jumping to her feet.

He stepped forward, spotting Lewis first, inching forward between the northbound and southbound lines. Further along, Billy being dragged backwards between the tracks of the southbound line, an arm across his throat. Then Dixon saw the scythe, the tip of the blade caught in Billy's T-shirt.

Dixon dropped down and began walking along the tracks. 'Quintin,' he said. 'Thomas Quintin was executed, wasn't he? Maybe I should call you Simon Bagwell instead?'

'Stay back!' Clean shaven this time, a black leather waistcoat over the same sleeveless T-shirt and fetid jeans.

The unmistakeable smell of slurry reached Dixon as he closed in. 'You see those lights behind me?' He was staring at Quintin; a hard, cold stare. 'Do you see them?'

Quintin nodded. He had stopped dragging Billy now and was standing between the rails, pointing the shotgun first at Dixon, then at Lewis.

'That's a train,' said Dixon, calm and matter of fact. 'Let the boy go.'

'It's over, Simon,' said Lewis.

'The train's coming!' screamed Lucy, up on the platform behind Dixon.

'Stay where you are, Lucy,' he shouted.

Quintin was pointing the shotgun at Lewis as he edged forward. Lewis glanced over his shoulder at the train. 'He's fired one barrel, Nick,' he said. 'You know what to do.'

'No!'

'We all have debts to pay.' Lewis stepped forward.

Dixon saw the muzzle flash but never heard the shotgun over the squeal of the brakes on the train and the wail of the police sirens. The blast hit Lewis in the chest at point blank range as he stepped over the offside rail, his arms outstretched towards Billy, and threw him back on the gravel in between the two lines, his body crumpling like a rag doll.

Dixon lurched forward, throwing himself at Billy, one hand reaching for the scythe, the force of his flying dive sending them both crashing over the rail and into the clear as the train screeched to a halt beside them. The scythe clattered on to the sleepers under the train as Dixon rolled away, dragging Billy with him.

He jumped up and ran around the front of the train, but there was no sign of Quintin; only the shotgun lying on the gravel in the gap between the train and the platform.

A trickle of blood was leaking from the corner of Lewis's mouth as Dixon knelt over him, several faces staring down from the train windows above. Lewis's chest was moving, almost imperceptibly, as the last of the air in his lungs escaped.

'Billy is safe,' whispered Dixon.

The ghost of a smile crept across Lewis's lips. Then he was gone.

Chapter Forty-Five

'We need an ambulance!' Dixon stood up when another officer took over the chest compressions; his hands dripping in Lewis's blood. He looked up at the uniformed officers now lining the edge of the platform, standing in silence, staring down at the body of Detective Chief Inspector Peter Lewis.

'And we need to get the trains stopped,' he said. 'This is a crime scene. I want the station sealed off. Some of you check along the river. Be careful. He's dropped the gun, but he may have another.'

'Yes, Sir.'

'Keep those people on the train,' he shouted to uniformed officers who had arrived on the other platform and jumped down on to the tracks. Then he helped Billy to his feet. 'Are you all right?'

'I think so.'

'That man gave his life for you,' said Dixon, looking down at Lewis, an officer still doing CPR as blood seeped into the gravel from the chest wound. 'Don't waste it.'

'I won't.'

Then Jane ran on to the platform and jumped down beside them, throwing her arms around Dixon. She looked over his shoulder at Lewis.

'Is he—?'

'Yes.'

'Oh, fuck, no.'

'Look after Billy, will you,' he said, glancing up at the footbridge where Lucy and Daniel Parker were now standing. 'You'll need uniform with you until we catch Quintin. Either that or take them all back to Express Park for now.'

Jane wiped her cheeks with the palms of her hands. 'What happened?'

'The train was coming. Quintin had one shell left, so Lewis took it in the chest to save the rest of us.'

'Where's Quintin now?'

'He went that way,' said Dixon, gesturing towards the river. 'Fuck knows. I'll worry about him tomorrow.'

Lewis's phone pinged, lying face up on the gravel next to his body, the backlight illuminating the cracks in the shattered screen. And the blood. The text message was readable all the same:

Waiting outside book club. Where r u?

'What are you going to do?' asked Jane.

'I'll stay here with him.'

A doctor was first on scene, taking over CPR from the uniformed officer, who sat back on the rail next to the body. 'What are we looking at?' asked the doctor, grimacing up at Dixon.

'A twelve bore shotgun at close range.'

A bloodied hand pressed against Lewis's neck; then the doctor grimaced. 'There's no pulse. How long have you been doing CPR?'

'Fifteen minutes.'

'He's not coming back from this, I'm afraid.' The doctor straightened up, ripped off his latex gloves and checked his watch. 'Pronouncing him dead at 11.04 p.m.'

'We'd better have the pathologist out here,' said Dixon, turning to the uniformed officer.

'Is he dead?' asked Charlesworth, appearing by Dixon's side.

'Yes, Sir. He—'

'I heard. He'll get a posthumous George Medal, if I've got anything to do with it.' Charlesworth turned away. 'Where's his wife?'

'She sent him a text about ten minutes ago saying she was getting a taxi home. He was supposed to be picking her up from her book club, I think.'

'I'll go and see her now,' said Charlesworth, walking back towards a small aluminium step ladder leaning up against the platform.

'Excuse me, Sir,' said the uniformed officer to Dixon. 'They're sending the junior pathologist, a Dr Davidson.'

Dixon slid his phone out of his pocket, dialled a number and held his phone to his ear.

'Are you at Highbridge?' asked Poland. 'I saw it on my pager.'

'It's Peter Lewis, Roger.'

'Dead?' A sharp intake of breath down the phone line. 'I'm on my way,' said Poland.

It was just before one in the morning when the mortuary van arrived to recover the body from the tracks. Dixon was still there, watching on from the shelter on Platform 1, sitting with Dave Harding, Mark Pearce and Louise Willmott.

Bad news travels fast.

'Where's Parker?' asked Dixon.

'Still at Express Park,' replied Louise. 'Jane's with them.'

'What's happening over at Ham Farm?'

'That's going to take days,' said Harding. 'Another Scientific Services team has been drafted in from Bristol, and Armed Response are on hand in case Quintin turns up. I was over there when I heard about . . .' His voice tailed off.

'Family Liaison are going to be busy.' Pearce had his head in his hands.

The train opposite was standing empty; witness statements had been taken from the passengers, who had all continued their journeys by taxi. The scythe and shotgun had gone, bagged up and on their way to the lab. Now Peter Lewis was on his way too, Dixon watching on as the mortuary assistants slid the stretcher with the zipped up body bag on it on to the platform in front of them, then climbed up the ladder, one by one.

'A bad business,' said Poland, putting his case down.

'They found an Airwave radio in his car, so he'd been listening in,' said Louise.

'What time's the first train through?'

'God knows.'

'You'd better get some sleep,' said Poland. 'All of you. You're welcome to come back to mine. There's plenty of spare beds, and whisky.'

'I'll go home,' said Louise. 'Maybe wake up Katie and play with her for a bit.'

'I'll be fine at home too,' said Pearce.

'What about you?' asked Poland, turning to Dixon.

'Me?' he asked, with a heavy sigh. 'I'm going to take my dog for a walk.'

Chapter Forty-Six

He woke slowly, Monty growling softly at a fisherman digging worms down by the water line, the incoming tide rolling up the flats a couple of hundred yards away.

He sat up and slid his phone out of his back pocket; the soft sand must have absorbed the buzzing – he'd missed three calls while he was asleep.

The first glow of dawn was creeping across the sky from behind the dunes, the sun still below the horizon; asleep on the beach . . . the only things missing were Jane and a barbecue.

Then he remembered.

Lewis was dead.

He'd forgotten for just a moment – an all too brief moment – then it all came roaring back: the high pitched squeal of the brakes, the muzzle flash; Lewis blown backwards by the blast.

The blood.

He wondered how Charlesworth had got on with Lewis's wife.

'I thought you were going home, Lou?' he asked, holding his phone to his ear.

'Couldn't sleep, Sir,' replied Louise.

'What is it?'

'Dave's got something on the phones.'

Dixon stood up, brushing the sand off his trousers. 'He's there?'

'We all are, Sir.'

'Put it on speakerphone, will you?' Dixon looked down at his shoulder, his shirt covered in fine blood spatter. He'd stopped to wash his hands and face when he'd got home to collect Monty, but it hadn't occurred to him to change his shirt. High energy impact spatter, the experts would call it, but it was a friend's blood all the same. 'What've you got, Dave?' he asked.

Harding was some distance from Louise's phone, shouting. 'His phone goes dark just before eleven – takes the battery out probably, so it's not hitting any mast, anywhere. Then it pops up again twenty minutes ago pinging the Vodafone mast on the A39 at Chilton Priory, so he must've put the battery back in for some reason.'

'What I don't understand is how he got there,' said Louise.

'He could've had a boat down on the Brue,' said Pearce, in the background. 'Along the Brue, then the Cripps brings him out at Gold Corner, and there's a rhyne on the South Drain that'd take him all the way to Cossington. Then it's on foot from there.'

'Have you alerted all units?' asked Dixon.

'Straight away,' replied Harding, louder this time. 'There are cars on the way out there now; I told them to cover the bridges over the KSD.'

'And the footbridge west of Bawdrip,' shouted Pearce.

'The helicopter's up with its thermal imaging camera,' continued Harding. 'I'm not picking him up on any other masts yet though.'

'If he's using the rhynes,' said Dixon, sliding down the dune on to firm sand at the top of the beach, 'then he's probably got a snorkel for when the helicopter goes overhead.'

'A snorkel?'

'A piece of water reed would do.'

'The teams at Ham Farm are keeping an eye out too, in case he's trying to go home,' said Harding. 'Armed Response are on scene there.'

'He's not going home; he's going somewhere to die. Has he made a call?'

'No, Sir,' replied Harding.

'He's put the battery back in his phone to tell us where he is.'

'He could be dead already then,' said Pearce. 'Fuck it.' A thud carried over the loudspeaker.

'Thomas Cornelius was hanged for murder, and back then he'd have been left hanging from a gallows oak, probably at a cross-roads.' Dixon was talking to himself, really. 'Justice seen to be done, seventeenth century style.'

'All the old gallows oaks have gone,' said Harding.

'Forget the bridges; he swims the drain to get to work,' said Dixon, running along the beach towards Berrow Church. 'Get a car over to his old family home at Bradney. And make sure there's someone in Chedzoy and Westonzoyland. Keep me posted, Dave. I'm on my way over there now.'

One junction south on the M5; Dixon's phone buzzed as he was racing down Puriton Hill.

'What is it, Dave?'

'I'm picking him up on Dunwear, Huntworth, and Westonzoyland airfield now; he's pinging all three masts, but the strongest signal is coming from the airfield. That puts him somewhere on the battlefield.'

'Where's the helicopter?'

'It left ten minutes ago for a pursuit out on the A30.'

The Duke of Monmouth had got a grandstand view of the battlefield and the Royal camp from the tower of St Mary's Church in Bridgwater on the eve of the battle, but then he didn't have motorways, railway lines and pylons to contend with. Dixon grimaced. It would be at least twenty minutes through the early morning traffic and the church was probably locked at this ungodly hour anyway.

Only one thing for it.

He screeched to a halt outside Lockwood's bungalow on the outskirts of Chedzoy, jumped out, leaving the engine running, and banged on the door.

'Who is it?' The shout came from a window at the side of the property.

'Police, Mr Lockwood. I need to use your telescope.'

The door opened. 'You said you had one in your loft conversion,' continued Dixon.

'The ladder's down,' said Lockwood, gesturing along the corridor. 'Just don't stand up – you'll bang your head on my train set.'

'Thank you.'

Dixon left the old man pulling on his dressing gown, sprinted along the corridor and climbed the ladder; ducking low, he crawled towards the light at the back of the bungalow, the legs of a tripod standing in front of a dormer window.

Once clear of the train diorama, Dixon stood up and looked out of the window. Mist was trying to form along the rhynes but was being carried away on the breeze; the pale light of dawn creeping across the sky as the sun came up beyond Westonzoyland. The church was visible behind the conifers, and the latticework of rhynes criss-crossing the battlefield. Timperley's gazebo was still there too, out beyond Fowlers Plot Farm.

Start with the rhynes, thought Dixon, stepping behind the telescope.

'I do a bit of astronomy, as well as snooping,' said Lockwood, appearing at the top of the ladder. 'What are you looking for?'

'I'll know it when I see it,' replied Dixon. He was looking into the eyepiece, panning the scope along the largest rhyne that crossed the battlefield; it followed the line of the original Bussex Rhyne, only further north.

Lots of cattle, grazing in the early shade; birds flitting in and out of the hedgerows; a fox – watching something further along the ditch. Dixon panned across.

Quintin: standing up in the rhyne, peering over the top towards Westonzoyland; water and duckweed pouring off his black waist-coat and T-shirt. Then he looked up, watching and listening for the helicopter, before crawling out of the ditch towards the hedgerow in front of him, a coil of rope in his right hand.

'Oak trees,' snapped Dixon, spinning round.

'The only two are at the memorial. Whoppers, they are,' replied Lockwood, quickly scrambling down the ladder as Dixon crawled towards it, dialling Dave Harding's number on his phone.

'I've seen him, Dave,' said Dixon. 'He's heading for the memorial.'

'On it.'

Seconds later Dixon was racing along the single track country lane, his foot flat on the floor, the diesel engine screaming in pro-test. He skidded on the mud in the road outside Fowlers Plot Farm but got around the corner, then accelerated hard towards the main road, the click of pedal hitting metal carrying over the revving of the engine.

He remembered from the maps he'd spent hours poring over that Sogg Drove met the main road just outside Westonzoyland. It would save going through the village, but could he get to the memorial that way?

Only one way to find out.

Sixty miles an hour along the farm track, the grass in the middle flicking the underside of his Land Rover. Sirens all around; the two giant oak trees at the memorial now visible ahead as he took the bend at the end of Sogg Drove with a bit of help from his handbrake. Then left on to Langmoor Drove.

Movement up ahead. 'Fuck it,' muttered Dixon, accelerating at the sight of legs flailing, Quintin swinging out across the drove on the end of a rope.

Dixon skidded to a halt opposite the memorial, jumped out and ran towards Quintin. He dodged the kicking feet, grabbed hold of him by the lower legs and lifted him.

'Oh no, you fucking don't.' Dixon grimaced. He was holding Quintin around the knees, keeping his legs clamped together; at the same time leaning back to avoid the fists now being directed at him.

Then a patrol car pulled up behind Dixon's Land Rover.

'Is this him?' asked Cole, running across the manicured grass at the entrance to the memorial. 'You should let the bugger swing.'

'Untie it,' said Dixon, nodding towards the rope, looped over the bough of the giant oak; Quintin had tied it to the gate of the memorial enclosure.

The rope slid through Cole's fingers when he loosened the knot, and Quintin dropped to the ground, unconscious.

'Better get an ambulance out here,' said Dixon, letting go of his feet.

'He's alive, Sir.' A second uniformed officer was kneeling down, his fingers pressed to Quintin's neck, checking for a pulse.

'Make sure you handcuff him.' Dixon turned away.

'I heard about Peter Lewis,' said Cole, staring down at Quintin. 'I still say you should have let him hang.'

'This is a battlefield memorial, Cole, not the place a serial killer committed suicide.' Dixon shook his head. 'And besides, there are too many people who need to see him in court.'

He left three uniformed officers standing guard over Quintin and opened the back door of his Land Rover, letting Monty out for a sniff along the hedgerows.

'Ambulance is on its way, Sir.'

'Go with him and arrest him the second he wakes up.'

Cole nodded. 'And Mr Charlesworth has arrived. He's walking out from Bussex Farm now.'

Dixon backed his Land Rover into the gateway of the field opposite to allow the ambulance through, and was still there when Charlesworth arrived with Deborah Potter in tow.

'So, this is him,' he said, sneering down at Quintin, now being attended to by two paramedics, an oxygen mask clamped over his face.

'Yes, Sir.'

'Peter's wife was in a hell of a state. I ended up staying with her until their daughter got there an hour or so ago.' He sighed. 'So, that's it then, presumably?'

'No, Sir.'

'Eh?'

'According to Spurway, there's no way Quintin would have parted with any of his mummified bodies. They were his family, which means that someone else buried Rory's body on the battlefield so that it'd be found by the archaeologists.'

'Is this true, Deborah?' asked Charlesworth, frowning.

'That's what his report says. It also says he would have worked alone though.'

'That's bollocks. There's someone else out there,' continued Dixon. 'Someone who knew all about Quintin – protected him even – and went out of their way to see to it that Parker's appeal failed. At worst it's a joint enterprise; at best they're assisting an offender.'

Charlesworth watched the paramedics lift Quintin, gently placing him on a stretcher. 'Find them, Nick,' he said. 'We can't afford any loose ends this time.'

Chapter Forty-Seven

'All spruced up,' Charlesworth had said; a shave, a shower and a change of clothes, although Dixon didn't feel overly spruced when he got back to Express Park at midday for the inevitable press conference.

All the relatives had been informed, family liaison officers drafted in from Bristol to make up the numbers; and although Rory had already been found, Dixon had called in to see Doreen Estcourt on his way home, as much to break the news of Lewis's death as to tell her that her son's killer was in custody. Bad news and good – ish.

Her relief had been tempered by the sadness, but there were no tears. Doreen had said she was all cried out, and she was right.

'Let me do the talking this time, all right?' said Charlesworth, as they waited in the small office behind the press suite at Express Park. 'Press suite' made it sound very grand; actually it was the conference room with the table taken out.

Potter dropped her phone into her pocket. 'He's regained consciousness and will make a full recovery. Unfortunately.'

'When do we get him?' asked Charlesworth.

'They're keeping him in overnight.'

'And what did the CPS have to say?'

'They're asking for an urgent hearing at the Court of Appeal,' replied Potter. 'They'll offer no evidence against Parker and the charges will be formally dismissed.'

'There'll be photos of him on the steps of the court all over the front pages.' Charlesworth grimaced. 'But I suppose we'll just have to take that on the chin. Are we satisfied he wasn't Quintin's accomplice?'

'He was in prison when Rory's body was buried,' replied Dixon.

'Of course he was.' Charlesworth put his hat on and straightened it in the reflection in the window. 'Right, let's get it over with.'

The prepared statement read more like a eulogy – the press officer, Vicky Thomas, had excelled herself this time. Dixon could see Charlesworth's lips moving, but all he could hear was the squeal of the brakes on the train; and he flinched at the first camera flash.

'Detective Chief Inspector Peter Lewis sacrificed his life to save . . . in the finest traditions of the Avon and Somerset Police Service . . .' The clichés came trotting out. No mention was made of the George Cross recommendation either, presumably in case it wasn't granted. 'The relatives have been informed and identification of the remains is ongoing,' continued Charlesworth. 'Further information will be made available as soon as the bodies have been formally identified. Right, we'll now take quest—'

'How many bodies are there?' The question shouted from the back of the room.

'Four,' replied Charlesworth.

'How was Quintin missed the first time around?'

'The previous investigation, led by Detective Superintendent Ridley, which ended with the arrest and conviction of Daniel Parker, is the subject of a review by the Independent Office of

319

Police Complaints and it would be wrong to speculate in advance of the findings of that investigation.'

'Was it bungled, Assistant Chief Constable?'

Charlesworth took a deep breath. 'An arrest was made, evidence gathered and presented to the court, which resulted in a jury arriving at two guilty verdicts. There is no suggestion whatsoever of any fabrication of evidence by any officer on the original investigation.'

'Peter Lewis was the original arresting officer, wasn't he?'

'The circumstances of that arrest are well known and it is a testament to his extraordinary courage and dedication that he pursued a dangerous suspect alone into the fog on a dark night. I would remind you that he was commended for his bravery at the time.'

'Was Quintin questioned by police during the original case?'

'He was interviewed during the early phase of the investigation and ruled out, but, again, I would emphasise that it is the subject of an IOPC inquiry and I am not able to release any further information.' Charlesworth leaned back in his chair. 'I would also like to add that it is testament to the dedication of Avon and Somerset officers and the very thorough investigation led by Detective Chief Inspector Dixon, sitting to my right, that the matter has been resolved swiftly and without further loss of life.'

'Inspector Dixon . . . ?'

The mention of his name jolted him back to the present. He stared at the journalist at the front of the room, an iPhone held in her outstretched hand.

'Where was Quintin detained?'

'At the Battle of Sedgemoor memorial.'

'What was he doing there?'

'Trying to kill himself.'

'Have you questioned him yet?'

'No.'

'Are you looking for anyone else in connection with the Scytheman killings?'

◆ ◆ ◆

'No?' Charlesworth dropped his hat upside down on the table. 'What d'you mean, "no"?'

'No point in letting them know we're coming.'

'You misled the press,' said Vicky Thomas. Dixon had spotted her watching the press conference from the back of the room. She reminded him of a primary school teacher at a nativity play, ready to smack the back of the legs of any child who fluffed their lines.

'Well, technically we're not looking for anyone else in connection with the murders, just the aftermath; assisting an offender, or how about the prevention of the lawful and decent burial of a dead body – carries a life sentence, that one.'

'Does it?' Charlesworth frowned.

'That's splitting hairs,' snapped Vicky Thomas.

'They'll get over it,' replied Dixon, opening the door.

'What about the interview when we get him tomorrow morning?' asked Potter.

'I think we should bring in a specialist interview team,' said Dixon.

'You're not doing it?' asked Charlesworth.

'No.'

'I agree,' said Potter. 'DS Sam West is a trained psychologist. I'll ring him now and they can come down today and get acquainted with the file.'

'They'll need to visit Ham Farm too.'

'That'll give them something to look forward to,' said Potter, rolling her eyes.

'You'll get used to him, Vicky,' said Charlesworth, his whisper carrying as the door closed behind Dixon.

He found Jane in the canteen, sitting in the corner, a strong black coffee on the table in front of her. 'Long night?' he said, pulling out a chair.

'I stayed up.' She took a swig of coffee. 'Just in case.'

'There was no need.'

'I know that now.' She reached across the table and took his hand. 'I'd have stood there and watched him die.'

'No, you wouldn't. It's what he wants, and he doesn't get what he wants any more.'

'Where's Monty?'

'He's at home, watching the tennis.'

Jane smiled. 'I spoke to Billy's social worker this morning and it seems the local authority won't oppose an application for revocation of the wardship and a residency order for Daniel. So, he's going to live with his father at last. Thanks to you.'

'Where are they now?'

'I left them at the vicarage in Westonzoyland.' Jane screwed up a Twix wrapper and dropped it in her empty coffee cup. 'It's like a morgue around here this morning,' she said. 'They're saying Lewis'll get a posthumous George Cross.'

'He bloody well should.'

'Ridley will try to blame him for the failure of the original investigation now he's not here to defend himself.'

'And how far d'you think he'll get?' Dixon was staring at the canteen staff behind the counter. 'Black armbands. Nice of them.'

Chapter Forty-Eight

He left his Land Rover in the field and walked the rest of the way down to Ham Farm, the track blocked by Scientific Services vans and police patrol cars. Roger Poland's Volvo was there too, up to its wheel arches in the long grass.

The boarding had been ripped off the old farmhouse, allowing light in for the first time in decades, no doubt. Several of the panes of glass in the old sash windows were broken, but otherwise the farmhouse had been well maintained; far better than the rusting static caravan adjacent to the overgrown hedge.

Bright light was streaming out of the windows from arc lamps set up inside; several figures in overalls and masks moving about. More in the farmhouse.

'I've never seen anything like this,' said Poland, ripping off his face mask. 'And I've been at this nearly twenty-five years now.'

'Are the bodies still in there?'

'Yes.'

'Make sure they stay there until the interview team get down here. I want them to see it for themselves before they question him.'

'You're not doing it?'

'We've got a specialist team and one of them's a trained psychologist.'

'Makes sense,' said Poland, sitting down on his aluminium case.

'Where's Peter?' asked Dixon, grateful that he had made it to first name terms with Lewis before he died.

'He's at Musgrove Park. His children wanted to see him; they're coming down this afternoon, so I'm doing the post mortem this evening. Cause of death won't be diffic—'

'I was there.'

'Of course you were. Sorry,' mumbled Poland, sliding on a pair of sunglasses.

'Was there anything upstairs in the farmhouse?'

'Nothing. SOCO are up there now, collecting samples of anything and everything, but on the face of it there's nothing.'

'What about the bodies?'

'All except one – that must be the Picton boy – killed with a single stab wound to the chest from a curved blade. All male. You know the age range. Plenty of DNA so we'll soon find out who is who.'

'Anything else I need to know?'

'Not really. The coroner's coming out later to have a look at the scene. Then we'll start moving the bodies, once your interview team have been in.' Poland leaned forward, a set of overalls in his outstretched hand. 'Do you want to take a look?'

Dixon curled his lip. 'I saw it last night.'

'Quite.'

'I'll take those though,' he said, taking the bag from Poland's hand and turning towards the caravan. 'I came to see where he lived.'

◆　◆　◆

The steps up to the caravan had long since rusted away, replaced by five breeze blocks neatly arranged on the ground. Dixon arrived at the top, blinking furiously in the arc lamps.

'It's quite clean and tidy,' said Donald Watson, the senior SOCO, watching him fumbling for his sunglasses. 'I'll switch the lights off. Hang on.'

A dinette at one end, bed at the other, kitchen and bathroom in the middle.

'It's all disconnected,' continued Watson. 'Even the chemical toilet. I reckon he must've been emptying it into the KSD. We can't find evidence of—'

'I get it.'

'There's no electricity, so the shower pump doesn't work. And the fridge, of course. There's gas in the bottle outside, though, and the stove works.' Watson gestured to an old plastic razor in the sink. 'Dry shaves with an old Bic razor,' he said, rubbing his chin. 'Doesn't bear thinking about.'

A sleeping bag on the bed not fit for dumping a body in, let alone sleeping in, but otherwise the inside was relatively tidy, if not clean.

'We put anything interesting in the crates outside,' continued Watson. 'All indexed.'

No television, no books. Dixon sighed. 'He'll have spent his evenings sitting with his family in the farmhouse.'

'Looks like it,' replied Watson.

Blue plastic crates had been lined up on the grass outside, a list of the contents of each on the lid, the code number matching the relevant evidence bag inside the crate. Dixon leaned over and looked down the list on the first crate:

Various cutlery
Mouldy bread
Tins of Spam and baked beans

Toilet tissue (unused)

He straightened up and squinted at Watson. 'Is any of this likely to be useful?'

'Try the end crate,' said Watson, his grin just visible behind his mask. Dixon ignored it.

Box of photographs (misc)

'Well?' he asked.

'It's a shoebox full of photographs,' replied Watson. 'Looks like the tercentenary battle re-enactment in 1985. The photos are grainy and the colour's a bit faded.'

Dixon opened the crate, took out the evidence bag and tucked it under his arm.

'Oi,' yelled Watson. 'You can't take that.'

'I think you'll find I can,' replied Dixon, striding off towards his Land Rover. 'D'you want me to sign for it?'

'We haven't catalogued them yet!'

Dixon was back at Express Park fifteen minutes later, the photographs emptied out on to a table in the middle of the Incident Room.

'We need to get them catalogued, Lou,' he said. 'Scan them on to the system, then we can blow them up and start identifying everyone.'

'It'll take ages.' Louise raised her eyebrows. 'If you say so.'

'Where's everyone else?'

'They're all out taking statements from the families, looking for any connection with Quintin. You did say that's what—'

'What about Dave and Mark?'

'Charlesworth sent them home when he found out they'd been here all night.'

'So have you.'

'I lied.'

'Lying to the Assistant Chief Constable.' Dixon smiled. 'Lewis would be proud of you.'

'Thank you.'

He spent the rest of the afternoon with the specialist interview team who had arrived at Express Park via Ham Farm, slightly ashen faced, if anything. Spurway had travelled back down from London to assist as well, although Dixon suspected he just wanted to know if his profile had been right. And to watch the interview the following morning.

He left them planning the interview strategy in meeting room 2 and walked back up to the Incident Room; the lights off in the Safeguarding Unit. He checked his phone as he arrived at the top of the stairs.

Home. All well. Taking him to the beach. Jx

Louise had been busy. 'I've scanned them all in and the originals have gone back to Scientific Services. Watson was bending my ear on the phone, so I thought I'd better.' She pointed to the whiteboard mounted on the wall. 'These are copies I've blown up and I've marked the people I think I recognise. I've only bothered with the ones where you can see faces.'

The whiteboard was covered in photographs, some black and white, others faded colour.

'That's just the printing,' said Louise. 'All the photos in the box are colour snaps.'

A panorama had been Sellotaped together before being stuck across the top of the whiteboard.

She jumped up and walked over to the board. 'That's Graham Ashton,' she said, pointing to a man in jeans and a T-shirt holding a clipboard. 'I found a newspaper report from the time that listed him as technical advisor to the Sealed Knot. They usually do Civil

War re-enactments, so I'm guessing they brought him in as the expert on the battle.'

The rest of the people in the photograph were in costume: leather boots, black breeches, blue or red jackets and black wide-brimmed floppy hats. Some were holding muskets, others pitch-forks and some scythes. It must have been a long, hot summer that year, thought Dixon; the grass looking dry and parched.

'The people look different in this set,' said Dixon, gesturing to the whiteboard on the left.

'There were two re-enactments,' replied Louise. 'The Sealed Knot Society did one and then the local schools did their own.' She was pointing at a black and white photograph, a yellow sticker on it with a large arrow pointing to a woman holding a child by the hand; a small boy, in costume and armed with a scythe. 'I reckon that's Doris Bagwell. He had a photograph of her in his wallet. And that means the boy could be Quintin. He's about the right age.'

'I hope that's a plastic toy,' said Dixon. 'He'd have been five.'

'The old Bedford van in the background dates it. I'm sure it's them.'

'They can ask him in the interview tomorrow morning. Is he in any others?'

'A couple. This one up here,' Louise said, pointing to another yellow sticker; the rebels lined up along a rhyne. 'This one of the cavalry is a bit of fun too. Looks like the local pony club had a day out.'

Dixon sat down on the edge of the workstation in front of the whiteboard and folded his arms. 'You go, Lou,' he said. 'Get some sleep, and I'll see you in the morning. We're not going to make much progress until he's interviewed.'

'What time does it start?'

'Ten.'

'I'll let Dave and Mark know.'

Chapter Forty-Nine

The sleep of the dead; it was an unfortunate term, but it fitted today. Not even the shouting had woken him up; that's if there had been any. Lucy had been all smiles when he finally crawled out of bed just after seven, even dropping her toast on the worktop and throwing her arms around him.

'I knew you'd do it.'

'You're all right?' asked Dixon, squinting at her.

'Fine.'

'You've given a statement about Monday night?'

Lucy nodded. 'I didn't see what happened right at the end though; the train pulled in and you were down on the tracks.'

'How was Billy?'

'A bit shaken up, but he's just grateful to be with his dad, I think. He'll be all right. Social Services have offered him counselling, but he said no.' She picked up her toast and took a bite, continuing to talk with her mouth full. 'I'm going to back off a bit and leave them to it.'

'What's on for today?' asked Jane, putting Monty's food bowl down on the doormat.

'We're interviewing him at ten. There's a specialist team down from Bristol.'

'Who is he?' Lucy sprayed crumbs everywhere.

'A farm labourer with a complicated background,' replied Dixon, scowling at Jane when she snatched away the sugar bowl.

'I've got one of them, but I don't kill people,' said Lucy.

'I can't eat cornflakes without sugar,' grumbled Dixon.

'Eat something else then,' snapped Jane.

'Have you finished your exams?' He frowned at Lucy, more in hope than expectation.

'Not yet; Thursday and Friday, then that's it and you've got me for the whole summer.'

'Right, that's it. I'll have breakfast in the canteen.'

And he would have done, had the queue not been out of the door and along the landing. It was standing room only in the Incident Room too, a screen set up at the front for the major investigation team to watch the interview.

'You got any food, Lou?' he asked.

'A Kit Kat,' she replied, rummaging in her handbag on the floor next to her workstation.

'That'll do.'

'Dave's got some more on Ashton that seems quite interesting,' she said, watching him rip open the wrapper. 'It was him at the re-enactment in 1985 and he even had a holiday cottage at Stawell until a few years ago. Kept that quiet, didn't he?'

'Any connection to Quintin?'

'Not yet,' replied Harding, sidling over. 'It was his parents' place and he kept it for a few years after they died, according to the Land Registry.'

'Find out who did the parents' funerals, will you? Start with Latham's.' Dixon glanced up at the whiteboard. 'More yellow stickers?'

'That's Mark,' said Louise. 'Members of the local history society.'

'We need to place Quintin at all the funerals. Latham's can't tell, but check with Lockwood's in Burnham to see if they've got any records.'

'Yes, Sir.'

'Where are the interview team?'

'Downstairs, getting ready. They stayed over at the Premier Inn.'

'Ah, there you are,' said Charlesworth when Dixon opened the door. The anteroom was small: a table and four chairs; Potter sitting to Charlesworth's right, DS Sam West and his colleague opposite. Three screens were lined up along a sideboard, all of them flickering; the interview room on the screens unoccupied. For now.

'Is he here?'

'He arrived about an hour ago and is in with his solicitor,' replied Potter.

'Any progress overnight?' Charlesworth glanced at the screens to his right.

'That's his solicitor,' said Potter, watching a man in a suit drop a blue notebook on to a chair in the interview room.

'We've got enough to charge Quintin anyway,' continued Charlesworth. 'There's your statement and the CCTV at Highbridge railway station. And we've got the gun too, so that's Peter's murder covered. Then we've got the bodies at his home.' He shook his head. 'He's not going anywhere, is he?'

'I want his accomplice,' said Dixon.

'Quite.'

'What do we do if he goes "no comment"?' asked Potter.

'Find them anyway. It'll just take a bit longer.'

$$\blacklozenge \quad \blacklozenge \quad \blacklozenge$$

Dark blue tracksuit bottoms and a light blue T-shirt – his own clothes gone to Scientific – Quintin shuffled into the interview room and sat down next to his solicitor. The laces had been removed from the trainers, but it was the deep bruising around his neck that caught Dixon's eye.

Yes, he had saved Quintin's life, and he was getting some strange looks from colleagues for his trouble, but most would have done the same, when it came to it. Could he have stood there and watched Quintin die on the end of the rope? It would have been easy – 'I was too late' – but easy for who?

Easy for Quintin. And that was reason enough to keep him alive.

It would not be an easy interview though, not least because of the layout of the room. Gone was the table between interviewer and suspect – too adversarial; they'd been replaced by chairs snugly side by side, opposite the tape machine. To build a rapport, apparently.

Designed by an idiot, thought Dixon, as he watched West and his colleague file in and sit down, West taking the chair next to Quintin.

West leaned forward and flicked on the tape machine. 'My name is Detective Sergeant Samuel West, and sitting to my left is . . .'

'Detective Sergeant Dominic Hands.'

Quintin was sitting with his legs crossed, leaning forward over his knee with his arms folded tightly across his chest. His head was almost resting on his kneecap, the mark on the back of his neck where the rope had dug in clearly visible.

'Identify yourself for the tape, please, Thomas.'

Silence.

'Or do you prefer Tom?'

West waited, patiently. It had been the right decision to bring them in for the interview.

'How about Simon? Simon Bagwell is your real name, isn't it?'

'No comment.'

'Shit.' Charlesworth was watching the screen with his hands behind his head.

'You went by the name James Scott for a time. What about James?'

Silence.

'Perhaps your solicitor would like to introduce himself for the tape?'

'Michael Salter, Michael Salter & Co.'

'Let's stick with Thomas,' said West. 'That's the name you've used most recently. You're under arrest, Thomas, and I'm obliged to remind you that you have been cautioned and remain under caution. Do you understand?'

'Yes.'

'You do not have to say anything, but it may harm your defence—'

'I've advised my client of all of that,' said Salter, with a heavy sigh.

'When did your father die?'

'No comment.'

Potter turned away from the screen. 'He hasn't even confirmed his bloody name.'

'It must have been difficult, watching him decompose?' continued West, undeterred. 'Describe it for me.'

'No comment.'

'How old were you at the time?'

'No comment.'

'If it helps,' said Salter, 'I have advised my client to answer "no comment" to all of your questions and he has accepted that advice.'

Quintin sat up, his arms still folded, and turned his back on West. 'I'll talk to Dixon,' he mumbled. Then he looked up at the camera on the wall. 'I know he's watching.'

'Detective Sergeant West is leaving the room,' said West, standing up.

'You don't have to go in there, Nick,' said Potter. 'Peter Lewis was your line manager; a close colleague. That could be interpreted as personal involvement.'

'If that's what it takes to get him talking then I do.'

'Just be very careful,' said Charlesworth.

'You saw that?' asked West, opening the door.

'We did,' replied Potter.

'Is there anything you need?' asked Charlesworth, turning to Dixon.

'A change of interview room.' Dixon stood up. 'The one with a table between me and him.'

Dixon sat down in the vacant chair opposite Quintin and stared at him, letting the silence hang.

West had moved the interview to the only room with a table, restarted the tape and then left the room.

'Acting Detective Chief Inspector Nicholas Dixon is joining the interview,' said Dixon, more to put Salter out of his misery than anything.

Quintin was sitting with his legs crossed, arms folded and eyes closed.

'It's for your benefit, not mine,' said Dixon.

'What is?' Quintin's eyes opened, fixing him with a hard stare.

'The table.'

A smile crept across Quintin's face as he watched Dixon watching him.

'It must've been quite a night.'

'What must?'

'The battle,' said Dixon. 'Would you have been a rebel, or would you have fought for your king?'

'A rebel; Somerset through and through.'

'Just like you were at the re-enactment?'

'Always.'

'So, who was Thomas Quintin?'

'A carpenter from Langport. He fought with Holmes's Green Regiment at the Upper Plungeon. I found his belt buckle a few years ago. His name was engraved on it.'

'Hanged at Ottery St Mary.'

'That's where he was captured.'

'The buckle would be worth a few quid, I imagine?'

'This isn't about money.' Quintin sat up, a look of disappointment replacing the smile. 'I thought you'd understand.'

'Tell me about Thomas Cornelius.' Dixon decided that a change of tack was called for. 'A hero of yours, is he?'

'So, you do understand.' Quintin slouched in his chair, one arm hooked over the back. 'He rode with Grey's troopers. He was at the rear with Appleby when that useless bastard of a guide, Godfrey, was stumbling about in the dark trying to find the Upper Plungeon. Appleby fired the shot and rode forward to alert the Royal camp. Cornelius went after him, but couldn't find him in the darkness. Then the battle started.'

'I thought the shot came from the Blue Regiment? One of their sentries out near Langmoor Stone.'

'Nope.'

Get him talking and keep him talking, thought Dixon, as long as he could stomach it. 'And the trooper who rode forward was one of Compton's patrol sent back to alert the camp?'

'You've been reading Graham's book, haven't you?' Quintin was shaking his head. 'There's nothing new in there. It was Appleby; a Somerset man too.'

'And Cornelius killed him with a scythe,' said Dixon.

'Revenge is sweet.' Quintin smirked. 'Kept his body in the house.'

'Just like your father.' Dixon watched the smirk evaporate. 'Tell me about his funeral.'

'It was a prepaid funeral plan. I wasn't allowed to go.'

'And your mother's?'

'I arranged that.'

'Which is when you got a taste for the funeral business?'

'We were having such a nice chat,' said Quintin, folding his arms again.

'There's a couple of things I don't understand.' Dixon leaned forward across the table. 'Why bury Rory's body on the battlefield?'

'The appeal . . .'

'Was it you?'

Silence.

Dixon was losing him, Quintin retreating into his shell once again. 'The appeal would have failed if you hadn't interfered.'

A look of resignation.

'And why Zak?'

'Ah, the boy in the slurry pit.' Quintin's eyes widened, offering a faint glimmer of recognition. A blink and it was gone. 'No comment.'

Chapter Fifty

The 'no comments' had come thick and fast after that, Dixon stalking out of the interview room and straight into the path of Charlesworth and Potter.

'You'd got him talking,' said Charlesworth.

'Only about the battle, and I wasn't sitting in there having a "nice chat" with the man who killed Peter Lewis. We've got more than enough on him anyway.'

'He's on first name terms with Dr Ashton.'

'He used his first name.' Dixon sighed. 'There's a difference, David.'

'Don't push it,' said Charlesworth, smiling. 'But I take your point.'

'We're just waiting for a charging decision from the CPS,' offered Potter.

'It had better be all of them.'

'It will be.'

'Shame you couldn't keep him talking, Nick.' Charlesworth turned towards the lift. 'His accomplice is still out there.'

'He was never going to give them up. And I already know what happened three hundred years ago.'

'You'd better come and see this, Sir!' Louise was leaning over the balustrade on the second floor as Dixon walked along the landing on the first, catching him just before he disappeared into the canteen.

'What is it?' he asked, when he reached the top of the stairs.

'We looked at Ashton's holiday cottage in Stawell on Google Street View, and, well, have a look. Dave took a screenshot of it.'

'It was taken five years ago,' said Harding. 'And Ashton only sold it two years ago. What can you see?' he asked, gesturing to the screen on his workstation.

'A quad bike towing a trailer.'

It was parked along the stone wall outside the cottage.

'It's the same colour as the one at Bussex Farm, but you can't see the number plate because it's pixelated out.'

'Can we ask Google? They've probably still got the original image.'

'I already have.'

'It doesn't really tell us much though, does it?' Dixon straightened up. 'Just that the Bussex Farm quad bike was there. It might have been visiting next door, for all we know. And we don't even know who was riding it, do we?'

'We can ask Ashton, surely?' said Louise.

'Let's go and rattle his cage anyway,' said Dixon. 'You can ask the questions, Lou.'

◆ ◆ ◆

Same field; different trench. 'Still digging, Sir?' asked Dixon.

'We've had to hire a small digger,' replied Ashton, gesturing to a trailer on the far side of the field. 'Seeing as we've lost the students and all their muscles.'

338

'Is Professor Watkins over at the other site?'

'Yes. They've dug a couple of trenches without finding much else, so our theory about the pit seems to be holding true, sadly.' Ashton dropped his trowel and climbed out of the new trench. 'I gather congratulations are in order?'

'Are they?'

'You've caught the Scytheman.'

'A colleague died in the process.'

'Yes, of course, sorry.'

Dixon dropped down into the trench and began scuffing the ground with the side of his shoe. 'Detective Constable Willmott has some questions for you, Sir, if that's all right?'

'Fine,' replied Ashton, turning to Louise. 'How can I help?'

'You used to have a holiday cottage in Stawell, Sir,' said Louise. 'And we were wondering why you hadn't mentioned it before.'

'Hardly a holiday cottage,' said Ashton, arching his back. 'I inherited it from my mother when she died. It was a bit of a liability, really. I had to hang on to it when house prices crashed, and wait for the market to pick up.'

'Why didn't you mention it before?'

'It hardly seemed relevant.'

Dixon was rubbing a pebble between his fingers, pretending not to listen too intently to Louise's questioning.

'Did you let it out?'

'No.'

'Allow anyone to stay there?'

'No.'

'Did you have any work done on the property?'

'No.'

'Deliveries?'

'I used to have wood for the fire. That came over from Bussex Farm.'

And explained the quad bike and trailer, thought Dixon.

'Does the name Thomas Quintin mean anything to you?' Louise was getting into her stride now, although Ashton seemed more interested in what Dixon had in the palm of his hand.

'He was a rebel; executed, I forget where. His name's in the *London Gazette*.'

'You've not seen the buckle engraved with his name?'

'No!' Ashton was frowning at Louise and Dixon in turn. 'Is there one?'

'What about James Scott?'

'Well, he was the Duke of Monmouth.' Ashton sighed. 'Is this a history test?'

Louise looked at Dixon and shrugged.

'Appleby,' Dixon said. 'He was a trooper with Lord Grey, at the back of the column as it tried to find the Upper Plungeon and cross the Bussex Rhyne.'

'Couldn't have been,' said Ashton. 'He must have been with the Blue Regiment. Paschall thought the shot came from over near the Langmoor Stone. His account from 1685 says so.'

'That's the same direction, though, isn't it?' said Dixon, spitting on the pebble in the palm of his hand. 'On a dark, foggy night, sound carries.'

Ashton shook his head. 'Look, I accept it was Appleby. We can infer that much from Paschall's letter to Durling, I think. But Appleby must have been the outlying sentry left by the Blue Regiment at the Langmoor Stone. He fired the shot, then either he, or one of Compton's patrol possibly, rode forward to raise the alarm.'

'But Appleby could have been one of Grey's troopers?'

'No, he couldn't. There's no mention of it in any of the contemporary accounts.' Ashton frowned, his hands on his hips. 'Where *is* this information coming from?'

Dixon dropped the pebble in the bottom of the trench. He looked back as he walked across the field to see Ashton on his hands and knees grubbing about in the dirt for it, then trying a metal detector.

'What was it?' asked Louise.

'A stone.'

'It'll keep him busy for ages.' She smiled. 'Bit of a waste of time, though, wasn't it?'

'Was it?'

'How'd it go?' asked Pearce, when they appeared at the top of the stairs at Express Park, Dixon heading for the photographs on the whiteboard.

'He's got something,' whispered Louise, her eyes wide.

Harding and Pearce both stopped what they were doing and swung round on their swivel chairs to watch; more heads popped up from behind computers on the other side of the Incident Room.

'Where did we get to with his parents' funeral arrangements?' asked Dixon, still facing the whiteboard.

Harding snatched a piece of paper off his workstation. 'The father was cremated and his ashes interred in Chedzoy churchyard. His mother was cremated at Taunton and her ashes scattered in the Garden of Remembrance.'

'The father's was prepaid, but who paid for the mother's?'

'Simon Bagwell, aka James Scott, aka Thomas Quintin.'

Dixon spun round. 'Where are the rest of the photographs?'

'On the file,' replied Louise. She picked up a yellow folder off her desk and handed it to him. 'You can't see any faces in them, so they're not much use.'

Dixon spotted Potter watching from the top of the stairs. It was the movement that caught his eye – when she waved to Louise, who ran over. He was flicking through the photographs in the folder, discarding them one by one, pretending not to listen to their conversation.

'We're charging Quintin with all of the murders,' said Potter. 'Firearms offences and kidnap; everything, basically.' A pause. 'And Parker's hearing at the Court of Appeal is at ten on Friday morning. Tell him, when you get a chance.'

'I will.'

No need, he thought, as he picked up a roll of Sellotape and stuck a photograph on the whiteboard; slap bang in the middle.

Black and white, printed on an A4 piece of paper, the picture was grainy. All the people in it had their backs to the camera: a line-up of the rebels facing the Royal Army, with marquees in the background and the same Bedford van.

'That's not the Sealed Knot re-enactment,' said Pearce.

'It's the locals'.'

'You can't see their faces,' sighed Harding. 'I don't recognise any of them.'

'If that's Doris Bagwell, as Lou says, then the child could well be Quintin, there on the end,' said Pearce, pointing at the boy carrying the scythe. 'She's looking up at someone out of shot. I can't make out what she's holding in her other hand though.'

'Me neither.' Louise was trying to hide her exasperation.

'You're sure that's Doris Bagwell?' asked Dixon.

'As sure as I can be,' she replied.

He took a deep breath. 'Those are reins in her other hand.'

Chapter Fifty-One

Dixon had organised a few funerals in his time as a trainee solicitor, where the firm had been appointed executors in the deceased's will and there really had been no one else to do it.

Sad situations, always. Sometimes he had even gone to the funeral, just to make up the numbers.

There would be more funerals to attend in the coming days. Five at least; six including Peter's, although there would be no need to 'make up the numbers' for Detective Chief Inspector Peter Lewis.

He parked on the far side of the car park at Taunton Crematorium, well away from the mourners; a crowd milling about outside waiting to go in, another filing out slowly. A conveyor belt in more ways than one.

The mourners waiting for their turn stared at him as he walked across the car park, wondering how he might have known their deceased, probably. He put his head down and walked straight past them into the chapel, the chorus of 'Bring Me Sunshine' fading out as the last of the previous mourners left.

Latham's again. He spotted Skinner standing by a CD player at the back, waiting for it to eject a disc.

'He was a fan of *Morecambe and Wise*,' he said, as Dixon walked towards him. 'Are you here for a funeral today, Inspector?'

'I'm looking for the Book of Remembrance.'

'It's in a glass case over at the Garden,' replied Skinner. 'Follow me.'

'I'm after an entry from 1996. Does it go back that far?' asked Dixon, following Skinner back out into the sunshine.

'Ah.' Skinner stopped in his tracks. 'You'll need the office then. That far back and it'll be there. Ted will sort you out. This way,' he said, setting off around the side of the crematorium. 'I've spoken to the Picton family and told them we'll do the funeral free of charge, even though the business has changed hands since . . .'

'That's a matter between you and them, Sir.'

'I just wanted you to know, that's all.' Skinner ignored the 'Please knock and enter' sign and barged into the office. 'This is a police officer, Ted, and he wants to see the Book of Remembrance,' he said. 'From 1996.'

Ted sighed, opening the top drawer of his desk and taking out a set of keys. 'Give me a minute.'

Dixon watched through the window as another crowd gathered outside the crematorium, a hearse pulling up, the coffin draped in a white ensign this time.

'Must be ex-Navy,' said Skinner, looking out of the window over Dixon's shoulder. 'That's the Lockwood's hearse. I wonder what they're doing here?'

Dixon spun round at the sound of a heavy book dropping on a table behind him. 'What exactly is it you're looking for?' asked Ted, flicking it open.

'Confirmation.'

'Maybe you should see a vicar, then.'

♦ ♦ ♦

Dave, Mark and Louise were waiting for him outside Express Park when he turned into the visitors' car park forty minutes later, PC Cole sitting in a patrol car in the shade with two other officers Dixon didn't recognise.

Charlesworth and Potter were standing in the floor to ceiling windows in the CID Area on the first floor, watching. It was a familiar sight, their conversation animated; the only thing missing this time was Lewis, fighting Dixon's corner.

'They'll all be at the rehearsal for the re-enactment on Westonzoyland playing field,' said Louise, when Dixon wound down the window of his Land Rover.

He nodded, then looked at Dave Harding.

'I checked it on Google Earth,' Dave said. 'There are three ways in. One for cars, and two on foot with those railings that stop bikes going too fast.'

'Get uniform to cover them – discreetly.'

'I'll tell them to drive round to the far side and park behind the hedge.'

The small convoy divided at the junction by the village shop, Cole following the lane that took the uniformed officers to the far side of the playing field. Dixon turned into the main entrance, paused while Harding pulled in behind him, then reversed across the gate, blocking it.

It was an odd scene – almost comedic: the Royal Army lined up in front of the pavilion, dressed in shorts and T-shirts most of them; five small groups, each representing one of the Royal regiments that took part in the battle.

The rebels were waiting in a column behind the cricket nets on the far side of the pitch.

'There's Ashton,' said Louise, pointing to a figure in a sun hat, holding a pint of beer. 'And that's Timperley and Watkins.' They were standing on the edge of a small crowd that had congregated outside the pavilion.

'Parker's there too,' said Pearce. 'With the vicar.'

'The bar must be open,' said Harding, as Dixon slid out of the driver's seat of his Land Rover.

'Do we wait?' asked Louise.

'No, we bloody well don't.' Dixon walked across the middle of the battlefield, straight towards Ashton, glancing across to check that Cole and the other uniformed officers were in position at the exits on the far side.

'Who's playing the part of the trooper who raised the alarm, Sir?' he asked, when he arrived in front of Ashton.

'I am.' Sandra Smith appeared behind him, a glass of Pimm's in her hand. 'I'll be on horseback on the day, of course; the local riding school usually lends me an old cob. And in costume.'

'Has he got you as one of the Blues or one of Grey's troopers?' Louise looked at Dave Harding and raised her eyebrows.

'I told you, Inspector.' Ashton sighed. 'The trooper who fired the shot was a sentry left by the Blue Regiment at or near the Langmoor Stone.'

'Not according to your brother, Mrs Smith,' said Dixon, loud and clear, turning to face Sandra.

'My brother?' She stepped back, her path blocked by Harding and Pearce. 'I don't have a brother.'

'He says the trooper who raised the alarm was William Appleby, riding with Lord Grey. He was murdered by Thomas Cornelius and his mummified body kept by Cornelius in his house.'

'I don't know what you're talking about.'

'Cornelius was hanged for his murder in 1696.'

'You still haven't told me where this information is coming from!' exclaimed Ashton, emptying the contents of his glass on to the ground. 'There's nothing about Appleby riding with Lord Grey in Paschall's letter to Durling.'

'It's in Paschall's diary,' said Dixon, taking a step towards Sandra. 'The missing 1696 diary that *you* said didn't exist.'

Sandra stepped back into Harding, then lurched forward. 'Have you found this *alleged* diary?'

'Not yet.'

'There you are then. You do know I'm the Deputy Lieutenant of Somerset?'

'I also know you're the Scytheman's sister.' Dixon slid a piece of paper out of his pocket. 'Doris Ruth Bagwell, died 17th September 1996, beloved wife of Frederick, mother of Simon and Sandra.'

The blood drained from her face. 'Where did you find that?' she asked, her eyes darting around the playing field, checking the exits.

'The Book of Remembrance at Taunton Crematorium. Your brother made the funeral arrangements.'

'The bloody idiot.'

'And your birth certificate will confirm it, won't it?'

Sandra slumped to the ground, her legs stretched out in front of her. 'I was supposed to be the Lord Lieutenant one day,' she said, visibly shaking.

'You were on horseback for the 1985 re-enactment. I'm guessing it was your own pony?'

'Frolic; she was lovely.'

'Best in show, no doubt.'

Sandra threw her head back. 'Beat your drums, the enemy is come,' she hissed.

'And you lied about the diary. You told me it didn't exist, but it does. Where else is your brother getting his information about Appleby?'

'The diary exists?' demanded Ashton.

Dixon's eyes bored into him, wiping the grin from his face.

'Simon found it in the crypt at Chedzoy when he was down there doing some odd job work.' Sandra's eyes glazed over. 'I've seen it, but not for years. The maps of the cornfield are in it – they're real enough – but you'll never find it; I've tried. He became fixated with Cornelius and seemed to think he was some sort of kindred spirit. He was never the same after our father died. He became . . .' Her voice tailed off.

Dixon waited.

'Cold. Distant. I went to his school a couple of times and he never said a thing about our parents.' Sandra buried her face in her hands. 'I didn't find out my father was dead until Social Services went in and took Simon into care.'

'Who buried Rory's body?' Dixon gestured to Harding and Pearce, who stepped forward and helped her to her feet.

'I did. I knew the bodies were in the old farmhouse, and the rhyne had been dredged so it was easy; the boy hardly weighed a thing. I had to keep Parker in prison.'

'And your brother killed Zak because you stole Rory's body?'

She nodded, slowly. 'I took one of his, so he took one of mine.'

'Do the honours, Lou.'

'Sandra Smith, I am arresting you on suspicion of assisting an offender.' Louise paused while Pearce snapped the handcuffs shut. 'You do not have to say anything but it may harm your defence if you do not mention when questioned something that you later rely on in court.'

Tears were flowing freely down Sandra's cheeks, bringing her mascara with them.

'Anything you do say may be given in evidence.'

'I never killed anyone,' she said, raising her voice. 'I want that clearly understood. And I made him stop – I told him I'd turn him in if he didn't. He was my brother; what else was I supposed to do?'

Chapter Fifty-Two

'What are we doing here?' asked Jane. 'I know Monty enjoys sniffing around a churchyard, but we could've gone to Berrow.'

'You'll see.'

'What does a Deputy Lieutenant do anyway?'

'They're the monarch's representative in the county, so they open things, I suppose.'

The mist had been spilling out of the rhynes and rolling across the cornfield as they drove out towards Chedzoy, the sun below the hedgerows but still lighting up the sky.

Red sky at night; the novelty was wearing off now. 'We could do with some rain,' muttered Dixon, looking around at the parched grass in between the gravestones.

'Are you going to tell me what we're looking for?'

'He was cremated and his ashes interred, so it'll be a small stone, lying flat; around the edge, probably.' Dixon was walking slowly around the outside of the graveyard, just inside the stone wall, one eye watching Monty who was weaving in and out of the graves.

'The profiler was right then?' Jane was leaning over a grave-stone, brushing back the grass with the back of her hand. 'There's a first time for everything, I suppose.'

'He said Quintin was an only child.'

'Someone said in the canteen she'd confessed?'

'I let the interview team from Bristol do it; thought I might as well, seeing as they're here.'

'She knew all along?'

'She was estranged from her parents, which is why she's not mentioned anywhere. They wouldn't have her in the house.' Dixon stopped and looked down at two lines of slabs lying flat in the grass; some had been cleaned and the grass trimmed, others were over-grown. 'But she always kept in touch with her brother. She bought him the caravan and rented the land he kept it on.'

'Here it is.' Jane was squatting down, brushing the grass off a piece of black marble. 'Frederick Jasper Bagwell, 31st July 1993, beloved husband of Doris; father of Simon.'

'No mention of Sandra allowed.'

'But still she covered for him?'

'That was for her own benefit. It was after Parker was arrested; she went to the caravan, saw a light in the derelict farmhouse and walked in on him with his new family. I got the impression we were supposed to feel sorry for her.' Dixon shook his head. 'She couldn't afford the scandal *in her position*, so she helped him stay off the radar; not difficult with the police investigation focused on Parker – even easier when Parker was convicted and we closed the file. It was her idea that he cut his finger off, believe it or not.'

'And he did it, just like that.'

'In case he was ever arrested for something else and the data-base threw up a match.'

'Found it then, I see.' Donald Watson was striding towards them along the path, a shovel in one hand and his case in the other. 'Jolly good.' He dropped his case in the grass and stuck the shovel under the edge of the piece of marble, levering it up. Then he leaned over and peered underneath. 'There's something in there,' he said. He opened his case, taking out a pair of latex gloves and an evidence bag before lifting the slab clear to reveal a Tupperware box, taped shut. He held it up to the last of the sunlight. 'Whatever it is, it's wrapped in plastic. I'll get it back to the lab.'

'What is it?' asked Jane.

'Paschall's missing diary from 1696,' replied Dixon, oddly matter of fact. He shrugged. 'We've looked everywhere else.'

'Dr Ashton is going to have to rewrite his bloody book pretty damn sharpish, isn't he?' said Watson, grinning. He dropped the Tupperware box in the evidence bag, sealed it shut, then picked up his case. 'Right, that's me done.' He set off towards his car. 'Slide the stone back for me, will you?'

Dixon puffed out his cheeks. 'Cheeky sod.'

'So, that's it then?' asked Jane.

'It is.' He looked down at the urn in the bottom of the hole in the ground, the wood mostly rotted away, leaving a rusted metal name plate and two hinges. Then he slid the stone back into position and tamped it down with his foot. 'I did tell you I want my ashes scattered, didn't I?'

'Oh God, not that again.'

'If we have a son, I'd like to call him Peter.'

'You want children?'

'Do you?'

'When the time is right.'

Dixon smiled as he took her hand. 'I'm glad we got that sorted out.'

He pulled in and stopped across the top of Frys Lane as they drove down through Chedzoy, the cornfield now hidden in the darkness and the fog.

'*Haec olim meminisse juvabit.*'

Jane frowned. 'I didn't know you spoke Latin.'

'It's a line from *Goodbye Mr Chips*,' he said, staring out into the gloom. 'It may please us, one day, to remember these things.'

Author's Note

Thank you for reading *Down Among the Dead* and I very much hope you enjoyed it.

I have always been fascinated by the Battle of Sedgemoor, and much of the information I have used is, I hope, factually accurate – as far as one can tell, given that the battle took place well over three hundred years ago.

The battlefield is a haunting (as opposed to haunted) place, and well worth a visit if you get the chance; the walk out to the memorial from Bussex Farm on a warm summer's evening being particularly evocative.

A replica of the sword twelve year old Mary Bridge used to defend her mother can be found in the visitors' centre at St Mary's Church, Westonzoyland, which is also worth a visit.

The identity of the lone trooper who fired the warning shot and galloped forward to alert the Royal Army is, perhaps, one of the most enduring mysteries from the battle, and I feel I should clarify that the version given in *Down Among the Dead* is entirely fictional. I suspect the truth of the matter is simply that the shot was an accidental discharge; not surprising with six thousand rebels marching out on to the moor on a dark and foggy night. The lone trooper was also, more likely than not, a member of a Royal patrol out on the moor who heard the shot.

Truth is often stranger than fiction – but, on this occasion, I fear not.

That said, a Thomas Cornelius did take part in the battle, fighting for the Duke of Monmouth. He was captured, tried and sentenced to death, his entry in the *London Gazette* confirming that 'no place nor time then order'd for [his] execution [he was] respited'. The Zoyland Heritage website includes his name on a list of those later transported to Barbados as slaves on board the ship *Happy Return*. I like to think he made a happy return home some years later!

There are several people to thank, as always, not least of whom is my wife, Shelley, who lives and breathes every page of every book with me. I would also like to thank my unpaid editor-in-chief, Rod Glanville. And David Hall and Clare Paul who, once again, have been extraordinarily generous with their time and knowledge of Somerset.

I am most grateful to Caroline Tagg for her assistance in accessing the digital archive of the 1985 tercentenary battle commemorations, which includes photographs of the Sealed Knot and village re-enactments.

I must also thank Andrew Jones of Devon and Cornwall Police for sharing his fingerprinting expertise with me.

And lastly, I would like to thank my editorial team at Thomas & Mercer – in particular, Laura Deacon, Jack Butler, Hatty Stiles and, of course, Katie Green.

Damien Boyd
Devon, UK
November 2019

About the Author

Damien Boyd is a solicitor by training and draws on his extensive experience of criminal law, along with a spell in the Crown Prosecution Service, to write fast-paced crime thrillers featuring Detective Inspector Nick Dixon.